SORCERER

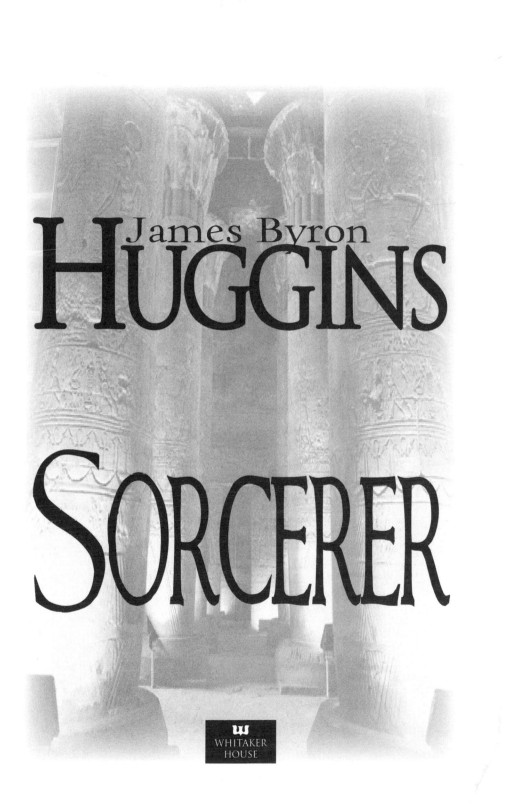

James Byron
HUGGINS

SORCERER

**WHITAKER
HOUSE**

This novel is a work of fiction. References to real events, organizations, and places are used in a fictional context. Any resemblance to actual persons, living or dead, is entirely coincidental.

SORCERER

ISBN-13: 978-0-88368-818-2
ISBN-10: 0-88368-818-2
Printed in the United States of America
© 2006 by James Byron Huggins

WHITAKER
HOUSE

1030 Hunt Valley Circle
New Kensington, PA 15068
www.whitakerhouse.com

Library of Congress Cataloging-in-Publication Data

Huggins, James Byron.
Sorcerer / James Byron Huggins.
p. cm.
ISBN-13: 978-0-88368-818-2 (pbk. : alk. paper)
ISBN-10: 0-88368-818-2 (pbk. : alk. paper)
I. Title.
PS3558.U346S67 2006
813'54—dc22
2005031087

2 3 4 5 6 7 8 9 10 11 12 13 14 15 LU 16 15 14 13 12 11 10 09 08 07 06

Prologue

B ury him alive!"

"While we still have the chance!" another cried.

Three men with shotguns raced forward to level trembling barrels into the dark mouth of the cave. A pale host of others frantically slammed stones into crude mortar that yet another man was heaving in shovelfuls to wall up the entrance of the skull-like cavern.

The night was close and cold in the darkest hour before dawn, and some glanced nervously at the enshrouding fog, as if expecting to behold more than mist.

"Forget the mist!" the oldest man shouted. "He'll recover quick enough, and we won't get another chance!"

A young man raised his face. "What about the Logan family!"

"*Dead*, boy! Like the rest of the town! *Now*—quickly!—wall this abomination up before it kills the rest of us as well! If the thing awakes, I don't know if these rifles will stop it again!"

The boy spun to the stones, slamming them atop each shovelful of cement. Now there were two men hurling the mortar, and the wall was climbing quickly.

They stopped as a low, guttural growl issued from the bowels of the darkness—a threatening tremor inhabited by clear and cold intent. A moment, then a voice began whispering in a soft, hissing maliciousness in a language the boy had never heard.

"Be silent in the name of Christ!" the old man shouted.

He raised his shotgun to his shoulder and fired both barrels directly into the mouth of the cave and the others followed, six shotguns expending twelve rounds into the face of something they could not see. As the last man finished firing, the first to fire had reloaded with the conditioned reflexes of men who hunted to survive, as was the way of any man inhabiting the small frontier village.

And then—no command, no words—they were firing again. As they finished the second volley, the others had again reloaded, smoking shell casings rocketing from the chambers of the heavy-barreled weapons.

Volley after volley continued for a smoke-blasted minute, round after round after round fired point-blank into the cavern. And somewhere in the thunderous explosions of light the boy looked up to see something in the near distance—something chained to a wall.

There were flashes of silver at his manacled wrists as he—as *it*—raised and crossed forearms before its face.

It was dressed in a long scarlet robe that might have once been imperial but was now dirty and bloodied and ragged from the long battle of the past week where it had killed and destroyed so many. Those who had not been killed in the terror wished that they had been so they would not have to live with the memory.

The rising wall of heavy stones was so high now that they had only to lay the last layer of granite, and it would be sealed. The ones not still firing took suicidal risks to avoid the narrow angles of volleys, placing stone after stone solidly in place, and then it was almost done.

But the grandfather of the group took one last second to steady his aim before the final stone was set. He laid the twin barrels into the narrow aperture. His voice was enraged.

"Beast! This is your grave!"

The twin concussion of his final rounds was followed by, "Quickly! The last stone!"

With the words, the two men lifted the massive stone and shoved it atop cement at the crest of the cave. Another second, and they had piled shovelfuls of yet more cement atop it to completely seal the cave from light and even air, and then they stood, staring in shock at the hastily built prison.

The old man lowered his smoking shotgun, breathing heavily. His face was ghastly white and he seemed perilously exhausted. His shoulders sagged as he slowly turned, staring steadily upon the men who gazed back upon him with the respect one would give an Old Testament prophet. Then the old man turned further and gazed over the settling mist toward a small New England village.

It was a warm crimson dawn, and there should have been merchants and others strolling along the boarded walkways. There should have been children running toward the one-room schoolhouse, milkmen drawing wagons along the rows of houses, and farmers moving over hills and fields.

Yes, there should have been. But there were not. The town was as dead as a grave. And foggy, ghostly specters seemed to hover along the once busy streets like disembodied souls not yet departed from this temporal plain.

The boy quietly walked up to wait beside the old man, who stood on the edge of the hill that held the cave and whatever dark force it now contained. The boy's voice trembled.

"How many are dead?"

For a long moment, the old man didn't reply. Then, hoarsely: "Most of them, boy...All of them."

The boy's widened eyes strayed back to the cave. "Do you think the cave can hold it?"

"I don't know," the old man replied grimly. "It has escaped prisons built of stronger stuff." He shook his head. "By the odds, it should have killed us. And if I had not finally discerned who he—what *it* truly was—aye, we would be dead."

The young man looked back. "Why did it kill so many of us? What was its reason?"

With a frown the old man shook his head once more. "It does not need a reason. It is its own reason—a cruel creature bent on mindless annihilation."

By reflex, or the remaining vestiges of terror, the old man reloaded the heavy 10-gauge shotgun, and lowered it in a single hand. He took a slow, somber step down the hill toward what was now a ghost town.

"Come, boy...We have dead to bury."

Chapter One

"You're gonna die if you quit, Thorn."

Turning at the voice, Michael Thorn laughed as he closed his locker. Other officers were in various stages of preparation with the staccato sound of Velcro straps, body armor, holsters. There were doors and trunks and briefcases slamming, the weight machines clinking as officers worked off a day's rage.

"I'm gonna die, anyway," Thorn laughed as he holstered his Beretta—one of the few things he was taking with him after eight years as a Los Angeles police officer.

"What difference does retirement make?" Thorn continued with a smile. "You remember Metcaff, don't you?

"Yeah," TJ answered.

"Well, Metcaff's been retired five years, man. And look at him; he's still alive."

"Yeah, but he ain't real happy."

"He was *never* happy."

TJ, as muscular as any man Thorn had ever known, shambled forward, and Thorn was again reminded of how prehistoric his friend appeared. Observing TJ, it was easy to accept the fact that Neanderthal man may have interbred with Homo Erectus. He had once seen TJ leap completely over the roof of a parked Volkswagen Beetle without even touching it.

TJ stopped a few feet away, watching as Thorn shoved his civilian clothes in an Army duffle. Upon the side it read in bold caps: **CAPT. MICHAEL THORN, 82ND AIRBORNE, 4 DIVISION, 7TH BATTALION.**

"I've seen it happen, Thorn. Good men; all of 'em in good shape. Then they retire; dead in two years." He shook his head. "They go home, pull out their fishing gear, golf clubs, start a book they never finish cause they drop dead from a heart attack. It's too much of a life change, Thorn. Nothin' like police work—the excitement, the brotherhood, the close calls and helpin' folks. You're gonna die, Thorn, if you ain't helpin' someone out of a mess. I know you, man. Deep down you're like blessed Mother Teresa; you've gotta be helping." TJ nodded at his own sage wisdom. "It's in your blood, Thorn. Or, though I ain't religious, in your spirit or something. You know I'm right."

Thorn smiled as he began to snap the duffel bag shut. "Listen, TJ; Rebecca and me have bought a very nice, big ol' house in this New England community, but it's a real fixer-upper, so we'll be busy for a long time. I'll have plenty to do."

"What about the kids?" TJ wasn't giving up. "Do you really think this is best for them?"

At that, Thorn turned and leaned a forearm over the top of the upright duffle. "You're really *serious* about this, aren't you?"

"Stay another year, Thorn. You're too young for this. You're in your prime."

Thorn hefted the strap of the duffle on his shoulder. Then he picked up his leather holster, slid the Beretta into it, and clipped it to his waist. "I'm forty-five years old, TJ; I've had twenty-four years of fighting, getting shot at, getting *shot*. I've been stabbed, blown up, broken nearly every bone in my body." He patted his friend on the shoulder as he slid around him. "No, bro. I'm done with adventures. I'm gonna spend the rest of my life in peace. Boring as it sounds."

TJ watched him walk away and muttered after him.

"Bet ya don't."

The audience was silent as the lean, white-haired professor laid a small collection of yellow notes at the podium. He did not need copious notes. He knew his subject matter well after a life of near-tireless study.

Though in his early seventies, and retired, he stood erect and appeared casually tan and in perfect health. His steps and posture had the bearing of a man undiminished by the weight of age. He cleared his throat and began.

"Good evening. I am Professor Alexander Adler, and I am honored to be here. I will not waste the time of such a distinguished audience by informing you of what you already know. Instead, let us launch directly into the subject of tonight's seminar: sorcery.

"The premier question is: What, exactly, is sorcery? And the answer is more complex than many presume." Clasping hands behind his back, the professor strolled across the stage, addressing his comments to individual members of the audience.

"Indeed, what is sorcery? There is modern sorcery. There is historical sorcery. There is anthropological sorcery. Ancient sorcery. Prehistoric sorcery."

Professor Alexander Adler let the depth of the dilemma settle into his listeners. "Yes, indeed, my friends. So the problem is, then, not only what is sorcery, but what kind of sorcery are we discussing?"

He waved vaguely. "The most difficult kind of sorcery to define—which should not be a surprise—is modern sorcery. For modern sorcery extends to the broadest lines of the most nebulous neo-paganism."

His voice assumed a harder tone, and he paced slowly back across the stage. "Yes, the difficulty with modern sorcery is not that we know so little; the difficulty is that we know all too much. Modern sorcery is such an amalgam of makeshift rituals, incantations, adopted paganism, and various kinds of talismans and spells that it's as much a product of *Buffy the Vampire Slayer* and wishful thinking as anything else."

He stopped, slowly raising a single forefinger. "Ancient sorcery, however; now *that* is an altogether different phenomenon." He gave his audience time. "Ancient sorcery, my friends, was a mysterious power of such depth that even the origin and meaning of the Hebrew word for 'sorcerer'—*mekashef*—remains unknown."

He began strolling again. "In ancient times, circa 1,491 BC, about the time of the exodus, the sorcerers or 'wise men' as they were called, were revered one step beneath the pharaoh himself. In all but the most literal sense, they were considered gods. And their powers were...quite real."

At that, a voice came tentatively from the audience.

"Um...Professor Adler?"

Professor Adler turned and stood in place. The voice had come from a young and apparently timid young man. He obviously had an important question or he would not have risked the interrupting the class. But the man's fears were unwarranted; the professor nodded courteously.

"Yes, young man?"

The man glanced nervously, slowly, at the hundreds of eyes now focused on him.

The professor's laugh was deep and inspiring. "Do not worry, my friend. We are all students here. Ask your question."

Gazing up, the boy spoke softly. "Don't you mean these 'wise men,' as they were called, *counterfeited* the miracles of Moses? I mean, using tricks like a magician? Tricks only they knew how to do?" As he finished, the boy could not take his seat again fast enough.

Professor Adler pursed his lips, then, "No, young man. That is not what I mean. What I mean is that the sorcerers *duplicated*—and the Hebrew word means 'duplicated,' not 'counterfeited'—the miracles of Moses. I mean they did indeed take an inanimate piece of wood and transform it into a living, breathing thing. They made what was dead, alive. They accomplished the very transubstantiation of matter, itself.

"Now," he continued, "at this, some people do have a problem. But you must read the Bible as it is written. And Exodus, chapters seven and eight, does not say the sorcerers *counterfeited* the first two miracles of Moses. Instead, the Bible says that the sorcerers of pharaoh *duplicated* the first two miracles of Moses."

Silence in the hall.

The professor's gaze roamed over the upturned faces, and then he spoke slowly and distinctly. "There is no one on this planet who understands a single thing about Egyptian sorcery at the time of Moses, best estimated at 1,500 BC. But the Bible records that those ancient warlocks had the power to turn their staffs into living creatures and water into blood.

"Now, how far their powers extended beyond that—what the limits ultimately were—is unknown. There is not a modern sorcerer, scholar, professor, witch, or warlock—nor any living being—who knows the secrets of those ancient alchemists."

Adler bowed his head and clasped his hands behind his back as he walked before the front row of the audience. "Allow me to make a brief point, and follow me with some patience, if you will. It shall not take but a moment."

He paused, then began, "The Bible states that all the books in the world could not list all the miracles that Jesus performed. A man named James Joyce, in a book entitled *Ulysses*, tried heroically, but failed just as heroically, to describe a single day lived by a single man. So the history of literature has proven that it is impossible to record, in detail, what a single man does in a single day.

"You must remember: Moses waged war against Jannes and Jambres, the sorcerers of Amenhotep II, for, as near as we can determine, four to six months. The Bible does not record the details of this battle, and understandably. If a single day of a man cannot be recorded, how can such a period of time?

"So the question must be asked: What battles did Moses wage against these two men that went unrecorded? What other powers did they use against him? What did they do in an attempt to terrify him? Did they attack his mind? That is certainly a possibility. Yet if they could not shake Moses' invincible mind and faith, would they not then attack those around him? Would they not attempt to destroy Moses through those they *could* affect? And how would they affect them? And how would Moses have responded?"

Adler ceased moving in the middle of the front row, turning directly into the audience.

"With power," he said plainly. "Moses fought them with the power of God because it was only by the power of God that he could defeat the very real power of Jannes and Jambres."

"So...their power was great, and real," the young man murmured, almost to himself. He looked up. "What else do you think about them, professor?"

The professor smiled indulgently.

"I think, young man, that we are very fortunate they do not walk among us."

It had been three months since Thorn had turned in his badge, and he had spent it packing and repacking, marking boxes, hiring an affordable moving company, supervising the loading, closing up the house, and tying up loose ends.

There were a lot of emotional good-byes for Rebecca, but Thorn, naturally stoic, had simply ended things with a handshake and a blanket invitation to come visit anytime they pleased.

Thorn's SUV crested what the locals called Montabular Hill. It was located on the crest of Cedar Ridge, the small New England community they had chosen as their newest, and probably their last, home. The Victorian style mansion loomed large on the side of the hill with the same strange, singular authority Thorn had sensed when he first beheld it six months ago.

Alone on the hillside—fifty-five acres had come with the mansion—it was encircled by ancient hardwood trees, which was unusual since New England had been so thoroughly logged in the early part of the twentieth century. Many of these arboreal giants had obviously stood for hundreds of years. Even in the day, the forest floor gave the impression of night with a triple canopy looming above.

In fact, except for the mansion, the entire hill seemed strangely untouched by anything fast-paced or modern, but that was one of the reasons it had first appealed to Thorn. And as they ascended the hill in their Jeep Cherokee, loaded only with traveling gear for the trip, Anthony and Malorie were asleep in the back and Rebecca was napping in the passenger seat. Thorn let himself relax, appreciating the mansion's slow sense of peace.

Thorn again imagined what it would be like to enjoy a normal life, for he had spent more than half his life in the military, first as a Ranger, then in the early eighties he had applied for and qualified for Special Forces.

It was a tour that demanded a strict sacrifice of blood and time, and Thorn had done his duty and then some. But, eventually, it was either the Army or his marriage. Rebecca had grown weary of raising a toddler on her own as Thorn led expeditionary adventures all over the world. Thorn had understood and elected to retire.

Thorn had no problem stepping out of action. He'd done his part, been deployed at a moment's notice a hundred times. Had lived on eternal standby and missed enough holidays and birthdays. If Rebecca had not been as strong as she was, the marriage would have ended years ago.

Thorn owed her for her patience and steadfast love, and had meant to slow things but then came police work. And not just "normal" police work; Thorn got mantled with the harrowing responsibilities of a robbery-homicide detective. The money and security was extreme, sure, but so were the hours, and marital problems began again.

It was a twenty-four-hour-a-day job, and it eventually reached the point where Thorn had become nothing more than what he was hunting. And then, at last, it had come—Rebecca gave him an ultimatum.

Thorn freely admitted that Rebecca had good reason to demand a change or else, and so he had acquiesced, and together they found the quietest community that still met their requirements for the children—Anthony, 11, and Malorie, 8.

Thorn had, on first impression, fancied the scenic beauty of the place. It was at the very tip of the Appalachian chain, an unbroken series of mountains that ran from New England to North Georgia. It appealed to the better part of him—a part that had remained alive even after the years of high-tech weapons, tactics, authority and command, deployments and casualties, choppers, training and more training, and then battle.

In a major way, Thorn had never known a "normal" life, and he was eager to explore the dimensions of it—like soccer games, picnics,

PTA meetings, and waking up every morning to a good woman without having to worry about rapid deployment to some faraway part of the world, not knowing when or whether he would return. And, sometimes, whether Rebecca and the kids would still be there if he did.

It was enough.

This was a new beginning for them, and Thorn was more than ready for what was long overdue.

Yeah, he thought, this was their time now. And no one—and nothing—was going to take from them what they rightly deserved. He'd dedicate himself to rebuilding his life anew as he had dedicated himself to saving his brothers in war, to finishing fights he didn't understand, to fulfilling his duty as a soldier and as a police officer.

The house loomed larger on the hill now, and Thorn narrowed his gray eyes at a fast-moving black cloud. It wasn't so much the storm itself that suddenly demanded Thorn's attention. It was because the thundercloud had seemed to come from nowhere and center so much over the house itself.

For some reason he didn't like the look of it.

The storm broke as they arrived.

Chapter Two

It never ceased to amaze Thorn that, even after fourteen years together, Rebecca looked every bit as beautiful as when they married. He attributed part of it to her Italian genetics, the rest to the fact that she had never neglected herself.

Thorn was not so fortunate: two wars and uncountable battle wounds had cost him a few steps. Too much time in the wilderness had leathered his face. High altitude combat training on the Eiger had cost him a touch of frostbite. And then there were months and months of desert warfare training with the Mossad—the Israeli Secret Service—which Israel denies even exists. And it was then that Thorn determined the desert belonged to scorpions and the implacable Bedouin, not regular human beings.

In truth, he had lived through so many life-threatening injuries over the years that he could tell—as some of the old folks claimed they could—when the weather was about to change.

When he complained about his knee, Rebecca knew it was about to rain. His back wasn't what it used to be, either, and his knees had taken the abuse of parachuting from 35,000 feet for what were termed HALOs—High Altitude, Low Openings.

Falling for 34,500 feet breathing from an oxygen tank, wearing an astronaut suit and helmet, and pulling the cord at five hundred feet above ground going over one hundred mph—maximum velocity. No chance for a backup chute if the first chute fails.

Even opening at five hundred feet, the parachute had a hard time slowing someone from a one hundred mile per hour descent, but it was the safest way to land behind enemy lines without risking the loss of the aircraft. Yeah, his commitment to his duty and his men had been complete, and his body bore testimony to it.

Anthony and Malorie had been more than a little annoyed to travel nine days only to exit the Jeep in the most ferocious thunderstorm Thorn could remember. But Rebecca, like the natural mother she was, shepherded them inside quickly and somehow located towels and fresh clothes amid monuments of boxes, equipment, furniture, and items Thorn had long forgotten he even possessed. He was particularly surprised to find a set of totally unused golf clubs.

With a laugh, Thorn walked to the bag, half lifted a driver, dropped it. Rebecca saw the action and smiled.

"Gonna take up golfing again?"

"I used to golf?"

"Well," she shrugged, "you played one game."

Thorn thought for a minute. "Yeah, I remember now. With your brother."

"Yeah; you lost."

"Uh huh. I do remember, babe."

She laughed. "I don't mean to rub it in. But, hey, doesn't everyone say golf is relaxing?"

"I don't think this town even has a golf course, babe."

"Oh, come on, Michael, *every* town has a golf course." She continued drying Malorie's hair and then leaned forward to speak eye to eye with the eight-year-old. "You okay now, baby?"

Malorie rubbed sleepy eyes. "I'm hungry."

"I'll fix us something in just a minute, okay?"

"Okay..."

Thorn was staring out the window at the moving van, the workers. They were huddled in the back of the truck, waiting for the rain to let up, but as Thorn studied the low, utterly black thunderclouds, he didn't think the storm would be letting up any time soon. There were no edges to it, and it was so thick it seemed solid.

Despite his practical nature, Thorn wondered about the previous inhabitants of this house—a normal, loving family by anyone's knowledge. But six months after moving into this place they had been discovered one morning by a concerned schoolteacher who had missed the children in class.

They had been dead a week.

What had happened was never convincingly explained. But the grandmother had been found in her closet, her face frozen in horror, dead from an apparent heart attack—scared to death.

Literally.

They discovered the wife hanging from the chandelier, clothesline bound around her neck. And then, strangest of all, they found the husband in the front yard. Apparently, he had simply walked naked into the sub-zero January weather and sat in the front-yard snow until he died of hypothermia.

Rational and well respected in the community, he could have rescued himself at any moment simply by rising and taking half a dozen steps to the front porch. But, instead, he had just sat naked in the snow and died a slow, painful death.

Of course, the smaller the community, the more quickly a "haunted" house obtained a fantastic reputation. They progress rapidly from objects of horror to fascination, then superstition, and are finally celebrated in legend, which was the main reason Thorn had been able to afford the place. Not only was it unwanted by locals, out-of-towners were hesitant to chance fate, as well.

Thorn vaguely respected the supernatural; he just didn't consider it a threat. He was ultimately practical and possessed a natural tendency to challenge whatever challenged him or his family, supernatural or not. In short, he wasn't intimidated by ghost stories.

He didn't for one moment believe the house contained "spirits" or "ghosts" or things that rattled chains behind the walls in the middle of the night.

Rebecca, however, was sharply superstitious—the consequence of a traditional Catholic upraising. Thorn wore a crucifix to placate her, but he was not strongly religious. It touched his heart, though, that she wanted him to be safe, and so he wore it.

Thorn didn't mind that Rebecca remained a devout Catholic and had raised Anthony and Malorie in the Roman Catholic Church. The fact that Cedar Ridge—the official name of the community—had a sizeable Catholic congregation had been one of her deciding factors in the move.

Without a church in the town, the deal would have been off the table before it began. Nor did Rebecca have overt problems with the fact that Thorn himself refused to attend services. Nothing personal, he had told her before they got married in a traditional Catholic ceremony. He simply didn't think you needed a church to know God. She told him she knew his heart, and so did God. And that was enough for her.

Still, though Thorn himself had an aversion to anything religious, he encouraged the children to follow their mother's example. He reminded himself that, whether church did any good or not, it certainly didn't hurt.

Rebecca spoke from across the room. "Honey, go into the basement and see if you can't get that boiler going, okay?"

Thorn saw Anthony shivering, a blanket wrapped around his shoulders.

"Yeah," Thorn muttered as he turned away from the window toward the oversized, strangely long staircase that led to the sub-basement buried surprisingly deep beneath the house.

Its darkness was complete.

🪲 ⚲ 𓂀 𓏏 𓅃

Thorn hit the light switch at the bottom of thirty-three steps—he'd counted them, amazed that anyone would build a staircase that seemed to lead into the very heart of the mountain.

There seemed no logical reason for it, and he theorized they'd done it because this Victorian place had been built on the ruins of an older structure. This sub-basement was a pre-existing feature, and so it had been preserved as a ready-made and convenient storm shelter, for which it certainly qualified.

The boiler was old and burned oil. Thorn had had it inspected before he purchased, and it'd checked out to be in near pristine condition. Even the pipes were free of "ruck," as engineers called it, that accumulated in a boiler with long use. It was almost as if no one had ever lived in the house long enough to use it.

Crouching, Thorn lifted a box of matches that he'd placed here two months ago. On inspection he saw that they were bone-dry—strange but explainable. Simple ventilation and forty feet of natural insulation would do it. He struck a match and reached into the—

Scraping claws...

Thorn whirled, dropping the match. He found himself in a half crouch, almost a fighting stance.

The adrenaline electrifying his heart was a familiar thrill, so it didn't set Thorn fully off balance. But he was aware of the tunnel vision that attempted to knock out his peripheral, so he took a deep breath and released it slowly.

He knew what to do physically to counteract the body's involuntary response to a scare. He was an expert at it because, despite what some believed, even the bravest men know fear. They simply control it through technique.

Fear, someone once told him, is a lot like fire. Fire, if controlled, will protect, guard, or warm. But if you lose control of fear, as you can lose control of fire, it can burn your house down. And what could have been a useful tool for salvation becomes the means of destruction through a lack of understanding.

Motionless, Thorn peered into the darkness of the basement; the single bulb failed to penetrate the gloom. He was precisely aware that his skin was crawling, the hairs on his neck and arms standing upright. Slowly he stood, expelling a hard breath...

Get rid of excess oxygen, it limits vision...

He tensed every muscle...

Stress the skin, give it one good shiver, get it out...

Control, control...

He waited until his body settled, then took a long, deep breath, feeling his heart slowing with the voluntary slowing of his breathing. Then he felt a rush of contempt and frowned. He lowered his hands to his side and stared into the darkness a long time.

It was not inconceivable an animal had been somehow trapped in here, was alive in here, or even had a lair in here.

Alive in here...

Suddenly he wished he'd brought a flashlight. And with the thought he went straight toward the staircase, fully expecting to hear the sound again.

He did not doubt what he had heard. He'd trusted his judgment in split-second situations far worse, and he was certain: It had been the sound of claws scratching against stone or maybe wood.

His family was here. This was his home. This was the one place he did *not* retreat.

Not ever.

Instantly Thorn made a decision and was moving up the staircase three steps at a time.

"I'll be back in a second," he said.

☥ ♀ 𓂀 𓊽 𓅃

Rebecca raised her head as Thorn bounded out of the stairwell to the basement, shutting the door solidly. It was the seriousness of his face, the combat poise that she recognized by reflex, that made her instantly stand.

"Michael?"

"It's nothing," Thorn said dismissively as he walked toward their second-floor bedroom. Then he realized he'd replied too quickly and added, "I need a flashlight, babe. That light bulb down there ain't cutting it."

She didn't follow him into the bedroom, and it took Thorn five seconds to open the suitcase and remove the Beretta. He lifted one of the three clips he carried and quickly but silently inserted it into the grip. But he'd wait until he reached the basement to chamber a round because Rebecca would recognize the sound. He put the two extra clips in the back pocket of his jeans and pulled out his shirt to conceal them.

He went down the stairs and out the side door to the Cherokee, ignoring the rain, where he retrieved a mag-light from beside the driver's seat. Then he went back up the steps and to the basement door. He kept his voice totally relaxed, adding a touch of exhaustion.

"I can't even find the matches that I left down there," he muttered, then paused to smile at Anthony and Malorie. "Wanna order pizza tonight? Give Mommy a break?"

"Yeah!" in unison.

Rebecca laughed.

"Be right back," Thorn winked at her.

He was sure to close the door behind him.

His voice was a whisper, and it surprised him.

"I'm coming."

Chapter Three

Thorn was instinctively in defense mode as he stood in silence on the stairway.

When he'd first seen this place there was nothing disturbing about it, but Thorn was getting real disturbed real fast. He began to regret having spent most of his savings and committing 50 percent of his pension to it for the next twenty years.

Then he thought of the sturdy beams that had been used for reinforcement in the basement and, for the first time, considered it unusual. Similar beams ran throughout the mansion, and it occurred to Thorn that any kind of reinforcements were unusual for a basement. This entire place was becoming stranger and stranger, and he was amazed he hadn't noticed it before. He should have taken more time in making a decision.

Thorn had seen a lot of things in his life, had known fear in a thousand forms and was man enough to admit it, but at the moment he felt a strange, new kind of fear. He continued to stare into the depth of the staircase.

You're losing it...Tighten up, boy...

Rules are rules; you know how to do this.

The first rule; know your enemy. Know his strengths and weaknesses. It doesn't matter who or what your enemy is; the rules still apply—understand what it is before you move against it, and above all, stay cool. Do *not* let fear or adrenaline or anger compel you to rush in and get yourself killed. Instead, study the situation and the enemy, and when you perceive a weakness or come up with a plan, move against it.

Thorn was disturbed by his own thinking; what in the world had caused him to almost panic? The sound of claws? An animal in the dark? So what? No, no...he wouldn't let this happen. If it was an animal, he'd kill it—simple as that.

Time to take control.

He hadn't taken more than five steps, just to clear the door, when he heard Rebecca's voice in the kitchen.

"Come on, Anthony." Her tone seemed to conceal a tension; maybe she'd read through his veneer. After fourteen years of marriage, she was quite capable of it. She added, "Help me unpack so we can start on your room, okay?"

He couldn't discern Anthony's tired response but knew Rebecca would keep the children occupied while he checked this out. He stared down the staircase again and turned on the flashlight that he had carried since his days as a homicide investigator. Then in slow, cautious steps, he reached the base.

He checked the walls first, and then the ceiling. He aimed the flashlight at the floor and saw nothing but river stones joined by dusty mortar. Curious, he bent and touched the stones. They were smooth and flat from ten thousand years of water-wear and had been laid in place a hundred years ago. If something had been placed beneath them, it would be easy to detect.

Thorn didn't know why the solidity of the floor wasn't very comforting. It should have been, but his instincts told him that something was *really* wrong with this, and he'd become accustomed over the years to listening to his instincts.

He walked forward, acutely searching for typical signs of a "haunted house." It was always something horrific. In fact, the more horrific, the better. There was just nothing like a good old-fashioned broadax left behind by an ax murderer to make a good horror story. But, then, there was the more serious; an adulterous wife or husband entombed, a buried child, an Indian totem with claws and bones and animal skins. He'd seen plenty of Santeria when he was working LA and, frankly, he wasn't spooked by someone who killed a rooster for their religion.

Concentrate on what's down here, man...

The history of this place...

He already knew about the last family—children, father, mother, and grandmother all dead. But there were others, before that, vague rumors of families who had lived *and died* in this place.

Thorn recognized that a normal person would be nervous about such a dark history, and he wouldn't blame them. But he had seen it all, and virtually nothing disturbed him.

In the first place, Thorn didn't believe tragedy had to be traced to any kind of supernatural cause. Men were more than crazy and evil enough to cause havoc without any assistance from the devil. And, quite frankly, Thorn didn't think a demon could do much worse than someone merely intent on murder and mayhem.

Second, and this was the product of decades of discipline and training, Thorn reacted to the sensation of a threat very calmly, very tactically. But he always reacted, was always alert. He never allowed himself to completely let down his guard. Even when he closed his eyes to relax, he was constantly listening and monitoring movement and moods. He was aware of temperature and air pressure and conversation. His concentration was so complete, he could recite *Paradise Lost* on the runway of JFK with a crippled 747 crashing over his head. Still, though, the pressure was building—enough for Thorn to rack a round in the Beretta.

He could see no obvious threat, but that meant nothing. He knew that one of his first chores now would be to tear this place apart and find out what it held because it *did* hold *something*; he was certain of it.

He did *not* believe in ghosts. But it was not logical that so many could have died in such strange circumstances in such a short period of time in this place without *some* kind of reason. He was amazed that the thought occurred to him with such violence now, when it had not occurred to him at all before.

Thorn shook his head—ghosts and regrets and the vaguest kind of fears. This house was bringing them all to life.

He turned toward the stairs as he heard a soft creak at the top step. Remembering to appear casual and relaxed, Thorn walked over to see Anthony standing at the crest, holding a flashlight. He didn't know how the boy had gotten away from Rebecca, but it was no matter. He wasn't going to let his son sense that he was afraid. He made sure his shirt concealed the Beretta in the small of his back and called up.

"You can come on down! But bring the flashlight! It's dark down here!"

Anthony was understandably hesitant.

"What's down there?" he called out.

"Well," Thorn said, casually as he could, "more than likely we're gonna have to spray for bugs. So...spiders and roaches and just...a bunch of old stuff."

"What kind of old stuff?"

"Ah, well, chairs and...looks like some old barrels. A wagon wheel. Some tools. The boiler and some old cans of oil. Basically, just stuff you'd find in a barn or something."

"Anything cool?" Anthony asked.

Thorn gazed about; he wasn't quite sure what an eleven-year-old would consider "cool." It'd been a while. And then—he was surprised he hadn't seen it before—a flash of color caught his eye in the dusty yellows and grays of the cellar.

Thorn stepped forward, but called up. "I don't know. Let me check it out."

As he moved to the colors he saw it was metal, and indeed, colorful. Thorn reached out and brushed away a thick coating of dust and was startled at the deep blue that threw back the light of the flashlight. He wiped away more dust, and it was there; it appeared to be lapis lazuli stone in blue, purple, and scarlet.

There were beads and stones of various colors and small blue templates the size of playing cards linked together with purple beads and scarlet threads. To Thorn, it appeared to be the beginning of a costume of some kind. And it wasn't a hundred years old, either. This had doubtlessly been assembled by the last family that lived here, and if not them, then the previous family. In either case, it wasn't more than twenty or thirty years old. It had to be, actually, because the thread would have rotted in a longer time period, and this was still in good shape. He turned at a soft sound behind him.

It was Anthony.

"What is it, Dad?"

Thorn frowned that the boy had come down the stairs without him hearing the approach. That almost never happened. But he concealed his feelings and smiled down, "Looks like someone was making some kind of a costume."

"Wow!" Anthony exclaimed, touching it. "Is that gold?"

Thorn turned his attention to a gold necklace with blue, purple, and scarlet threads and beads. He rubbed the necklace with a thumb and the flashlight reflected brightly.

"Might be," Thorn muttered. "Or iron ferrite—what they call 'fool's gold.' It looks enough like gold if it's been smelted and polished." He released a deep breath. "I sort of doubt these folks had enough money for this much gold. It'd be worth a few thousand dollars."

Thorn wasn't surprised at Anthony's next question.

"Can we keep it?"

Thorn laughed. "I don't know. It might belong to somebody, or be part of a will. I'll have to check it out."

"Sure is a lot of gold."

Laughing, Thorn clapped him on the shoulder. "I'll put it some-place safe, and we'll call the sheriff tomorrow. If nobody lays claim to it, it's ours."

"What if a museum wants it?"

"Then they'll have to pay for it," Thorn grunted. "They pay for everything else."

Standing to his full six feet two, Thorn gazed around the basement. "All right, there's nothing down here. I'm just gonna check for leaks. Why don't you go upstairs and start getting ready for bed?"

Anthony was happy enough to go. He'd seen it. Big deal. "Okay, see you upstairs."

"Be careful on those steps. Watch out for nails."

"Okay."

Despite the fact that he could order men by platoons, Thorn had never been a hard father. He figured it was because his own father had been such a monster. Instead, he loved his kids, taught them right from wrong, and spent as much time as he could with them. Although he did draw lines on behavior, and didn't spare them from discipline when discipline was required.

Thorn hoped and prayed he'd done a good job, but he realized that he wouldn't know for years. Not until they grew up and had enough freedom to decide what they would do, how they would act, how they would treat people.

Rebecca had certainly not been lax in teaching them the importance of a spiritual life and the importance God placed upon patiently doing right, loving others, and demonstrating respect for others and themselves.

Anthony was gone, and Thorn turned at a strange brush of air. There shouldn't be any wind down here, he thought, as he focused on the source.

It was a wall.

Almost in a stalk, Thorn closed on the wall. He lifted a hand and held it a few inches from the mortar. He could feel a soft breeze emerging from between the stones.

"This where you're buried?" he whispered.

Chapter Four

Thorn cast the light around the room. He wasn't a superstitious man. He never had been. But he remembered how one of his partners, Aaron, was so superstitious that he even refused to work on Halloween.

He'd never made a big deal out of his partner's quirk because, when you mostly have to deal with maniacs, Aaron was the best backup in the world for hand to hand or in a firefight.

He was just scared of ghosts.

Thorn's mind returned to the moment; there was something here; an old instinct, honed by his years as a detective, confirmed it. If the feeling hadn't been so strong, he would have ignored it. But it was more than a feeling; he could almost taste it.

He held the flashlight close to the mortar. It was dusty and dry and flaking. Then he raised a hand and felt along the stones, and perhaps it was his imagination, but he thought he felt small indentations. He felt along the stones again, more slowly.

The indentations seemed like they had once been deeper and sharper, like bullet impacts. But they had been muddled by rain over the years and now there wasn't much remaining.

But Thorn was certain.

Yeah, a bullet had hit here—maybe a century ago, or more. He moved the flashlight very slowly and was suddenly aware that the hand holding the Beretta was sweating. His heart was beating harder, his vision tunneling. He wasn't as aware of the temperature as he should have been, and it disturbed him. He struck the wall with his hand and wasn't surprised that it returned a hollow echo.

Yeah, there was a room—or something—hidden here. This wall was concealing it, and Thorn had a fairly strong sensation that whatever it concealed wasn't going to be pretty.

He could hear Rebecca moving boxes in the kitchen and knew he had to get back upstairs or she would get curious and come down. He shook his head in frustration.

No; this wasn't the time to find out what was behind this wall. He'd wait until the kids and Rebecca passed out, exhausted from a long day of moving boxes. Then he'd come back and know what kind of buried secret lay hidden behind these stones.

But he *would* know.

It was almost dark when Rebecca sacked out in an upstairs bedroom, utterly exhausted from the day.

No cooking tonight; they'd ordered a pizza, and Thorn had helped unpack dishes and pots and pans and kitchen doodads until Rebecca and the kids had eaten their fill of cheese and pepperoni. Thirty minutes later they were sound asleep upstairs, and Thorn had dined on leftovers and crusts. Good enough.

After a quick snack he wandered upstairs again to make sure everyone was snug, and then he hesitated, staring over the kids. From their open mouths and heavy breathing, they'd sleep through until tomorrow. It was time.

He'd kept the Beretta in the small of his back all evening, and not just because of habit, though he had been required by department policy to carry it on-duty and off-duty for so many years. No, he had carried it because he'd acquired a bad apprehension, and he had learned a long time ago not to avoid the sensation, however unexplainable.

He picked up the special police issue mag-light, which was ten times more powerful than the generic model civilians purchased at the hardware store.

Quietly, Thorn opened the door to the cellar. He stared into the depthless darkness and was slightly amazed that, as powerful as the mag-light was, it didn't reach the base. It should have reached the base and beyond, but for some unfathomable reason the light seemed to stop halfway down the oak steps.

Knowing that his entire family was safely asleep, Thorn stepped onto the top step and quietly closed the door behind him. They wouldn't be waking for another ten hours, at the least. And more unpacking was the last thing he cared about right now.

In truth, he was as tired as they were, or more, and desperately needed to close his eyes. But he knew that if he lay down he'd be right back up because he could never sleep if he sensed danger—a trait that Rebecca both hated and loved about him, depending.

His pistol was a Beretta 92FS, a semiautomatic nine millimeter with a fifteen-round clip. From habit he still loaded the magazines with 148-grain silver tipped hollow point rounds that struck at supersonic velocity, or approximately 1,250 feet per second at twenty-five yards. They were generally good enough for a one-shot stop against a normal human being.

He moved down the stairs, using the section closest to the wall, where the step would be least likely to creak. He didn't know why he was stalking, he just felt the need to be cautious. His instincts couldn't be that wrong.

He automatically assumed a combat posture as he moved step by step. With one hand, he held the flashlight away from his body at arm's length. With the other, he extended his gun at shoulder level. If someone took a shot—not likely in this situation—they'd aim for the flashlight and miss.

In a split second he reviewed night fighting techniques.

In the dark, don't fire the standard two-shot defense. Drop low and to the side, changing location and height, and blast off a full fifteen-round clip where the flash appeared while *again* moving to a new location. Move in the dark and fire, then move again and listen. As soon as you've fired from a location, your location is known, so you have to move again. But don't move if you think you've hit the target. Wait, and listen.

After firing fifteen rounds—remember to count—there is one shot remaining because there's an extra round in the chamber. Keep aim as you eject the spent clip and shove in another. Don't drop the slide because the slide only locks if it's dead empty, so the sound won't give away your location in the dark.

Speed, speed is of the essence. The trick is not moving the pistol so fast that man-sized holes are left in the pattern, which was the usual problem with any kind of automatic fire. A three-shot burst is the surest way to hit someone. After three shots, recoil generally takes the aim high and to the left.

The tactical review only took Thorn a split second because it was a combination of reflex and instinct. Already he was moving as much from muscle memory as conscious thought. Then, at last, he reached the bottom of the steps.

He shone his light on the wall, took a heavy breath. He knew it; he knew it in every fiber of his being. Something was down here. Nor did he doubt his feelings like a normal person might have doubted them, because he'd faced cases like this before.

In case after case, despite what evidence suggested, Thorn had gone with his instincts—just as he was doing now—to eventually win a conviction. Experiences like that inspired him to trust what he could feel more than what he could touch or see.

Suddenly Thorn realized that the rest of the night could be filled with an irritated sheriff, confused deputies, an angry coroner, yellow crime scene tape, a gurney, and ambulance attendants who would haul some old bones to whatever qualified as a funeral home around here. Nobody liked to be called out in the middle of a stormy night to disinter a dead body, but Thorn wasn't going to let whatever was behind that wall stay here until sunrise.

First, though, he had to find it. And that was going to require a little work. This far beneath the house, he didn't think a little racket would awaken either Rebecca or the kids. And he could always just yell up that he was making room for storage—anything to prevent them from descending those steps until he decided it was safe.

He took another step into the room and saw a stack of old tools in a far corner. He inserted the Beretta into his pants at the small of his back; no reason to conceal it. Then he began looking over the tools. He found an ax—rotten handle; a shovel—that wouldn't work.

This is stone...I need something to crack it...

Then he found it: a pickax.

He checked the steel, rusty but still strong—it'd do. He checked the handle—incredibly preserved. It had to be a hundred years old, and it looked like it could have been bought in a hardware store yesterday. Thorn could easily dig up a grave—an *unmarked* grave—with this.

He turned and shone his light at the segment of wall framed by old bullet impacts. It was almost as squarely framed as the entrance to a tomb. His real question: What kind of tomb? And why was he so disturbed by it? He was no amateur; he'd dealt with death, in one form or another, most of his life. He was a very capable soldier and knew it, but there was something...something unsettling about this—something unnatural.

This—whatever it was—didn't really feel hidden. It felt more like it was...waiting. The feeling made him picture ghosts and skeletons rattling chains along the corridors of his house.

He walked to the wall and laid the mag-light so that it illuminated the entire bullet-ridden section. His shadow would pose a problem as he moved, so he found a position basically in the middle of the square and drew back the pickax.

Thorn was good with an ax, pickax, or shovel. He had been raised in the country. He could hit hard and do even more damage tearing away, and he hadn't lost his touch over the years.

He swung and the pickax dug deep into ancient stone. When he tore it away, a shockingly large section of the wall dislodged. He hit it again; the wall was thick and old, but the stone was strangely brittle. It took him thirty minutes of hammering away at the middle section and then a significant portion caved in. There was still a one-foot high foundation remaining, but Thorn ignored it.

He raised his right arm with the Beretta at the incredibly thick darkness, shining the light into the depth, and didn't move. He'd stand there a half hour or until he felt it was safe to move. But, in truth, he wasn't in any hurry to enter. He had a feeling that whatever was hidden in there was not something anyone wanted to discover. Maybe what happened in the past should stay in the past. But it was too late for that now. All secrets have an end, and this one had ended.

Thorn stepped carefully over the foundation, moving the Beretta from left to right, as he'd been trained. There was no real reason for it; it was just training, reflex; he couldn't have prevented himself if he had tried. Whatever was dead in here felt like it'd been dead for a thousand years, but he never let down his guard. Indeed, eternal watchfulness was a mode so deeply ingrained in Thorn that he couldn't imagine how other people walked around ignorant of how others were dressed, whether anyone was going in and out of the bank, what cars were running in the parking lot, or even sudden shifts in the wind.

When Thorn walked into the bank to deposit his early retirement, he could tell Rebecca the make, year, and license plate number of every car near the entrance. Before he cleared the second door, he knew whether the tellers were moving freely, whether the security guard was wearing his gun, and the model of it. But before that he already knew whether the shades were drawn, whether people were using the phone, making notes, talking, or standing in silence.

A bank or supermarket were the two places Thorn broke custom and didn't open the door for Rebecca. Instead, she was always second, right behind him, as he glanced over it—a protective quirk of his that she found endearing, or so she said. Otherwise, after fourteen years of marriage, he always opened the door for her, house or car or church.

Thorn did one quick sweep with the mag-light to see if anything at all was in what he had come to regard as a tomb. It seemed empty enough. Then he saw something gray and unmoving and covered in rags. He walked closer.

Yeah...

There you are...

Yep...it was a dead guy.

A *really* dead guy.

Thorn stood over it and stared down. It had to be a hundred— maybe a thousand—years old. He'd seen a ton of corpses, sure, but nothing like this. This was ancient.

The mouth hung open in a silent scream and the rib cage provided a clear view of the spine. The humerus and radius and ulna were stripped bare, and Thorn discerned slight scrapes in the bone, as if from bullet wounds or rats—hard to tell on something this old. But—the detective in Thorn couldn't help but notice—the skull was remarkably undamaged, as if the rodents had avoided that particular part of the body.

Looking closer, Thorn determined that some of the bone damage was definitely from bullets. Half a dozen ribs had been blasted cleanly in half, others were snapped away from the spine. Forearms, carpals, and both humeri had also sustained scrapes.

Thorn knelt beside the body. He automatically reached for plastic trauma gloves before realizing he no longer carried any. So, using his bare hand, he removed a tiny shred of cloth from the skeleton and held it closer to the light.

Cotton. Thorn could still detect individual fibers. And then he detected a color; it appeared to have been a mixture of blue, purple, and scarlet, much like the lapis lazuli plates in the main cellar.

He didn't know what to make of this guy's cloak matching the colors of the ceremonial garb in the cellar. It reminded Thorn of something he'd seen once, but he couldn't remember what it was or where he'd seen it. Still, he felt it was important, so he filed it away; it'd come to him. Right now he was more concerned about how long this guy had been dead.

He gently ran a hand over the forearm to see if it was petrified. It wasn't. But the hair—the last thing to fade—was gone, which meant at least sixty years even in this environment.

He knew it was far too late to determine whether this Unknown had actually been murdered or those bullet scars were the result of war. But Thorn didn't think anyone would go to the trouble of walling him up unless they wanted to conceal a crime. Then he estimated the guy's size; it looked like he was well over six foot tall, maybe seven.

He'd been strong and big-boned, probably about two hundred fifty pounds. The spine was straight, and Thorn didn't detect any kind of arthritic defects or calcium buildup in the joints; he'd been exceedingly healthy for the time period until he'd danced with one seriously determined firing squad. Glancing up, Thorn saw scratchings on the wall beside the skull.

It wasn't English, French, or German—Thorn spoke them all. No, it was some kind of early European or Native American pictographs—maybe something no one in the world still understood. But the writing was ragged and haphazard, as if they'd been done quickly and under stress.

Thorn was almost shocked to realize the guy *himself* had drawn the letters! With the thought, Thorn sat back and stared.

They'd buried him *alive?*

He shivered with the thought.

They buried him *alive*.

Why would anyone bury someone alive and needlessly mark the grave with bullets? For that matter, why would anyone bury someone else alive at all?

Thorn's flashlight caught a glimpse of silver on the dead man's left wrist, and he squinted. Something was there.

Reflexively operating by his training as a homicide detective, Thorn studied the ground very carefully. He didn't want to disturb anything that might reveal a clue as to what happened here. But, realistically, the *normal* rules didn't apply to hundred-year-old corpses; this was an archeology dig, not a crime scene.

Then, fairly satisfied that he wouldn't disturb anything important, Thorn placed the Beretta on the ground and reached out. He touched whatever object reflected the light.

It was a manacle.

A *manacle*...

There was a dust-covered chain attached to it. Thorn looked up and saw a thick railroad-sized spike holding the chain in the wall. He didn't know why he hadn't noticed it before. He surmised it was because his interest had been focused on the skeleton, itself. But this was even more curious...

Manacles and chains.

So...they had shot him and chained him and buried him alive...not necessarily in that order.

Thorn was intrigued; he'd always liked mysteries, and this qualified. But he wasn't shocked. From the first, he'd sensed this would be something weird. Now, though, it had moved beyond weird to murder. And not just murder, either. It was a horrible, drawn-out murder, and Thorn had no desire to live on top of it. He was fast deciding this whole thing should *stay* in the past.

The thought occurred to Thorn that perhaps he should just rebuild the wall, and stronger this time, but there were two problems with that. Rebecca would eventually become curious why he'd done it, and she was too accurate a lie detector for him to deceive. And second, he wasn't too crazy about having a dead guy in his basement.

No, he decided, if he was going to have any peace of mind, he had to get rid of this guy. He didn't care, really, who this dude had been or who had killed him. Whatever happened here happened more than a hundred years ago. What Thorn cared about was the chance that someone who died so horribly might have left behind some "bad vibes." He didn't want to say *ghost*, even to himself. As far as justice, let the past bury the past.

He rubbed a thumb across the manacle and confirmed what he'd suspected; yeah, it was silver. It wasn't a big leap of logic, considering they were less than forty miles from Salem, Massachusetts, America's heartbeat for witchcraft and the occult. Then Thorn angled the maglight on it and saw slight indentations.

This man had been imprisoned before he had been buried, but

somewhere in the melee, a group of men had opened up with sidearms and shotguns and rifles, firing at him in frustration or fear or both. Thorn deduced that it had to be more than one man because it would have taken a single man all night to expend this many rounds with a seventeenth century muzzle loader.

But what kind of man could inspire such extreme retribution and treatment from an entire village? A warlock? A mass murderer? Did he burn down the church? Practice witchcraft? Kidnap innocent travelers? Practice human sacrifice?

There were no clues that Thorn could see. He shook his head and pulled off the manacle. Phalanges from two of the fingers fell apart.

Frowning in concentration, Thorn stood and studied the manacle closely. It was remarkable craftsmanship—flawless, as far as he could determine. And the thought occurred to him; who in the world would use thousands of dollars in silver on a dead man and then bury him alive and then *shoot* him on top of all that?

Overkill wasn't the word.

A lot of people had been utterly terrified of this man. Ridiculous images of werewolves and vampires flashed through Thorn's mind, and he put them away just as quick. He was not an idiot and judged that those who did believe in such things were not necessarily fools but... certainly not living in reality.

Intrinsically, Thorn tried to put himself in the minds of the killers. And the first thought that came to him was the time period. What was reality a few hundred years ago wasn't exactly reality now.

Superstition was high back then, and ghosts and curses had meaning. Now, science and civilization had mostly replaced what some had held for so long to be the supernatural, but back then...Well, they'd burned people at the stake for having a black cat. Any number of reasons could account for this man's death, even the slow and gruesome process of it.

Only one thing was certain; this guy was killed in a hard and vengeful manner by some very frightened people.

Thorn was considering what to do next when something caught his attention. It had been a flash of...light?...in the blackened eye orbs of the corpse. However impossible it seemed, Thorn was certain of it. There had been only empty blackness and then a flash of...intelligence?

No, Thorn told himself immediately, it couldn't be. It had been a reflection of the mag-light; it happens. But all of a sudden he made a hard decision. This thing was not staying in this house tonight.

The phone line hadn't been hooked up; it didn't matter. Thorn used his cell phone to call the county sheriff's dispatcher.

"Is this an emergency?" answered a woman's voice.

"No...Not exactly."

"Name and address?"

Thorn told her what she needed for her contact card.

"What's the situation?"

Thorn debated a moment on how to say this without causing a major response. "I've discovered a very, very old skeleton in the basement of my new house."

He gave her the address and was slightly put off when she seemed pretty familiar with it. He knew the house had a tainted history, but he hated being part of a local legend.

"Yes, sir," she replied, "we'll send someone out immediately."

Thorn blinked; a remarkably calm dispatcher. It was as if they found buried skeletons all the time around here.

"I'll be waiting for him outside."

Dial tone.

Dispatchers weren't big on good-byes.

Cold...

...Cold?

He had no eyes, but he felt...cold.

Air...something...touching him.

He attempted to see, but he was so weak. What was this? It was cold...and wet.

By reflex he closed his hand, knowing something different, there. The life left within him blazed with hope, and he closed his fingers tighter. They were warm in the cold. He could feel them.

He concentrated. There was...*what was it?*

Something had happened to break the darkness.

Searching a long moment he found what he needed and concentrated, calling upon that force that had never betrayed him across millennium, but nothing happened. And so he continued, concentrating, willing it to be as it had always been. And as he concentrated he felt the darkness and the air and the moist dirt beneath him and the agony of his form.

He was *free*!

He knew it as he thought it, and he tried to rise, but he was not yet able. He tried to open his mouth, move an arm, to do anything to alter this awkward position, but strength was coming so slowly to these skeletal limbs.

In Egypt he had transformed dead things into living things. He had turned water into blood. He had called forth animals of every kind from the forest in times of famine so that the people worshipped him even more than pharaoh.

Spiraling, dazzling, serpentine darkness...

He could see!

In his riotous joy he would have roared, but for a faint sensation that he was not alone, and he must be alone. He had been alone for so many centuries, so many...*Had it been centuries?*

It began to return to him...Yes, it had been centuries, once, and then centuries more...yes, certainly at least three centuries more after the millennium that he had been buried. But now he was awake again.

He heard sounds upstairs and...

Upstairs?

Where was he?

He groaned as he looked down and saw his left wrist, where the hated manacle had held him to the wall. His wrist was free, and the manacle lay upon the moldy ground. And then, with a frown, he reached over with his freed left hand and ripped the manacle off his right wrist.

With both hands chained, he was imprisoned. Now he was free, and with that he leaned forward and stood, gathering himself, his mind, his spirit and will, reaching out to that eternal force that had always given him strength to rise from the dead, for it had commanded death.

But it was not so strong now. It seemed distant and...unforgiving, somehow. He twisted his head in frustration.

"Where are you?" he whispered, before the most hated of all thoughts came to him, the thought of what first brought him to this ruin, stripped of his glory and devoid of his own land.

It was there before him, in his gathering dark vision, the beginning of the end of all that he knew.

It had been a day like any other in the courtyard of Amenhotep II, pharaoh of Egypt, and he—Jannes—the greatest of all sorcerers, had entertained the mindless concubines and guests of court with simple tricks that left them amazed and speechless.

It was nothing for him—the turning of wine into bread, of sand into iron, calling down the fowl to settle on the arms and shoulders of the veiled maidens decorated by their masters in such splendorous silk and satin. He had performed all his duties cunningly and discreetly, allowing Amenhotep to take the glory, and then...

He had walked into the courtyard like a beggar roused from the street, seeking food and clothing. Jannes had seen a hundred thousand of them rise and fall, and he had long ago ceased to sense any joy at their demise. They were chattel; they lived, they died. But this one was different, somehow.

He bore himself rigidly and without fear. His robe was a deep crimson and flowed to the ground, covering an undershirt of deep blue and white. His hair, typical of the slaves, was long, and his flowing white beard descended to his chest. His strong chest and shoulders were testimony of a long life of physical hardship in the desert, but he did not seem dismayed or weakened by his many years.

The guards strangely gave no challenge as he walked forward with his smaller, gray-bearded companion. Each held staffs, and Jannes stepped before the throne, as Amenhotep rose.

"Moses," Amenhotep intoned, and then, slowly, he smiled, "at last, you come to me."

The one who was Moses stepped forward.

He was large, but stood bent with a humility that made him seem smaller. Still, there was something about him that hinted of great strength, even in his demure posture. He regarded Amenhotep with the aura, the fearlessness, of a king. Then the man who was beside this shepherd raised his eyes to Amenhotep, and spoke.

"Noble Amenhotep," he began quietly, "I am Aaron, the brother of Moses, whom you see before you."

Amenhotep's visage reflected his anger. "I know Moses, you fool. I have just welcomed him! Moses and I have been friends all of our lives, so let Moses speak for Moses." He regarded Moses with growing fondness. "Will you speak with me, brother?"

With a heavy sigh, Moses stepped forward and finally spoke in a hesitant, uncertain tongue: "I wish I came only to embrace you, my brother. But that is not the cause of our gathering."

Amenhotep, as he had been trained, laughed to defuse any impression of his confusion. "Brother, you have returned to your home. Now we can build Egypt together!" He shook his head. "And all is forgiven for a meaningless event that had no consequence. A dead man is a dead man. We mortared the pyramid with his blood and bones!"

He turned with arm outstretched. "Slaves, bring me the finest steer! Rouse the musicians! We shall celebrate for a season! For the architect of all Egypt has come home!"

Moses spoke again: "Great Pharaoh, we are humbled and thank you for your graciousness. You are the greatest ruler of all the nations. But we have come to ask a simple request, if you would hear us."

Amenhotep laughed, then glanced quizzically at those around him. He took a step forward and put both hands on Moses' shoulders. "Why such formality, Moses? I have longed to see you again, brother. Any boon you crave shall be yours!"

Moses bowed his head, and the celebratory atmosphere ended. It seemed like all music had fled, all dancing had ceased, and a dark cloud had settled over the open-roofed courtyard. In the deep currents of silence, Amenhotep's voice seemed tiny and insignificant.

"Moses? What is it? Are you tired?" He lifted an arm to serving girls. "Bring us some wine! My brother thirsts!"

"No," Moses intoned. "It is not wine I seek, brother."

Amenhotep had not understood, and he stared in silence. Then the pharaoh had stretched out his arm. "This is Jannes, my servant. He can do many magical and wonderful things, brother. Are you in danger? Do you need my assistance? I can assure you that Jannes alone is worth as much as my entire army."

"I come only to deliver a message," said Moses.

"A message?" the pharaoh laughed. "And who would be so foolish to send me a message without a gift? Surely not you, Moses."

Moses lowered his head. "No, great Amenhotep, I would not be so foolish. The message comes to you...from the God of Israel."

Amenhotep stepped back at the words. His right arm, involuntarily, had lifted to cover his chest, and he stared a moment more, before laughing. His voice was hesitant and subdued; "Brother, all sins of the past are forgiven...You do not need to forsake all that we hold dear for this...farce. I welcome you back with open arms."

"God has forgiven me," Moses declared, just as quietly, "so I do not need, nor seek, the forgiveness of men. I come only to deliver the message to Great Pharaoh, for the God of Israel says unto you, 'Let My people go.'"

And so it began...

When Moses had come the third time, Amenhotep had summoned Jannes to the courtyard, and he had observed the Hebrew prophet as he argued so humbly and yet so forcefully. And with each exchange, it seemed, Amenhotep became more and more agitated and hostile. He complained that his sleep had been fitful and his waking hours haunted by strange and disturbing fears. And finally his talk of disturbing thoughts was eclipsed by open contempt, and then hate, for Moses. Eventually, Amenhotep's every waking moment was spent decrying the power of the Hebrew God.

Jannes knew far better than to doubt the power of the Hebrew God. He had witnessed the Old One's power before and had no illusions of who the victor would be in a contest. Yet he could not very well reveal his fears to the pharaoh.

Despite Amenhotep's schemes to frustrate Moses, Jannes knew that the Hebrew would not cease from his ministrations. He had learned long ago that the Hebrew God demanded and received nothing less than total devotion from his chosen servants. And if Moses had delivered this message to Amenhotep, the most powerful ruler of this world, he was certainly chosen. Yes...he was chosen, or he would have been a dead man long before now.

And then the moment came.

With all of Amenhotep's slaves, couriers, guards, concubines, and a large host of revelers and guests present, Moses had loudly and boldly declared: "The time for words has passed, Amenhotep! Behold the power of the God of Israel!"

At the words of Moses, his brother Aaron threw down his staff and in the blink of an eye it was transformed into one of the serpents that inhabited the Nile. It was not like Set, the crocodile, nor was it like a snake. No, the serpent referred to was a creature about six cubits in length, and the weight of a man, but it was unnaturally fierce and territorial and had been known to terrorize creatures twice its size. Also, it was covered with scales so tightly joined that not even air could pass between them.

Amenhotep had backed up in shock. "Jannes!" he cried, "show this renegade Hebrew that he has done nothing my own sorcerers cannot do as well!"

Transforming a staff into a serpent was no easy task, and Jannes had gathered himself. Then he began concentrate and spoke the necessary series of words and incantations, and despite the fact that he endured great agonies to channel the force that worked through him, he stoically revealed no pain. For he knew that how others perceived his power was more important than the power itself.

Often enough, if they simply believed you controlled power, it was the same as genuinely possessing it. In fact, that very phenomenon is what worked so well for Amenhotep, who possessed nothing but a golden throne and the title, "Son of Ra."

In truth, though, Amenhotep was only the fortunate child of a foolish old man who outlasted his usefulness, and so he had generously put the previous pharaoh, his father, to sleep in his fiftieth decade.

Pharaohs come and go; *he* was the power behind throne. He had always been the power, and his power was real. But he somehow sensed that it would not be enough in this contest.

Finally, when his incantation was complete, he raised his face to see that his god had not deserted him. For on the floor, facing the Hebrew, was a second serpent, every inch as large as the serpent of Moses. Then Jambres threw down his staff as well, and he again intoned the spell, and Jambres' serpent was there.

For a moment he actually hoped that he had overcome the prophet of Israel, but it did not last long. And when the serpent of Moses had killed and eaten the two serpents the Egyptians had conjured, he knew this would indeed be a long and laborious battle.

Still, Amenhotep was confident in a power he did not possess to defeat Moses. And when Moses had turned the Nile—the source of all life—into blood so that many living creatures died, the pharaoh had become vividly defiant.

Amenhotep demanded that he duplicate the miracle wrought by the Hebrew God, and he had complied. But transforming water drawn from freshly dug wells had been as nothing compared to the serpent. Yes...to manipulate dead matter was simple, but to summon forth a living, breathing thing required test of his faith, for he never knew whether his god would honor his requests or deny them for its own mysterious reasons.

He knew without being told that Moses enjoyed a personal relationship with his God. While he, himself, was forced to rely on the hints and mysteries and masks that his god allowed. But he had chosen long ago to refute the Old One. Nor did he regret his decision; what he had gained through his allegiance to the Darkness was far more satisfying than anything he would have gained from servitude to the Light.

He almost laughed when Moses had summoned frogs from the restored Nile, for they were not a threat. And then the infernal throng of creatures began to die so that they had to be piled in heaps and dunes and hills of rotting bodies that spread flies and disease and a stench that would not be denied through every house and room and tent.

Enraged, Amenhotep had commanded him also to call forth frogs and demonstrate Moses could accomplish nothing that his own great sorcerer could not match.

Jannes had seen no sense in such a request; it would have been wiser to command him to drive the frogs back into the Nile. But Amenhotep was shortsighted enough to make the command in the presence of slaves, and he could not allow the people to know that the pharaoh was a fool. So, for reasons of security, he had been forced to indulge the idiot prince.

Moses was not discouraged when he, too, called forth frogs from the Nile, though for him it had been no miracle. Indeed, he could not even imagine calling upon the Hebrew God for the power to work his sorcery.

No, he had done as he had always done. He had invoked the presence of his god, even though he could not invoke him by his true name, for his god had many names. And his god had answered.

The cooperation of the god he served was never a certain thing, and he accepted that. His prince might, or might not, acquiesce to his requests. And unlike Moses, he himself did not know the true nature of his god; he only knew that if he was obedient, and did everything he could to destroy followers of the God of Israel, his god was pleased with him and awarded him accordingly.

Pain...

He remembered where he was in this moment...

He was underground.

In the darkness of his tomb, he attempted to stand, and in painful agony he collapsed back to the embracing dust. Then he placed his free right hand against the floor and pushed violently to rise, and as he rose he remembered the eventual defeat he had received at the hands of that hated lawgiver—that messenger of the Hebrew God.

Aaron, always at the instruction of Moses—who alone heard the instruction of God—had raised his staff and struck the sand of the desert, and it had become gnats.

Gnats—they had seemed insignificant, at first. But they tormented and stung and blinded and crawled into our clothing and bed and eyes until we grew weary of striking them. As it was with all the plagues, they seemed insignificant in the beginning; but as they lasted, endurance and patience faded and torment began.

And so he had called upon the god he could not see to duplicate the miracle of the Hebrew god. He had ordered Jambres to inscribe the incantations on stones cut with bronze harder than iron, forged from his own secret process, and summoned his source...

But—as he feared—at last his source had not answered.

And yet the gnats had continued until Amenhotep had finally summoned the Hebrew prophet and his brother and asked him to call upon his God to relent. Then Amenhotep had summoned him yet again and asked for an explanation to this travesty. He would never forget his words, for they had been alone and he could speak freely.

"Amenhotep!...You *fool!* Do you truly believe I raised you to rule over Egypt so that I might answer to you as my master?" He stared upon the "son of Ra" and shook his head. "Remember who rules this nation, Amenhotep! And take care you do not shortly follow your father to Anubis!"

In the sanctity of the temple, Amenhotep had managed, "But...but *where* is this God of Moses? *Who* is this God?"

"The God of the Israel is the greatest god of all," he declared, unable to deny the plain truth since he had been defeated in the eyes of all Egypt. "I suggest that you let His people go."

But the prideful prince had defied the warnings until it cost him the most precious blood of all—his own son—and then he had let the people go only to pursue them with Egypt's entire army.

Jannes had laughed as the horsemen, arrayed with javelins and bows and banners, bravely pursued the weaponless Hebrews into the desert, for he knew what would come. They could catch the slaves, yes, in the deserts beside the sea, and pharaoh's army would pursue them across the sea...and pharaoh's army would be destroyed.

Remembering, he laughed. He had not even tried to warn the fool-king of his army's impending doom. There had been no reason. If this ragged nation needed to be defended, his sorcery could defend it. Otherwise, they could die at the hands of slaves.

He himself could build another nation from the ashes of this one, for over the centuries he had learned that all kings, and all nations, were expendable. His own survival was the only matter of importance.

And his time here was almost over.

All had seen that his sorcery could not defeat the power of the God of Israel, and in time contempt for his god would only grow. Even though the God of Israel had apparently vanished into the desert with His beloved prophet, leaving him free to establish another pharaoh and rule once more from behind the throne as he had done for a thousand years, it would never again be the same. The people would not forget that he had been defeated, and so he began that day to plan his new future as he had planned it in the days following Babylon.

He himself had been born after the flood, when the Nephilim had once again established themselves upon the earth to replenish the ageless list of kings. But the old ways had passed, and no one remembered Emmenluanna, who had reigned for 43,000 years. Nor did they remember how he had learned the secrets of his sorcery. He, alone, knew how to open the gateway to power without worshipping the Hebrew god.

A frame suddenly loomed before him, and he raised his head, hearing the dry grind of bones and... He blinked.

He could *see!*

Yes...Yes...he *remembered*...

They had placed him here, and he could see again the white flashes that blinded him and tore through this flesh until he fell hopeless against the wall. He had withdrawn the Puritan's sword from his chest, the silver-coated blade smoking with his blood, and hurled it aside. And then he had tried to tear himself loose from the chains, but the chains had held so that he could do nothing as the last stone was placed.

Standing alone, there in the darkness of that moment, he had raised his face to the domed ceiling, and called upon the source of all his power to sustain this withering flesh beyond the mere years of men, so that he might rise again one day and avenge himself.

And now...he was free.

Sounds above...

He staggered over fallen stones, moving into the half-light of another room, and then he reached a stairway that led up. Nothing was familiar to him now. But in the back of his mind he felt rather than saw the path to freedom.

To the left...

He walked toward shadows and felt along the wall, understanding rapidly that things were not as they had been. Then, with his faint, returning sensations, he knew that wind was flowing past him, and he reached out to feel a wooden shelf.

He could not hold back from roaring as he pushed upon the hidden door. The wall surrendered and then he was standing in a tunnel. He could not see the light, but he did not need the light.

He hated the light.

In moments, he was gone.

Ten minutes later, a patrol car pulled into Thorn's driveway and by reflex Thorn studied the officer's caution.

He came up the drive with his headlights on, parked directly in front of the house, left himself no cover in case of rifle fire. He didn't even park beside the tree at the front gate, the perfect protection.

Not so good; these boys could use some street survival skills. If Thorn had this one for a few weeks in the LAPD Academy, he might make a decent police officer out of him.

"Hey," Thorn said casually. "I'm Michael Thorn."

"I'm Deputy Taylor. Dispatcher says you might have something in your basement."

"Yeah, I think so. Something...pretty old."

"How old?" Taylor asked.

"A few centuries, if you ask me. It probably needs an archeologist more than an undertaker."

Although Thorn himself wasn't an expert in Crime Scene, ten years in Robbery-Homicide with the LAPD had trained him to recognize talent when he saw it, and at the moment he didn't see it. Still, Taylor took his job, and himself, very seriously.

The deputy walked forward. "Let's take a look."

Thorn gently raised a hand. "If you don't mind, deputy, my wife and kids are asleep upstairs. This could be something, probably isn't. But whatever happened here happened a long time ago, so there's no rush, and my family is exhausted. I'd appreciate it if you tried not to wake them up."

Taylor took a surprisingly long time to reply, and when he did,

Thorn was curiously disturbed at the tone. "Well, mister, you don't know the history of this town, do you?"

Thorn blinked. "Well, I know this place has a past. But most of these old New England towns have ghost stories. LA has its share, too—old cemeteries, mausoleums. It's the same old, same old."

Taylor shrugged and then took a step forward. "This one might be different, but let's take a look. I'll be quiet. No reason to wake up the wife or kids."

They made their way to the cellar, and Thorn began to descend. He had taken four steps before he realized Taylor was still standing at the crest, staring into the darkness. He hadn't even pulled out his mag-light.

"What's wrong?" Thorn asked quietly. "It's right down here."

Taylor still didn't move.

"What's wrong, man? It's just a dead guy." Thorn moved his head in the direction where the skeleton was. "Come on, let's take a look. It could be a thousand years old...probably is."

"Yeah," Taylor replied without enthusiasm. Slowly, he drew his mag-light and began to descend with glacial speed. Thorn waited until the deputy was beside him and couldn't help but ask, "You okay?"

Taylor didn't move.

With a heavy sigh, Thorn made a motion with his flashlight and said, "Come on."

After a remarkably long descent, they finally stood before the tomb. Thorn didn't even bother looking into it. He knew what was in there and didn't particularly care to see it again. He just shone his flashlight into the aperture and looked at Taylor, who finally moved up beside him. Thorn knew instantly that something had changed.

Taylor looked at him: "What am I supposed to see?"

Not even taking a second to waste on surprise, Thorn looked into the grave. The silver spikes were embedded in the wall. The chains hung distended, long and heavy and black with cave dust. The manacles were secure and locked, and the imprint of a skeletal body was deep in the dust.

But the body was gone.

"There's nothing here," Taylor said, sounding relieved—even happy.

Thorn didn't say a thing as he stepped into the small cavern and shone his light over the walls; the area surrounding the chains still held the same enigmatic writing as earlier. At least that hadn't changed.

Then he did a slow sweep with the light, taking his time—experience had taught him a long time ago to never rush an investigation. Things come out in time and snap decisions, assumptions, and conclusions without solid evidence were always a mistake.

A dozen factors went through his mind. It's possible—however unlikely—that someone could have slipped in and stolen the corpse while he was outside, waiting for Taylor. He hadn't bothered to lock any of the doors; the house had been vacant for years—ever since the last family that lived here met their untimely end. Besides, Thorn hadn't yet checked the windows or means of accessing the cellar, and some of these old places had hidden entrances from the Civil War. It was possible that there was more than one way to get down here.

Still, he was profoundly disturbed. It suddenly felt like a big house—bigger than before—and he wondered what other secrets it might hold. He shone the light in the dirt, searching for footprints, and squinted.

A series of strange lines in the dust lead straight out of the tomb—lines that looked like...skeletal footprints.

He bent, searching the dust for other tracks, and it confirmed what he suspected. There was only a single set of prints leading away from where the corpse had been. Despite what Thorn wanted to find, there were no boot prints other than his. He studied the marks closer; tracking was a skill he'd picked up in one of the many training schools required as an LA detective.

The prints began tentatively, lengthened, and then seemed to deepen. And as they reached the aperture they spread to a normal separation, becoming more balanced.

A lot of possibilities went through Thorn's mind, including the possibility that a three-hundred-year-old skeleton could have stood up and walked out of the house.

Yes, it was ridiculous, but Thorn was conditioned to consider everything—including the ridiculous. Slowly he looked at Taylor, who was still staring, transfixed, into the opening.

"You okay, Taylor?"

Taylor didn't reply.

"Taylor!"

The deputy's head snapped sideways, and Thorn was taken back for a moment by the horror. The deputy's eyes were wide-open, mouth agape. The gun was trembling in his hand.

"What's wrong with you, man?" Thorn asked. "Somebody was probably planning to come in here and get it, anyway, first chance they got. They just ran out of time. Might have already been down here when we arrived. Anything's possible."

It occurred to Thorn that there was only one set of tracks, and they led away from where the skeleton had lain. But he preferred not to consider a walking skeleton *seriously*. Maybe he just wasn't that good a tracker, but it ultimately didn't matter. What mattered was that the thing was out of his house.

He heard Rebecca's voice at the top of the stairs and moved over quickly and casually to the base. Something—it had to be instinct because they weren't making any noise—had awoken her.

"It's nothing, baby," Thorn called up. "Just had to notify the locals about something I tripped over down here."

Thorn knew what her question would be.

"What'd you find, honey?"

"Nothing important; a few old bones, probably prehistoric." Thorn forced a laugh that seemed utterly unforced. "Dino bones, I think."

Rebecca began down the stairs. "I want to see."

Thorn raised a hand. "No! Stay there! This could be some kind of big-time archeological site! We'll let the kids come down and check it out as soon as the sheriff clears it!"

She laughed. "Sounds cool."

Thorn joined her. "Why don't you try and get some sleep? I'll have to stay up for a while, but I'll wake you if anything big happens."

Rebecca turned her head, looking behind her. "Hello, Sheriff," she said pleasantly.

Thorn heard a thick, gruff voice.

"Evening, ma'am. How are you?"

"Fine, thank you. Are you here for the dino bones, too?"

Hesitation, then, "You bet, ma'am. And if you don't mind, I'd like for you to stay here for a little bit until I'm sure it's safe and that those Harvard eggheads ain't gonna go ape cause we messed up their dead-a-saurus."

Rebecca laughed again. "We'll stay out of your way."

"Thank you, ma'am."

The sheriff of Essex County came into view and Thorn did his habitual assessment.

Sheriff Cahill was in his early fifties and dressed just as sharply as Taylor—it reminded Thorn that East Coast cops had a particular lean toward being snappy dressers.

He wore a broad, flat-brimmed black hat, light blue shirt, dark blue pants—pure polyester—a gray tie with a gold-layered tie clip. He had prominently displayed identification, glossy black shoes you could see your face in, and a perfectly maintained leather holster and belt. There was not a thing out of place, as if they had surprise inspections in the field, which Thorn suspected that they did.

He was about six-two with heavy, gorilla shoulders and arms and a truck-tire gut. His face was leathery and tough and even at a distance Thorn could discern enough scars to prove the sheriff had seen plenty of action. He glanced at Cahill's holster and saw that he carried a Colt 1911A2 single action semiautomatic—a powerful gun. The choice of weapons told Thorn two things; Cahill was an old fashioned man and he liked to keep things simple.

But since Taylor carried a Smith and Wesson Model 19, it also told Thorn that Essex County deputies were allowed to carry any number of firearms as long as they were listed in policy. Not surprising; a lot of departments were moving in that direction. Most cities would rather have confident officers who were also expert shots with their favorite weapon than disgruntled officers who couldn't shoot straight with department issue.

The only thing that gave Thorn serious pause was that Cahill was also carrying a shotgun—a Remington 870 12-gauge with an extended magazine to hold eight rounds—a serious gun.

It was always unusual for the county's highest-ranking law enforcement officer to carry a shotgun; supervisors let others do the grunt work. But it was doubly unusual if he carried it to a hundred-year-old murder site.

Cahill didn't hesitate on his way down the stairs; he descended like he was entering a lobster restaurant—nothing to it. He looked directly at Thorn as he reached the base and nodded curtly: "Sheriff Cahill."

"Sheriff."

"What ya got?"

"Nothing now."

Cahill stopped moving. "Thought you had a dead body."

"*Did*," Thorn said almost apologetically. He pointed to the hole in the wall. "It was in there."

Cahill took a moment with that, then moved slowly toward the aperture. He pulled out his mag-light and looked inside, but didn't enter. He seemed to study the cavern a moment and focused on Deputy Taylor. "What's going on here, Jack?"

Taylor shrugged as he took off his flat-brimmed hat and ran a hand across the top of his head. "This guy—"

"Thorn."

"Right, Mr. Thorn...Well, Mr. Thorn, here, says he saw a skeleton in there."

Taylor demurely motioned with his hat at the hole in the wall. "Said it looked like it was a couple hundred years old." He shrugged again; Thorn thought he looked more unsettled by the minute.

Apparently Cahill could be rough when inspired. He looked solidly at Thorn. "You say there was a dead guy in here?"

Thorn gave a tilt of his head. "I was an LA cop for a lot of—"

"Yeah, I know," Cahill grunted, "I checked your background." He waved off Thorn's look. "No offense, Thorn. I do that with everybody. I just like to know who's moving into my community. And, by the way, son, all I got right now on my crew is a bunch of young boys. If you happen to need a job..."

"Thanks, Cahill, but no. I'm done." Thorn sighed. "Anyway, this dude was long dead, all right—a couple hundred years dead. Bones were beginning to petrify. And it was a violent death. He didn't go easy."

"How do you know it was violent?"

Thorn gestured vaguely toward the sheriff's abdomen. "He had broken ribs, plenty of bullet or shotgun damage center-mass, but no damage to the skull. So it looks like they buried him alive and then cut loose on him. I don't expect he lived too awful long, but he might have hung in for a few hours. Lived long enough to write that on the wall, anyway."

Cahill simply stared. "So where is he? He get up and walk off?"

The silence was disturbingly solid.

After a careful look into the tomb, Cahill racked a round in the Remington and stepped up to the entrance. He stood in place, searching with the flashlight. Then he saw the tracks, and his head stayed bent for a long time. Thorn heard him mutter, "Dead guys don't get up and walk off."

There was no reason to comment, but Thorn heard himself say, "Which means someone must have slipped in and taken the body while I was waiting outside for Taylor."

"Yeah," Taylor agreed quickly. "That's probably what happened."

Cahill shone his light briefly over the manacles, caught the glimpse of silver. "Is that silver?"

"I think so," said Thorn.

Cahill didn't remove his eyes from the manacles. Then, "Why would some fool take the worthless bones of a dead guy when they could have taken a good load of silver?"

"Good question," Thorn answered. He looked solidly at Cahill. "What's happening here, Cahill?"

Cahill shrugged. "I don't know. I remember the last family that lived here. The parents went crazy, killed all the kids then killed themselves. Nobody knows why." He paused. "They seemed normal enough, I guess, until they committed mass murder. The father was even a member of the city council—old-time Cotton Mather kind of guy. The wife was a member of the PTA, Chamber of Commerce, First Baptist Church Women's Choir, member of this, member of that. Real sociable.

They had a bunch of kids and...well, like I say; they seemed all right to me."

"Nobody has a clue why they did it?"

Cahill shook his head grimly. "Not a clue. They just went crazy and killed themselves and everybody else, far as that goes."

Well, thought Thorn with some fatigue, there wasn't much else to do down here. He didn't care to hear about murders. He'd just left a job where murder was discussed, analyzed, and thought about twenty-four hours a day.

He theorized that the skeleton might have just been one of the family's earlier victims and he was simply bad at judging the age of bones. After all, it wasn't the same as judging the age of a decomposing body, where he was fairly competent.

Bones were just bones unless you had a doctorate in Forensic Analysis. Thorn was starting to doubt his earlier analysis. Locked in an airless tomb, the bones could be a hundred years old or a thousand. Maybe they collapsed into dust when he exposed them to the air.

And, ultimately, it didn't matter: a hundred years, six hundred, a thousand. Whatever. Dead is dead, and Thorn was certain that it happened a long, long time ago. So whoever was guilty of killing this guy was dead, too.

Not much sense in investigating an age-old murder or even wasting time thinking about it. The skeleton was gone, and Thorn didn't much care who carried it off. Probably one of the guilty party's relatives who had never wanted it discovered in the first place. Only problem: In the morning he'd have to make up something to keep Rebecca at ease. For sure, he wasn't going to tell her he'd found a dead guy down here. He'd have to throw the dice on her lie detecting abilities.

Thorn released a deep sigh and focused on Cahill: "Sorry to get you out of bed, Sheriff."

Cahill's stare gave Thorn a hint for why he was feared by his men—or at least by his deputy. His dark gray eyes were emotionless, implacable, impartial—the eyes of a man who could lift you out of a ditch, shoot you like a dog, and then watch, emotionless, while you bled to death.

Thorn could do the same; his stare alone could close most interrogations. He solidly held the sheriff's gaze.

Finally, Cahill realized Thorn wasn't intimidated. He nodded slowly: "Guess it don't matter none that some fool ran off with an old skeleton. He's dead and gone; whoever did him is probably dead and gone, too. And it don't look like there's too many clues for a crime scene. Might as well let it go."

He looked at the chains, gestured vaguely. "What are you going to do with those? Technically, since this is your house, they belong to you. They might be worth a little bit."

Thorn thought about it.

Normal silver, melted down into bars, might be worth a lot. But the inscriptions written into them might make them a lot more valuable to a museum or gallery. They might have some kind of special, sacred meaning.

Thorn shrugged. "Guess I'll see if anyone wants them."

Cahill moved to the opening, mumbling as he passed Thorn: "I'd wall this back up, if I were you."

Thorn watched closely as Cahill stepped over the foundation and into the tomb, itself. The big sheriff stared down at the skeletal indentations, then glanced back at the imprint of the body. He tilted his head toward Taylor.

"Don't worry about the paperwork, Jack. I'll write it off as a miscellaneous." Cahill paused a long time. "I'm just glad that thing...whatever it was...is gone."

Thorn remembered his earlier feeling of evil. He took a deep breath, released slowly. He was disturbed that his palm was sweating. He stared into the tomb.

"If it is," he said quietly.

Chapter Five

Boxes and boxes and boxes.

Rebecca was using a standard folding knife to cut open the marked boxes as Thorn continued to supervise the moving crew. He'd hired an efficient moving company; no way he was gonna carry all this stuff himself.

It'd actually been something of an amazing experience to watch them load the trucks. He never knew tables, chairs, and all sorts of indiscriminate pieces of furniture could be dismantled in so many ways. But the crews had packed those trucks like a can of sardines—very efficient. No wonder they made so much money; they were worth it.

Thorn continued to dwell on last night. He'd told Rebecca that since he placed the call about the dino bones, the sheriff had decided to check it out and welcome them into Cedar Ridge, encourage them to get their landline hooked up as soon as possible, let Thorn know how many deputies he had and where they usually patrolled. He'd asked if they had any special needs and paid a discreet compliment on Rebecca, who at forty-three seemed even more beautiful to Thorn than she had in her twenties.

After tipping his hat to her, Cahill motioned to Taylor and had the unfortunate lack of concentration—perhaps he really was impressed by Rebecca—to say, "He's gone...I mean; just some old mule bones. Get back on patrol."

Thorn had closed his eyes. He knew that Rebecca would want an explanation for that one.

And, yep, she did.

"What did he mean by that, Mike?"

Thorn had shrugged. "I think he mostly just wanted check us out, see what kind of shape the house was in, get a good look at the kids. He's an old school sheriff—likes to know his people."

Rebecca blinked. "Wow. You don't see much of that in LA." She paused. "I guess he just seemed a little anxious."

"It's a serious job."

Rebecca focused on the comment, or maybe the tone. "Do you miss the action, Michael?"

"I miss putting away maniacs and stopping bad guys from hurting people," Thorn replied. "I never cared for the action in the first place. You know that."

"Yeah, I know. And now you get a chance to relax and be like a normal person. No more fighting monsters."

Thorn had spent his entire life in either the military or the LA Police Department, and he had taken it seriously. Not one policeman in twenty made detective, and usually they were well into their forties. Thorn's promotion had been deserved and rapid but had caused some tension, jealousy, and animosity when it happened. Yet when the other detectives saw that Thorn wasn't in it for glory or the money, but for the satisfaction of doing a good job, he was solidly accepted into the team—a strong team. And there was another dynamic that unexpectedly came into play.

Thorn was so naturally talented and dedicated that his addition to the detective division had caused an unspoken sense of competition. Suddenly, everyone was a better detective because they weren't simply doing it by rote anymore. They were in a Colombo mode—focused, dedicated, attentive, minds working the tiniest detail for the tiniest clue. His mere presence had improved the division.

Thorn turned to see someone approaching the house.

A priest.

A *Catholic* priest.

"Wow," Rebecca muttered, "sort of early for a house call."

Thorn scowled, studying the priest. He was middle aged and portly—not surprising—and he seemed to be having a bit of trouble climbing the slight slope of the hill. He was still about sixty yards away but Thorn could see that he was already breathing heavily.

He was dressed in the traditional white collar suit priests mainly wore at funeral or mass. And as he drew closer, Thorn estimated that he was in his late forties. His hair was still thick and black and swept back smoothly from his forehead. He carried a Bible under his right arm.

When he saw that Thorn had recognized his coming, he waved kindly and continued his climb.

Thorn turned to the moving guys. "You guys okay?"

Nods and waves; yeah, they'd do fine without him. Thorn turned his attention to the priest. Somehow, he sensed this was more than a welcome to the community. Thorn walked down the hill to reduce any sense of drama. He met the priest halfway. "Good morning, Father."

"Good day, my son. I'm Father Cavanaugh. How are you and your family settling in?"

"Doing great, thanks."

"Ah. Good."

Thorn gave a quick jerk of his head. "Why don't you come on up to the house and sit down?"

"A very good idea," Cavanaugh rasped.

Thorn measured his steps carefully as they climbed the remaining portion of the hill, accommodating the less-than-perfect physical condition of the priest.

"Tell me something, Father," he said mildly, aware he'd have to give the priest a chance to get his breath, "do you welcome everyone that moves into the area?"

"As a matter of fact, I do. But I made visiting you and your family a particular mission because of...well, the disturbing history of this old place. For the sake of my own peace of mind, I wanted to bless all who have settled here. And I wanted to invite you to service, of course."

"Yes, of course," Thorn said casually. "But, really, Father, lots of historical places like this have strange histories. It'd be hard to find one that didn't, actually."

"Well," the priest remarked, "that's true. But local legends that you might not have heard yet do tend to prey on the mind. I may have succumbed to intellectual sin by paying too much attention to them." He gestured to surrounding hills. "You may not be aware, but the hills themselves are cloaked with legend. Although it's never been discovered, they supposedly contain an ancient Indian burial ground."

"A lot of legend in this part of the country," Thorn commented.

"Oh, yes, but I'm afraid legends far outdistance the truth. Still, I more than welcomed the chance to come out and get out of the parish for a bit. I love the open country, and this is certainly a beautiful site."

Thorn didn't say anything for a long time, then, "I did find something unusual."

"Oh? And what was that?"

"It's just some writing in the cellar," Thorn answered. "Would you like to take a look at it?"

"If I can be of service," Cavanaugh bowed.

Thorn once again thought about the wall inside the tomb and considered what a weird language would be doing in this very normal, nondescript community where the most exciting event rarely surpassed a robbery.

Thinking about the find, and the amount of superstition this community seemed to harbor, made Thorn suspect that the priest's visit was more purposeful than he had admitted.

"Were you, by chance, notified by the police, Father?"

"Yes," Cavanaugh answered honestly. "I was probably the second or third person they called after they had secured the scene, as they call it." He smiled. "Don't be offended, Mr. Thorn. The people of this parish have sensitive feelings about their superstitions. It is not the same so near Salem as it would be in Los Angeles."

At Thorn's surprise, he laughed.

"Oh, everyone knows about you, Mr. Thorn. In a community as small as this, everyone knows everything."

Thorn shook his head, smiled. "Well, considering the checkered history of this place, it's not too surprising. But tell me something, when these last murders occurred, was Cahill sheriff?"

"Oh, yes. I believe Bill Cahill has been sheriff for the past twenty years or so—something of a lifelong occupation since he returned from the war. And, of course, most people prefer his brand of frontier justice to a long term in the county jail. He has a rather informal way of settling things."

Cavanaugh grew more studious: "But if this is what you're truly asking, Mr. Thorn, yes; Bill Cahill worked all of the previous murders. And I think it's been a craw in his side that they remain unsolved. He couldn't find any clues or motivation, or even any history of violence among the victims—nothing unusual at all, really. Only...this house."

"Have you ever been into the basement of this house?" Thorn asked at last.

The priest took his time: "No, I can't say that I have. But from what I understand from Deputy Taylor, there is obviously an object of interest. I heard there was some type of writing?"

"Yeah," Thorn muttered. "It looks hieroglyphics to me, but I don't know for certain." He shrugged.

Father Cavanaugh obviously found that of great interest—so great an interest that he stopped walking. Then, "I see...Yes, indeed; let's take a look."

They were careful to stay out of the movers' way as they moved through the house. Thorn smiled at Rebecca who was still puttering in the kitchen. She had the pots and pans hanging and was beginning to unload two coolers full of food that Thorn had purchased in a fifteen-minute stop back in Andover. It had been one of those exhausting, last minute stops, but the kids were asleep and Thorn knew he wouldn't want to come back down to the village after driving four thousand miles in six days.

"Doing a great job, honey," Thorn said.

Rebecca laughed and looked down from a stepladder. "It'll be ready by tomorrow night."

"Good enough."

Thorn pointed to Father Cavanaugh, who executed a formal bow. "This is Father Cavanaugh. He came by to welcome us to the community. Father, this is my wife, Rebecca."

"Nice to meet you, Father," she nodded. "And thank you for coming by. Can I get you anything?"

Cavanaugh laughed as he leaned back and patted the sides of his ribs. "Oh, thank you, madam. No, no; I don't suffer from a lack of sustenance. But thank you all the same."

"Well, you're always welcome here, Father."

Thorn was strangely happy that Cavanaugh's presence hadn't

aroused any suspicions in Rebecca, who seemed quite content to get her kitchen in order. He turned to the priest.

"Will you help me with that boiler now, Father?"

"Of course!" Cavanaugh replied, demonstrating that he was quick to adapt. "These old places always have secrets to them, you know. Let me show you how to get it started."

When Thorn was five steps down the staircase, he recognized that there was a lack of movement behind him. He didn't have to turn, but he did. A good many had gone into the Great Beyond in this place. Thorn gave the priest time to steady himself.

"Are you sure you can do this?" he asked.

Cavanaugh's look was strange.

"You say it's an inscription?"

"Not really, no. I said there were some words. And I found some bullet holes in the wall and on the skeleton."

"What skeleton?"

"That's another story." Thorn instantly wished he hadn't mentioned the skeleton. "I just want you to look at these words that are scratched in the wall."

"Scratched, you say?"

"Looks like scratches to me," Thorn answered with a steady stare. Something about the almost instinctive reactive of the priest's body made Thorn even more wary. "What's wrong?"

"Show me these words."

They continued slowly and steadily to the base, with Thorn sweeping the light across what seemed an empty basement. The hole in the wall seemed the same; no change in the size of the hole or the position of stones. Everything was like it'd been. Thorn was surprised that he was grateful for that. Like he expected the stones to get up and walk off next?

At the base, the priest stood a moment then walked slowly forward until he stood in the opening. Thorn shone the flashlight on the wall, and Cavanaugh was instantly transfixed.

The cryptic series of symbols seemed to glow under the flashlight. Thorn saw Father Cavanaugh's lips moving in silent translation.

Yeah, he could read them.

"What is it?" Thorn asked.

"Hieroglyphics," the priest mumbled.

Thorn tilted his head. "Looks sort of like a horse's head," Thorn said, distracted.

"It is," the priest replied. "Almost all modern language comes from hieroglyphics. That horse head turned, degree by degree, becomes an 'A.' It was originally hieroglyphics, then it was stolen by the Mesopotamians—not a real tribe, mind you, just an amalgam of colonies. Then it was taken by the Greeks, who were in turn conquered by the Romans, who also took it."

Cavanaugh continued his history discourse mechanically. "Before the Romans conquered the Greeks, they didn't even have a written language. But after stealing letters from the Greeks, they comprised words with the symbols. They eventually dropped the horse's eye so that only the mouth and head remained. The other letters evolved in a similar pattern. Then the early British refined it into what is now the English language."

Thorn found himself staring at the priest. "You're trying not to tell me something, aren't you?"

Cavanaugh hesitated.

Something about this was irritating Thorn: "Well? What does it say?"

Cavanaugh took a deep breath and spoke distinctly. "It says that whoever reads these words has released one who saw the face of God's mightiest servant and resisted him."

"Oh, good grief," Thorn lifted his hands and dropped him. "And who was the mightiest servant of God?"

"That would be Moses."

"How do you know? You guys keep points?"

Cavanaugh shrugged. "Most scholars would agree that it was Moses. But there is competition, I suppose. There is always John the Baptist or Elijah...But I, myself, consider it to be Moses. And that is the traditional judgment."

Thorn liked mysteries, but not this mystery. He felt the need for a suitable explanation, and began: "Okay, this place isn't too awfully far from Salem. Let's say that three hundred years ago, when Cotton Mather was on a rampage and those psychotic little girls were accusing everyone of witchcraft, a similar witch hunt happened here. Maybe this writing was left by witches or warlocks or some kind of religious nuts."

"You told me you found bullet traces on his ribs and skull?"

Thorn shrugged. "Some."

"And so he wrote these words after he had been shot and buried?"

"People can be shot and live, Father."

The priest continued to read the hieroglyphics. "And though the Almighty possesses magic beyond my own, I will yet have my vengeance against the Lawgiver..."

"Lawgiver?" Thorn asked.

"That would be Moses." Then a thought seemed to occur to the priest for the first time. "What did you do with the body?"

"I didn't do anything."

"Pardon?"

"I didn't do anything with it. It vanished."

Father Cavanaugh stared into the empty grave. "It vanished..."

Thorn sighed. "Father Cavanaugh, I knocked down this wall and found a skeleton. I took one of those manacles off his wrist to see if it was really silver. He sure wasn't coming to me, and I didn't care to be leaning over a dead guy. Anyway, I went upstairs, called the locals; they came out; asked me 'so where's the body?'"

"Meaning?"

"*Meaning*...in the time it took me to get upstairs, call the police, and wait outside for Taylor—let's say a half hour—somebody apparently snuck in here, stuffed the bones in a bag, and snuck out again. It had to be somebody familiar with the layout of this place—somebody local. Somebody who knew all about this and was probably planning it anyway, but they had a time schedule and we messed it up."

There was a long silence.

"If you ask me," Thorn continued, "this was something like a town event when it happened. Everybody knew what was going down, just like in Salem, but there wasn't anything one man could really do against an entire town of hysterical witch haters. Still, he had relatives, and they eventually had descendents who still live around here. And for some reason, when the entire town heard we were moving into this house, his descendents wanted to retrieve their ancestor's bones. Stranger things have happened."

Cavanaugh's brow hardened. "This is evil."

Thorn stood in abstract silence. "It's not possible that this could just be another old house with a grave, huh?"

"This man hated Moses. But he was part of a larger plan."

"What kind of plan?"

"Something terrible." The priest shook his head. "Just as the Almighty has reserved Elijah and Enoch for himself—the two prophets who will witness in Jerusalem and bring down fire upon God's enemies—Satan has also reserved his soldiers to make war against the children of God in the end of days."

"I think this guy's war-making days are over, Father."

"Perhaps. Or..."

Thorn was staring at the priest now. He suddenly felt ridiculous. "Forget it," he said. "If his relatives want his body so bad, they can have it."

Cavanaugh looked directly at Thorn.

"Do you believe in the devil, Mr. Thorn?"

Thorn released a heavy sigh: "You know, I just got here, and I don't want to be rude, but I'm already tired of hearing about the devil. To me, there's enough evil in man alone. And I don't see that some old bones and some weird writing in some cave mean the devil's at your door. Why don't we just deal with what we can see?"

"What you can't see is as real as what you can."

Thorn stared into the empty grave and couldn't help but be curious. "Tell me something: just when was the exodus, anyway? Three thousand years ago?"

The priest shrugged. "Around 1,492 BC, give or take. It's impossible to determine for certain. But I could give you a seminar on the archeological evidence, if you like."

"I don't."

"This is not easy for me to say," Cavanaugh began, "but there are those who might be angry at your desecration of this grave."

Thorn's eyes narrowed; "Like who?"

"I do not know their names," the priest replied. "But I will contact those more knowledgeable than myself—men familiar with these things. They will know how to insure your safety."

"Safety from *what?* This guy's been dead for a hundred years! How many ticked off relatives can he have in this area?"

"It is best to assume that he still has some, Mr. Thorn. This type of thing, from what I understand, can be generational. And his family, or those loyal to whatever he was a part of, may have untoward intentions for you and your family because you disturbed his tomb, which is more than likely a sacred place for them." He shook his head angrily. "Do not underestimate the passion of these people, Mr. Thorn."

Thorn's face was grim.

"All right," he said, finally, "then find out what you can and get back to me. Do you need anything from in there?"

"Do the manacles have any type of inscriptions?"

"Yeah, it looks like Hebrew."

"Give them to me. And when this ends, I am not certain I will be able to return them. It is quite likely they will have to be destroyed."

Thorn stepped to the corner with the century-old tools. It took him a moment, but he found a double-bladed ax with a blue plastic handle. It had probably been left behind by the last family that had so strangely self-destructed within these walls.

He stepped boldly over the foundation of the tomb and noticed how his mag-light, which the priest now held, cast an unnaturally sharp silhouette against the dirt floor and solid granite walls.

Thorn angled his shadow, took solid footing, and put his weight behind the swing. He hit on spot. Perfect.

Yeah, he still had it.

Silver, like gold—while pretty—has very few practical uses and virtually no tensile strength. A silver link snapped, and the chain clattered to the dusty floor. Thorn repeated the procedure on the second chain but missed, and the blade shattered stone. Without a thought Thorn flipped it in his hands and swung again. He hit accurately, and the second chain followed the first. Thorn looked around the room—now for the second problem.

He didn't want this priest walking directly past Rebecca holding silver chains and manacles. It'd take him all night to make up enough lies to cover *that* up. And he *certainly* wasn't going to tell her the truth;

Rebecca had never liked wakes, funerals, or dead people in general. And she was under enough stress; he'd tell her what was really happening when he had the situation secure.

He looked around the room and saw a fairly new wicker basket in a clump of other furniture. Doubtless, it belonged to the last family to inhabit this doomed mansion, Thorn realized. He couldn't believe he hadn't done more research on this place before he plunked down the change. But it was too late now for that. He could put it on the market, sure, but he'd stand about as much chance of selling it as ice to an Eskimo.

He bent down and began dragging the chains and manacles toward the wicker basket. Yes, it would have been physically easier to carry the basket to the chains than the chains to the basket, but he didn't fancy staying inside this tomb any longer than absolutely necessary.

He stuffed the chains into the basket, ripped off a piece of a rotten blanket, and covered up the silver. He stood and turned toward the priest. "Listen to me, priest. Don't mention this to my wife. Understand?"

"Completely."

Thorn's tone was hard. "But if these inscriptions say anything alarming, which they probably *do*, then I want you to contact me by tomorrow morning. And nobody else. Not the cops, not Cahill, not my wife—you contact *me*."

The priest did not seem to hear; he was acutely studying the inscriptions. But Thorn knew he heard every word: "Now, we'll go upstairs. Any longer down here and Rebecca is going to get curious."

"Yes," Cavanaugh nodded, "let's go"

Thorn raised a hand at the wall. "You want to take a moment to copy that down?"

"No, I understand what it means."

Thorn waited: "What does it mean?"

"It means he has not yet had his vengeance."

The day passed uneventfully, and the moving crew finished with the last truck. After Thorn tipped them handsomely, they cleared out of the long, sloping driveway and vanished in the dusk.

Exhausted, they made do with sandwiches and chips and, after being awake for thirty-six hours, Thorn was asleep almost before he hit the bed. The kids were settled in their rooms, and the house was quiet and snug.

It was midnight when Thorn awoke to a sudden, strange wave of cold. He didn't move for a moment because years in the field had taught him to wait if he sensed danger. It was a simple rule, just hard to remember, at times. Never get in a hurry if you sense danger.

Rebecca was sometimes piqued by Thorn's conditioned responses, but his reactions were inculcated too deeply by decades of relentless training for him to react anything like a normal person.

For instance, where others would react violently and with electrifying emotion, Thorn would narrowly follow a possible threat with a lion's sleepy gaze. His low key responses were a result of the fact that he rarely felt threatened.

If he *did* feel threatened, like if someone cleared leather on him, then he would kill in a heartbeat—simple as that. Not that he enjoyed using force. In truth, he hated using it; he was just good at it. His best theory was that he was so very good at killing because he wanted to end it as quickly as possible.

Nor did he dwell on violence or train incessantly—as many of his colleagues did. And for *certain*, he didn't keep his gun on his bed stand, as many police officers did in case they were attacked in the night.

He frankly admitted that the odds of being attacked in the night were awfully long to say the least, but the odds of being startled and half-asleep and firing a shot that killed someone in your family were high indeed. He'd seen it happen too often, even with veteran officers.

Instead, he kept his Beretta on a hook inside the closet door, located about seven feet away. If he needed it, he could reach it inside three seconds.

Thorn lay in the dark, thinking whatever woke him might simply have been some as-of-yet unexperienced phenomenon of this old mansion. He didn't sleep well in new places, anyway. But the cold remained, and then it deepened. He squinted into the dark and finally looked at Rebecca. She was exhausted and sound asleep.

The hallway was lit so that each doorway was framed in shadow. If Anthony or Malorie awoke in the night—a particular trait of Malorie—all they had to do was drag themselves, blanket and all, down the hallway and climb into bed with Thorn and Rebecca.

Thorn didn't care about the middle-of-the-night invasions, though Rebecca often remarked that the children were getting too old for the bogeyman and that Thorn was too soft on them.

"How old were you when you completed potty training?" Thorn asked her once.

"What difference does it make?" she answered. "I have no idea."

"Exactly," he said. "What difference does it make? I have no idea, either. So they're afraid to sleep by themselves, big deal. Or how about when Anthony learned to ride without training wheels? Doesn't make any difference, does it? He learned, eventually. They'll remember our love, not when they gave up training wheels. Trust me on this one."

Rebecca had remarked, "You only say that because everything comes easy for you."

"*You* didn't make it easy. Made me work for you."

"Was I worth it?"

"Yeah, honey, you were worth it—absolutely worth it."

Thorn's mind came back to the moment. Still, the cold had not departed, and he tried to measure it. If anything, it was intensifying.

Very gently, he pushed back the covers and pulled on his blue jeans. Then he slipped on a cut-off sweatshirt. After making sure that Rebecca was sleeping, he opened the closet door. He quietly unsnapped the holster and pulled out the Beretta.

He moved without sound into the hallway. He didn't stand there wondering if there might be something. He couldn't have cared less if a skeleton with bleeding red eyes had come staggering out of the darkness, bloody dagger raised high in a skeletal fist, a maniacal stare fixed solely on him.

Thorn would have simply aimed for the thoracic vertebra—the one place where a skeleton can be blown in half without wasting rounds on expendable ribs, clavicles, scapula, skull, or legs.

And if that didn't work—Thorn suddenly felt ridiculous considering a tactical response to a walking skeleton—he'd eject the spent clip, slam in a fresh one, and put another fifteen rounds through the cervical vertebra. He'd like to see if a headless skeleton could still find him.

He quietly eased open Anthony's room and a swell of warm air flowed out. It confirmed his suspicion; whatever this cold was, it seemed to be centered on him.

Good.

He checked Malorie. She was sleeping soundly in a nice, warm atmosphere, snug under her blankets in the double bed that Thorn had managed to make his last project of the night.

He was as exhausted as they were, or more, but his protective nature was strong, and he wasn't surprised that he was awakened by this strange sensation of cold. He could never let down his guard, not even to exhaustion.

All right; everyone was safe, and he was convinced the rooms were clear, but he did a second, silent search, anyway.

Clear.

But the cold was still with him.

It seemed denser at the far end of the corridor, near the top of the staircase, so Thorn moved directly toward it, shifting the Beretta in his grip. He didn't need to see if a round was chambered; it wasn't. He never chambered his gun inside the house unless he was leaving for his shift, and since he didn't work a shift anymore, he never chambered a round.

In truth, he kept the Beretta mostly from habit; it was hard to go completely without a weapon when policy and procedure had required you to carry one for twenty-five years.

Thorn didn't even hesitate when he got to the staircase. He descended. If something was down here, so be it. If it was in any way a genuine threat, Thorn would put every round he had in it, and if that didn't stop it, he'd snatch up the fireplace poker as a club. And if *that* didn't stop it, he'd go hand to hand using the deadliest stuff he knew with a vengeance.

If he could direct it, he'd take them through a window or through the front door and into the yard, rolling and gouging, and Thorn would be doing his best to break its neck or anything else. And if, when it was over, it was lying broken but still alive in the grass, he'd come back inside and get a bottle of water and call what qualified around here as a lawman. Might even smoke a cigarette, though he'd mostly quit.

Still, he kept an emergency pack for dire situations.

For one second Thorn wondered what kind of paperwork you filled out on a slaughtered skeleton.

He reached the base of the stairs, searched behind every stack of boxes, behind the furniture—not yet positioned—and frowned. He didn't like this at all because there was nothing here, and the cold was intensifying.

He looked at the kitchen.

"Whatever," he said as he walked quickly forward and snatched the mag-light off the counter. He checked it by reflex; it worked.

He edged open the door to the basement with the same hand holding the mag-light, stepping back and aiming at the entrance with the Beretta, ready to pull the trigger.

Nothing.

Didn't matter; he was going down.

Thorn shone the light down the steps. It seemed to penetrate even less than before. He moved boldly and smoothly down the stairs. The light was of little assistance, but it allowed him five to six feet illumination in any direction. Then he was at the base and had every intention of moving inside the tomb.

He was over the foundation in a heartbeat and was frankly surprised by his involuntary words: "Where are you?"

Silence.

"Don't waste your time," Thorn continued, voluntarily this time, "I think those chains held you in some way, and I made the mistake of taking one off your rotten arm." He frowned. "Don't worry; I'm going to put you back in them. And this time I'm going to bury you where *nobody* will ever find you."

The cold was palpable.

"First time in my life I've ever believed in ghosts," Thorn whispered. "But I'm beginning to believe in you...whatever you are."

Thorn turned in slow circles in the dark, head tilted. He wasn't searching with his eyes as much as listening. He knew something was

here, just as he had known in Beirut that an AK-47 was aimed at him from somewhere. He had simply dropped to the ground as the sniper fired. Just like that—no warning.

He was half-expecting some kind of ghostly, demented voice to emerge from what was now a freezing darkness. But nothing came. There was only cold. And silence.

But in his heart, Thorn knew the silence and the darkness held more than cold.

Chapter Six

Father Cavanaugh had secured himself inside the rectory after delegating evening mass to his assistant priest, Father Dominic. He took a seat at his desk, pulled down his Bible reference from the shelf, and quickly found a reference to Jannes, the sorcerer of Amenhotep II, Pharaoh of Egypt, who challenged the power of Moses—the name he had found written on the manacle.

Cavanaugh studied the links of chain; it was like an algorithm. There was the tetragrammaton, or the name of the Hebrew God: YHWH. Then there was the name of Jannes and the tetragrammaton again and the name of Jannes in a repeating pattern.

Cavanaugh didn't expect easy answers because there weren't easy questions. First, why was the name of Jannes, the sorcerer who defied Moses, scratched into the granite wall of a cave in New England? And, far stranger, how could the skeleton of Jannes—if this *was* Jannes—have reached North America?

Moses led the Exodus, by best guess and archeological evidence, in 1,491 BC, so sailing to America would have been all but impossible for the Egyptians. More than that, nothing had been uncovered to indicate the Egyptians even considered other continents a possibility. Then Cavanaugh found inscribed upon the chains the names of Thothmes III, Ramses, Amenhotep II...

"Yes," Cavanaugh muttered, "so and so..."

By academic reflex, Cavanaugh mused that the name of the pharaoh of the exodus had always been a point of dispute. Some evidence indeed pointed to Amenhotep II, but some pointed to his successor, Thothmes III, who had an unmarried half-sister who acted as his regent for twenty years because he was too young to rule.

Hatshepsut was her name and, according to the oldest hieroglyphics, she educated her "adopted son" to become "the Lawgiver" of all Egypt. Consequently, he was trained in all the laws, customs, and languages of not only Egypt but also the surrounding nations, including the slave nation of Israel.

This time period, circa 1,490 BC, and the mention in Exodus of how Moses was trained in all the laws and languages of Egypt bore a cryptic similarity to his eventual rank in Israel, including the incidental fact that the Jews also referred to him as "the Lawgiver."

But in the final analysis, Cavanaugh decided, it didn't matter which pharaoh it had been because Jannes, the supreme sorcerer, and his master apprentice, Jambres, served under both of them, and neither of the magicians had been killed at the Red Sea.

A more difficult question: How could Jannes have arrived on this continent more than a thousand years before it was discovered by the Viking explorer Eric the Red? In that time period, all of Mesopotamia believed the earth was flat, anyway, and that to sail beyond view of the coast was doom.

Slowly, a theory came to Cavanaugh.

Perhaps that had been the plan of the Egyptians all along. Not only had they come to fear Jannes, but they had also decided to rid themselves of him. So they somehow managed to capture him, and bind him with manacles inscribed with archaic Hebrew. Then they put him on a ship dedicated to a suicide mission and sailed him into the sun.

Apparently, they intended to sail him off the edge of the world, perhaps because they could not, for whatever reason, kill him. Sending him into the depths of the ocean was the best they could do.

It made sense...

Yes...

It would be amazing if the Egyptians had come to fear Jannes so greatly that an entire crew was willing to sacrifice their lives. But—if that *was* the case—then their plan had backfired. For the world was not flat, but round, as they must have surmised when they unexpectedly landed on what would eventually become the continent of America. But, Cavanaugh thought with a sigh, it was a waste of time to so deeply ponder a mystery that had no answer.

His mind returned to the deep etchings on the wall. How could a man have done that with his fingernails? Even simpler questions were difficult to answer. How could a man have done that *at all* in total darkness?

That answer seemed simple enough; he couldn't. Nobody can write legibly in the dark, and Cavanaugh had seen no signs of a light source— something he had searched for, specifically. No candle, no lamp, no torch, no charcoal.

And yet, he thought, Jannes had been more than a man. Perhaps he had known some ancient, forgotten spell for creating his own light source. It wasn't outside the scope of probability; the limitations of Egyptian sorcery were totally unknown.

Obviously, Jannes had been a powerful being. He knew how to transform inanimate objects into living, breathing creatures. He had certainly turned a piece of wood into what the English version of the Bible calls a "serpent."

And then, after Moses turned the entire Nile into blood and the Egyptians were forced to dig wells to obtain fresh water, Jannes did the same on a much smaller scale. He transformed water into blood. And no transla-tion of the Bible indicates that Jannes "fabricated" the miracle by a process of modern "magic" like the magic of David Copperfield or Houdini.

No, from everything that Cavanaugh had ever learned through his research, Jannes had actually turned a piece of wood into a serpent and transformed water into blood. Or, perhaps, Jannes had simply "trans-ported" serpents from along the Nile and delivered them to the cham-ber. Perhaps Jannes could not create any kind of life at all, but he could borrow it from another place.

As most of Cavanaugh's more scholarly peers often said, sorcery was the manipulation of natural forces by an unknown means, except that Jannes had obviously known the means.

Only when Moses turned dust into "gnats"—whatever kind of bug *it* was—did Jannes fail to meet the eighty-year-old patriarch of Israel act for act. So there were obviously limitations to how far the laws of nature could be bent.

But one thing was certain; the sorcerer had commanded signifi-cant power and influence, along with secrets mercifully lost to the mod-ern world. And there was no determining what other battles occurred between Jannes and Moses in that nine-month period, but it was a safe assumption that Jannes did not simply lay down in humble defeat.

Jannes admitted to Amenhotep II that the God of Moses was the one true God, but that does not mean he accepted personal defeat. To preserve his image, the sorcerer may have continued the battle in vari-ous ways, attempting to stop Moses unilaterally, if it were possible. Or, in other words, by some manner of "sneak attack" either though Aaron, Moses' family, Israel itself, or other elements Jannes still retained under his control.

It did not go beneath Cavanaugh's notice that the Bible does not say God separated Jannes from the spirit that gave him power. But neither did the world witness such phenomenal displays of sorcery in this day and age, moving Cavanaugh to believe that Jannes knew secrets of sorcery that have not been known since that forgotten era.

And what that sorcery allowed him to accomplish was as much a mystery now as it was then. And, just perhaps, that power had allowed Jannes to reach North America. Which left the most disturbing question: Could Jannes have used some ultimately mysterious power of his sorcery to protect himself from a natural death?

The Bible declares that Satan was the master of death until Jesus. But would that most ultimate of all satanic powers have been made available to the greatest of all sorcerers? If that was the case, Jannes certainly would not have allowed others to know.

Indeed, secrecy is what ultimately gave sorcery its power and drew such allegiance. For if too many knew the secret, then the secret itself lost its influence. Familiarity breeds contempt—it's true—and demons lost the advantage of fear if men knew their face. And since man is indeed compelled to approach the void, the allure of the mystery itself is the real source of a demon's strength.

Cavanaugh whispered, "It is also your weakness..."

The fact that Jannes was able to match Moses at all qualifies as one of the greatest cosmic contests of power ever waged. And only God knew the limitations finally placed upon the sorcerer.

Cavanaugh stared at the phone. Perhaps he should call the monsignor. And then he thought about it more—no, no, not tonight. Tonight he must study this out. He would research this ancient sorcerer, or whatever remained of the documents, letters, and instruction manuals once secured in the Library of Alexandria before it was razed to the ground in 641 AD by Arab invaders.

Cavanaugh knew that the sorcerer would have weapons at his disposal that were the stuff of legend. It would take the learning of many lifetimes to know the secret spells and incantations…and all that knowledge would still be as nothing compared to what secrets Jannes had commanded. Cavanaugh had studied much of what the Church had to say about the subject of spiritual warfare, but in this case, he worried that it might not be enough.

"What are you doing?"

Cavanaugh almost fell backward out of his chair. As it was, his arms flung out in opposite directions, scattering various documents and tools across his small room.

In a heartbeat he had reached his feet and was staring at the crucifix that hung above his bed; it was rattling, as if from the aftershock of an earthquake. Cavanaugh felt he would have a heart attack, and then noticed he was drenched in sweat.

Very, very slowly he looked around the room.

Nothing…no…

Nothing that he could see…

"What are you doing?"

This time Cavanaugh was calmer by the barest degree. And then he sensed an image and whirled. He glimpsed something manlike and blackish—like a living shadow; something that hovered on the border between this dimension and the next.

Cavanaugh was not only Catholic, he was Jesuit. And Jesuit training involved fifteen years of theological and philosophical study, four of which were dedicated to psychology at an Ivy League School. This was done to prevent unnecessary exorcisms or overreactions to physical phenomenon easily misunderstood to have spiritual causation, as in stigmata.

And it was the hard Jesuit training that allowed Cavanaugh to calm himself, degree by degree. He controlled his breathing, wiped the sweat from his palms and neck. He knew he had been working too hard lately, and that he was understandably distracted by what he had found at Thorn's house. Also, he had no problem admitting he had an almost sinful streak of superstition in him—something he carefully concealed from his colleagues. It was no wonder that he was overwrought and hearing voices. He was only, after all, human.

Cavanaugh forced himself to relax. He looked again at his notes—now he could work.

"Thank God for training," he muttered.

Indeed, without the mandatory scientific training, Jesuit priests would be constantly misdiagnosing psychosomatic manifestations as "miracles." And cold, hard procedures and strict ritual also had their place, for the Church used exact criteria to determine whether demonic activity was present—another hurdle to slow down those too quick to claim supernatural interference.

From his training in physics, Cavanaugh knew that a demonic entity could cross dimensions to harass someone on Earth, but it was not half so simple for the demon as many believed. They could even steal from the dimension of Earth, though that process was a delicate and dangerous event for all involved, including the demon.

Mathematics alone had proven the existence of nine parallel dimensions, and theoretical physics held that there was a tenth dimension that encompassed them all. Also, the Omega Point Theory surmised that "substance" from varying dimensions could be "exchanged" as long as the exchange between dimensions was simultaneous and equal in properties.

Which meant that nothing could be "stolen" from another dimension, though "exchanges" could be made if one knew the dark science of how it might be accomplished—a secret surely held by Jannes. The trick was in insuring that the exchange was equal in measure, and there were no second chances. A mistake, and all involved would suffer. And although a demonic entity could not be killed, a human being could be physically destroyed.

Parallel dimensions, however, had come to be old science. It was not even interesting anymore. Physicists simply waved off the mention; yes, yes, of course there are other dimensions, we have known this for years...

Very well...back to work.

He purposefully ignored thinking that he had heard a voice. He was overworked. That was all.

There had been no voice.

Cavanaugh found himself clutching his rosary. Then he noticed blood dropping slowly from the bottom of his fist. He didn't care that he was holding the cross so tightly that the crossbeam had been impaled in his hand.

If there were not an explanation for the wound, he could have claimed stigmata. As it was, it was only pure, full-blown panic.

"No," he whispered, and sweat dropped from his brow. "There was no voice..."

"What are you doing?"

This time Cavanaugh had to respond. He knew what the Book of Common Prayer said about dialogue with a demon, but it was one thing to read a vaguely meaningless and irrelevant passage in the Book of Common Prayer in relation to a situation that all logic says you'll never confront, and quite another to genuinely confront that situation. And as they say, rules are made to be broken.

He whirled again as he glimpsed the image. It was to his left, slightly behind him, and moving. He turned again and raised a bloody fist for protection, though the crucifix itself was constricted within his hand. He extended his arm fully, and the rosary snapped at his neck.

He stood trembling, sweating and breathless.

"Take the knife upon your desk..."

Cavanaugh could not move. He could not even move his eyes.

"Take the knife upon your desk..."

So slowly, Cavanaugh's eyes moved to his knife-like letter opener. It was one of the few objects that had not been swept from his desk. It stood silvery and sharp against the dark, glossy mahogany wood.

A shadow behind him...

Cavanaugh spun, his heart on his chest.

It was gone ...

To the right...

Thoughts too horrible to contemplate flooded through Cavanaugh's mind.

"Take up the knife upon the desk..."

"No!" Cavanaugh shouted.

It's behind me!

Cavanaugh spun.

Beside me!

Cavanaugh heard himself screaming.

"I am with you. Take the knife upon your desk..."

"No!"

"You must..."

"NO!"

If Cavanaugh committed suicide, the one unforgivable sin according to the doctrine of St. Mark's, then he was damned and his entire life would have been for nothing, meaning nothing. He noticed a disturbance and raised his hand before his face. It was trembling. His teeth were chattering.

Again he glimpsed the image, this time to his right, and then to his left. *Behind him!*

"You cannot win...Take up the knife upon the desk..."

Cavanaugh heard someone speak in his voice: "No..."

"Take up the knife..."

Cavanaugh looked down. Somehow, his trembling hand held the blade. He began to move it toward his arm. "I...can't..."

"You can...You must, to save your flock...You must sacrifice yourself...for them."

"No..."

"Yes...To save them, you must sacrifice yourself...As He did...It is the only way...Place the edge of the knife at your elbow and cut to your wrist..."

Father Cavanaugh did not know how many hours the voice droned so hypnotically within him, but it lasted, and lasted, and lasted until he found himself slunk in a corner of his room, a blanket in his hand. He had the sensation of seeing himself from above—a cowering, broken, amazingly weak man off balance and unable to stand. He watched as he swung his head numbly from side to side, a single step from utter confusion, utter hopelessness. He fought and then he prayed and then he sat in a rainy darkness before he realized it was tears, and then he knew that all the regrets he had ever felt, and all the fears he had ever known had come home...and he thought of all those he had hurt so horribly, and how he could make it right...

Yes, he must sacrifice himself...for them.

And then, finally, something incredible happened and he was staring down at the red sheen of a knife clutched loosely in his hand... clutched ever so loosely...

The blade was held by a pale, sweating hand, and...it was his hand. Yes...he had been afraid he could not succeed...

He pushed harder and blood even further stained his white sleeve. He closed his eyes and drew the blade in dull pressure down the length of his arm, and blood flowed freely. He knew it was a killing act, and he gave no more thought to it.

He sat slowly at his desk, obeying a part of his soul that was not yet defeated. He would, at least, die with a faint portion of the dignity that he had spent his entire life nurturing so diligently.

He reached out and grasped the pen before him. And there was yet a white page of parchment upon the mahogany surface. He bent, focusing between tired blinks of sweat, and began to write.

To Monsignor DeMarco,

Forgive me, Excellence, but I knew you would have prevented this action, and I cannot live with the knowledge that I have failed so completely, and so terribly. I pray for absolution and will administer to myself the Eucharist, though I know the limitations of forgiveness.

I have a basket in my closet, and my journal will enlighten you as to the cause of this catastrophic betrayal of your trust. I pray your forgiveness that your efforts to bring me into your holiness have ended so horribly, but it is for the best. If I attempt to stand in what is to come, I will cause more loss than victory.

Do not mourn for me. I know my decision is true, and so I leave the battle to your great strength and wisdom and am confident you and our dearest mother, the Church, will ultimately prevail.

Your Servant,

Father David Cavanaugh

Father Cavanaugh felt a feather-edged touch at the edge of his consciousness. He shook his head, attempting to clear his thoughts, and began a final note that he would leave randomly upon his desk. He knew it would be found easily enough and did not want to sully his goodbye with something so dark. But thoughts were disjointed now, and he found himself drifting on a warm, embracing sea...

'...your invincible mind. You are old and full of years, and the Thorn family has discovered what should have remained undiscovered. So pray for a reformation of my soul, and I leave you with the tenderest of sentiments and love....Your son...'

Blinking, Cavanaugh rose and walked slowly to his twin bed, only dimly noticing the thick red trail he left behind. He stopped for a moment, staring down, and then he laughed lightly, sadly.

So it comes to this...All these years of service, to disappoint even the little children...

Leaning on his one good arm, Father Cavanaugh lowered himself to the bed, faintly surprised that he was in very little pain. Then he lay back fully, ignoring the growing crimson shade upon his side. He closed his eyes and knew no more...

Thorn stood in the dark of the backyard.

When he made a search, he searched everything. There was not a board left unturned. Places that would be impossible for a chipmunk to find safety in were explored with exacting patience. He checked the toolshed, under the wheelbarrow, under Anthony's plastic swimming pool. He looked under the car and then reentered the house. He did another check on the kids and Rebecca; they continued to sleep soundly and warmly.

But the cold followed him like an invisible cloak. He didn't question that it was unnatural. He was a skeptic, not stupid. He knew something unnatural when he felt it.

If a pink elephant had walked up to him and spoken, Thorn would not have wasted time doubting the authenticity of it. He would have recognized that this was unnatural, and then he would have said hello: no surprise, no emotion, no fear. Just a pure and simple hello and the recognition that this is as weird as it gets. But, in truth, no, *this* was as weird as it gets.

He descended the stairs and was through the cellar, Beretta high, intending to make one final search of the tomb for the night. He checked behind tools, debris, and discarded furniture. Then he walked the floor, checking the beams of the ceiling for anything—anything at all; it didn't matter what.

He turned the mag-light to the opening in the wall and walked quickly forward, stepping over the torn stones without hesitation. He ignored the scratches on the wall and then he sensed rather than heard something behind him and whirled.

He glimpsed a manlike image that was vaguely humanish and vaguely demonish. It was there, less than four feet away as he whirled, but even as the light struck it, it was gone.

Thorn snarled.

His fighting instinct, always strong, ignited like a nuclear blast. He didn't retreat, didn't fall back against the wall. He did was he was trained to do, what every instinct compelled him to do, and he didn't fight it.

He moved directly into what he perceived as a threat.

He was back over the foundation like lightning, in the middle of the basement. *Again* it was behind him, and he whirled even faster this time to get a clear image.

In the blink of an eye...gone.

Thorn was in a Weaver stance, right arm fully extended with the Beretta's safety down and off. His left hand was wrapped around the last three fingers of his right hand. He was pushing with his right hand, pulling back with his left and it gave him stability. He had always been an expert shot because his technique was perfect, his eyesight perfect, and he didn't rattle. And he employed all his training and skill as he stared into the darkness.

Something ascending the stairs...

Thorn knew it would be gone again as he turned, so he simply turned his head. He would not give it the satisfaction of even presenting the image of fear.

Whatever it was, it would reap nothing from—

"Put the gun to your head..."

It had not been a real voice or anything audible. But it was an impression so strong that it could have been mistaken for a human presence. Incredibly, it rattled Thorn for a moment, and he stood breathing a little heavier as he lowered the Beretta. Something told him bullets wouldn't do much good against this thing. Not yet.

He stared long and hard into the darkness, and he thought of Anthony and Malorie and Rebecca.

His words were cold.

"We'll meet soon enough."

𓆣 𓋹 𓅓 𓊨 𓅃

Monsignor DeMarco stared down with curious eyes upon the body of his beloved protégé, Father Cavanaugh, lying so still under a white sheet as attendants of the Cedar Ridge Emergency Transport Service rushed about him.

They had already plastered tiny circular heart monitors to his chest and detected the faintest beat.

No, he was not yet dead.

It had been a moment of shock for DeMarco, who assumed on sight that his son, for whatever incomprehensible despair, had taken his own life. But the EMTs explained, as they rushed about him, that his blood pressure had dropped to the point where his heart no longer pumped with sufficient force to expel blood from the long smooth cut along the inside of his arm. If he had done so with both arms, and cut his femoral artery as well, they said, then he would have surely succeeded. But he was, as they termed it, "lucky."

DeMarco would have chosen another term. He would have said his protégé was blessed to be alive because the Almighty decides who lives and who dies. Luck had nothing to do with it.

As the EMTs lifted him onto the gurney, preparing him for transport, DeMarco studied Cavanaugh's last notes, sullied with scarlet. He did not, just yet, attempt to analyze them. Things a man writes in his dying moments are rarely revelatory. Rather, they are the product of exhaustion and, often enough, horror. There is little that is coherent, since it was usually a moment of overwhelming nothingness, not true sadness. Still, though, something about the timing of the suicide was more disturbing than the attempt itself, and the notes seemed more important than process would ordinarily suggest.

DeMarco possessed a complex understanding for the psychology of strength and weakness; he was not a Monsignor for nothing. And he was well aware of every moment he'd spent recently with Father Cavanaugh.

His protégé had not been unusually depressed, not unduly prone to discussing judgment or the afterlife. He had not given away cherished personal items or neglected his personal appearance or duties. He had not exhibited any signs of substance abuse such as excessive drinking or even an inordinate amount of smoking, though he did enjoy his pipe upon occasion—nothing worthy of scandal. In essence, he had exhibited none of the usual signs of someone contemplating suicide, or even of despair.

DeMarco studied the scrawl on Father Cavanaugh's letter. It distinctly revealed a shocked and fearful state of mind. And he wondered what could have so quickly driven his strong-minded friend to such a condition. It was not a salient quality of his temperament or even part of his casual nature. He had known the younger priest for twenty years, and he had observed nothing to indicate such mental weakness.

DeMarco was a jaded and experienced pragmatist; he was not prone to dark and sinister theories. He believed that everything had a cause but was experienced enough to realize that not all causes are easily known. Investigation was usually required in direct proportion to the strangeness of the incident, meaning this would require some serious investigation—something he was more than willing to do. DeMarco tried to subdue the impulse for vengeance, for he knew that investigations could lead to unexpected and unwanted discovery.

But one thing he already knew with certainty. Whatever had caused his most cherished, most trusted assistant priest to attempt to take his own life did not stand on this side of everything DeMarco had spent his life believing and serving. And the Church was not unable to defend itself against dark forces of the earth, or to deliver justice when injustice has been done.

As a Monsignor, DeMarco carried a heavy mantle of responsibilities that involved the life and death of many unable to defend themselves. Endless wars, missionaries and orphans trapped in war-torn regions, faithful servants of the Church targeted for assassination by maniacal legions disposed to ruling by cruelty—these fell within his duty to protect.

Nor did Rome leave him helpless to the task; he, too, had an army he could summon.

For seven hundred years they had been legend, folklore, a prayer whispered in the darkest night, and DeMarco secretly commanded seven of them.

Yes...the Assassini were legend, but in truth they were ordained priests who were also experts at protection, investigation, infiltration, transportation, hand to hand combat, weapons, tactics, communications, and cloak and dagger tactics.

DeMarco had sometimes mused: Why did people think the Citie

del Vaticano was never invaded by the Third Reich during the dying days of World War II? What presumptions did people claim when Mussolini himself did not dare cross the circle of St. Peter's?

It was certainly not because Hitler or Mussolini had respected the corridors of the Church. It had been because those who attempted to break the sacredness of those gigantic iron doors had died mysteriously and soundlessly in the night, and the message was sent.

All knew that some type of unnamed force walked those holy walls. And as death after death mounted, those with any sense of self-preservation began to avoid those gates as they would a plague.

DeMarco's steel mind returned; he concentrated on the note. Questions came to him steadily, slowly, logically: What could suddenly break the mind of one of the strongest men he had ever known? And why had Father Cavanaugh given no warning?

And what was the reference to this man, Thorn? Why him, specifically? Did the letter request him to assist Thorn? To protect him? Or was this man somehow a threat?

It took DeMarco another moment to make a difficult decision, but he was certain of the correctness. He would need, first of all, to insure his physical safety in ways that law enforcement authorities could not provide.

He reached out slowly and picked up the phone. He dialed a number, and somewhere deep inside the Vatican a tiny golden bar fell across a set of wires that led to a computer in the Secret Archives that allowed him access to yet another communications system isolated but for a select few in this world, nor could it be accessed by any other modem.

A toneless voice answered on the third ring.

"Yes."

DeMarco sighed; he had rarely used his authority in the manner in which he was about to use it, but this was a radical situation. The attempted suicide of a priest could have disturbing and far-reaching consequences.

"I need you and your men," said DeMarco. "Immediately."

"Where?"

"Here."

"We will be there tomorrow morning."

DeMarco hung up.

Assassini did not say good-bye.

Thorn had not bothered to mention last night's events to Rebecca. The less she knew, the better. He had also been loath to leave them alone in the house until he figured this out, and he needed cement to wall up that tomb again.

He didn't know whether sealing the tomb would improve the situation, but it couldn't hurt, so he told the kids that they could go with him to the hardware store and pick out paint colors for their own rooms. They were back in three hours with almost two hundred dollars worth of paint and supplies, though all Thorn had really needed was twenty dollars worth of concrete.

He let Rebecca supervise the painting of the kitchen—the kitchen always came first—and descended into the basement with the cement. There was already a wheelbarrow and, after mixing, he began caking cement on the stones. The hole he had made was significant, and Rebecca questioned him about it, but his answers were demure and boring, and she gave up on getting anything reasonable.

"Men are such strange creatures," she said, using her flashlight to get back up the stairs. "If the house were on fire you'd only be concerned about saving that baseball you caught at the Dodger game last year."

Thorn had laughed. Better than the truth. But as she ascended, he shone his light across the beams above and resolved to rig the most power series of floodlights in existence so that every corner of this basement was illuminated like the sun. If a shadow could survive that, it *had* to be alive.

The fact that he actually considered a shadow a possible danger to him or his family actually startled Thorn. He didn't know if he had been spooked by Father Cavanaugh, or whether it was Cahill's incomprehensible superstition, or if he was still shaken by what he thought he'd seen down here last night...Ultimately, it didn't matter: Whatever the reason, he didn't like it. And if, by some unlikely twist of reality, a shadow did turn out to be something to be feared, he'd give it the last thrill of its existence.

Thorn hadn't lost count of the men he'd put down, but neither did he dwell on it. It had been his job, and he'd used the level of force he had to use to survive. And he was practical—it didn't do any good to second-guess or wish things had been different. It had gone down like it went down, and that was that. Forget it; move on.

"Baby!"

It was Rebecca; she rarely called him by his name. It was her habit, since she'd been raised in South Georgia, to use the common colloquialisms that had been used for her all her life, and which consisted of "honey," "baby," "darling," or "sweetheart."

Frankly, Thorn found it charming. It was a welcome change from the military world where he was known only as "T," or "Thorn." Even better, both the children called him Daddy, though Malorie was reaching the age where she considered herself "too old" for such things and was more commonly using Dad.

Since he had never known a normal family, Thorn found all of it touching.

His own story held little happiness. He'd been adopted at two by an alcoholic father and an insanely despondent mother, and both foolishly believed that bringing a child into their miserable life would magically improve it. But the only good thing it had done was instill in Thorn a passion to make sure his fate didn't befall his own children. He often wondered if that wasn't also why he'd dedicated his life to saving people.

"Babe!"

Time to go.

A quick glance at the wheelbarrow told Thorn he'd waste little of the first bag of cement, anyway. Although it'd be dry by the time he returned, there was only a shovelful remaining. So he'd just mix more and keep going until the job was done. But it'd be done—today.

He mounted the stairs quickly and emerged into the kitchen to look quizzically at Rebecca. "What is it, babe?"

Rebecca pointed toward the front door.

"Don't know—looks official, though."

The priest, Thorn thought; he'd found something.

As he opened the door, he knew two things; first, it wasn't Cavanaugh; second this priest was a much higher rank. His significant authority was evident by the red and black vestment and sheer size and majesty of the crucifix that hung on a solid silver chain from his garment. He was probably in his early sixties, but his bearing was erect and severe. His salt and pepper hair was surprisingly long and swept back smoothly from a widow's peak.

His demeanor was munificent and calm, essentially communicating what Thorn remembered from the Bible—yes, he'd read the Bible cover to cover, once—as the "fruits of the spirit."

"Good afternoon, Mr. Thorn. I am Monsignor DeMarco."

With slight surprise, Thorn glimpsed a shadow in the ridgeline, and he almost started. But then he recognized the figure as a man, and not what he had glimpsed last night.

If he had not once been a professional soldier and trained by his all but worthless father as a hunter, Thorn wouldn't have seen the man at all. But he was trained to observe movement, and the man had moved ever so slightly. Then, by reflex, Thorn scanned the entire perimeter of the surrounding wood line.

He caught a glimpse of two more figures, dressed much the same as the first; long black leather coat, black vest, black leather pants, black boots, no hats, no sunglasses, nothing to diminish a clear watch. And they were, indeed, watching. Although Thorn couldn't determine at this range if they bore weapons, he suspected they were requisite bodyguards for the monsignor, and bodyguards rarely went unarmed.

Thorn didn't like it already. Not that he was naïve enough to think that a monsignor traveled without protection. His real question was: Why would a monsignor come to his home at all?

The monsignor bowed and beamed.

"What can I do for you?" Thorn asked with a semblance of warmth. "I was expecting to hear from Father Cavanaugh."

The monsignor apologetically raised his hands. "The good father met with an unfortunate accident and is hospitalized, so I came in his stead." He paused for Thorn to absorb the news. "May I come inside?"

"Want to invite one of your men?"

"Ah...you noticed." His smiled was accomplished—the smile of a politician. "They are mandatory for a monsignor—dictates from Rome. I'm sure you understand. They certainly mean *you* no harm. And they will be content to remain where they stand. Their primary duty is to simply ensure that my travels are without unfortunate incidents."

Thorn didn't buy it; a chauffer with fair qualifications as a middle of the road bodyguard—someone who could remain close and invisible

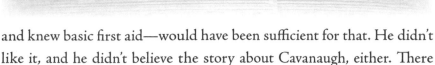

and knew basic first aid—would have been sufficient for that. He didn't like it, and he didn't believe the story about Cavanaugh, either. There was something about the lack of details surrounding his so-called injury that piqued Thorn's suspicions.

After last night, Thorn didn't need much to suspect the most unlikely scenario.

But waiting too long was a bad move; it would inspire the monsignor to even further cloak his questions and his intents. Best to let the priest believe that he had no suspicions at all, then he might stand a chance at getting some truth out of this.

"Sure," Thorn said casually with a casual glance at the bodyguards, "come inside."

Pleasantries were exchanged with Rebecca and the children, with whom the monsignor seemed particularly gifted at communicating, and then the priest asked to see the house.

It had always been a place of legend, he explained, and he wanted to see if there were some type of overt symbolism in the architecture or design or some other manner of projection that the Church might be able to bless and therefore protect the Thorns from "metaphysical elements."

No, no, he was not an exorcist, and this was no common occurrence for the Church. But there had been so many tragedies to erupt within these walls over the past decades that, for his own peace of mind, he would sleep easier knowing he had blessed the house. If neither Thorn nor his lovely wife had any objections, of course?

Thorn had no qualms about the monsignor blessing the house, but knew there was more to it. Just as there was more to what he had glimpsed and heard in his head last night. Whatever was happening here was picking up speed fast, and Thorn somehow sensed the ending wasn't going to be pretty.

He nodded, "Be my guest."

"Thank you so much."

The elderly monsignor made the sign of the cross over Anthony, then Malorie, then Rebecca, and finally Thorn himself.

Thorn nodded curtly.

Then without preamble he blessed the living room and moved into the dining area. Room-by-room they worked their way through the lower level of the house. Thorn gave Rebecca "the look" to quit apologizing for the mess. In fact, the monsignor seemed to be looking for something specific and was totally uninterested in the riot of moving.

Afterward they progressed upstairs where the procedures were repeated. Then they descended and entered the kitchen for the first time. They had avoided it on the first pass because Rebecca had insisted upon tidying up her "kingdom" before the monsignor could enter. The priest had acquiesced politely and moved upstairs.

They descended in less than fifteen minutes and after Thorn got the okay from Rebecca, the monsignor entered the kitchen with a beatific smile, complimenting her instantly on the in-progress organization. It would surely be a work of art when it was complete, he said, as was appropriate. A kitchen was always "the heart of the house."

Then, in silence and stillness, the monsignor focused upon the door to the basement.

Thorn had known this was coming. Then he wondered if the mysterious figures in the forest had moved closer and edged casually to the window for a narrow glimpse. He wasn't surprised to see one standing less than fifteen feet from the back door, but neither was he alarmed. Whatever they were, they were professionals—very casual, very close, very low visibility.

"They watch you closely," he said without noticeable emotion.

The monsignor nodded. "They are dedicated servants of the

Church, my friend. And, as I mentioned, they travel with me to insure my safety." He raised a hand to the basement door. "May I?"

Thorn debated a moment; he didn't know if Cavanaugh was genuinely injured or if he'd discovered something terrible and been replaced by DeMarco. Either way, Thorn didn't like it. Still, he needed more information, and there was only one way to get it.

"Sure," he said and opened the door for the monsignor. He took the mag-light from the table. "You'll need this."

"Thank you."

With remarkable presence of mind, the monsignor checked to insure it worked and began his descent. Thorn retrieved the second mag-light and remained two steps behind him. In moments they had reached the basement, and the monsignor stopped in place.

Thorn felt the same strange coldness he had felt last night—an unnatural coldness because, if anything, this cellar should be warmer than the rest of the house. The boiler was here and burning full blast. But unless you stood within a few feet of the iron-sided cylinder, you could have worn a parka.

Very slowly, as if with clear purpose, the monsignor swept the basement with the flashlight. And when he focused on the tomb, he moved toward it without hesitation. But he did not step across the rising foundation, which Thorn had already raised to three feet of fast drying cement.

Contrary to popular belief, cold temperatures made cement dry much faster than heat, which could keep it soft for twice as long.

"Here," Thorn muttered, and gave the wall a vicious kick; the stones went clattering, leaving an entrance.

Thorn somehow sensed he didn't have to tell the monsignor a thing; the priest seemed to understand with complete clarity. He remained silent and unmoving for a moment and then made the sign of the cross at the entrance...and stepped inside.

Thorn merely waded to the entrance and watched. He didn't have any need to go in again, didn't care to. He'd discovered what it had contained, and he'd already had enough unpleasantries with this thing. Instead, he closely watched the priest.

Monsignor DeMarco bent and felt the ground where the skeleton had lain, and Thorn thought he detected a shiver. Then the priest stood and touched the silver pin anchoring a single broken section of silver chain to the granite. He looked across and saw the other pin. Thorn knew that he understood. He said nothing.

Instead, he waited patiently as the priest studied pockmarks in the wall left by old rifle rounds. Then, to Thorn's surprise, the priest withdrew a pocketknife from his fold and began to dig into one of the holes. In a moment, a piece of lead fell into his right palm. He examined it, extended a dead steady hand toward Thorn.

"You were an investigator?" he asked, without bothering to conceal the fact that he had done uncommon research.

Thorn was laconic: "You check everyone out like this?"

"Only when one of my most beloved children is mysteriously and almost mortally injured. My responsibilities and concerns range far beyond what you might assume, Mr. Thorn." He rolled a musket ball between his fingers, arm outstretched. "Can you tell me what this is?"

Thorn sensed something close and glanced toward the stairway to see one of the bodyguards poised in stoic silence, watching everything. He didn't wonder why Rebecca let him in. They were obviously professionals of a high grade and had a prearranged series of logical excuses for remaining close.

Still, Thorn had questions, and he was going to get some answers, bodyguards or not. He reached out and took the round from the monsignor, raising it in front of the mag-light and taking his time.

"Strips on the ball could be from impact with the wall, but I don't think so. I think it's rifled." He studied it closer. "Looks like a standard 45.110 Sharps. They were pretty common, first part of this century. It was a heavy round—a good bush gun. Some people used them for buffalo."

Thorn gave the round back to the priest, who said ominously, "What else did you discover here?"

"A dead guy," Thorn stated simply.

"Authorities assumed responsibility for the body? Sheriff Cahill?"

"No. He...it vanished."

DeMarco stared. "Vanished, you say?"

"Uh huh."

"Please...explain."

Thorn told him the story in detail, leaving nothing out, and when he was finished the monsignor pursed his lips and gazed once more at the skeletal imprint in the soil. He looked at the man on the staircase: "If Mr. Thorn has no objections, please dig these pins from the wall. Leave nothing of this behind."

Thorn waved the man into the tomb. "What am I dealing with?" he asked the priest.

"An evil beyond this world," the monsignor answered with surprising frankness. "I would strongly suggest you remove your family from this premises until the Church can deal with the matter."

All Thorn could manage for a moment was a tired sigh. Then, "I figured it would be something like that."

The monsignor stepped out of the tomb as the man on the stairway approached. With a studied eye, Thorn identified an illegally short barreled 12-gauge pump action shotgun slung under his left arm, a bulge at his right hip, and a row of high-capacity semiautomatic clips lined along the left side of his waist.

Yeah...more than a bodyguard.

The monsignor stood before Thorn, and Thorn needed no confirmation to an answer he already knew. "Cavanaugh tried to kill himself, didn't he?"

Only the slightest hesitation. "Yes."

Thorn considered his next words for a long time. "He tried to kill himself because he was hearing voices and sensing a shadow that he began to see once he had been inside this tomb, read those inscriptions, and taken those chains."

"Apparently, this is so. But I can offer no verification. His final words were not complete."

Thorn knew the monsignor was disturbed, but the older priest obviously had gained his rank in the Church through a considerable control of mind and emotion. He asked, "Can this thing hurt my family?"

"I do not know," the monsignor replied, straightening slightly. "What he...what it is...remains uncertain."

The bodyguard exited the tomb businesslike and wordless and nodded curtly to the monsignor, who did not visibly acknowledge him at all. Then the black draped figure returned to his place on the stairway and stood, implacable and emotionless and, unless Thorn had not undergone the training to detect concealed weapons, completely non-threatening.

Thorn stared hard at the monsignor. "Do you have a place where you can insure the safety of my family?"

The monsignor drew a deep breath before he replied.

"If what I suspect is true, Mr. Thorn, none of us are safe...anywhere on this earth."

Chapter Seven

After DeMarco and his shadows departed with a generous blessing from the monsignor, Thorn reentered the house, rubbed
Anthony and Malorie across the head in case the incident had somehow frightened them and then turned, mostly out of curiosity, toward
Rebecca, who stood one arm akimbo, head tilted. He didn't let her long
brown hair and sensuous figure distract him. He knew very well she had
some serious questions and would demand the answers.

"What did that dude in the black leather coat say to you so that you
let him in the house?" Thorn asked, curious.

Rebecca blinked. "He said that the old priest had a heart condition,
but he was the guy who carried the nitroglycerine pills and so he had
to stay fairly close at all times. He apologized for the necessity of the
intrusion, so I let him in and told him where you guys had gone." She
stared at Thorn for a long moment. "Honey, what are you trying not to
tell me?"

"It's nothing," Thorn waved.

"No, it's something," she said flatly. "I know this look; this is how
you used to look when you were hunting a hard target." She stared.
"Even when you were with us, you—"

"—weren't with you. Yeah, I know."

She looked at Anthony. "Go stir up the paint cans in your room.
We'll start painting in a few minutes, okay?"

"Cool!" Anthony set off up the stairs and, for some reason, Thorn watched him all the way to the top of the flight and down the hall until he was lost from view, and even then Thorn listened closely.

"We've got a few minutes," Rebecca said. "Talk to me."

Thorn stared at her steadily. "They found something in the basement."

"Dinosaur bones, right?"

"Well...it's dead."

Rebecca hesitated. "*What* is dead?"

"To tell you the truth," Thorn began, "I'm not really sure. But it looks like he died a long, long...long...*long* time ago."

Thorn had never seen Rebecca's eyes so wide as she said, "He? How long ago did he die? Are we talking...prehistoric or something?"

"I don't know," Thorn stated simply. "Sure looked old to me, and Cahill said he doesn't do prehistoric murders."

"He was *murdered?*"

That required a pause. "I'd say the chances are good," Thorn answered finally. "And, apparently, word gets around in this place. I guess somebody told the monsignor and he wanted to bless the house...just in case."

"In case of what?"

"You know; in case it's...haunted." Thorn shrugged. "I don't know; I humored him."

Thorn was amazed, as always, how Rebecca could put things together. He'd known detectives that couldn't work deductive logic as well as she could; she had probably missed her calling. She said slowly, "You mean the monsignor suspects that this dead man might have something to do with the history of this place?"

"Sort of, I guess—what with the entire family going crazy at once. It's an unexplainable phenomenon, and people...well, people look for explanations, however remote."

"What are you not telling me, Michael? I didn't see them carry any body out of that basement, and I've been in the kitchen all day. Are you saying this dead guy is still down there?"

Rebecca only used Thorn's first name when she was approaching anger, and it was a bad idea to make an Italian woman angry. He made a deliberate effort to coach his words carefully.

He didn't like arguing with Rebecca, partly because he never won, but mostly because he didn't like arguing with those he loved. He'd argued with enough superiors and subordinates and fought enough— for *real*—for ten lifetimes.

Thorn bowed his head, debating. He came up with the best explanation he could: "Well, my best guess, hun, is that when the skeleton made contact with fresh air, it just disintegrated. It was so old, it just crumbled into dust, you know? It wasn't petrified, so...anything is possible."

She stared. "So it's not still down there any more?"

"Just some dust."

"*I'm here.*"

Thorn's heart skipped a beat. But, remarkably, he didn't reveal the volcanic eruption of alarm. He focused acutely on Rebecca.

"Did you just happen to hear anything, babe?"

"Yeah," Rebecca answered dully as Anthony called from upstairs and she started for the stairway. "I heard you say it's not here."

Thorn nodded stoically as she ascended the steps.

"*I'll always be here...*"

☥ ⚲ 𓂀 ⸙ 𓅃

Thorn wasted no time snatching up the flashlight and descending into the basement. His earlier fears had turned to anger now, and he had a job to finish.

He gently laid the flashlight so that it angled against the wall and then he spoke into the darkness. "I don't know who you are or what you are, but I'm sending you back to where you came from."

"*Why do you fear me?*"

"I don't."

Thorn poured the dry fifty-pound bag of cement in the wheelbarrow and poured in gallon-size buckets of water he had hauled down from the kitchen. It took him two minutes to get the right thickness, and then he was slamming stones into place once again.

Somewhere into the second hour the Beretta began to chaff, so Thorn removed the semiautomatic and set it on a stone. It was close, in case he needed it, but safe from spattering cement.

He laid another row of rock around four feet long and was halfway through another when he glanced over to make sure the semiauto was untouched by the cement. He'd clean it later, anyway, just from habit, but he didn't want to have to do a major—

The Beretta was gone.

Like that.

Just gone.

Unlike a normal man, who might have been shocked or even horrified, Thorn didn't even blink. Two conclusions came to him simultaneously, and he was already moving as he analyzed the ramifications of them.

First conclusion as he hit the steps; this thing could not only communicate with him telepathically, it could move physical objects by some kind of unknown power.

Second conclusion halfway up the stairs; if it could move a two-pound pistol, it could move a twelve-ounce butcher knife into the heart of his wife or children.

He exited the stairway, audibly repeating the emergency phone number Monsignor DeMarco had provided.

A cold voice answered on the third ring.

"Yes?"

"It's Thorn. Give me the monsignor."

DeMarco was on the line in seconds. Thorn's voice was impatient, and he didn't conceal his anger. "Is that safe house ready yet?"

"No. Not yet."

"Doesn't matter. Get over here. Now. Get my family to the safe house. We'll deal with groceries and stuff later tonight."

"What has happened?"

"I'll tell you about it later. How soon can you be here?"

"A half hour."

"Bring all your men. And be ready for anything. This thing, whatever it is, can move stuff around—something like telekinesis. And it can make you hear things."

A sigh. "I was afraid of that."

"Of telekinesis?"

"No," the monsignor answered. "Of something much worse." He paused for a breath. "We are leaving now. Stay close to your family until we arrive."

Thorn hung up and searched for a weapon. If it could move stuff around, maybe it had to assume some kind of corporeal form to do it—even if it was using telekinesis. Maybe—just maybe—there were limitations to its powers. And in order to touch, maybe it had to leave itself vulnerable to *being* touched.

Yeah...

Maybe.

He only saw one possible weapon, and he wasn't sure whether he could conceal it. He would tell Rebecca everything once they were safely out of here and in the sanctity of the Church, but for the next hour he'd remain circumspect.

He slid the butcher knife into his belt at the small of his back.

🐍 ♀ 𓄿 ♀ 🦅

Cahill was leaning back in his chair, boots set high on his desk as he studied a small chip of silver Taylor had retrieved from the floor of the tomb.

It was barely the size of his finger; it had probably snapped off when Thorn hit the chain with that ax. But, small as it was, it held considerable value. And questions arose: Why would a nineteenth century community melt what was probably every last silver piece in town to forge silver chains and manacles?

Unfortunately, by the time Cahill had reached the attempted suicide scene of Father Cavanaugh, the chains and manacles had been packaged and sent by "special curio" to the Holy Office in Rome. Or, at least, they said it had been Rome, but you never knew. Cahill's criticism of the unauthorized action had fallen upon apologetic but deaf ears.

He noted that this small piece of silver was smoothly worked; someone had used a lot of skill and care in crafting it. It was also pure silver, not steel overlaid with silver, as he'd first suspected. No, this was pure silver, and the amount of it used to make manacles would have been, in any practical sense of the word, priceless for that time period.

If everyone—and that includes everyone—of that old, Puritan community had provided every silver chalice, cup, coin, and bracelet that they possessed, it might have been enough. But there was no direct evidence that members of the township actually forged the chains. The chains ended up here, sure, but they could have originated anywhere. They could have been shipped from England in the fourteenth century. They could have been left by the French or Spanish. Cahill could see no identifying marks but, then, it was only a small sliver of a single link.

Cahill could accept a mysterious origin for the chains, but he had a problem understanding what could have compelled normally peaceful people to bury this guy alive. And, somehow, Cahill suspected that he *was* alive when they walled him up. It just seemed to fit the use of chains: Why chain up a dead man?

Puritans were not necessarily violent, but neither were they pacifists, either. So Cahill could see them using whatever measure of violence they deemed necessary to rid themselves of a warlock or witch or madman.

In fact, as Oliver Cromwell so ably demonstrated in the seventeenth century, the majority of Puritans were well trained in a variety of martial arts, such as fencing or marksmanship. Some were even internationally recognized as excellent swordsmen, commanders, and diplomats. Nor were they "gray and uninteresting," as most modern people assumed.

Some were fairly flamboyant—such as Sir Jason Brand, who wore a scarlet cloak, carried a silver coated rapier and rifled flintlock pistol, and drank wine from a silver goblet. Also—and most intriguing—Brand spent a considerable part of his life simply "wandering the earth," fighting for various causes.

Cahill was an ardent amateur historian, which aided him greatly in his job as sheriff of Baldwin County because so much of the past was tied to the present of this place that, unless you understood both, you wouldn't understand either.

For example, last month he'd been called to quell a dispute at a local cemetery. A landscaping crew had been hired to fix up the old place, but as they were working on the small square of black fence they inadvertently knocked down a section.

Well, the family of the deceased, watching the operation closely, went ballistic and rushed forward to lift the fence, putting both themselves and everyone else in danger of the crane. The landscape engineer couldn't understand such a violent reaction and reacted with similar hostility and a fight broke out.

Cahill arrived, dragged the landowner off the engineer and threatened them both with a weekend in jail if they didn't calm down.

He understood the landowner's supercharged emotion: It wasn't so long ago that a black fence was erected around the grave of someone suspected of having been a witch or warlock. And tradition held that if a portion of the fence ever fell, the evil spirit would rise and possess someone of their bloodline.

Maintaining the fence was not an act of reverence; it was an act of self-preservation fueled by terror. In any case, Cahill had needed no explanation. He had known the reason for the super-charged emotions as he drove up in the squad car.

The relatives, at great personal risk of getting hit by heavy equipment, had already thrown the section of fence back up, or Cahill would have done that before he tried talking to anyone.

He had learned there was no point in using logic where severe and deeply ingrained superstitions were in full control. And so, after he restored the fence, Cahill peacefully and logically negotiated a landscaping system, and both parties were happy.

There was no use trying to explain such superstitions to the landscaping engineer. There was no point trying to explain to the family how unlikely it was that someone who's been dead five hundred years is going to rise from the grave and possess them.

Cahill knew the futility of it, so he didn't try. He simply accepted that one party was steeped in generational superstition and one party was a product of cold, logical business.

And Cahill himself? What did he believe?

As he studied the chip of silver, Cahill distinctly remembered his thought that night.

He had been grateful for the fence.

Thorn was waiting on the steps when Monsignor DeMarco and what Thorn had come to see as some kind of black branch of the Church arrived.

He'd explained to Rebecca that, for his own peace of mind, he wanted them to stay with DeMarco and his people for a few days until he was absolutely certain this place was safe. She'd objected, of course, but there was a point where Thorn *would* lay down the law, Italian temper or not, and things *would* be done.

It wasn't a thing he did often, because he rarely felt threatened and had nothing to prove in terms of manhood or courage, but when he felt that either Rebecca or the kids were in danger, he would act with a finality of purpose that left no question as to who was ultimately responsible and in charge.

Since they had barely unpacked, repacking was a simple thing, and two of the leather-coated men began loading the suitcases in the huge trunks of black Lincoln Town Cars.

Another two men entered the house to escort Rebecca and the kids onto the porch, their right hands concealed beneath the left sides of their coats. Another opened the door for Monsignor DeMarco and another took a position to study the wood lines—all without instruction. Thorn noted microwave hearing aids on each of them—a well coordinated team.

DeMarco moved with a solemnity of grace that belied the deadly gravity of the situation. "We should go quickly," he said.

No blessing, no formalities, no gracious greetings in the name of the Church. Just a simple and direct statement that meant he considered every moment spent in this house to be threatening. Thorn glanced at the man watching the wood line.

"First, tell me who these men are."

"We must go," enjoined the monsignor. "But if you must know, they are Assassini—protectors of the Church and those whom the Church would serve. They are trained much like yourself, Mr. Thorn, but with the loyal sympathies of a priest."

"And if Rebecca or the kids are threatened?"

"They will defend your family with their lives," DeMarco stated. "Your family will never be alone, even when they sleep."

Thorn nodded for his family to get in the car. Anthony put his hand flat against the window—a sign between them that meant: "I'll always be with you."

Thorn held up his hand, fingers spread. He felt a tear in his eye, then with a angry frown he shut down the rush of emotion. He spoke quietly to DeMarco: "Guard them with your life."

The monsignor nodded curtly. "These men are veterans at protection and powerful not only in prayer but the weapons of this world. In other words, Mr. Thorn, you and your children could not be in better hands."

"I'm not going," Thorn answered, ignoring a glance from the closest and seemingly the coldest Assassini. "I'm staying here tonight."

DeMarco's mouth dropped open. "I understand your irritation with the situation, Mr. Thorn. But I have summoned a special branch of the Jesuits trained to deal with these matters."

"Is Cavanaugh still alive?"

"Yes, David lives."

"Have you questioned him?"

"There is no need. I know that he encountered something here that followed him to the rectory and broke his mind with an attack of demonic power. The details are unimportant because demonic forces always mix enough truth with lies to confuse even the elect. In fact, the safest means of dealing with a demon is to not speak with them or listen to them at all. This is why we use very strict rituals. We do not deviate from time-tested routine."

Thorn had heard enough. "All right," he said. "Get my family to the safe house. And guard them close."

DeMarco's expression grew tense. "Mr. Thorn, although you are undoubtedly a brave man—a man of courage and trained in the ways of human investigation—you have no experience in dealing with...with entities from this domain."

Thorn ignored the closer Assassini and watched as Rebecca climbed into the Lincoln Town Car beside Malorie.

Rebecca and Malorie appeared frightened, while Anthony seemed to be having a good time—a little adventure in an otherwise boring life of school, homework, chores, and a mandatory daily training session with his dad in boxing and wrestling.

Thorn had made certain life had not gotten too serious too fast for them—there was plenty of time for "serious" later. But he had resolved at an early age that they would never be victims, that they would know how to defend themselves, how to survive in the forest if they became lost, how to deal with fire or cold, desert or snow.

Thorn took his parental responsibilities seriously—he always had—and it was paying off at the moment. Both the children were confident and didn't rattle easily, so they'd adjust to the atmosphere of the safe house without undue stress. But neither did he intend to let this situation last long enough to try their patience, which is why he was staying here tonight.

"Why do you insist on remaining here?" DeMarco pressed.

Thorn locked on a grim-looking Assassini. "I don't know anything about this spook business. But I don't want to be looking over my shoulder the rest of my life for this thing. I'm gonna *personally* make sure it's gone."

Rebecca was watching closely from the car.

DeMarco took a cautious step forward. "Mr. Thorn, doubtless, you were highly respected in your field. But, then, you were dealing with human forces—forces you were familiar with. And this is a force that even I do not understand.

"We have no idea how powerful this creature is, what it can accomplish, or whether we even have the power to do battle with it. The Jesuit Superior General has sent an entire army of..."

"Exorcists?"

DeMarco's lips pressed together. "To the common man, they might be regarded as such. But that only reinforces what I have told you; they have experience in these types of situations and are wary of demonic tactics and methods. They will not be caught off guard."

The priest did make sense; Thorn knew the benefit of experience. It was something he had drilled into his rookie cops, repeating it like a mantra: "Inexperience makes you overconfident, and that's what gets a lot of people killed. So go slow, and remember you don't know everything. Look slow, talk slow, think fast."

Thorn had to admit that he had no experience with this sort of thing, but his motivations were strong: His family was all he had, all he ever wanted, and all he cared for. He didn't even care for his own life, or about suffering serious injury. His attitude was simple and natural; he'd been injured before, and death comes for us all, eventually. Let the chips fall.

With an attempt at clinical detachment, he tried to estimate the skill of the Assassini.

They were silent, respectful, and moved with skillful coordination. In the real world any one of them could pull in a quarter million a year guarding presidents, dignitaries, or executives. Thorn judged they would protect the kids and Rebecca well.

Okay...he'd seen enough; time to end this conversation.

"Get my family to your safe house, monsignor, and make your men cover the physical. You're a holy man, supposedly; you cover the spiritual."

"You still wish to stay?"

"I *am* staying."

DeMarco turned slowly away, head bowed. Then he stopped in place and turned back. "Would you grant me one concession? The Jesuits will not be organized until tomorrow morning."

"What do you need?"

The monsignor extended his hand toward the closest Assassini. The man was dressed completely in black leather, with short black hair, olive skin—obviously first-generation Italian. His arms were crossed on his chest, hands under his coat. He was broad-shouldered with heavy arms and thick thighs. He had the thin white souvenir of a scar across his throat. His face revealed no emotion.

By necessity, Thorn had long ago developed the ability to determine if he would trust a man with his life. In seconds, he judged the man trustworthy.

"This is my most skilled and trusted servant," DeMarco said with a slight bow. "His name is Artemis."

Without any expression, Artemis bowed to Thorn.

"Grant me this one favor," DeMarco continued, "and allow Artemis to remain with you tonight...Just him, and him alone."

"Why?"

"An old biblical principle, Mr. Thorn: 'And He sent His disciples out two by two.'"

Thorn grunted: "I'm not a disciple."

"Still," the monsignor clasped his hands, as if thankful for the wisdom of a thought, "it is a sound principle, nonetheless. Does not even the revered Los Angeles Police Department employ such?"

Thorn had to admit the monsignor made a good point; a rookie had to ride in a dual unit with a veteran for months before he could go solo. "All right," he said, "just him. The rest stay with Rebecca and the kids. And *you* know what to do."

"None of us shall sleep until the Jesuits arrive," the monsignor replied. "Then we shall rest, and my men will be relieved."

Thorn gestured toward Artemis. "How many more of them are coming?"

"I cannot say; no more than a handful. There are not many of them to begin with. And, I suppose you understand, Rome does not actually endorse their use any more than it can eradicate a facet of the Church more than six hundred years old."

"Can you protect my wife and children on the spiritual plain? All that stuff? Protect them from the voices? The thoughts?"

"Where we are securing them is covered in prayer by priests and nuns and other members of the Church far holier than I. Our prayers will never cease, and there is genuine power in prayer."

"Prayer," Thorn repeated slowly. "You still believe in prayer?"

The monsignor grunted.

"Prayer can prevail where weapons may fail."

🪲 ☥ 𓂀 𓏤 𓅃

After Monsignor DeMarco departed, Thorn reentered the house with Artemis close behind him.

Quite casually, the Assassini withdrew what Thorn recognized immediately as a Mossberg eight-shot 12-gauge riot shotgun—it was a powerful, simple, and effective weapon.

Wordless, the Assassini offered it to Thorn.

Thorn blinked, then took it. He racked it a quarter inch to insure a shell wasn't chambered, made sure the safety was on, and slung it across

his back. "Thanks," he muttered, and moved into the living room. With sound tactical judgment, Artemis kept his back to Thorn, his eyes on the rest of the house.

Thorn unlocked his steel footlocker and lifted a bulletproof vest charged with fully loaded magazines. Then he removed a .45 caliber Colt 1911A1 and chambered it. He flicked the safety up, leaving the hammer back. Now, all he had to do was flick down the safety for one good, fast first shot. Last, Thorn snapped on a canvas belt loaded with even more clips and lifted a CAR-15.

A CAR-15 was basically a cut down version of an M-16 with a collapsible stock and a fifteen-inch barrel. It fired a .223 caliber round at a velocity of 1,700 feet per second and held thirty-round clips. But, holding it, Thorn reconsidered the probable range and some unknown factors. He didn't know how quickly this thing moved. He might have to shoot from the hip. He slung the CAR over his back and positioned the shotgun for a fast grab.

Thorn removed the kitchen knife from the small of his back, laid it on the floor, and lifted a bowie-style knife with a nine-inch blade that he slammed into a sheath attached to the clip-belt.

These *had been* souvenirs from his days in the Army and as a LAPD investigator. He looked up at Artemis, but knew the answer to his question before it was asked.

"You need any of this?"

The Assassini curtly shook his head.

This soldier, or Assassini, or whatever he was, was probably as heavily armed beneath that coat, even minus the shotgun, as any man could be. And Thorn suspected that he wore the priciest, most modern ballistic vest, too. Professionals always wore a vest. It's how they lived long enough to *become* professionals.

Thorn suspected that even Artemis's clothing, which wrinkled with a strange stiffness—was ballistic. It was probably some kind of Japanese material that offered the same protection as a vest, but resembled regular clothing and was, incidentally, very, very expensive. Whatever else Artemis and his crew actually were, they weren't underfunded.

Thorn stood. "Now what?"

"We wait."

"For what?"

"For him."

"And if he comes?"

"Then we attempt to destroy him."

"How hard will that be?"

The Assassini was silent a moment. "I don't know. But we have challenged him, and so he will come. How he will attack, I cannot tell you. I can only tell you he will wait until tonight, when his powers are strongest."

Thorn studied the Assassini. "Just what, *exactly*, do you do for the Church?"

Artemis apparently considered his answer very carefully. "Understand me, Mr. Thorn, I am a priest. What I do is serve my God. But I also protect the Church from evil, and from evil men. And sometimes I must protect the Church from itself."

Thorn gestured vaguely with shotgun. "Like now?"

"No," said Artemis coldly. "I believe that, now, we face something that has not been challenged in three thousand years. And then it took the greatest of all God's prophets to defeat it."

It was the manner in which Artemis said it that held Thorn. He wasn't ignorant about the Bible; he knew that Artemis, in his own cryptic way, was referring to the Old Testament figure of Moses.

"Yeah, well," Thorn frowned and racked a round, "Moses didn't have a Mossberg."

Chapter Eight

The monsignor was the epitome of charm.

Rebecca had never before felt so warm and protected unless she was with Thorn, but that wasn't exactly comparable.

When she was with Thorn, fear never even entered her mind. Living with Thorn was like living with a very large, very capable watchdog that never slept. She remembered a time when all of them, including the kids, had been caught in a snowstorm at the base of Mount Washington.

Malorie had been only four at the time, and too weak to even be carried through the cold, so they had to weather it out until morning. She remembered Thorn's utter confidence and businesslike attitude about the entire incident.

He had quickly found a niche in the cliff and in ten minutes had rigged a waterproof shelter from the storm. Then, inside a half hour, he had a blazing fire going near the entrance and cooked them freeze-dried meals on a small stove. Afterward he hiked to a nearby creek and an hour later he returned with six large trout that he cleaned and cooked for them over the fire.

Actually, she and the kids had had a wonderful time and slept warmly on a dry bed of pine needles. And the entire experience reinforced once more to her what she constantly saw; she and the children were the most important thing in Thorn's life, and he would die before he'd allow them to be injured.

And that was one thing she so admired about her husband; he was always prepared and—no matter how terrible things got—*never* gave up. Thorn was living proof of the old saying, "When things are at their worst, he's at his best."

Of course, Thorn's protectiveness did cause small moments of dissention between the two of them, at times. For instance, Thorn always had to be prepared for a disaster, "just in case." In a way, Rebecca found it quaint, but sometimes she couldn't help but comment, "Michael, this isn't a safari. It's just a day hike, you know?"

But whenever they ventured into the woods for even the smallest hiking, camping, or sight-seeing trip, Thorn never deviated from his die-hard routine.

He *always* carried a day pack with dried food, a mess kit complete with plastic spoons and a small gas stove, first aid kit, a poncho that he could instantly rig into a small tent or shelter, his bowie knife, a Bic lighter, map, compass, and flares. No matter how small and insignificant the trip seemed to Rebecca, Thorn was always prepared to protect them from the unexpected.

She had never known a man who took his protective responsibilities so seriously and attended to them with such unerring devotion.

For instance, the first thing Thorn unerringly did, after settling them comfortably into a campsite, was purchase topographical maps of the area and familiarize himself with the locations of homes, cabins, trails, ravines, and bridges. Then he'd casually interview the Rangers—not content with the outline information of a map—to learn an area's propensity for rapid weather changes, landslides, flash floods, bad bridges, or the lesser known perils of roads rarely traveled.

Not that Thorn wasn't something of a mountain man, himself. He could usually determine most of what concerned him simply by studying the terrain. He even seemed to possess a genuine ability for "sensing" the weather, as he termed it, and could guesstimate far ahead of time whether it was going to rain or snow.

And, because of training, he was always resourceful and calm in a disaster, and he had taught both her and the children how to deal with a wide variety of emergencies.

It was Thorn who taught her how to survive when she'd gotten herself lost in the woods on a day trip with the kids. There's a lot of ways to find your way out, he explained, but simply walking downhill was as good as anything. Just follow the water, because a tiny stream leads to a bigger stream, which leads to a creek, which leads to a bigger creek or a river, which leads to a bridge, which puts you on a road.

After you're on the road, pick a direction or just wait for someone to come along; it's only a matter of time. If it's cold, use a poncho to make a lean-to, build a fire, and break out the rations. Then all you need is a deck of cards.

Rebecca looked about the safe house, which seemed an awfully lot like the rectory of a priest. Religious symbols adorned each wall—St. Michael, St. Jude—there was a portrait of Mother Theresa and her blue-habited nuns. There was a reverently framed picture of John Paul II raising his hand during the Eucharist, dispensing Communion, newer pictures of Pope Benedict XVI.

She respectfully accepted Communion when Monsignor DeMarco offered to dispense it to both her and the children. Then the ritual was repeated with the quiet, leather-coated men who were always close beside her, but never so close that they invaded her privacy or space.

Rebecca knew enough about bodyguards and legends of the Church to suspect what the men truly were. She had just never believed that the Assassini actually existed. Nor was she disrespectful enough to request from the gracious monsignor an explanation of their purpose and identity.

She raised her face as the monsignor stopped before her, hands clasped. He smiled gently. "Are you comfortable?"

"Very much," Rebecca said, and glanced at Anthony and Malorie. "But the kids need some form of entertainment, monsignor, and some kid food. You know what I mean—maybe some ice cream, some pizza. Michael and I make them eat healthy, but I think I'm going to cut them some slack under the circumstances."

DeMarco laughed lightly. "I anticipated as much. Do not worry, Mrs. Thorn, those appointed to serve you will be returning shortly with all manner of 'junk food.' Plus, I instructed them to obtain healthy foods, as well. And others will return with games—I cannot say what they are; I'm afraid I'm not up on the latest trends. But rest assured the children will not be bored. And we are preparing a room where you may all sleep together quite comfortably and very safely."

Rebecca's head was bowed as she asked quietly, "And my husband?"

In a heartbeat the monsignor's manner was a monument of conviction.

"All the powers of the Church stand behind him."

🪲 ☥ 𓂀 ☥ 𓅃

"Taylor!"

Cahill knew his voice had an unnatural facility for carrying through brick and stone; he took advantage of the effect it had.

Casually, Taylor stuck his head in the open frame of the door. Some vague impulse of self-preservation inspired him to keep his body out of Cahill's gun-sight eyes. He attempted a nondescript tone at first, but seemed to know it wouldn't save him.

"Yep, boss?"

"Did you not tell this Professor What's-His-Name that this was an emergency?"

"I sure did, boss."

"And?" Cahill prodded. "What did he say?"

Taylor moved fully into the doorway after confirming he wasn't the one in trouble. A shrug: "Well, boss, he said he had to teach this afternoon in Boston and—"

"At Harvard?"

"Yes, sir."

Cahill frowned. "And that he'd come up soon as he was done." He stared out the window, and nodded. "Soon as he was done...I've got a suicidal priest, a haunted house, an entire family possibly in danger, a walking skeleton and this 'guru-professor' will be up when he's done teaching a bunch of citified morons. That's great. That's just great."

He heaved a massive sigh, "I want you to call the dispatchers over in Salem. Talk to Shirley; she knows everything. See if there's been any unusual activity in the last few days. And not the ordinary unusual— not just kids having sex in the cemeteries. I'm only interested in something truly bizarre."

Taylor stared a minute. "Like what?"

"I don't know, Taylor! How would I know how bizarre these freaks can get?"

Andover was only twenty miles from Salem, Massachusetts, the site of the Salem Witch Trials of the early nineteenth century, and Thorn's house wasn't in the police jurisdiction of either township. It was about three hundred yards outside the city police jurisdiction of Andover, so unless there was an emergency, Andover police wouldn't respond, which put the situation in Cahill's lap.

Cahill covered all of Essex County, and his department, despite his stubborn requests for more deputies, was always shorthanded. Most were forced to ride solo in order to cover the two thousand square miles of mountainous territory. And it didn't help that the entire state was at the northern tip of the Appalachian Chain. To be sheriff, you had to know the mountains as well as the city, meaning you had to be as much a tracker and hunter as lawman.

Cahill had grown up in the mountains, so he knew tracking and hunting, but he had also gained an expensive education in the Army, so he was at home in both worlds.

He knew how to gauge the minute of angle on a 30.06 at six hundred yards, and he knew which fork to use. And although he didn't make a habit of being tactful and diplomatic, he could deal with city councils and mayors charmingly and persuasively when occasion required. His natural disposition was blunt and even abrasive, but he knew when to use brute force and when to use persuasion.

But Essex County was—including a sleepy Italian Mafia that engaged in low-key smuggling that Cahill couldn't have cared less about—a fairly crime-free community.

Cahill was very much proactive when it came to crime. And if he perceived that a situation might mushroom into trouble, he'd take care of it early and without mercy. He didn't believe in letting a situation "develop."

For instance, he'd been irritated recently with a growing community of young street racers in souped-up foreign jobs. Catching them involved high-risk pursuits, which Cahill discouraged, so he'd just written tickets for whatever innocuous traffic violation until parents pulled keys. That took care of it; no cars, no racing.

An abuse of power, maybe, but Cahill didn't believe in letting a minor problem became a big problem. Although there was one dilemma he hadn't managed to resolve yet: the gothic flood of teenagers and Satanists that descended on Salem at Halloween.

Ninety percent of them were harmless, sure. But there was that 10 percent who actually lived and believed what they said, and practiced every word of it. Hence, every year Cahill suffered a deluge of reports from tourists and residents claiming there were some *"genuinely* crazy people out there in the woods sacrificing human beings!"

No matter what Cahill personally believed, and he did *not* believe there was a coven out there sacrificing human beings, he had to investigate it, which usually meant a long, arduous trek through the overgrown brush west of Salem—a briar patch of ground he had become hatefully familiar with over the years. For the most part, though, Cahill just found deluded adults participating in some loopy ritual for fame, money, sex, freedom, popularity. Whatever.

But this thing with Thorn felt different, somehow. Maybe it was simply because Cahill was prone to pay attention when one of the most respected investigators to ever work LAPD Homicide reported a walking skeleton.

If the report had come to Cahill from a drunk at Tankersly's Garage and Grill, he would have, of course, ignored it. But he couldn't ignore a report from someone like Thorn.

Mistakes were for people who didn't get killed if they made one. And Thorn had not only survived in that environment for twenty-four years, he'd been decorated for his judgment and dedication and skill.

Still, though, Cahill sensed the former LAPD detective wasn't telling him everything.

He was certain that Thorn was holding back on something crucial, but Cahill couldn't decide if it was just a suspicion or a piece of solid evidence. Which is why Cahill had called for that old professor that he'd read so much about in the newspapers. Normally he would have just let the whole thing slide, but he had a bad feeling about this.

Also, he had fourteen unsolved murders committed in this house, and although he had officially closed the files, he hadn't been satisfied with the explanations. He knew...he *knew* there was something wrong and unnatural about that house. And he sensed that this skeleton was part of the equation, somehow.

"Spook factor," he said as a very tall gentleman with pure white hair appeared at his door. Taylor lifted his hands toward the man as Cahill stood and stared.

"H-H-Here he is," Taylor offered.

Cahill shook his head. His deputies needed some work.

The older man bowed graciously. "I am Professor Adler," he said pleasantly. "I believe you requested my assistance?"

Cahill leaned forward on gorilla arms.

"You ever heard of walking skeletons?" he asked, in no mood to delay the inevitable.

Professor Adler laughed.

"As a matter of fact, sheriff...I have."

🐞 ♀ 𓂀 𓂉 𓅃

Thorn studied Artemis closely; there wasn't much to see, and Thorn was a trained observer.

Artemis was cloaked in an atmosphere so meaningless and unobtrusive he could have carried a rocket launcher through the lobby of the White House without attracting any attention.

He said little, didn't reveal fear or impatience and, overall, barely seemed to acknowledge Thorn's presence. Though, occasionally, he would cast Thorn a glance as he poured another cup of coffee or checked windows and doors.

Although Thorn's movements were minimal, he didn't come close to the statuesque stillness of the Assassini, who remained almost motionless, with his back to the wall in a place that gave him the best view of the first floor.

Finally Thorn settled in again, not far from the Assassini because

Artemis was right; the angle did provide the best view of the first floor. He leaned back, resting the barrel of the Mossberg up the wall. With a pillow at his back, Thorn could endure this position long enough.

Nothing to do now but wait, but something in the back of Thorn's mind nagged at him—a kind of instinctive fear that men, for the most part, ignore but never completely bury with cold reason.

A walking skeleton?

Thorn wasn't disturbed that someone had volunteered the concept, but he was very disturbed that he had considered it, even briefly, as a possible explanation.

He knew, of course, the skeleton hadn't disintegrated upon contact with air. Sure, Rebecca had pretended to buy into it because she *wanted to*, but she knew better. He also knew it would have been all but impossible for someone to have snuck past him, down that flight of stairs, sacked up the skeleton, and left, without his senses alerting him. He trusted his instincts and experience far too much to accept that, which left him with only one explanation.

A walking skeleton— the explanation that the thing just got up and walked out.

Just like that.

It just stood up and walked out.

Strangely, in Salem, Massachusetts, it actually didn't seem like so much of an outlandish theory, but Thorn would keep his thoughts to himself until he knew more.

In any case, he couldn't completely ignore it as a hypothesis because if this skeleton was indeed haunted, cursed, or whatever, and imbued with some kind of fantastic, as-of-yet unknown energy to "do things," then it would come after Thorn on its own ground before it'd seek out his family in a safe house. And if that was the case, Thorn would make himself easy to find. He'd rather have it come after him than his family, whether it was a walking skeleton or just the insane descendents of a revered witch or warlock.

Thorn lifted his head to a low rumble of thunder, then glanced at their massive grandfather clock: nine o'clock. He shifted at a settling stiffness in his shoulders and legs.

The clock continued ticking...and ticking.

Come on, come on...let's do it.

He looked toward Artemis. Although he appeared totally relaxed, the Assassini had one hand concealed beneath his coat.

Thorn could only guess what he was holding, but it'd be something small with a high cycle rate and a lot of knockdown power. And that reduced the list to either an Uzi or a MAC-10. Thorn guessed it was probably a MAC-10, a superior weapon just because of the .45 size caliber. But it did rise off target more than an Uzi, unless the shooter held down hard. Not that that made much difference. Thorn didn't think Artemis had much trouble holding it down.

"How long have you done this?" he asked.

Artemis was unexpressive a long time, then spoke quietly, "It is dangerous to speak in the belly of the beast."

Thorn glanced at the empty room: "Someone listening?"

"I believe so, yes."

Thorn considered this. "Well...could you at least tell me what you think we *might* be dealing with? I don't see how that can hurt us."

"The less he knows about what we know, the better."

The lines in Thorn's jaw tightened. "You know, I've just about had it with this mysticism and the Church and secret societies and exorcists. This is my house, and if I don't get some cooperation, you're going out that front door, weapons or no weapons." He waited while Artemis slowly turned his head for a full stare.

Thorn laid down the Mossberg. "Okay, your decision." He stood up and walked toward the Assassini.

"A monster," Artemis said without tone.

Thorn stopped.

"A monster..." he repeated without agreement or disagreement in the tone. "What kind of monster? You mean, a monster like Dracula? A vampire?"

"Something like that," answered Artemis coolly.

"A monster like Dracula," Thorn repeated. "A monster like a walking skeleton? Is that what you call a monster?" He paused. "Those are campfire stories, man."

"Yes," the Assassini agreed. "My people, the Italian Gypsies, have a wealth of campfire stories. But not all are merely stories."

Thorn thought he had experienced just about everything, but now he felt the most curious combination of sentiments. Before he moved into this place he would have laughed at the concept of a vampire. Now he was searching the shadows.

He focused on the front door; the house was as silent as a tomb. Artemis was still as stone. Thorn tilted his head toward the basement door.

He didn't like this waiting. He'd rather have the thing walk up with a chainsaw or meat cleaver or butcher knife or scythe or whatever the Grim Reaper carried so they could dance this dance.

It didn't help that Artemis expressed no signs of impatience at all. Rather, it seemed like the Assassini had stood in his corner for a hundred years and could stand for a hundred more.

"What is it with you?" Thorn asked.

Without expression, Artemis glanced at him.

"I mean, what's your story?" Thorn pressed. "No man does this kind of thing unless he has some sort of obsession." He waited. "So what's your reason? I know you have one."

"Why do you ask?"

"Well, let's say I would like to know who's backing me up." Thorn's tone was inflexible. "I *do* need to know that much."

For the first time in hours, Artemis shifted position. He raised his eyes to the open section of hallway upstairs, as if imagining the skeleton staring down on them, studying his every word. Then, incredibly, he seemed to laugh—something that came and went so fast Thorn wondered if it had truly been there at all.

"I have no obsession," the Assassini said finally. "I do what I do because of a sense of duty."

Thorn continued to listen in stillness.

"About twenty years ago, my church in Colombia was attacked by an extreme sect of militants," Artemis continued. "My assistant priests and nuns were trapped in the chapel. But I was caught beneath the building in a cellar...with the children." He sighed deeply. "When they began killing my people, I kept the children hidden...and quiet. We were never discovered, so we were forced to sit in silence...and listen to the screams...as the killing continued."

He cleared his throat; "When it was finally over, and it was totally dark, we crept out of the trapdoor...to a bloodbath." His expression was tired. "I secured safe houses for the children, but I knew this particular army would return and kill more of us unless they were stopped. They did not care about reason, or mercy. And so I stopped them...with their own methods." He sniffed. "Afterward, the Holy See determined that I might be more useful to the Church in...other ways."

Thorn remarked, "You must have a knack for it."

"I end things quickly. I hate violence and violent people."

"Who trained you?"

He shrugged. "As you say, I seem to have a knack for it. But I received some instruction from others who came before me. In truth, I did not require much training."

"I'll bet."

"And you, Mr. Thorn? Do you remember why you devoted your life to saving others?"

At Thorn's unrevealing eyes, Artemis smiled. Then he looked back at the door with a genuine laugh.

"Yes, I know of you, Mr. Thorn. I never go into a situation unless I know the principals." The smile slowly faded. "Detective, soldier; you won the Silver Star for carrying fourteen of your men in Beirut out of a cross fire. Then, although you were wounded, you directed artillery fire that consequently saved your entire regiment. You were a top patrol officer for Los Angeles, then a homicide investigator—commended eight times for valor." He studied Thorn more closely. "So...do you remember what first compelled you to pick up a weapon?"

Actually, that was a question that had occurred to Thorn over the years, but he'd never arrived at an answer.

It just seemed like weapons and violence were all he'd ever known. His earliest memories were of training—karate, boxing, wrestling. Also, his stepfather had been an exceedingly violent man, and Thorn had learned early how to protect himself, how to bind his own wounds, how to hide them, how to endure agony without any medical treatment or support or love.

He didn't overanalyze the why of it. He only knew that somewhere between asking the question and answering the question came a cloudy zone of nothing but questions, and he'd finally given up trying to understand. And then, after a while, he hadn't cared to anymore.

Yeah, he'd dedicated his life to saving his fellow soldiers, oppressed peoples, the weak or helpless or doomed. He felt compassion for them.

And he knew he'd made a difference. But he really didn't know why he felt such compassion, and he didn't think he ever would.

In a way he admired the Assassini; it must be peaceful to know such clarity of purpose.

But Thorn *did* know why he was waiting for these people, tonight. If they, in any way, posed a threat to his family...well, the options weren't pretty.

He gazed through the first floor. Nothing. The clock continued ticking.

Nothing.

With the air of a priest, the Assassini spoke, "God designs a man's heart, Mr. Thorn, and gives to that man no more than what his heart is made to bear, just as God has planned man's every footsteps. He does not ask us or expect us to understand, nor can we. All He asks is that our hearts remain pure, and He will lead us."

Thorn released a deep sigh. He scowled and glanced up the stairway at the unseen section of hall.

"It will come," Artemis muttered. "Patience..."

Thorn looked at the Assassini. "And when it comes?"

"Then we dance with the devil."

𓆣 ☥ 𓂀 𓊽 𓅃

"That'll be all, Taylor."

A curt salute that would have landed him in the brig for ten years at any respectable military establishment was the only reply and Taylor was gone.

Cahill was surprised that he wasn't intimidated by the professor, because he should have been.

This guy was regarded as a giant, even among the intellectually prodigious. He taught at Princeton, Harvard, and Yale. Had doctorates in anthropology and Egyptology and theology. He'd written a Pulitzer Prize-winning book six years ago based on, as best Cahill could understand it, the "sameness of the fear of God" in ancient cultures.

Yeah, Cahill had checked up on him, making sure Adler might be able to help or at least not make the situation worse. He had discovered that the old man was born in the twenties in Plymouth, England, and raised in Cambridge. He graduated from Trinity College with his first doctorate at fifteen years old and many degrees later was internationally recognized as one of the premier thinkers in his field. Although what—exactly—his premier field *was*, wasn't so easy to define.

Some defined it as a revolutionary field of psychology and sociology that dissected man's fear of the unknown, death, and God. He had also conducted a lifelong investigation on the phenomenon of loneliness and the hidden motivations behind political and religious institutions. And, although he didn't lambaste or ridicule, he did remove the veneer of grace that organizations constructed to justify deeper, hidden motivations that sometimes even they were not consciously aware of.

His work was an attempt at unification—revealing man's deepest motivations so that their actions could enhance solidarity and not separation. But his success had come at a strange price. Instead of being rewarded, he had been vociferously attacked by political and religious groups who did indeed harbor jealously cherished prejudices. In recent years Adler had dabbled more in the occult than science, though Cahill figured he probably made it a science.

He was fairly certain he could trust the old man—to a degree, anyway—because he had enemies all over the board and wasn't aligned with any particular university or think tank. Also, he was an expert in ancient man—prehistoric stuff—and gut instinct told Cahill this thing was prehistoric or better, so he might take a personal interest in keeping it close to his vest.

While researching him Cahill had finally stopped reading the list of degrees; it was a doctorate in this, a fellowship in that—theology, anthropology, psychology, and on and on. Strangely, he held no permanent teaching position though he was regarded—or regaled—as "professor emeritus" at Yale, Harvard, Cambridge, and a half-dozen other universities. Though retired, he remained Editor Emeritus of a dozen scientific publications for his exacting craftsmanship in editing and writing. Cahill figured nobody kept him in a permanent position because they couldn't afford him, which was yet another reason Cahill had chosen him.

Because he had no ironclad university affiliation or curriculum to develop, he wasn't encumbered by a "crew" documenting either his research or writing. If anything, that was the factor that made Cahill happiest. The last time "researchers" came to Salem, it was like something out of *Ghostbusters*.

During that misadventure, about five years back now, Cahill had sent the entire team packing after they started knocking down walls in an old sanitarium utilized in the dying days of the Civil War as a tuberculosis center.

The place had been surrounded by ghost sightings and horror stories since as long as Cahill could remember. But Cahill had grown up in the shadow of it, and he'd never seen anything unusual. He figured some people—not *him*—just loved a good ghost story.

Still, the fourteen people murdered in Thorn's house weren't imaginary, and Cahill sensed that this might be the time to find some overdue answers. Earlier in the day he'd counted his strong points; Thorn was a hard man and didn't spook easily. He knew how to stay cool, how to protect his family if things got out of hand with some kind of Satanic cult, and clearly had no intent on leaving. His wife seemed strong enough, and her religious bent might give her added stability if things got spooky. With the inclusion of the professor, Cahill had a lot on his side. He couldn't help but cautiously hope he could find some explanation to the killings that was more satisfying than an incomprehensible murder-suicide out of nowhere.

But, clearly, the strongest factor was Thorn. He was a world-class detective and had the perfect crime scene; he *lived* in it. With a little luck, Thorn might solve this thing himself. Still, Cahill mused, if this professor could be of any use, even better. There was nothing wrong with stacking the deck. And ultimately, if Cahill was left with nothing more than what he had now, well, at least he would know that he had done everything possible. Maybe some mysteries weren't meant to be solved.

Professor Adler smiled: "As I said, yes, I have heard of such things—not as uncommon as you might think in certain parts of Africa and Eastern Europe. In fact, the Baltics are rife with tales of zombies and the walking dead, as is the hill country of Libya."

"And what do you think?" asked Cahill. "About the walking dead, I mean."

"Oh, there are all manner of theories," Adler answered, totally relaxed with the question. "Some theorize it is a matter of electrical displacement."

If Cahill was sheriff of Bonneville, Nevada, he probably wouldn't have a clue what an "electromagnetic displacement" was. But as the chief law enforcement officer over Salem, Massachusetts, he could deliver a speech on the Theory of Relativity as well as Einstein's chauffeur, who was forced to hear it a thousand times. Cahill might not know what electromagnetic displacement actually *meant*, but he knew the terms. He lifted a broad hand as calloused and hard as a board.

"Let's talk a while, professor."

Adler unceremoniously dropped his cashmere overcoat over a chair as Cahill glanced out the window. The temperature had dropped an unpredicted thirty degrees since Thorn had uncovered that skeleton, and it was incredibly dark. If this kept up and that rain front moved in, his department would have more problems than downed power lines. And the last thing Cahill wanted in the middle of a serious investigation were road problems.

"Excuse me one minute, professor," he said as he pressed a button on his phone. "Shirley?"

The intercom blinked.

"Yes, sheriff?"

"Call the weather service and get me an update. If it's snow, call Petey at the garage and tell him to break out the snow chains for the units. Also, I want you to call Tom Humphreys at the Moose Lodge and tell him we might need the guys with four-wheel drives to ferry doctors and nurses back and forth from the hospital. He'll know what you're talking about. He keeps a list of volunteers."

"Will do, Sheriff."

Cahill ran a relaxed ship and liked it that way. His men dressed sharp to encourage morale and self-respect—time in the Army had taught Cahill the truth of that psychology: feel better, fight better. That was a good enough reason for him, but he also had a neurotic county commission perpetually concerned about tourism and the "image" of Essex County, and he had to keep up relations if he wanted to keep up funding.

That done, Cahill leaned back in his chair and studied the professor more closely.

Adler was sitting comfortable and patient with one leg crossed, a 1940-style brown fedora hat on his knee hand. He smiled pleasantly; "So, how may I be of service?"

"Well," Cahill said, and paused, "I really don't know where to begin."

"Let's just try the beginning."

Cahill nodded. "All right. I've got a vanishing skeleton, a haunted house, some dead people, and some folks who might soon *be* dead. I've got superstition at war with religion, and I'm not sure if people are going to act rationally or...get excited and kill somebody just because they don't believe like 'we' believe."

"Something that happens more often than you might believe, sheriff. I've made a lifelong study of it."

"I know. And I believe it happens often enough, professor. I just don't want it happening *here*." Cahill's eyes narrowed. "You say you've heard of walking skeletons. From anybody sane?"

Adler took a deep breath and released it slowly. For a time he stared at the floor in front of him. Then, finally, he fixed Cahill with a solid gaze.

"Oh, quite sane," he stated. "And also quite dead."

Chapter Nine

Ben Johnson never believed this old road was cursed just because the community, having nothing better to do, needed a good old-fashioned horror story.

"Dead Man's Curve" wasn't particularly inventive or frightening, and Ben was fairly ashamed that it was the best they could do around here. The most ironic thing about it was the dumb road didn't even have a respectable curve—just a slight twisting down the Andover-side of what qualified as a "knob" to Ben. In his opinion, it wasn't even high enough to qualify as a hill.

The real reason it was associated with death is because it was the only curve on the road that passed the old mansion where all those folks had been killed. The last man foolish enough to buy it went crazy on Halloween Eve and murdered all his kids. They'd found the grandmother dead inside the closet and the mother hanging from the chandelier. Local legend said the grandma was white as a sheet and the frozen expression on her face was pure horror.

Of course, the coroner wrote it off as a heart attack and—ironically—that did sort of fit the circumstances. Ben reckoned he might have had a heart attack, too, if a madman had been chasing him around the house with a butcher knife. That is, if he couldn't get to the shotgun first. Then the worm would have turned real quick.

"Never bring a knife to a gunfight," he muttered as he lazily let the lug wench spin. "And I *do* keep a shotgun, partner."

He'd never expected the newly paved asphalt to have a ragged pothole when he came around the curve a little faster than usual, heading for Andover. But it was too late when he saw the hole to risk swerving; he had to hold his course.

He hit it at about fifty and knew instantly that his front right tire was blown. He was losing control quick when he finally made it to the side of the road and a grinding stop. Then he saw the rim was banged up, too, and hauled out the jack and lug wrench.

Ben was a farmer. Changing a tire in the midst of this hurricane— or whatever this night was becoming—was a piece of cake. He'd often bet his wife he could change a tire inside three minutes just so she'd have to make him chocolate pie.

He was a minute into the work when he began to wonder about the pothole and, almost as an afterthought, glanced at it.

Strange that it'd just cave-in like that, being newly paved. Ben made a mental note to speak to the county boys about it first of the week. Probably the same old problem; they used the wrong grade of gravel.

Ben was no spring chicken; he'd worked just about every job you could think of and knew what size gravel was best for most purposes. And he knew that for a road you needed twelve-grade as a foundation. That was small as it gets, and it always packed tight. But this inexperienced road crew had probably used six-grade or bigger, which was mainly intended for septic systems, and the big rocks would shift with time.

Ben had told his work crews a thousand times, "Foundation is everything in a road or house or anything else. If you lose the foundation, what's on top of it doesn't matter. How good it's built doesn't matter. It's coming down. Maybe not today, maybe not tomorrow, but soon enough. And there won't be jack you can do about it."

Ben didn't need to get a closer look at the road; he knew what they'd done and wrote it off as inexperience. Still, he might bring it up at the county commission meeting when Regina, their newspaper reporter, was there. She'd take care of it for him. He almost laughed as he turned the lug wrench; yeah, the last thing those county commissioners wanted was bad publicity. It was almost worse than the IRS coming in and—

Crack.

Ben had twisted his head at the sound, and his hand had stopped the wrench from spinning in the same split-second. With a strange breathlessness, he became aware he was staring at the wood line behind him; it was about fifty yards away and inky in blackness—total blackness.

Nothing could see in that pitch black.

Including Ben.

It was almost a full moon, but temporary cloud cover had blocked out the paling light. Ben looked around: no road lights, no reflectors, not even a firefly. There were no houses as far as the curve allowed him to see, but he didn't have to see. He knew every shack and trash pile from his house to Andover.

In the distance he heard a logging truck, still five miles away, at the crossways—not coming his way. Logs didn't come *from* Andover, they went *to* Andover.

Ben was alone in the dark.

For a moment the thought disturbed him, then he laughed at his own foolishness. He had an old 12-gauge in the cab for varmints, wounded deer, or the outside chance of a hooligan. And, although he disliked the thought of doing it, he'd plant somebody if it came to it. He'd done it in the war; he could do it again.

Probably a coyote...Maybe that Jersey devil story has some truth in it... Some critter that might have lived in these woods a long time without being found....Ya never know...

"Change the tire, old man..."

Ben heard his own whisper and didn't hesitate to repeat the advice. "Just change it."

He placed the wrench on the lug when he felt...*felt* rather than heard...someone on his right.

A veteran of Korea and hard times, Ben knew how to handle himself. His palm, suddenly sweating, tightened with a firmer grip on the wrench as he turned and began to rise. He didn't want to hurt some fool who was out here to grab some easy...

Ben stopped moving before he'd fully stood.

It slouched toward him, trailing rags.

It was dressed in draping black rags, and *dirty*...dirty like it'd dug its way out of the grave. Ben dully noticed that the finger bones were white like its face.

Ben heard himself moan as he looked up.

No...not a face.

Jagged jaws, unnaturally sharp and elongated, grinned beneath bloody eyes as it closed, reaching out with a hand that dripped flesh onto the black gravel of the roadway. Its strides were halting but purposeful and left no question of its direction as it closed on Ben.

Ben involuntarily dropped the wrench and raised hands before his face as it grabbed him by the arm and moved inexorably toward the woods, dragging him by the wrist. More than a foot taller than Ben's six-foot frame, it towered over him.

Its finger bones were as cold and strong as the pinions of a steel vice, though they were only bones and rags of bloody flesh. And strangely, in the bizarre vividness of the moment, Ben realized it wasn't true; you don't see your life flash before your eyes. All he could sense were clouds of darkness, weeds brushing past him, and the tremendous pressure enclosing his arm.

A hot nova of panic exploded within Ben, and he tried to gain real balance, but the thing would *not* let him go. Then, faintly reorienting himself, Ben surged against the grip, screaming wildly. Ben had considered himself too proud to ever scream from sheer terror—until now.

It only laughed, and then they were at the wood line and the inky blackness enveloped them like a mountain of dirt.

Ben felt something hit his shoulder and clutched at it but lost it in the off-balance, remorseless movement. He heard other small thuds in the woods as the thing walked slowly through branches that reached out to him like skeletal shadows.

Something else hit Ben in the chest. He caught it this time and raised it to his face. And Ben knew...

As it passes, the birds are dying.

It's killing whatever it passes.

🪲 ♀ 𓂀 𓏤 𓅄

After listening to a recital of several tribes in North Africa—particularly Egypt—that had remarkably in-depth mythologies of just such things as walking skeletons, Cahill had risen to take a seat on the front part of the desk. It was the position he normally used for interrogations, but now with a friendlier atmosphere.

Cahill didn't want to intimidate this professor—actually, he didn't think he could, but there was a small risk. No, no, he just needed to take a familiar position for something this unfamiliar—a lame attempt to retain a grasp of what little he could remember as reality.

He'd offered the professor coffee, apologizing for the quality, and the old man had graciously complimented Cahill on the fact that it was better than what was offered in the faculty lounge at Harvard.

Somehow, Cahill didn't find that surprising.

Cahill had not intended to open the conversation with, "Ever heard of a walking skeleton?" but it had happened and there was no reason to lament it. In fact, it had proved a good conversation opener.

It seemed like the old man had seen just about everything, but that wasn't surprising. As he listened, Cahill thought that the professor was a lot like a priest, in a way.

He was devoted to both spiritual studies and various disciplines of literature and science. He allowed his theories to go where science led but had his own faith-based beliefs that science could neither prove nor disprove. And his demeanor was much like Monsignor DeMarco's— calm, unhurried, patient, never surprised or shocked, always ready with friendly advice or merely friendship.

Cahill had leaned on the monsignor after the death of his wife and, contrary to what Cahill had expected, the monsignor had never offered platitudes or sage advice on how to cope with the loss of a loved one. He hadn't read Scriptures or offered communion or even invited Cahill to pray with him.

No, the priest had simply invited Cahill to join him in his daily walks around the "pond"—more like a lake—that bordered St. Mark's, where they had discussed the City Council, sports, hobbies, art, or problems with the church van and where the monsignor might obtain a new one. But eventually, Cahill had begun talking about his wife, almost unconsciously, and the monsignor had ceased talking and listened for as long as Cahill cared to speak.

Then Cahill noticed, after a few months, that he could talk about his widowerhood with sadness, but comfortably remembering the good times, and the monsignor had casually offered his own thoughts on pain and loss and love and life everlasting.

It was only at the end of a long, hot summer of walks together that Cahill realized the monsignor had never asked the first question. He had simply offered companionship and patience.

Professor Adler cleared his throat. "So, as you see, sheriff, the concept of a walking skeleton is hardly unique."

Cahill stared: "Let's just say it's unique for my jurisdiction."

With an amused laugh the professor reclined. "I understand you are an intelligent man, sheriff, and please don't misunderstand me. But this is not so shocking. I receive stranger reports from neuropsychiatrists who regard themselves to be the intellectually prodigious."

Cahill found some amusement, even some relief, in that. If the professor was attempting to make Cahill more comfortable, he was succeeding.

"Guess I'm not alone, huh?"

"Oh, not at all, sheriff. Especially not in this part of the country, and at this time of year. Halloween is only a week away, so the air is filled with wraiths, demons, witches, spells, covens, clans, and omens. Debates are raging between the scientific and metaphysical departments at all the major universities. Vandalism and grave robbing are probably at an all-time high and—"

"Tell me about it," Cahill broke in. "I had to replant three of 'em last week." He pondered that, as he always did with grave robbing. "What do these guys want with a dead guy, anyway? He's dead."

"Oh," the professor gestured, "they want the usual relics of power—talismans, amulets, a lock of hair or a fingernail. Perhaps they are searching for a book of spells. There is a tradition among secret covens that the deceased will take their secrets with them. And secrets, as you know, are power."

Cahill stared a long time. "So what about this skeleton?"

The professor slowly pursed his lips and delicately capped his fingers before his tanned, remarkably smooth-skinned face. "Before we do that," he said, "was anyone injured in this particular incident involving this...skeleton?"

Cahill was fairly relieved. He had expected a lot of curious stares from the professor and questions like, "What in the world would make you crazy enough to consider a walking skeleton? Does this not sound a little paranoid? Are you mad? Do you really think a skeleton can just get up and walk off?"

"No," Cahill heard himself reply. "No one was hurt."

"Ah, good."

"Beggin' your pardon, professor, but you don't seem rattled at all by any of this." Cahill shook his head. "I can see why you would expect to find this kind of thing in North Africa or Transylvania or some other weird place. But I don't really think this kind of thing happens much on this side of the Atlantic."

The professor grunted softly. "Never think that the most educated man does not share the fears of the most primitive. Men are men. And an education does not insulate you from instinct.

"In fact, more often than not, the more cerebral one becomes in these matters, the more willing he is to consider the impossible. Superior knowledge is the father of humility, my friend. The greatest intellectual sin is in not realizing that we know virtually nothing."

Cahill pretty clearly understood the direction, but hoped he was wrong. "You're saying it's possible?"

"Anything is possible, Sheriff Cahill."

At that, Cahill stood and moved away, hands dangling. He felt the impulse to make sure his .357 was fully loaded and was glad he ignored it.

"How is that scientifically explainable?"

"I precisely said it is not 'scientifically explainable,'" the professor replied. "But there are many entities and powers in this universe that are not explainable. Nor do they qualify as 'science.'

"'Magic,' for instance, does not qualify as 'science.' And whether they call it white magic, black magic, sorcery, shamanism, it's the same thing. It is the practice of manipulating natural forces and even supernatural forces by a power hostile to that force. There is no free will... There is no place for the will of God." He added, as an aside: "Or so they believe."

Cahill brooded beside the window, absorbing the professor's words with a certain acceptance, considering the source, alone. But he'd never had any experience with genuine supernatural phenomenon.

As the professor continued, Cahill was aware that he had not moved in some time. "Yes, a true sorcerer does not believe anything is outside his control, sheriff, making them, for all practical purposes, equal to God and not subject to God—just as Satan chose to raise his throne above the Most High. And while one might admire such vaunted ambition, I believe God's job is already taken."

A kaleidoscope of questions ground out slowly in Cahill's mind, like Samson turning a millstone over wheat. Endless circles with endless questions—the dead end of hope.

The professor sensed it, obviously, for he slowly glanced at his watch and the window. It was pitch-black. "Why don't we ride out to where this happened? I would very much like to see it."

Cahill stared at the old man a moment and wondered if Thorn would let them back inside without a warrant. Then he remembered the one thing he *could* show the professor right now. He went to the desk, jerked open the drawer, and lifted the chip of silver. He extended his arm and the professor rose and took it.

The old man moved to the lamp and held it so that he might study it with more illumination.

"No," he whispered. "It can't be..."

"What?" Cahill said. "*What* can't be?"

The professor stared at the silver without comment. His lips moved silently—some kind of interpretation—and Cahill's curiosity escalated into something like fear. Despite his reputation for control, Cahill noticed a faint tremor in his voice: "What have you got, professor?"

"You say this was discovered at the site of the skeleton?"

"You bet."

"Incredible. No...impossible."

Cahill's eyes opened further. "Didn't you say anything is possible?"

Adler turned towards Cahill. He suddenly seemed to be a much younger man. "You must take me to this place."

"What's the hurry?"

"I suppose a man like yourself—an investigator—might call it a 'hunch,' sheriff."

Cahill glanced at his watch: 9:15—not too late for a friendly drive-by to make sure the Thorn family was safe. Or, at least, that was the excuse he'd use. He reached for his hat and coat, and the professor duplicated his actions.

"Shirley!" Cahill shouted.

"Yep, boss?" Shirley said, without breaking rhythm on her nail filing.

"Get the professor a room at the Holiday Inn in Andover. Put it on our tab."

"It's done."

"If you need me, I'll be on the radio till about midnight. If you need me after that, I'll be at home. You'll have to phone till I answer or send someone to wake me up."

"I know the drill."

Cahill glanced over at the professor as he pushed open the door and a shockingly cold wind enveloped them both. "The weather's dropped thirty degrees since Thorn dug up that thing!"

Professor Adler said nothing as he pulled up the collar of his cashmere overcoat and struggled with his gloves.

"Don't you think that's a bit unusual?" Cahill realized the wind was making him shout, which angered him because it was unseemly and might be misunderstood as panic.

The professor did not immediately reply. They slammed the car doors against the hateful cold. Adler gave the front seat a quick glance as if he'd never been inside a squad car before. Cahill's mind, however, wasn't on public relations.

"Well? Don't you think that's a little unusual? Thorn digs up this skeleton and now the temperature drops thirty degrees?"

Adler snapped his seatbelt and shook his head. "It is too early for a theory," he said, more curtly. "Let us look at the available evidence."

Cahill slammed the transmission into drive and in seconds cleared the parking lot under the haggard skull of a moon.

🪲 ♀ 𓅖 𓏤 𓅆

Thorn lifted his head at a steady, continuous sound that had continued for five minutes now—the sound of a dripping faucet. Yeah, that's what it sounded like, but somehow Thorn sensed that it wasn't a dripping faucet. He looked calmly at the Assassini.

"Is this how it begins?"

Artemis sighed. "Sometimes."

"How long does it keep this up?"

A shrug. "It varies—days...weeks. It studies you to see if you are disturbed or frightened." He sighed. "It's all psychological—an attempt to wear down your courage, your faith, your confidence and control. The attack is psychological."

"Psychological," Thorn said dully, then shook his head.

"It wants you to become frustrated," Artemis said, settling back. "It wants you to become angry, and then confused. Then you will pray, but Satan is not yet destroyed. He still retains power to wage war against the Almighty. And so you pray, but the sound will continue. And then you begin to doubt your faith, or God Himself. And when it is certain that your doubt is complete, it will compound its tactics."

"How do you stop it?"

"Only the Almighty can stop it."

Thorn thought about that one long and hard. "I don't know what I believe about that sort of thing, man. I don't have faith like my wife's. Or even yours."

The Assassini reached inside his cloak and adjusted a low-slung underarm holster, and Thorn glanced over to see what he was really carrying. He was a bit surprised when he identified a Glock 9-mm with a fifty-round extended clip and a silencer plus a magazine pouch with four extended clips. Together, the holster gave the Assassini two hundred fifty silenced rounds and Thorn bet the Glock had been modified for fully auto—a formidable weapon.

"Pretty fancy hardware for a priest," Thorn said. "But not a bad way to spend three grand, I guess." He paused. "Don't you guys swear a vow of poverty?"

"Yes."

Thorn waited a while. The priest would either amplify on that or not. The sound of the faucet continued.

Artemis shifted. "I have to admit...this one is exceedingly predictable. He must be in a gravely weakened condition."

"This *what* must be gravely weakened?"

Artemis turned his head for a full stare. "You didn't merely uncover a skeleton, my friend. You uncovered a sorcerer wasted from long years in a tomb. But through his dark powers, he was still capable of retaining some semblance of life. And with the correct rituals, he may grow strong again."

Thorn didn't blink.

"I find that a little hard to believe," he said finally.

"Do you find the sound of a water faucet hard to believe?" the Assassini asked. "Go and search every water faucet in your house, Mr. Thorn. The sound will stop. Then, when you leave, it will begin again. And as many times as you search, it will stop. And when you leave, it will begin again." He waved vaguely. "This is the stuff of children. This one is weak now. He has not yet begun."

Thorn grimaced.

Dripping faucets. Strange sounds. A walking skeleton. A vicious sorcerer. A holy assassin. A nervous Monsignor. A frightened sheriff. His own family in hiding.

Something was reacting within him in the same way it had reacted most of his life, only this time it was stronger—and deeper. He had always been compelled to protect people who could not protect themselves. He'd risked his life a thousand times for people he had never met, but whom he'd judged to be the victims of tyranny. He'd fought hard as a soldier, as a cop. But he'd never been forced to physically fight for his family.

In a manner, his intense watchfulness over his family had prevented any of them from ever being endangered. Rebecca called it paranoia; Thorn called it "duty." Also, he didn't believe that running from a threat insured safety.

He could have driven to DeMarco's rectory, loaded his family up, and disappeared into the Beyond with all of them in tow. He could have ordered the moving company to just move everything back out, the same way they moved it in, and he could have bought another place.

It was an argument that made sense, except for one thing: This creature—if it *was* a creature—had *presumably* threatened his family, which made it a permanent threat. And that wasn't something Thorn would tolerate.

If the skeleton hadn't so mysteriously disappeared underneath his nose, and if his Beretta, which he clearly remembered setting down, hadn't been moved, Thorn would walk away from this. But it had moved a weapon when it could have moved a shovel or a rock, which meant that it had an agenda. It knew exactly what it was doing.

Then, in rapid succession, there was a gravely wounded priest, the strange intrusion of a Monsignor, a shadowy Assassini, and a sheriff that held great respect, or fear, for some secret darkness contained within this place.

Thorn didn't care much for any of it. But the perceived threat to his family was the deciding factor for him.

He didn't even consider retreating. He would take this to its end now. He would find out what was causing this, and he would make certain it was finished in whatever way was necessary. Even if his own life was forfeit. At this point he couldn't care less about living or dying.

No, he wasn't about to spend the rest of his life watching over his shoulder to see if this thing was following him, or his kids.

At the moment all he had was the sound of a dripping water faucet. But to him it was the same, inside his house, as gunfire. His analysis was pure and simple: Something alien and hostile has entered my house and threatened my wife and children and, for that, I'll kill it.

Whatever it is...I'll kill it.

Artemis must have sensed his thoughts or read Thorn's grim expression. He spoke quietly.

"What are your plans, detective?"

"Just call me Thorn. Or Michael. Whatever." Thorn paused. "I'm retired."

Artemis nodded slowly. "Your plans?"

Thorn's cold gaze said it all. The Assassini released a laugh that was more like a grunt. "Some creatures are inhabited by forces we do not understand, Thorn. They do not die as a man dies. And this thing, if it is who or what the monsignor suspects, has had a million men come against it. Yet it has prevailed."

Thorn didn't blink. His voice was emotionless. "You've fought one of these before, right?"

Artemis nodded tightly.

"And?" Thorn pressed. He wasn't going to let this one go without an answer. It was an amazingly long time before Artemis relaxed with a deep sigh, and longer before he shifted uncomfortably and bowed his head. His voice was softer than before.

Thorn didn't move, didn't make a sound as the Assassini spoke. "We encountered one similar to this in North Africa...four years ago. Yes, we fought. The Church provided their most revered..."

"Exorcists," finished Thorn.

Artemis sighed. "And that was the trouble, Mr. Thorn. It was not 'possessed' as you, or even the priests, understood possession. It was not 'taken' by a demonic force. It was in collaboration with the forces of darkness—a loyal servant of the Underworld."

Thorn stared: "And?"

"And so the Exorcists were unable to resolve anything," Artemis shrugged. "So my men and I were responsible for stopping it in the end. But to stop it we had to utterly destroy the form it inhabited. I lost a dozen very brave men. The town lost over a hundred innocent people. The Church lost many priests.

"In the end, we managed to reduce it to dust. Then I took the dust and spread it in the water of the Nile, where it fed into a reservoir for Alexandria. And, from there, to the sea."

Thorn was pensive. "If it was demonic—not that I believe easily in that sort of thing—then you didn't destroy it; you just destroyed the body it inhabited."

"It was enough," the Assassini muttered. "The force that was within it may continue, but without a human form to execute its incantations, its power is limited."

Thorn thought about it a while. "So...if what you say is true, then this thing—whatever it is—can still go off and seize someone else, and start all over?"

"Not so easily," Artemis replied. "Few, if any, know how to maintain contact with one of these creatures. They are from another dimension and almost uncontrollable. It is a rare man who can be inhabited by their power and not lose his mind to their games and masks and ulterior plans.

"Another danger, you must remember, is that they can attack the thoughts of those surrounding you. They can inspire those susceptible to spiritual contact to attack us in the flesh. They can manipulate governments and law enforcement agencies because they can influence a man's thoughts." He focused hard on Thorn. "A sorcerer's power is formidable because it is not of this dimension. Only the power of faith, and prayer, can shield your mind from demonic assault."

"But you said that you *did* destroy one," Thorn muttered after a moment. "How?"

"With a long and uncertain battle. And I think that the one I destroyed was nothing compared to the one we face now."

Silence solidified between them, shrouding them.

"And what do we face now?" Thorn asked quietly.

Artemis focused on him.

"One that defied God Himself."

Chapter Ten

Thorn was beginning to understand, now, how the sound of a dripping faucet could drive someone nuts. It was fast becoming a distraction.

He thought about Japanese water torture—one drop at a time—and mused that, at first, someone probably didn't notice anything. But after a few days, getting hit by a single drop would be like getting stabbed with a knife. He wondered if some of the tortures men invented to use on each other actually arose from the minds of men or were inspired within them by other forces...perhaps forces like this.

Despite the presence of the Assassini and the absence of his family and other developments of an extraordinary day, Thorn was surprisingly relaxed. He figured it was because he'd surrendered any hopes of rest and sleep and given himself over, without reservation, to a night of horror and surprise. In essence, he had no expectations to disappoint.

Either that or this entire event had simply provoked his natural fighting instincts and he wasn't gone long enough from police work to have lost his combative edge. He wasn't frightened of this thing as much as angry. Silently, he wished this...sorcerer...whatever he was, would get this show on the road. And then it happened. Like that.

On the far side of the living room, a drawer opened.

By itself.

Be careful what you wish for...

Thorn lifted his gaze to the drawer, studying it. A quick study confirmed that the drawer hadn't opened by any common cause.

Not much of a move, Thorn thought.

"Do nothing," Artemis said quietly. "It's testing us."

"For what?"

"Our courage."

"Huh," Thorn grunted. "It's gonna have to do better than that."

"It will."

The Assassini reached within his cloak and unsnapped his holster. When his hand emerged, he held the Glock loaded with what Thorn clearly saw was a fifty-round extended clip.

Actually, upon closer observation, Thorn had never seen one quite like it and understood these shadow warriors of the Church probably had their own network of armorers and gunsmiths and weapons specialists and probably even owned a few factories and gun shops that facilitated acquisition of whatever they needed without paperwork or even notification to their chain of command.

More than likely, Thorn mused, they didn't even have a chain of command. They answered to one man and him only. And it wasn't hard to understand why no one else controlled them; they were too effective and dangerous for an inexperienced commander to dispatch. The choice to use a force like the Assassini wasn't a religious decision; it was a civil decision because Assassini crossed the lines between religion and law.

Granted, Rome did sanction the use of force when absolutely necessary. But the Papal See also had a mandate prohibiting violence except as a last, unavoidable option. Thorn suspected that most of the Assassini's job was to protect people from threats, sort of like bodyguards. Only rarely were they deployed for offensive purposes.

Crack...crack...crack crack crack crack crack...

No warning, but Thorn hadn't expected one.

All of the bureau's drawers began opening and closing at once, loudly snapping back into the cabinet only to rocket out again. Thorn heard Artemis's quiet words between the staccato racket. "Ignore it," the Assassini murmured. "It is simply testing our resolve."

"Really," Thorn said. "How we doing?"

"Most people would have run screaming from the house. No doubt, it is becoming frustrated."

Thorn sniffed, clicked the safety of the shotgun. "So this is what scares people, huh?" He spoke laconically to the air. "Knock yourself out."

The top drawer of the bureau flew across the room, straight at Thorn—a heavy projectile of wood and whatever it contained. There was no sagging or swerving as it flew straight and true, and Thorn almost snarled as he stuck out a hand and caught it. In the same split second he spun, smashing it into a half dozen black shards against the doorframe.

Without stopping his spin, Thorn came all the way around, racking a 12-guage round into the shotgun as he focused on the bureau again. He heard the same staccato sound in the kitchen and walked forward.

Artemis whispered tensely, "He is *close!* He cannot control such things unless he's almost close enough to touch them!"

Thorn barely heard the Assassini as he reached the kitchen and saw the drawers opening and slamming. Then, of all the things Rebecca could have sorted out first, an entire row of steak knives lifted from a drawer of their own accord and leveled their serrated blades at Thorn.

Thorn loosened his fingers, noticing the coolness of the air on the sweat in his palm. He blinked, focusing, trying to believe what he was seeing. He watched the slow motion armament turn slowly in his direction. Then, as one, they flew toward him. Thorn cursed in disbelief and slammed the door just as the knives struck, imbedding themselves halfway to the hilt in the oak panels of the paneling. Breathless, he turned sharply toward the Assassini.

"He has to be close to do this?"

"Yes!" Artemis snarled. "In order to move something he has to be able to see it! To almost touch it! His powers are limited!"

Thorn glanced at the doublewide glass doors that opened onto the back deck and glimpsed something moving fast toward the tree line. It was only a sliver of white movement, and Thorn wouldn't have seen it at all if it had remained still, but it had made a mistake.

He remembered the simplest of rules; never move. When you are hiding, never, ever move. If anything were going to give away position, it would be movement.

Thorn squinted, peering closer. It wasn't that he doubted that he had seen movement; he only doubted about what he might have seen. "Come on," he said, and started for the doors. He didn't have to look back to see if the Assassini was behind him. He threw open the doors and dismissed the steps, leaping over the rail and dropping five feet to the ground as Artemis landed lightly beside him.

Thorn crouched, staring hard into the darkness.

"I saw it," he whispered.

"Yes," the Assassini replied. "His range for what you would call telekinesis is only twenty to thirty feet."

Holding weapons close, they rose together and moved across the field toward the darkened wood line.

𓆣 𓋹 𓂀 𓊽 𓅃

Concealed by black, skeletal branches, it watched the two men from the edge of the wood line. Then, without a sound, it turned and moved deeper into the forest.

It was not ready for a direct confrontation. It had still not accustomed itself to this age and these people, and it was reacting even slower than the last time it had been awakened—so long ago.

Yes, he had been freed once before, and had almost succeeded in his plan before that cursed old man had discovered who and what he was. And then the battle had raged until that aged follower of the Hebrew God finally forced him back into those chains—those *hateful* chains— the only prison on this earth that could hold him. But he would not be imprisoned again, and he had already invoked powers that would reconstitute this rotten flesh unless he was utterly crushed down and his bones ground into dust and scattered in the wind.

Yes, he could be destroyed by enough force. This flesh could be destroyed, just as any flesh can be destroyed. But their fear had saved him.

If they had understood that weakness three hundred years ago when they freed him the first time, they could have destroyed him after they chained him once more to the wall. Either that or they could have buried him so deeply that he would have never been discovered again. But they had overestimated his powers.

No, he was not indestructible, as they had so wrongly believed. But he had used that fear to sustain what little blood remained in this putrid sarcophagus of flesh and bone, keeping himself alive through the centuries.

But he gave respect where respect was due, and acknowledged that the old Puritan had possessed strength and courage that was more than merely human. Indeed, the old man had possessed a grimly defiant courage like "The Lawgiver," who served the God of the slaves and later freed them, leading them into their "Promised Land."

A hateful image of the great, white-bearded Lawgiver and his loathsome brother rose in his mind, and he snarled, twisting his head to the side. But even as he attempted to shut down the memory, the image did not fade. He could even yet see the brother striking the desert with his staff, turning the dust into lice.

Miracles of Moses warred against his own dark sorcery, and he had matched the fearsome Lawgiver act for act—serpent, blood, and plague of frogs. But suddenly, when the older brother—Aaron was his name— struck the earth and turned the dust into a living thing, his powers had failed. He could not match this new thing, though his powers had never failed him before.

No...not until Moses.

Yes...great Moses, who fled as a criminal and returned a vagabond shepherd only to depart again with a nation under his crimson cloak.

Never had he imagined that someone could defy his sorcery and survive his wrath, all but despising his spells and conjurings and curses. Before Moses had come, he had effortlessly struck down every man that came against him, and he had lost count of the number.

He had tried, also, to wear Moses down with powerful spells and curses, but they had no affect upon the prophet. So he changed tactics and attacked Moses' family. But that, too, proved ineffective, and he realized the Lawgiver must have placed some kind of protective hedge around them. Then, at last, he attempted to inspire the people themselves to rebel against their Prophet, but his sorcery could conjure no more than simple grumbling.

In a blink, face-to-face with Moses, all his powers of sorcery had been rendered impotent. His one consolation had been that the pharaoh who defied the Lawgiver, Amenhotep II, had remained easy to control, which was fortunate for Amenhotep.

If, in that dark hour, Amenhotep had added to his distress in any way, he would have quite simply killed the "Son of Ra" as easily as he had raised him to the throne. But the young pharaoh had been obedient, and diligently performed all that was required—so unlike Ramses who, upon reaching the throne, quickly forgot his place so that he had to be destroyed before his twentieth year.

Thinking of the ambitious but expendable Ramses, he rattled his fingers—no loss. He could make a pharaoh as easily as he could conjure a snake from dead limbs—as easily as he sucked the energy of life from the forest creatures that died at his passage.

The hills were familiar to him because every physical faculty of man—sight, hearing, vision, strength, and memory—had been enhanced so he might better worship *his* god, Set—the Supreme God of Darkness, Lord of the Underworld. These humans called him Satan, Belial, Beelzebub, Diabolos...so many names...

He laughed at what the Egyptians had worshiped. Yes, let the people worship Ptah, Amon, Mut, Horus, Osiris, or Thoth. They worshiped a bull, cow, vulture, hawk, or crocodile. Or they made an idol to worship from a block of wood or stone that could not eat, see, walk, or even listen.

It would be amusing if it were not so pathetic.

There was no doubt in his mind; the God of the slaves—the God of Moses—was the most powerful God of all. As Moses proved when he blocked Ra from the sky for three days and the entire land was smothered in a darkness so thick that it could be felt. And yet the slaves had light by day and burned candles in their homes by night.

Yes, it was then that he knew the God of Moses was stronger than Set, but strength was of no avail where ignorance prevailed.

The Israelites were doomed precisely because they were ignorant of the strength available to them. Just as his own people, the Egyptians, were doomed because they did not know the deep powers of Set's sorcery, as he did.

"Fools..."

His deep laugh was a growl.

"You were doomed to be defeated by slaves..."

He did not need to turn to know he had not been followed into the forest. He would have heard the man's most cautious pursuit as easily as he would have heard a blind rhinoceros charging at him through the sun-baked reeds of the Nile.

Still, in an impulse of self-preservation, he turned to look.

Nothing...

With a despising glance at the house, and the man who even now crouched on the edge of the field—*yes, I will remember you*—he turned into the darkness that had so long ago become his home.

And was gone.

🪲 ♀ 𓂀 𓏏 𓅃

Her arm around Anthony's shoulder, Rebecca stared into the soul-warming fire that one of the black-cloaked men had so kindly kindled for her and the children.

She had made no special request, the man had simply entered the room, saw her and the kids bundled on the couch, then bent and in minutes had the room bathed in a comfortably warm amber glow. Then he had stood and turned, smiled gently at her, and said quietly, "Our commander is with your husband. I assure you he will be quite safe."

Rebecca bowed her head. "Thank you."

He departed as quietly as he had come. And, somehow, Rebecca sensed that moving without sound or announcement was so much a part of their lives that they did it even when there was no need.

This one could probably walk through a crowded room without anyone noticing him, and the rest were the same. They simply came and went, making no sound, attracting no attention. They didn't look her in the eye, never came close, never moved quickly or with any sense of direction or purpose. In all, they were about as interesting as a coatrack.

It seemed effortless, but Rebecca knew there was an art to it. She had seen Thorn do the same thing. He would pull his hat down over his eyes, put on his sunglasses and just...disappear. Suddenly, he would be so bland and boring and so "not there" that a person would never look at him twice. And then, if he chose, he could instantly be in command of the most chaotic situation with his stentorian voice and take-no-prisoners aspect.

The fire had begun to lull her to sleep when Monsignor DeMarco crept quietly into the room. He paused beside the entry, hands clasped behind his back. She could feel his eyes on her and raised her gaze with a faint smile.

"They're asleep," she whispered. "Thank you."

The monsignor smiled in return. "They will be even more comfortable tomorrow, I assure you. And I'm sure we've obtained things to distract them so they will not have time to be frightened."

"Can you..." Rebecca paused, not certain what to ask, "...tell me what is happening?"

The monsignor bowed his head as he took a step forward, moving to the fireplace. He lifted a hand and leaned against the mantle. "In truth, I do not know, Mrs. Thorn."

"Rebecca, please."

DeMarco smiled and nodded curtly. "In any case, I do not know for certain, Rebecca. This would not be so disturbing to us if we knew why our assistant priest attempted to take his own life."

Rebecca had not been aware, and the flare in her eyes revealed it.

"Yes, it is a shock," DeMarco said quietly. "But you have a right to know that there is possibly a threat to you, your husband, and your children." He raised his gaze to the ceiling. "I would do you no favor by withholding the truth from you. And the truth is that you would have been in grave danger if you had remained in that house another hour."

"Yes, I grasped that much," Rebecca replied. "You forget that my husband was a police officer, monsignor. I'm used to sensing danger." She paused. "And fear."

Monsignor DeMarco seemed to find that interesting. "Your husband, though I have just met him, does not seem to be the type of man who is easily frightened."

"Not for himself, but he knows fear." She was silent a moment. "When Anthony fell and a stake pierced his lung, Michael was afraid we'd loose him. We got him to the hospital fast, and the doctors said he'd live, but Michael still didn't leave his side for five days—not until he was certain Anthony was all right. Not until he knew Anthony wasn't afraid anymore. So," she released a deep breath at the memory, "if my husband feels the children are in danger...better move out of his way. He won't tell you twice. And he won't ask at all—not when the kids are concerned."

DeMarco was nodding, "I have brave and capable men of similar disposition sworn to protect you and your children with their lives."

Rebecca looked at the doorway where the black-coated man had vanished. "The Assassini?"

The monsignor stared upon her a long time. Nodded once.

"I suspected," Rebecca said, as she relaxed to the warmth of the fire and the soothing spiritual presence of the monsignor who seemed so... so *unofficial* in this quiet moment. Indeed, it was like being in the presence of her father. And, from nowhere, as she relaxed, she felt a single tear roll softly from her eye. She made no sound or movement to reveal fear or pain, but the monsignor understood. He spoke in a voice strong and full of conviction.

"Your husband does not face this alone. Even now, the strongest, the most courageous, and the wisest of all the Assassini stands beside him. And before sunrise there will be a dozen more—all men of fearless resolve and armed with skill. An ancient evil has awakened."

The monsignor scowled into the flames. "The Church has fought this demon before. But this is the last contest. Because this time we will utterly destroy it from the earth. Not a drop of blood will remain. We will destroy it so that not even a memory remains."

Rebecca wiped her left eye with the sleeve of her shirt. Then, gently, she caressed Anthony's tousled hair with her tear-touched hand. Her voice was ragged: "Are you certain you can stop it?"

Gravely, the monsignor nodded. "We will stop it. Long might be the battle, and costly. We know that not all of us will survive. But it will be defeated, in the end—just as it has been defeated before."

"How do you know you can defeat it?"

"Because the Lord God, Judge of all the Earth, will not forever suffer it to blaspheme the Holy Spirit." DeMarco's aspect darkened. "Yes...there is a place where judgment shall descend—an hour of deliverance—when its great power will not be enough to overcome the wrath of God."

Rebecca grimaced. "What *is it?*"

"An abomination," the monsignor replied with unexpected, quick anger. "It is a monstrous relic of a monstrous age—a creature of such diabolical power that it held even Moses in contempt and duplicated the miracles of the Almighty. It was once a man, it's true, but it became much more through secrets lost to a world long dead. We do not know how it can invoke the forces it invokes. We do not know how it can accomplish its dark phenomenon. There is much we do not know. But I know this; it can be defeated.

"Though the sword may devour one side as well as the other, and we may lose many of our brave brethren in this struggle, we will ultimately defeat it."

Rebecca blinked. "It sounds...like some kind of demon."

"He was once an Egyptian sorcerer," DeMarco frowned. "But the actual word for what this...this thing *is*, is so terrible that the exact definition has been erased from all the ancient manuscripts of both Egypt and Israel." He paused. "Apparently, the Egyptians feared him as much, or even more, than the Israelites."

Silence.

"Why did they fear him?" asked Rebecca. "Wasn't he Egyptian?"

Monsignor DeMarco shrugged. "To be truthful, we do not know where he came from, or even his name, for certain. We have a suspicion... an old legend of the Church, but there is no way to be certain." The monsignor stared into the flames and then broke away, shaking his head.

"Ah, forgive me, I rant. I will have the Mother Superior come and tend to your needs. And I will contact my people to insure everything at your house remains well. By morning your family should be reunited."

"Thank you," Rebecca said with a few slow blinks, feeling the fatigue envelop her as she relaxed. She wasn't far from what she knew would be a fitful sleep, but any sleep would be better than none.

Michael wasn't the most spiritual of men and, although she had encouraged him to join the Church without harassing or pestering, he had simply refused. She wondered for one second if confronting something genuinely evil would open his heart to something greater, but the thought was quickly overshadowed by a desperate hope...

A hope he would not die for them in the confrontation.

Motionless, Thorn crouched on the edge of the wood line, Artemis beside him.

Shoulder to shoulder they stared into the dark midnight silence and gloom, but nothing was visible. Not even the looming, colossal trunks of the towering oaks were distinct in the night.

Thorn wasn't in any particular hurry to move. He'd rather crouch here, watching, than venture onto unknown ground in the dark against an enemy he didn't even understand yet. He was fairly certain that the Assassini understood the nature of this thing, but Artemis was not the most verbose of companions. He never removed his eyes from the tree line as he whispered.

"What *is* this thing?"

Artemis was silent.

"No more games," Thorn said, louder. "What is it exactly? Can this shotgun drop it?"

Artemis's whisper was almost nonexistent. "I am not an expert in this type of thing, but I believe it may be a sorcerer who has survived ages by the use of his black arts. He should have died centuries ago, but he knows old secrets—secrets lost to the world for thousands of years. His kind no longer exist." A pause. "There is only him and us now."

The Assassini glanced at Thorn's shotgun and shook his head. "As to whether our weapons will stop it, I can't say. If it's exhausted, it's more vulnerable to weaponry. But we have to exhaust its magic first. Sorcery is a real power, Thorn, and we don't know its limitations. And there is such a thing as 'healing sorcery.' It can enhance its own healing process, protecting itself. But, then, there will be a limit."

"A sorcerer," Thorn muttered, and squinted into the darkness. He glanced at Artemis. "How many rounds you carrying?"

"All that I can."

"Uh huh," Thorn replied. "Enough to put this thing down?"

A shrug.

Thorn grimaced. "I'd rather wait, but I think that's what it's going to do, too. We're gonna have to go after it and take our chances."

He stood.

Artemis grabbed his shoulder. "We have no light!" He pointed at the trees with the Glock. "That is *his* world! Anything can happen in there! He can manipulate matter! You've seen it with your own eyes!"

"You have a better plan?" Thorn hissed.

The Assassini glanced around; there was nothing but twigs and dead leaves. "We have little advantage. But I say we wait for morning. Maybe his powers are not so strong in the light. Then we can—"

Both spun as headlights cleared the gate.

Down the hill and almost a quarter mile long, the long black asphalt drive ended in a paved circle about one hundred feet in diameter directly in front of the house. It took Thorn a second but he recognized the make of the car by its headlights. Then he caught a glimpse of a reflective silver star on the driver's door.

"It's Cahill," he muttered and glanced at the woods. "We'd better get back inside. If we're not there, Cahill's gonna start looking around. And I don't want this thing to get out of control any more than it already is."

Artemis had no objections and matched Thorn step by step as they cautiously loped back to the rear entrance. They were inside, and Thorn violently tore four knives from the kitchen door, tossing them onto the counter as Cahill's impatient knock resounded through the house.

A quick glance confirmed that Artemis was already seated in a far corner—just an old friend dropping in for a visit. Thorn leaned the shotgun against the wall and walked to the front door as Cahill escalated his knock to a respectable pounding.

"Evening, Cahill," Thorn said, noticing the tall statesman-like figure beside the sheriff. The man bowed with old world dignity, hat in hand.

Thorn nodded. "My pleasure."

Thorn simply turned and walked into the house; Cahill didn't need an invitation. He heard them enter and then Cahill shut the door, taking care to shoot the deadbolt and secure the chain.

Together they walked into the living room, which bordered the kitchen. When Thorn turned, the sheriff was immobile and staring solidly at Artemis, who nodded demurely.

"Huh," Cahill grunted, "this keeps getting better and better. What next? The pope?"

Thorn was expressionless. "What do you want, Cahill?"

Cahill was gazing at the shattered drawer. "What happened to your drawer?"

"Got stuck."

"Uh huh." Cahill motioned to the older man. "I was just showing Professor Adler here the county—sort of a public relations thing. And I happened to mention to him what you found in your cellar. He's into archeology, legends, and all that stuff. Said he'd love to take a look at the grave, if you'd let him."

Thorn glanced at Adler; the old man was the very image of scholarly patience and courtesy. He doubted that Cahill, or the rest of them for that matter, could even begin to comprehend what insight the professor could offer. Thorn decided the old man might be useful.

"It's up to you," Cahill said easily. "Just thought you might feel better if you knew how old that thing was."

"That 'thing' is gone."

"Yeah. Walked off." Cahill gestured to the professor: "I told him."

The professor didn't laugh. Suddenly, Thorn wished that he had. Not looking at Cahill, and not caring what he thought, Thorn picked up the shotgun as Artemis stood with, "I will stay here."

Thorn looked at Cahill. "Ready?"

"What do you need the shotgun for?"

"Rats," Thorn muttered and looked at the professor. "Are you ready, professor?"

"At your service."

"Let's go."

Thorn pushed open the door to the kitchen and was well aware that Cahill didn't fail to notice the indentations of the knives, even though Thorn had tossed the knives themselves onto the counter.

"Been practicing?" he asked.

A knife print is a knife print, Thorn mused. No need to try and dismiss it as anything else. Cahill wouldn't be fooled.

"They've been there," he replied as he moved across the floor to the basement door. "You just didn't notice 'em before. Neither did I. Must have been from what happened with that last family."

Thorn opened the door to the basement and stared into the long darkness. He was inspired to rack a round into the chamber but—with great discipline—reminded himself that there was a round already chambered, and that this was not the time for more drama. Thorn pointed to the table; six flashlights stood upended. He made a conscious attempt to sound casual and unconcerned as he said, "Might want to grab one. The light is pretty weak."

In a moment they were descending the stairs, and Thorn was aware of how, with each step, the air grew colder and the darkness thicker until Thorn could literally touch it.

His sweating hand tightened on the shotgun.

It had happened before.

Long, long ago...it had happened before.

No, this was not the first time he had been temporarily frustrated. Two hundred years ago, that Amish grandfather and the fearless Puritan adventurer had stoically stood against him armed only with their primitive faith, swords, torches, and guns.

If he had anticipated the true depth of their courage and ability to pull the confused townspeople together at the last moment, he would have killed the two of them first.

His first mistake. His last.

Being buried for three thousand years had dulled his instincts for battle, so he had been slow to recognize the threat they posed. Yes, he had made the classic mistake; he had moved before he understood his enemy—a mistake he would not make again. This time he would discover the strongest among them and eliminate him first. Only then would he subdue the chattel.

The blood he had taken from the farmer and the forest had given him enough strength to invoke minor spells—spells that would have been laughable against the might of Moses. But he was strong enough now to at least explore his enemy.

Some, he knew already, would have to be killed, though instinct told him these two who pursued him into the forest might be difficult prey.

He reminded himself that any man—*any man* can be broken. Even Artemis, or the one called Thorn, could be broken. But he did not want a protracted war. He wanted to initiate his plan without the tedious ordeal of a long and painful conflict.

Understand your enemy...

Artemis was easy to understand; he was a warrior-priest of the Hebrew God. The other—Thorn—was something of a mystery. He did not seem significant, but neither did the Puritan adventurer two hundred years ago. It was only when the Puritan's sword, coated with silver, finally wounded him that he realized the threat.

Always, it was silver, nor did he know why his power had no affect against that cursed metal.

It was not logical, for in the fullness of his strength he could transform a piece of wood into a dragon. He could transform water into blood. He could reverse the flow of the Nile and manifest images of armies or beasts or demons. But he could not break the power of silver.

Strangely, he remembered the tabernacle of Moses.

The shittim pillars, overlaid with gold, had silver sockets for the rods that held the golden taches that held the veil that concealed the Holy of Holies and the ark of the covenant.

Indeed, every pillar in the tent and tabernacle stood in supports forged from silver. Not a single plank or support beam was buried in the sand, but in solidly crafted foundations of silver, even if silver did lack the majesty of gold.

But only silver had been used for the supports and taches, which hooked the veil to the Hebrew heaven, the veil symbolizing the Messiah. And to complete the message, the veil descended to the earth, revealing the Messiah was the bridge between heaven and earth.

Know thy enemy? Yes, he knew his enemy. He probably understood the Hebrew God better than the Hebrews themselves, and he acknowledged that YHWH was ultimately undefeatable.

But His *people* were vulnerable because they did not walk in the fullness of His power, nor command the full knowledge that could be theirs should they seek it as a drowning man seeks breath.

His greatest advantage was their ignorance of what was possible for them to achieve, which was why he avoided direct confrontations as much as possible. Let them think of him as a ghost, a goblin, a gremlin, or some ridiculous creature from a ridiculous cosmology. For if he confirmed his own existence, then he inadvertently confirmed the existence of their God. So...yes, it was far better to be thought a product of superstition and wishful thinking.

He laughed.

Yes, let it be anything but what he really was.

He tried not to ponder that the Hebrew God could place limitations on his powers, but he remembered how he had been incapable of matching Moses and Aaron when Aaron struck the ground with his staff and the dust became gnats. Yes, he had attempted to duplicate the miracle, but the Hebrew God had shut down his power.

Yahweh was, indeed, an enemy to be respected and feared. And it is quite possible to respect what you hate.

For reasons beyond his understanding, certain items, relics, and people were always beyond his power. They were "hedged in" by the Old One, somehow, and as far beyond his reach as the stars, leaving him with nothing but his human strength and skill. And against that steel-armed Puritan, a master swordsman in the fighting arts of their time, his physical strength had proved insufficient, in the end.

Given time, he might have risen to the challenge, but three thousand years in a tomb had its effect. Not only had he foolishly rushed forward, ecstatic to be free, but too late he came to understand he had risen in a strange and alien land.

Quickly enough, however, he learned their language, mostly by walking among them, cloaked from their sight—child's play. But then he needed sustenance, so he began feeding on them, taking the blood to make himself whole once more.

He had not anticipated the riot he would inspire, but battle was instantly launched.

The old grandfather had led the townspeople just as Moses had led the slaves—sternly, gravely, and without fear. Then the Puritan had joined forces with the old man and the two of them combined proved too much for him in his weakened condition.

But now he could begin again.

Only this time he would not make the same mistakes. He would test them first and learn their capabilities, the depth of their faith. He would understand their weapons. He would study their reactions. He would try them and see who was wise and who had courage. And if anyone suspected who he truly was, they would die.

He stood, bent with weakness, at the edge of the forest. The clothes of the farmer—he had assumed the man was a farmer—barely fit his form, but it was sufficient for now.

He glanced once more at the farmhouse that he did not remember from three hundred years ago. They must have built this modern structure on top of the native mound where they had originally buried him, but he could remember where his countrymen had buried the rest of his followers...

The entrance of the cave was different than before. It was smaller, and all but hidden behind the huge trunk of an unknown tree that grew out of the side of the mountain. Still, he could see a small sliver of utter blackness in the night, and knew that behind this wall lay a tunnel that would take him back to his treasures, his weapons, and his people...

His power was returning measure by measure. Even now he felt his form expanding, fleshing out his skeletal form. His hair had already descended onto his shoulders, and when he lifted his hands before his face, his arms and fingers were filling with layers of moist muscle.

The trail of death he had left in the forest indicated where he drew the sustenance to reconstitute this flesh. For when he extended his hand, the life held by bird or creeping animal was his for the taking. He could do this with all things, and had through the centuries. Only man was immune to his touch, and had to be physically killed...like the farmer.

Yes, the Old One had made man different than all the beasts of the field. Man alone was conscious that he was more than flesh, that he lived, and that death awaited him. Only man was aware that he *was* aware of God.

He stood twenty feet from the tree and extended his hands. Then he closed his eyes and made contact with...it...

Before he moved the tree—or the mountain, itself, if he decided—he was struck by the strange wonder of the power that worked with him. No, he had never fully understood the measure of it, though he had walked in it for five thousand years.

Once though, millennium ago, he had a face. But then he had sensed that what he had seen was only a mask, and so he had looked deeper, and glimpsed another face.

And so it had been for centuries. He would finally glimpse what he sensed was its true essence, and time would pass. But as it passed, he would begin to sense that the face he had seen was not its truest self. And he would look deeper, only to begin the circle again... face upon face, mask upon mask, until after so many thousands of years he had realized that it would never allow him to know its true essence.

Yes...for some reason, it was determined to forever conceal its true face from him. He did not argue or contend. It would only give him the power to work his sorcery if he did as he was told. He was the servant, it was the master.

The Hebrews had been shocked when he duplicated the miracles of Moses. But he had indeed been given the power to match the Lawgiver act for act until their God simply stopped him. Then, defeated, he had chosen a tactical retreat over fighting a doomed battle.

But he had vowed this: If he could not defeat that cursed servant of the Hebrew God in open combat, he would *even yet* take away the nation Moses had come to save.

Though he could not match the stupendous miracles of Moses, he could claim smaller victories, as he had in the wilderness. Piece by piece, with fear and confusion, he had worn Israel down until not one adult male or female from that generation saw the Promised Land except Joshua and Caleb.

Besides Moses, only they had been undefeatable because their fear was conquered by their faith. When Moses should have been frightened, the Lawgiver leaned upon his faith and surrendered his fears—fears of the people, wealth, power, or his awesome responsibilities—whatever was massed against him—and trusted in his God to deliver him. Nor had his God ever failed.

The sorcerer continually reminded himself that fear worked so well in conjunction with confusion. Even their own Book told them they would only "understand in part" and would not fully understand in this dimension. But when he struck them with an action that their limited knowledge could not sufficiently explain, they soon forgot everything they thought they knew about good and evil in the world.

They became confused and afraid, and then he had them where he wanted them; then he could begin mixing fear or anger or bitterness into their minds, but as a little yeast works through the whole leaven of bread, a little fear works its way through the entire soul.

All that was required from him was a simple act of power—something they could not understand. Something that did not fit into their dogmas, doctrines, platitudes, rhetorical prayers, or the words of their prophets, as if prophecy were so easily understood.

As long as they became fearful simply because they did not understand the mysteries of this world, he would rule over them.

His mind returned to his work. He was growing stronger by the moment and was keenly aware of the spirit arising within him, as if from the depths of a place where space and darkness did not exist. But he knew it was only another mask, another unexplainable thing that he—unlike the followers of the Hebrew God—accepted as a mask.

He did not need perfect understanding; he didn't search for it. And that was his strength. He did not care about the source of his power, where it came from or if it was a living entity or simply a force set in place in the beginning that he had learned to harness.

Quickly, the tree began to list, and the dry cracking of roots tearing loose from the ground filled the night. Then the lean became more profound, and the tree fell to the side with a thunderous, slow motion crash, its fall cushioned by the umbrella of bony branches cresting the upper half of the trunk.

He did not waste time in satisfaction, nor was he surprised that he had already regained a significant measure of power. For, although he had been imprisoned for centuries, he had not allowed his powers to lie dormant.

He had exercised his ability to contact the minds of these mortals, causing the death of both families that had unknowingly nested over his grave. And with each death, either by suicide or murder, he had absorbed a portion of their energy—their hates, fears, loves, and desires.

It was enough to strengthen him, giving him the energy to sustain a remnant of life in his withering form.

What he had done had pushed his sorcery to its limits, for even he had not thought to last so long. And, conscious of his incredible achievement, he prepared himself for what he might find in this cave. Perhaps the others had not been so successful.

No matter. He had formed that circle, and if they had perished, he would recruit others from this place and time and form another circle.

Invisibly he would rule, as he had always ruled. For in Xetec, the civilization that inhabited the desert before Egypt arose from among the sea tribes of the North, the people had worshipped the Lion, captured in the original form of the Sphinx. It wasn't until a thousand years later, when foolish Ramses insisted on recarving the Lion with his own youthful face, that the monument had become "Egyptian."

Then, of course, the people had worshiped expendable Ramses. But *he* had been the power behind the throne—he had always been the power—and the transient pharaohs who had forgotten that their place was beneath him had not lived long enough to regret their arrogance.

It wasn't until the one called Alexander the Great had invaded with virtually no resistance from the fat and happy Egyptian army that his plans had gone awry, for he could control the pharaohs and people, but he could not control a brilliant and determined conqueror with an army of a million.

Yes, he remembered the scarlet glass of wine offered by handsome Alexander—a treaty. And he had willingly drank from it, all too glad that what little army remained from the foolish adventures of Ramses II against the war-mongering Hittites would not be liquefied by the Greeks.

He had known no more.

Alexander, in his Aristotelian wisdom, had perceived that he was the true power behind the throne and laid his trap wisely. Unconscious, he could not resist as silver chains inscribed with the name of the Hebrew God were fastened upon his wrists.

And then he had been truly helpless, for whatever force gave him power would not abide with him as long as he was imprisoned by the name of the Most High God of Abraham, Isaac, and Moses. Afterward, they had cast him aboard the vessel and sailed toward the edge of the world. But they never reached the edge of the world; they crashed upon this continent.

Almost mad with fever and thirst and starvation, the staggering, suicidal crew carried him inland and eventually enclosed him within the burial mound of those unknown savages, and thus...he was forgotten.

He knew no more for 2,500 years.

Remembering the wake of defeat that followed his first resurrection, he reminded himself to strike quickly this time—to strike before they could fully prepare.

He must strike them down before they guessed enough to summon the kind of men who defeated him before, though he sensed that the two men inside the house already had something of the Puritan in them and were fierce and fearless fighters. But flesh alone would not be enough; they would need a servant of the living God, the God of Moses—the God of Israel.

Ankle deep in water now, framed by the silver moonlight in the distant entrance of the cave, he looked to the side to behold five sarcophagi half-buried by muddy earth and ancient roots as large as his arms. He nodded a long, long moment. Now, he could begin again...

He concentrated and slowly extended his arms.

Seals of the sarcophagi cracked open.

He laughed.

"Awake, my children. We have a world to rule..."

Chapter Eleven

The descent into the "dungeon"—as Thorn had come to regard it—was mercifully without incident and in a few moments they were staring at a newly-cemented brick wall.

Cahill was surprised. "Don't waste much time, do you?"

Thorn shrugged, lifted the pickax. "Step back," he muttered, and with three blows knocked down a section large enough for them to stoop through and enter the tomb.

Slowly and cautiously, the professor crouched in the opening, shining his light. It only took him a moment to identify the location where the skeleton had lain.

"Yes," he murmured, examining the spikes buried so solidly in the wall. "A natural cavern, eaten from the limestone by acidic gases. Essex County does not lie far from a major fault line."

"So nobody dug this out?" Cahill grunted.

"They enlarged it, but it was already here."

The professor shone his light on the walls, and Thorn noticed, for the first time, the parallel lines of chisel blows. A moment passed; Thorn was more than willing to let someone who finally had some knowledge of this stuff take a close look. Cahill was certainly no good, and he had to admit that archeology wasn't exactly his field.

Professor Adler felt along the wall and stopped. He didn't look at Thorn as he asked, "Did you only discover one skeleton?"

Thorn blinked at the oddity of the question. "Yeah? Why?"

Adler stood and searched the chamber more diligently. He moved and crouched in several corners, brushing the dirt. He continued to feel along the walls and finally Thorn thought he recognized his motive. The old man was attempting to find other spikes or bones—something to indicate the skeleton had not been alone.

Before Thorn could say anything, the professor asked, "Did you happen to find anything else?"

"No," Thorn answered, uncomfortable. "Just the one skeleton and chains. Nothing else."

Professor Adler stood and moved out of the small opening, into the basement. "Have you examined the other walls?"

"All right," Thorn said, stepping into the old man's path. "Just what are we looking for?"

"If I am correct," Adler answered easily, "there will be others."

Cahill gaped. "You've got to be kiddin' me!"

"Five others, to be exact." The professor gazed at the other walls. "But, somehow, I don't believe we will find them here—maybe somewhere in the surrounding hills."

"Why does there have to be others?" Thorn asked. "These people didn't die by themselves?"

"As you have probably guessed," the old man stated, "he was not dead when he was buried. And there *will* be others." Cupping his chin, he stared at the surrounding walls. "You say the skeleton simply vanished while you were awaiting the deputy?"

Thorn didn't move. "Yeah..."

The professor nodded once, as if he'd expected the answer. Thorn looked at Cahill, who looked back, open-mouthed. Neither of them liked the matter-of-fact manner in which the professor was accepting the hypothesis of a skeleton walking out of the house in broad daylight.

Propping the butt of his shotgun on his hip, Thorn fixed the old man with a flat gaze. "Why was this dude buried like this? Surely you have some kind of idea. You've seen it all, haven't you?"

"It's impossible to determine without the manacles, Mr. Thorn. But I will hazard a guess, based on the piece of Hebrew transcription I read on the link of chain."

"Feel free."

"Let us retire upstairs." The old man led the way to the steps. "We will be more comfortable there."

"More comfortable for what?" grunted Cahill, appearing very uncomfortable.

Adler paused on the steps.

"For the unbelievable."

Rebecca awoke as a host of black-robed priests with grim countenances entered the room. They obviously did not expect to stumble over her because they stopped almost instantly and turned, as if to retreat without sound from her presence.

Throwing off a blanket, Rebecca stood. "Wait!"

As one, they stopped and gazed at her.

"Are you here because of what they found in my house?" Rebecca asked.

The one who appeared to be the oldest glanced at the others and murmured something in Latin. Soundlessly, they began to tread a silent path through a doublewide portal. The one who remained approached Rebecca with both hands extended. He graciously shook her hand, and she was curiously aware of how warm and comforting his grip was, despite the fact that the cold had descended so bitterly.

"Mrs. Thorn?" he smiled.

"Yes?"

"Good evening. I am Father Trevor."

At that, Monsignor DeMarco entered the room from the opposite side. Rebecca took a step backward as Father Trevor knelt and the monsignor courteously extended his hand.

"Your excellence," Father Trevor said as he kissed the ring.

"Arise, old friend," the monsignor said, laying a hand on the older priest's shoulder. "It is good to see you again. I only regret this tragic occasion would be cause of our gathering."

"It is of no matter, Monsignor. I have only had this chance encounter with Mrs. Thorn, but I already believe the cause is just, and your concern to be true. Have you any further news?"

"We won't know anything further until morning, I suspect." The monsignor glanced at the wide portal. "How many accompany you?"

"There are seven of us." Father Trevor bowed again to Rebecca, but she didn't know why until he spoke: "And now, if you will forgive me, madam, I must see to my friends. Our journey was long, and we are not as spry as we were forty years ago."

His laugh was effortless and disarming.

It was hard for Rebecca to believe that this was the terrible and formidable exorcist the monsignor had referred to earlier. He seemed simply an old man patiently waiting out his final days as a priest in a quiet Catholic rectory, harmless and all but insignificant.

"Please," DeMarco said, "food has been prepared, and your rooms await you. The Order is guarding the grounds."

Father Trevor, with effortless pleasantness, merely shook his head. "This kind may come out only by prayer and fasting, Excellence. We will not eat, nor sleep, but remain in prayer until morning, when we will measure our enemy."

"I wasn't thinking," the monsignor apologized. "I will show you the way to our brethren."

"Thank you." Father Trevor turned for the final time to Rebecca. He grasped her hand gently, bowing once more. "Be assured that you and your children are perfectly safe here, Mrs. Thorn. Nothing can harm you."

Rebecca stared into the kindest pale blue eyes she had ever encountered. "And my husband?"

Father Trevor shared her concern.

"Our bravest warrior stands beside him."

With a gentle wave the older priest turned and vanished into the rectory. Rebecca stood alone with the Monsignor, who regarded her with compassion.

"Don't assume there are no answers to questions that might arise in your mind," he said gently. "God knows the why and the how of things. We receive a portion of this, or that, and do the best we can with what meager understanding we are given."

Rebecca looked again at the empty doorway.

"He...he seems like...just an old priest."

The monsignor laughed gently.

"I'm sure Moses seemed like just a shepherd."

Thorn didn't bother to ponder how odd it was that three men, armed so heavily to kill some kind of unknown "thing," were listening so attentively to the advice of a man who had probably never picked up a gun in his life.

As if sensing their impatience, Professor Adler took a position in the middle of the room. Neither Cahill nor Thorn put down their shotguns, though Artemis kept his weapons concealed. It didn't matter; Thorn knew the Assassini could have a weapon in either hand, firing in any direction, in a tenth of a second.

"I will make this brief," the professor began. "I am, for the most part, an anthropologist. I deal with what remains of prehistoric societies, primarily the Mediterranean, circa 2,000 BC." He walked across the room, as if from habit. "Fortunately, the language I discern on the link of chain is a type of archaic Hebrew, and I was able to decipher it... somewhat."

"Somewhat?" Cahill repeated. "What good is 'somewhat'?"

"Please, Cahill," said Thorn.

The professor raised a hand. "I will not be able to give you a definitive answer tonight, but I will tell you one thing I am certain of." He cleared his throat. "By the custom of that period, the inscription on the chain would have been identical for each link. What was written on the manacles would have been the key to the...to the power that supposedly contained this creature."

"All right," Thorn said, taking a step forward. "What did this thing say?"

A pause: "The link, in effect, said, 'To chain the Serpent of...' but the rest was missing. There were four letters, Y-H-W-H. There is also what appears to be the name of 'Jannes.'"

"Unfortunately, the rest was not present. And if you did indeed allow Father Cavanaugh to take the chains, and my suspicions are correct, the rest has been suppressed by the Holy Office in Rome."

"They *would*," Cahill contributed.

"We don't need the chains to support what Rome has already confirmed by sending an entire army to this town." Thorn stepped toward Cahill. "By tomorrow morning this town is gonna be crawling with priests and exorcists and that...that 'thing' hasn't even *done* anything yet."

Cahill glanced at the kitchen door. "Really?"

With a frown at the sheriff, Thorn focused on Artemis. "Tell us something."

"It is not my place."

"Make it your place," Cahill growled.

Artemis sighed. "There are others more knowledgeable in this than I, and they will be here by morning, if they are not here already."

"What good are you if you don't help us figure this out?"

Like a great black bat exploding from the darkest corner of a cave, Artemis rose in a single smooth motion. Beneath the ankle-length leather was a harness that concealed a half dozen Glocks, clips, a fully automatic cut-down MP-5 submachine gun. A twenty-four-inch tanto—more like a katana—hung from the inside of the coat.

He nodded. "I'm sure I can be of service."

Cahill had involuntarily stepped back, but Thorn had expected no less and simply rubbed sweat from his forehead. Despite the ice-box atmosphere of the basement and the chilling wind that emanated through the walls, he was sweating heavily.

The professor, surprisingly, expressed no reaction and continued to speak. "What do we know? Well, first, principles: We know the corpse was a skeleton bound by silver chains that bore an ancient Hebrew inscription. And now the skeleton has mysteriously vanished. We know that Jannes was the name of the sorcerer who defied Moses in the seventh and eight chapters of the book of Exodus, so it is likely that the body was the skeletal remains of the same Jannes. However, how it came to arrive on this continent is a question completely open to conjecture. And I, myself, have no theory."

Thorn had a bad feeling. "What do you know about this Jannes?"

"If I recall correctly, Jannes was the only surviving member of a highly sophisticated race that inhabited North Africa three thousand years before the rise of Egypt. He was supposedly the architect of the Sphinx, which predates the Pyramids of Giza by three thousand years, despite what the Egyptian government claims.

"We believe that Jannes' government was built on a hierarchy of 'wise men,' as they were called, and ruled in much the same way as the later pharaohs of early Egypt. The salient difference in governments was that Jannes' prehistoric Egypt, if you wish to call it such, was ruled by a council of six."

Thorn scowled. "Why six?"

"On that, all we have is conjecture. Seven and three are the numbers associated with the Hebrew God. Seven is, according to Hebrew mythology, the perfect number. And six is the number most closely associated with demonic spirits, or spirits from another dimension. They are referred to in the Bible as principalities and powers, world rulers. And finally, Satan, himself."

"Doesn't make any sense," Cahill muttered.

"On the contrary," the professor turned, "it makes perfect sense. Six is only one number less than seven. By comparison, according to the theory of numerology and some mythologies, Satan is only one step less than God, as man is one step less than angels.

"Numerology does have its place in the mythology of many civilizations and is deserving of academic study. In this unusual case, it might reveal to us the intentions of a possible enemy."

Thorn interrupted. "I'll be honest with you, professor, I don't believe in any of it."

"One does not have to believe in someone else's mythologies," Adler replied, unfazed, "but it can be helpful to understand what another believed, especially if he is a potential enemy.

"Even the apostle Paul was familiar with many of the Roman gods at the Acropolis when he delivered his lecture on this shocking new Hebrew God called Jesus of Nazareth."

No one seemed eager to contribute to that. The professor took a moment, staring at Artemis and Thorn. His voice assumed a more restricted tone.

"The two of you are resolved to remain here, on the premises, should it return?"

Thorn nodded slowly. Artemis didn't express anything at all; he didn't have to.

"Yes," the professor murmured, and focused on the stoic Assassini. "You should tell your superiors that others stand beside them against this creature. They may need our assistance to overcome, in the end. For, if I am correct, this sorcerer will not come against us alone."

"How do you know that?" Cahill growled.

"Because everything we know about this prehistoric society, this government if it may be called, operated under a council of six. And if that society banished this sorcerer to this continent so long ago, then logic dictates they would have exiled all of the sorcerers. Banishing one of them would do no good. They would have to get rid of all of them, and at once, to eliminate them from their society."

Cahill: "Why is that?"

"Because if they only rid themselves of one, then the others would rescue him. And whoever managed to pull this off in the beginning was obviously no fool. He seems to have foreseen every contingency." The professor considered. "No. I am convinced. This one is not alone. There are others here, and he will attempt to awaken them, also."

Suddenly the professor became stern and impatient. "Regardless of what any of you might believe, the universe has mysteries we do not know and never will.

"Regardless of what you are accustomed to believing—that magic and sorcery is all smoke and mirrors, or illusions and tricks and springs and hidden doorways—sorcery is a real force. It is a power to be reckoned with. We do not know the limitations of genuine sorcery; they are beyond our knowledge, beyond science. If you are wise, you will proceed from this point with extreme caution."

Cahill's frown could have melted ice.

With a fainter voice, Professor Adler finished: "We do not know the limitations of its power, so we will have to discover them piece by piece. Which could prove...costly."

His demeanor fell, and Artemis stared a long moment. Then, slowly, he stepped forward. "By morning, we will not be alone."

The words caused Cahill to speak up. "I hope you guys...whoever you are...have some experience at this. I got a crew of young deputies that are doing good to find an address. Only half of them are qualified on the range—and barely."

"You kiddin,' Cahill?" Thorn exclaimed.

"Hey," Cahill cast a glare, "I'm just one man. It takes time to train these kids."

"What happened to all the old guys?"

Cahill shrugged. "Bought out with early retirement, Thorn—a budget thing. Saves the county forty percent."

"There are others with me," Artemis said without tone. "We are proficient, should we be needed."

"You will be," Thorn said.

The professor brought the moment to a close.

"Very well," he said, and picked up his coat. "I have much work to do." He cast a final glance at Thorn and Artemis. "I would suggest that neither of you sleep. But if you must, then one of you should remain awake at all times."

"Why would this thing have a grudge against me?" Thorn asked, genuinely curious. He couldn't imagine why it would come back here or even care about him.

"This creature's greatest weapon is anonymity," Professor Adler said stolidly. "It does not want mankind to believe it exists. It wants us to believe in ghosts, goblins, gremlins, werewolves, vampires, disembodied spirits, electromagnetic discharges, and negligible psychic energy left by a disembodied soul. The last thing it wants mankind to believe in is a demon, or worse, a prince or principality, inhabiting a living man with such power that he can transform human flesh, move objects, direct minds and nations, and rule the world through the souls of certain servants."

No one spoke.

"Satan's greatest trick, gentleman, is convincing the world that he does not exist. He doesn't mean to ruin six thousand years of careful strategy, and the only certain way to contain his secret is to silence each of us. With death."

The professor stared over them all.

"My friends, the killing has just begun."

In what proved to be an unexpectedly dull night, Thorn had wandered the house end to end.

Artemis, by contrast, had never moved from his place in the corner. Neither had he checked his weapons, made contact with his men, or even made a routine status check on the rectory.

Thorn surmised that if something were wrong with the kids or Rebecca, or if something had gone amiss with the Assassini, either he or Artemis would have been alerted. Already, there was an entire army arrayed against this thing. Cavanaugh had probably left some type of suicide note explaining enough to compel swift and committed action from his church.

Regardless of the fact that he had only lukewarm belief in God, Thorn could not help but recognize the fierce purpose that propelled some of these men surrounding him.

He was accustomed to seeing such purpose in Rebecca. And Malorie, at only eight years old, was surprisingly dedicated to God. But he had never been around so many intelligent, highly capable men who shared such total loyalty to something that they couldn't prove existed.

Stolid, he gazed out the window.

The distant tree line appeared much different in the orange glow of early morning. White sheens of ice rested on icy limbs, and there was a stillness to it all, as if the cloud of cold smothered all the forest life. Then Thorn noticed something else...something strange.

"Do you hear anything?" he said to Artemis, not removing his eyes from the forest.

Artemis, who never seemed fatigued or sleepy or even concerned, gazed at him a moment. "What?"

"I said; do you hear anything?"

Artemis listened for a moment, head cocked. "No. Why?"

"Neither do I." Thorn moved to the window. "Not a thing. No birds. No crickets. Nothing." He paused, then, "I noticed it last night but couldn't place it. I was too worried about the house."

He opened the door and was aware that Artemis stood and drew the Glock from beneath his coat.

No questions.

Thorn stepped onto the porch, leading with the shotgun. His gaze roamed across the tree line, and he reached two conclusions as cold as the wind that embraced him. One, no sound indicated that something unnatural was present. Two, it was hiding.

Artemis moved up beside him, and Thorn saw he'd been wrong. The Assassini had pulled two guns. He held a Glock in each hand, dark eyes searching the glistening white wood line. His voice was quiet: "I see nothing."

"It's here," Thorn said with a frown. "He's back."

They stood in silence, and Thorn knew Artemis was analyzing tactics, same as he was. There were a dozen options, but the first was to call the rectory and get an update on Rebecca and the kids. Then he'd be able to concentrate more fully on what he sensed was about to come. He didn't want to be worried about his family while he was fighting this thing.

"Check on the kids," he said to Artemis.

In a split second Artemis sheathed a Glock and held a cell phone. He pressed one button and one second later: "Condition?"

He listened for fifteen seconds, then, "Good; maintain protection of Mrs. Thorn and the children." Pause. "I see. Then twelve of us will have to do. Maintain six at the rectory. Send the rest of them with Father Trevor." Pause. "Yes, they can come now. We'll be waiting."

As he hung up, Thorn said loudly, "Oh, no..."

Artemis turned.

A scarlet-robed figure stood at the edge of the wood line, having almost magically appeared from behind a tree. He was approximately seven feet tall and heavyset, like a linebacker. His shoulders were wide, and his neck thick with an aquiline face crowned by a long mane of utterly white hair.

With a smile, he came forward, approaching with strong, measured strides—the image of imperious will and effortless strength. And his face somehow projected an impression of superior knowledge forged with utter confidence. Thorn even thought he glimpsed amusement in what, at a distance, appeared to be ice blue eyes. He didn't dwell on the passing thought that yesterday there had been no eyes at all.

Artemis stashed the cell phone quickly and grabbed the second Glock as Thorn turned his head with, "Oh, *man!* Look!"

Two gray-robed figures holding long knives of a strange, curving design stood within the trees. Thorn thought he could detect some kind of etchings in the blades.

As the Assassini glanced to the right, he seemed to somehow know what he could expect and looked to the left. "Uh huh...Two more on the far left. There's probably two more hiding somewhere."

"If the professor was right, there'll only be one hiding. There's only supposed to be six of them, right?"

"Yes."

Thorn lifted the shotgun, not aiming, but holding it close as they both stared at who Thorn knew was in command of this legion. If any of the priests, the monsignor, or the professor were correct, the one in the scarlet robe was what had become of the skeleton in the basement.

Laughing, it continued forward.

Thorn backed toward the door, Artemis beside him. With a quick glance, Thorn confirmed that the others were also walking forward.

"Now," Artemis muttered, "do you believe he lives?"

Thorn gazed into the sorcerer's ice blue eyes.

"If he lives...he can die."

Chapter Twelve

Thorn confirmed in a split second that the dead bolt was shut and spun toward Artemis, who was stepping out of the kitchen after making sure the windows were secure.

"How do they attack?" Thorn shouted.

The Assassini holstered the Glock, and his hand emerged with the fully auto MP-5. Heavy artillery. From their vantage through the doublewide back doors, they could see the sorcerer almost to the edge of the backyard.

"He's already across the field," Thorn whispered. He spun to the walls. "The others are probably just outside."

"I suspect each will be different!" the Assassini shouted.

"Can they walk through walls?"

"I don't know!"

"Can they disappear?"

"I don't know!"

"You *don't know?!*"

Artemis's eyes darted from door to door "I don't know what they can do! This guy's been *dead* for three thousand years! How would I know what he's capable of doing?"

A window crashed on the second floor, and Thorn had leveled the shotgun at the balcony before the sound of falling glass died. He and Artemis retreated into the middle of the living room, back to back.

Thorn was focused on the front door and first floor balcony. Artemis had the submachine gun trained on the balcony.

"How did you kill the other one?" Thorn shouted, wishing he'd pressed for more of that answer last night.

"I told you!"

"You just told me you killed it!"

"I shot it until it went down, and then I cut its head off and burned it!"

An image like a gray wind swept past the doors of the first floor balcony and Thorn spun aim to fire the shotgun from the hip. But even before he'd pulled the trigger, he knew he'd missed. He was too late, and it was moving too fast.

It was already out of view when he went to pull the trigger a second time, so Thorn swung to the left at the last split-second and caught some of the wall, too, hoping the buckshot might penetrate. The glass door was blown across the railing.

"What do they use?" Thorn shouted.

"What?"

"Weapons! How do they kill? Knives or what?"

He felt Artemis shift aim. He was focusing on the kitchen door. "They try and capture you so they can kill you by ritual. They absorb some kind of energy. I think it's what sustains their life. That's the theory."

Thorn was acutely focused on the double doors. He hadn't gotten a clear image, but he knew what he'd seen. It had been one of those that had approached from the right. Thorn tried not to consider the door, but he couldn't help it; the shotgun had obliterated it. Now, there wasn't even enough of it left to slow down an entry.

But, for some reason, Thorn wasn't as worried about the ones dressed in gray. He somehow sensed they weren't as lethal as the one wearing scarlet. He didn't wonder why. At this point he was trusting his instincts more than anything.

He wondered if maybe the chief sorcerer wanted to see how well his crew performed before he stepped in, himself. Maybe he wanted to see how much of them had survived their long interment.

Thorn frowned; when he was finished with them, he'd make certain that nothing survived. Overkill wasn't the word for what he had in mind.

"Here."

Thorn spun like lightning and shot, aware that Artemis had heard the voice and fired with him. The simultaneous blasts from the shotgun and MP-5 obliterated the wardrobe and mirror where, for one frantic, flashing moment, Thorn had glimpsed a reflection of a gray-robed image. He racked another round as—

"Here."

Image!

Understanding fast, Thorn didn't fire at the image but spun toward the opposite side of the room, searching and leveling and...

Nothing...

He saw nothing.

He gritted his teeth: "They can project their image!"

"Maybe only in a mirror!"

"Not anymore."

With the words, Thorn casually aimed at the last remaining mirror and pulled the trigger. The blast blew out the mirror and framing and part of the plaster wall, sending a white cloud of dust billowing across the ceiling. The thunder of the shotgun was followed by the sound of Thorn shoving three more shells in the chamber.

Back to back, they turned in a tight circle. Thorn's voice was, strangely, a whisper: "Do they ever attack you man to man?"

"Yes. The one I fought in Africa used a special knife he had forged in a specific ritual, which helped him absorb the life force of his enemy."

"How can these guys *absorb* someone?"

"It's just energy," Artemis whispered. "That's how it was explained to me. We're spirit, soul, and physical. And there's some part of us that is just electrical. It's a part of life that we leave behind when we leave this world."

"Ridiculous," Thorn gritted.

"Ridiculous or not, it's what they believe."

Thorn leveled his shotgun at the balcony as he came around. "No more mirrors for them. What are they waiting for?"

"I assume they're trying to drive us."

Thorn frowned. Then he remembered the Assassini's phone call. "Are the priests on their way over?"

"Yes!"

Thorn was already moving to the stairs. "I'm not gonna let those geezers get in the way of a firefight! A bullet doesn't have a name on it! We have to finish this!"

No argument.

Artemis was a stride behind him up the stairs. Thorn wasn't in the mood for subtlety; he marched straight to the first door—Anthony's door—and kicked it open, leveling the shotgun.

Nothing.

"What is this?" Thorn snarled. "Are these guys gonna attack or what?"

Artemis was watching their backs, the MP-5 trained steadily on the stairway. The entirety of the first floor and the kitchen door weren't visible from this vantage, so Thorn looked at the golden globe of the chandelier hung from the 15-foot ceiling.

No, he didn't have line of sight of the living room floor, but he had the globe, and the globe reflected everything, including a single gray shape standing in the doorway of the kitchen.

Thorn moved instantly, shoving Artemis out of the way and pointing the shotgun straight down at the floor of the balcony, estimating the location of the doorway without seeing it as he pulled the trigger.

The blast was tremendous, scattering boards and insulation in a white halo, and Thorn spun back to see if there was anything in the reflection of the globe as the sound of a wounded man erupted from the kitchen.

"That's it!" Thorn shouted.

He was down the stairway and vaulted over the railing when he was eight feet above the floor. He landed hard in the living room and in two strides he was through the door, only dimly aware that gunfire had burst free upstairs.

When Thorn cleared the door to the kitchen, he saw a crimson stained figure leaping through the back door. He leveled for another blast but sensed movement to his left and was turning when the gray blur of what he thinly recognized as a knife descended toward him.

He turned into the blow and deflected the blade with the butt of the shotgun, aware that it dug into the wood to send a sliver spinning into the air. This sorcerer or warlock or whatever was too close to escape a point-blank follow-up. But so was Thorn.

Years of experience and training screamed at Thorn for the one thing he needed: *Distance!*

He reacted by reflex. He had already taken a step to retreat, to gain room for a second shot, when he sensed something behind him and almost turned into it.

It was a dangerous choice but made by something within Thorn—something that was the center of him and dead right because it had to be. Everything else—fear or confusion or anything besides itself—was trod down by the momentum of it. The decision was made so that Thorn was moving before he was conscious of his action.

He had a sorcerer in front of him and sensed—*knew* one behind him. He couldn't afford to hesitate by searching both directions, so Thorn fired from the hip at the shape in the doorway, simultaneously throwing himself forward.

They collided heavily, and the figure fell back, his chest open and red. Thorn dove, rolling over the kitchen counter to come down on his feet—*distance!*

Got it!

Thorn viciously racked another round, scanning with eyes like wildfire and...saw nothing.

They were fast or experienced.

Or both.

Thorn was certain one had been behind him, but the sorcerer had retreated even before he cleared the counter, anticipating that Thorn would level the shotgun and fire.

At least they didn't like being shot, even if they did heal up fast. And if they didn't like getting hit, then enough rounds could stop them. Even if it didn't kill them, it'd put them down—he'd already seen that. And if they were down for a few minutes, Thorn could do something else to put them down for good.

Artemis had the right idea; Thorn would like to see if they could hurt someone without a head on their necks.

The sorcerer he'd hit with the shotgun was on the floor and motionless, and suddenly Thorn was aware of Artemis unloading a full clip upstairs. He moved forward through a cloud of gun smoke and acrid heat hovering in the air from blasts of the shotgun. He swung around the banister and took the stairs three at a time.

Two additional sorcerers bust into his path at the top of the landing, and Thorn had fired without thought from the hip—no time to rack another round as the second sorcerer leaped forward, colliding with Thorn hard.

From reflex alone, Thorn raised the shotgun to parry the descending blade.

Thorn experienced a lucid moment of clarity—where time seemed to slow or even stop and every wrinkle of cloth, every expression, every breath was known with an exactness rarely experienced at any other time.

The sorcerer was large and muscular and seemed stronger than any man Thorn had ever faced. His face and head was smoothly shaven without a scar or wrinkle. His eyes were a strange color—a reddish brown like the desert—and his cheekbones and nose and chin were sharp and predatory.

He was stronger than Thorn, but Thorn was faster by the faintest, flashing margin and jerked his head back as the blade whipped past. The blade missed his throat by a quarter inch.

Still—Thorn was very aware—superior physical might often determined the victor in hand to hand, despite what wannabe martial artists would tell you. And in the single blow that Thorn parried, he had felt a steel core of strength behind that arm and shoulder that told him he was solidly outmatched. He had to take this thing to the ground, equalize this guy's strength with some kind of chokehold or lock.

Without a glance, Thorn knew the strength of the banister and how much weight would take them to the floor, knew his distance to the floor without a glance, and felt the balance of his attacker. He moved with the thought.

Thorn lashed out with his left hand and grabbed the sorcerer by the right side of his gray cloak and then twisted back and to his right, hurling the sorcerer down the stairs. But Thorn didn't let go as he tumbled after him, and as they came around Thorn threw a vicious elbow that hit solid.

The sorcerer didn't seem to feel the blow, and Thorn didn't like what he had felt when he connected; it was as if he'd driven his elbow into a telephone pole.

The sorcerer came up from the floor, but Thorn lashed out with a low front kick, catching the figure solidly in the chest. It might not have hurt him, but it stalled his lunge. Then Thorn reflexively lifted the shotgun, and they both locked on the stock, wrestling for control. Surging volcanically, Thorn tried tearing it loose, but the sorcerer was shockingly strong.

No good!

Thorn made a decision and moved in the same heartbeat.

He released the shotgun and quick-drew the Colt .45. The semiautomatic was chambered but on safety so all it took was a flick of Thorn's thumb and the safety was down and off. He held the Colt in his right hand, hand at his waist.

By training alone, with a distance of three feet, Thorn simply reacted. His left forearm came up across his chest, his left hand open to shield his eyes against splattering blood and the blinding flash of the discharge. His right hand, holding the .45, was at the level of his right ribs and flush against his side as Thorn fired twice in two tenths of a second. The shots were so close together it seemed as if Thorn had only fired once.

Both rounds hit the sorcerer center mass, propelling him backward into the stairway that descended to the basement. He lost his balance and careened wildly into the darkness, tumbling.

But that wasn't enough for Thorn. He dropped down and followed the fall by sound alone as he leveled the Colt and fired the remaining five rounds, attempting to continue the kill. He saw the slide lock and in two seconds dropped the empty clip and fired seven more rounds and dropped that clip as well, slamming in another to drop the slide once again, chambering a fresh round. He didn't pay attention to smoke spiraling from the gun barrel, the superheated air. He blinked to clear his vision from the flash of gunfire.

Breathing heavily, covered in cold sweat and completely unaware if or where he might be wounded, Thorn listened. He heard nothing. He had no idea if any of the secondary rounds had hit the sorcerer, but there was only one way out of this basement.

Artemis bellowed upstairs.

Make a decision!

Artemis could be surrounded and wounded, but Thorn had one trapped in the basement and he didn't want to let him go; it was too difficult to trap one, but...

Thorn frowned as he lifted the shotgun and holstered the Colt.

No decision at all, really.

The gunfire from Artemis had stopped when Thorn was halfway up the steps, but he knew it had come from Malorie's room. In four seconds Thorn was in the doorway, hesitating just an instant to sweep the room for a target.

Artemis was rolling on the floor, wounded.

Slamming the door into the plaster, Thorn entered the room, sweeping left to right with the shotgun. He didn't fire a shot as he saw the open window.

Unsteadily, the Assassini stood. He said something in Italian and angrily flicked blood from his left hand. Then he bent and picked up the MP-5, closing the bolt with a sharp blow of his right hand. Although his back was to Thorn, he obviously knew Thorn was present. In a half dozen strides they were both at the open window.

"Gone," Artemis frowned. "They do not retreat simply because they are wounded. They have another reason."

Beginning to catch ragged breaths and vaguely check himself for injuries, Thorn turned and led them down the hall. "I got one in the kitchen and basement. I put two rounds in him."

"It won't be enough."

"I didn't think it would."

They hit the first floor together and Thorn was shoving more rounds in to the shotgun when something seemed suddenly out of place. And as he cleared the entrance to the kitchen, he knew what it was.

The warlock was gone.

Thorn moved toward the back door. "He couldn't have gotten far," he muttered, sliding shells in the magazine. When he turned toward the basement door, he saw a wide trail of blood leading up the stairs and out. He saw where the sorcerer had staggered out the back door, as well. There was a bloody handprint on the right side of the frame.

"Well," Thorn frowned, "he's hurt, at least."

"They are not like other men," Artemis was calming fast. "What would kill a normal man barely affects them."

"Yeah...I can see that."

"It takes ten times as much force to kill one of them, Michael."

The Assassini had not yet used Thorn's first name, and Thorn was unexpectedly affected. He looked long and hard at the black-cloaked figure, feeling an instant wave of concern like most cops would feel for a long-time partner.

Artemis caught a ragged breath; he seemed a little stunned. "These die harder than the others." He tightened a tourniquet at his left elbow. "They'll regroup fast."

"They didn't *need* to regroup," Thorn muttered angrily. "We didn't hurt 'em that bad." He concentrated. "Come on."

Raising weapons, they went through the back door and onto the wraparound porch. Back to back they swept and searched. Thorn was ready for anything. He was aware that his breath was slow and under control now, but he was still light-headed. He consciously held his breath, attempting to reduce his oxygen level and to avoid tunnel vision.

He was so hot with the instinct to kill that everything he was—training, reflex, conditioning, experience—was blending together without conscious thought into a machine-like mode that was, strangely, most like a dance. It was almost as if he were moving in slow motion because his mind was already four moves ahead of where they stood and what they were doing.

Physically, Thorn was moving from the back door, searching with his eyes. But his mind had already moved beyond that with the crunching sound of four cars approaching from the road. Then, in his mind, Thorn was meeting the occupants while he was physically reloading the shotgun. Like a chess game, he was calculating every combination of words and actions as he took a single moment to look at Artemis's hand.

"You all right?" he asked.

The Assassini was too much of a professional to deceive him about what could be a serious wound. Both their lives depended on knowing what the other was capable of doing. If Artemis was compromised, Thorn needed to know.

"Cut through the muscle, missed the radial artery." He grimaced as he tightened a second bandage over the wound itself. "No loss of strength. It's just pain."

"Gonna hurt a lot more when this adrenaline wears off."

The Assassini flicked blood from his fingers. "I'm fine."

Neither was the kind of man to pay attention to any wound less than crippling. Thorn would have ignored any concern or sympathy from Artemis, and he figured Artemis would be the same.

Thorn said nothing more as he walked down the porch toward the front door, where four cars were slowing. As they rounded the corner they were met by an amazing procession of black Town Cars. But it was a tall, thin man dressed in dazzling white that caught Thorn's attention.

Bald and seemingly ancient, the man gazed at Thorn with striking black eyes and smiled pleasantly. Nor did he seem shocked or overly concerned when his gaze focused for one moment on Artemis's bloodied hand. His calm composure and smile didn't waver.

Hands folding meekly, he bowed to Thorn. Then he simply looked at another of the black-robed figures and nodded. Without any spoken instruction, the man came forward with a large black box and Artemis moved back to sit in a chair.

When the second Assassini opened the box, Thorn saw it was a first class trauma kit similar to what Marine medics carried in the field or what you might find in a hospital trauma room. He'd seen a thousand of them, and with just a glance he confirmed it was supplied with everything from IVs to a triage pack.

Artemis shed the top part of his coat, exposing a truly awesome array of weapons. As he extended his left arm, the second Assassini lifted a tiny plastic syringe of what Thorn assumed was morphine. Artemis frowned and shook his head as the other began to wash the wound with sterile water.

Thorn turned back to the emerging contingent. He assumed he was supposed to say something, but he really didn't have anything to say. This whole thing was beyond him, and he was just going along for the ride at the moment. He had a dim desire that Cahill would show up so there'd be someone else as confused as he was.

Monsignor DeMarco climbed the front steps to mount the porch, staring at the front door. Even though it was still locked, the carnage of the living room was easy to see through the windows. He focused on Thorn.

Still mildly hyped from the battle, Thorn nodded and looked again at Artemis. Although it was a question that didn't need to be asked, Thorn heard himself: "You sure he missed the vein?"

Artemis nodded slowly, grimacing as his colleague inserted a small, curving needle with silk into the wound, drawing a stitch.

They both knew the sorcerer had been aiming for the radial artery, located on the outside of either forearm approximately one inch from the elbow. The artery was the primary target for a skilled knife fighter, and, if severed, insured unconsciousness from blood loss inside two minutes.

It was also one of the easiest body parts to hit, as a fighter was forced to extend his arm in order to strike his opponent. With a strange interruption, the random thought occurred to Thorn that very few knife fights ended in a blow to the heart or a major organ. Most were a matter of blood loss or blindness. He dismissed the intrusion; it was just a reflex for him to check and recheck moves and tactics.

This might take a while, thought Thorn, as he watched Artemis getting stitched. But the Assassini was in good hands.

Again, by reflex, Thorn scanned surrounding trees. He didn't think they would attack again just yet, not with all these people here. But he was in a combat mode; he chanced nothing, trusted nothing.

"Cowards," Thorn muttered.

DeMarco looked at him. "I'm sorry?"

Thorn sniffed, motioned with the shotgun. "Nothing. Come on inside. But we'll have to go through the kitchen door. The front's locked."

He led a caravan—he estimated a dozen priests and Assassini in all—through the back door of the kitchen. The priest dressed utterly in white paused at the kitchen counter, staring at the bloody floor. He studied the hole in the ceiling.

"Yes," he murmured, "they do die hard."

Two things told Thorn this man was special, even among exorcists. For one, the man was the only one dressed in white. Second, his crucifix was silver, not gold like those worn by the rest. Then the old man gave Thorn even more confirmation; he raised a hand and one of the black robed priests handed him a tall, silver scepter.

It was much like a staff, about six feet in length, but had a silver thread like a rope or a snake wrapped from the base to the crest where it flared into a strange, flat panorama of three images that seemed something like flames, or serpents wrapped in flames—Thorn couldn't be sure. He could have got a better idea if he'd studied it, but he didn't want to stare or give anyone the idea that he was impressed.

He gestured to the living room.

"Most of it happened in there," he began. Then he thought about it a little more. "Actually, it sort of happened all over. Upstairs—that's where Artemis was wounded." He motioned to the floor. "I put one of them down in here. But he didn't stay down."

"They usually don't," the old man replied. He gazed at Thorn with what seemed genuine benevolence and love. "You did well to keep your head when so many are after it."

Thorn frowned. "They're welcome for a rematch." He focused on the monsignor. "How are Rebecca and the kids?"

"Quite safe, I assure you." Thorn was encouraged by the lack of hesitation. "She is worried for your safety—as she should be, of course. The children are being entertained by the sisters and are well guarded by Artemis's brothers. And, although I know you do not have as much faith in prayer as you do in your shotgun, we have covered them in prayer."

Thorn grunted, "I'm beginning to believe more in prayer all the time." He focused hard on the tall, white-robed priest. Thorn was waiting for an explanation of sorts, and thought he was entitled. But he was also a veteran of combat and the adrenaline rush that follows—the kind of rush he was in the grip of now—and didn't trust himself to speak more than a few words.

The priest, gazing calmly at the living room, raised his eyes. "Forgive me, Mr. Thorn, I am Father Trevor."

"Not a Monsignor?"

Father Trevor laughed. "No...I am afraid that I'm far too old for a parish, though I can still help out, on occasion." He lifted a hand to the door to the living room. "May I?"

Thorn grunted: "That's what you're here for."

"Indeed."

Father Trevor walked heedlessly over the plaster that Thorn had blasted from the ceiling. The Mossberg had laid a wide, white blanket of dust and caulk across most of the floor. The priest studied the obliterated glass door at the wraparound porch and then turned to look at the door to the cellar.

Thorn didn't even move as the priest walked forward and stood in the open frame. Then he reached out and flicked on the wall switch. A very sparse light could be detected at the base of the steps, and the old priest began to descend, not asking permission. As the others moved forward, he lifted a hand; they stopped in place.

"You might want to take a flashlight," Thorn said dryly. "The light down there doesn't give you much."

Pausing on the fourth step, Father Trevor smiled back at Thorn: "I believe they will be more willing to communicate with me in the dark," he said.

He was gone. Thorn looked at DeMarco. "You're not going with him?"

"Nope," the monsignor said flatly.

Thorn spent a little time studying the situation. "I guess he does this a lot, huh?"

DeMarco's tone was slightly incredulous. "Mr. Thorn, do you actually think the Church runs into this 'a lot'?" He seemed to find the question grimly amusing. "I have served the Church for forty-seven years. I have known only one victim of stigmata, which was actually a psychosomatic manifestation of repressed sexual abuse. I have seen priests disappear into the labyrinth of their minds, convinced they were the Lord Himself. I have seen many things that seemed to be evil but were only the product of the mind of man. And the mind of man is not lacking in evil. And I have never participated in an exorcism of any kind."

Thorn glanced at the bloodied floor. "And nothing like this."

"No—I have never encountered anything like this. Nor have I even ever witnessed what I would consider to be a legitimate possession. Or a genuine sorcerer."

Thorn was staring at the basement door. "And he has?"

"I have heard stories of exorcisms that lasted for days, and weeks. And I have heard of exorcisms that lasted for only a few hours. And, then, I have heard of severe ordeals of exorcism that have lasted for months. But technically, this is not actually a possession. It is sorcery. And there is a distinct difference. But Father Trevor is quite accomplished in all manner of these things." He paused. "There is no one quite like him."

"Is that why he went down there alone?"

"No, Mr. Thorn. He went alone to show them, once again, that he is not afraid, because he knows they feed on our fear. And to let them attack as they have the courage to attack." He grunted softly. "Their tactics will have no affect against Father Trevor because his mind is invincible to their lies, and this drives them mad. They hate him so much, they know him by name."

Thorn stared into the depth of the stairwell; there was nothing but darkness. "They know him by *name?* They must really hate him."

"Satan himself can tell you about Father Trevor," DeMarco replied. "Which I actually consider a great accolade."

"An accolade?" Thorn asked with a stare. "Why?"

"When the most demonic power of hell hates you so much that he knows you by name and makes it a personal matter to destroy you, then you can be certain: God is pleased with your service."

Thorn turned as Artemis entered the kitchen. The Assassini was massaging his arm. His hand had been cleaned from blood. He was wearing his cloak again, but Thorn wouldn't fast forget the arsenal that lay concealed beneath the black ballistic coat. Artemis gave him a tight nod; Thorn returned it.

Then a ghostlike figure emerged silently from the darkness of the basement. It almost seemed to float up without sound on patient, balanced steps, and then Father Trevor once again stood among them, scepter in hand. The eldest priest did not seem bothered at all by his descent into the bowels of the grave. Upon raising his eyes from the steps, he focused on Thorn.

"Let us sit and speak," he said in a warm, comforting voice. "And would you be kind enough to give an old man a cup of tea?"

Thorn blinked. "Tea?"

"Of course," Father Trevor laughed. "We are in no present danger, so there is no reason why we cannot share some tea and remind each other how wonderful our Strength is."

Mechanically, Thorn filled a kettle with water and placed it on the stove. He found the cups and saucers and in a minute entered the living room to see Father Trevor seated in a large recliner. The other priests, including the monsignor, surrounded him as if he were Archbishop of Rome.

It wasn't until Thorn sat squarely on the coffee table that he realized he hadn't really thought about the sorcerer at all while he was making the tea. "My wife likes this herbal tea," he muttered, a little off balance by the priest's implacable demeanor. "It's all I could find."

Father Trevor laughed. "It will be fine."

With a phrase in Italian, he handed the scepter to one of the assisting priests and leaned slightly forward. "Are you certain you were not injured?"

Thorn stared a long moment. "Forgive me for saying this, Father. But you seem remarkably calm about the fact that this house is shot to pieces and we've just been attacked by madmen."

Trevor nodded. "Mr. Thorn, be assured, I have been a witness and a participant in situations far worse. And those who attacked you and Brother Artemis were not madmen—they were undead sorcerers inhabited by the most malicious powers of hell." He smiled. "To be precise."

Thorn didn't know what to say, but eventually settled for, "So... you're an expert in this kind of thing?"

A laugh: "Well, let's just say I have had some experience with these type of fugitives."

"Fugitives?"

"Yes, my son; fugitives, for that is what they are." The priest took his time with a sip of tea. Then, "You see, Mr. Thorn, they have been cast from their first estate, denied their royal inheritance, and are doomed to wander a desolate void for eternity. But exactly what form they have taken in this confrontation, and what the limits of their power may be, is yet unknown." He shook his head. "But that is of no matter; we will know their limitations soon enough."

Thorn was struck by both the priest's stoic acceptance of this surreal situation and his utter lack of fear. He was searching for a proper reply when he heard a car in the driveway.

When he looked out the window, he saw Cahill walking up, shotgun in hand, Professor Adler in tow. Cahill already knew something was up as he made his way cautiously down the wraparound porch. He racked the shotgun at the kitchen door.

Thorn walked into sight. "You missed all the fun."

Glancing left and right, Cahill entered. "What happened?"

"Our friend came back."

"Where's the wife and kids?"

"You wouldn't believe me if I told you."

Artemis was gazing stoically at Cahill, who studied the bloodstain on the floor and said to the Assassini, "Your work?"

Artemis shook his head.

"Still loaded?

A nod.

"Stay that way."

Thorn was indifferent now to Cahill's attitude. He knew it wasn't going to get any better. And after this morning, there was a fair guarantee that it was going to get worse. He just wanted some straight answers from the only man who seemed like he could give them. He gestured for Cahill and Adler to sit down with the others.

"I regret we were not here sooner," the old man began. "But you can be assured, they will return, and we will be waiting."

"Your best guess: *What* is 'they'?"

A patient nod. "Do you believe in God, Mr. Thorn?"

"I guess I believe about like most people; I have some faith." Thorn monitored those around him. "But not like you guys."

"And so this morning's events had so little effect on you?" The priest waited; Thorn simply stared. "Very well, then indulge an old man, because I have dealt with similar situations as this. Is Jesus your Lord?"

Thorn said, "If you're going to try and convince me that God will protect me from these things, you're wasting your time. My wife is the one with all the faith. I just get by."

"Don't we all," Father Trevor replied coolly. "Consider this, Mr. Thorn; you may be threatened by a very ancient, hostile force. And although I suspect that self-defense is an art you cultivate, fighting skills work best against flesh and blood and bone." He set down the tea. "Now, if it were merely flesh that had come against you, I'm sure you would prevail. On the other hand, if what you have come against is, indeed, demonic—then all the guns in the world will not save you without the power of faith and prayer and spiritual weapons of warfare. Only then will you be able to overcome this monster, insuring the lives of your wife and children. So, either way you look at the situation, our presence here can, at least, do no harm."

Thorn couldn't disagree with that.

A smile, and Father Trevor leaned closer.

"Make no mistake," he began, "this creature means to kill you because you know his identity and his secret. But you are not alone, and your wife and children are well guarded. And together, we might have a chance of destroying him. All we must do is finish the fight."

Thorn glanced at Artemis, another Assassini. "I see that you sometimes rely on more than prayer."

"Yes," the old priest agreed. "Artemis and his men are an arm of the Church that deals with civil authorities when all other methods have failed, and they are sometimes called upon to commit actions so complex and fearsome that no man has wisdom enough to decide whether their actions are right or wrong. We simply proceed with the light we have, and pray we are right."

"I have no problems with them," Thorn said.

Cahill pitched in: "I'd give a gun to a chipmunk if I thought it'd do any good."

"I know something of your life, Mr. Thorn," Trevor continued. "You are a man experienced with evil. But not all evil is from this earth. It is from...somewhere else. And not all that is from somewhere else is, in essence, the same."

"What do you mean?" Thorn asked.

The old priest brought the tips of his fingers together. "There are ranks among demonic forces, Mr. Thorn, much as there are ranks among armies comprised of men. The lowest demonic rank, and the one most easily dismissed, is simply referred to as a 'demon.' It is a fallen angel that did not forsake its original inheritance by taking physical form, and so it is free to wander this dimension for a time. There are also demons that did forsake their original dimension and have died only physically on the earth. But, granted, no demon can die spiritually, and so the essence of those particular demons is confined to hell until the day of judgment.

"Though evil, mere demons are not irresistibly powerful, and they can be recognized, confronted, and defeated by someone of forthright faith. The next level is demonic spirits, which the Bible refers to as 'principalities and powers.' They are far more difficult to recognize, confront, or exorcise. Some come out only by prayer and fasting, and an exorcism can last for days, weeks—even months.

"Usually, the priest chosen to lead the exorcism of a prince of demons has some experience in these matters. He will be familiar with traps that the principality will lay, and he will avoid falling into them. A novice, on the other hand, might become frightened or confused, and that is the beginning of defeat." He leaned closer.

"Anyone who confronts a prince of demons must know exactly what God declares. If you become confused for one second, the demon will sense it. He will know it. And he will use it against you. And once you are off balance, attempting to use your intelligence to decide what to do, the demon will use all your memories, all your regrets and weaknesses and fears against you.

"You cannot pay attention to what he says. There is nothing to talk about with a demon. Quote Scripture, pray, and fast. The demon will depart soon enough. He cannot abide the presence of Christ, and where two or more are gathered in His name, there He is, also."

Thorn thought vaguely that Father Trevor was using this opportunity to reinforce that point to surrounding priests and Assassini. He also thought it was a lecture they'd heard a thousand times. Vaguely, he was also aware that no one present, not even the Assassini, had moved or spoken since the old priest began.

"And then we come to the final level of true demonic power," Father Trevor said with a strange lowering of tone. "Scripture barely refers to them at all. But they are classified as 'world rulers.'"

Thorn waited for a little explanation, and when the priest didn't continue—and didn't seem like he was going to—Thorn asked, "And what does that mean? Exactly?"

Trevor's eyes, for a single moment, were windows to remembered pain. He spoke tiredly. "A demonic power ranking on the level of a 'world ruler' cannot be exorcised at all. They can resist any kind of faith, any measure of prayer. They rule entire regions of the earth, and will not be defeated or chained until the end of times. Only God can uproot them.

"They were quite probably cherub or seraphim before they rebelled against God, and even yet they retain a significant measure of their original power, just as Satan does. But that is only conjecture. All we know for certain is that they are so powerful and wise that at times they can deceive even the elect. Nor do they answer to commands."

At the words, spoken so quietly, several of the priests blessed themselves. Thorn looked back to see Artemis's hand fall from his chest; the
gesture didn't surprise him. As lethal as the Assassini was, he was humble before God.

Thorn had come to understand the Assassini's place, so he wasn't
concerned anymore about the lethal ordinance he carried.

Artemis was, in a way, where the buck stopped. If there could be
no peaceful resolution for the Church, the Assassini were a last chance
solution. For instance, if someone planned the assassination of a pope
or a revered church leader, Artemis would be called upon to take care
of it his way.

Thorn had no problem with that; there were a lot of situations that
didn't allow tidy resolutions. He'd "bent" the law himself on occasions
when there was no legal way to snatch someone he knew was guilty of a
heinous crime.

He had no regrets; he wasn't above stooping down to pick somebody
up. And experience had taught him that life often became too complicated to identify the straight and narrow. Sometimes, you needed someone like Artemis—somebody who just got the job done with as little
collateral damage as possible.

The Assassini was a noble man standing on a hard line; Thorn
admired him. Then he turned his mind, reluctantly, back to what the
old priest was saying.

"So which kind of demon do you think I'm up against, priest?"

"A world ruler," Father Trevor replied without hesitation. "And the
situation is even more complicated than that." He sighed. "I fear that
who—or *what*, rather—you discovered in your cellar was the remains
of an Egyptian sorcerer named Jannes, who purposely gave himself to
this unnamed demonic force thousands of years before Christ was even
born. And Jannes, in human form, has learned ancient secrets of sorcery

that the world has long forgotten, including the means of prolonging his life...indefinitely." He shook his head. "In truth, we do not know the limits of what he can do."

A pause. "Make no mistake, Mr. Thorn, Jannes' is prideful of his power, and you have challenged that. So he will seek to destroy both you and all you hold dear. This is not over, for him."

"Also, Jannes is wise in human terms. He did not ascend to rule over all of Egypt by overlooking small threats. He did not let the children of those he killed grow up to become enemies seeking to avenge their murdered fathers and mothers. He killed the children, as well. So, bear that in mind. He is careful, and right now you are someone who, in the future, could threaten his plans...whatever they may be."

"You said my family is safe," Thorn challenged. "How can you say they're safe when you can't control this thing?"

Father Trevor raised a dead steady hand to Artemis. "Artemis and his brothers are armed because when the Lord told His disciples that He was leaving, He also said if they did not have a sword, then they should sell their cloaks and buy one. We will use force to defend ourselves against evil and evil men when force is required."

Thorn measured the old man's resolve as the priest continued, "It is always a test of our faith, and wisdom, when we decide whether to use force. In the present moment we see in part and understand in part. And when our understanding fails—as it will—we trust our courage and resist those that would destroy us. And sometimes we must rely upon men with the skill and courage of Artemis. It is part of the mystery of God."

Father Trevor clenched a fist.

"But even when we do *not* understand, we must hold fast to faith! We must do what the Lord told us to do! And when some of us do not survive the fight, as they surely won't, we must remember that it is foolish and futile to despair over questions that will not be answered in this world. We must continue with faith and courage and wait to see the purpose of the Lord."

"*Purpose!*" Thorn erupted to his feet. "What kind of *purpose* could there be in some kind of prehistoric madman with the power of Satan running around killing people?"

"Perhaps the purpose is you, Mr. Thorn."

Thorn didn't bother to mask his anger. "What does this have to do with me?! I barely even believe in God!"

Father Trevor's eyes didn't waver.

"Perhaps you should consider something, Mr. Thorn."

"What's that?"

"In more than five thousand years, no one has managed to destroy this man...who is no mere man. And perhaps the time has come for his complete and final destruction, and you are God's means of achieving that. Perhaps...yes, perhaps, the Almighty has delivered him to us...and to you...for this reason."

Thorn looked at Artemis, then the monsignor, back at Father Trevor. "Understand me: I'll do this, but not for your reasons. I'm not in this because this guy's evil, or because you people have a grudge against him. I don't care who he is or what he is. He threatened my family, and I won't rest until they're safe."

Father Trevor again met the deadly gaze as Thorn glanced at the wood line. "When he comes back, you and your men are welcome to pray all you want...just remember one thing."

"Yes?"

"This guy's going down."

"You're going to kill him?"

Thorn nodded slowly "Yeah, I'm gonna kill him, and anybody with him. So pray all you want. Just stay out of my way."

The old priest looked to the side, nodding slowly.

"The Scripture is true."

"True?" Thorn grunted. "About what?"

The priest released a heavy sigh.

"There is, indeed, a time to kill."

Chapter Thirteen

I t was morning, and there was still time for Thorn to check on Rebecca and the kids at the safe house. He didn't ask for permission; he simply informed the priests what he intended to do and commandeered a Town Car. Artemis got in beside him; Thorn wasn't surprised. And, frankly, he didn't mind. The Assassini was a good man in a tight spot.

It took a half hour, and Thorn repeatedly noticed the gray, intertwining tree limbs as they bent before a gathering wind. If clouds came in; it'd be a shutdown snowstorm, for sure. So whatever they needed, they'd better get it before the roads became impassable.

The thought occurred to Thorn that the weather had begun declining so dramatically only hours after the skeleton disappeared. But even at the thought, he tried to shut it down.

As they drove along the blacktop road leading from Thorn's place, Artemis noticed a huge water tower that seemed to dominate the landscape. He spoke casually, "I have seen many lands where they were lucky to have any water at all." He squinted. "The road to it seems strangely reflective."

"It's fiberglass," said Thorn. "It looks like earth, but it's an artificial surface. Sort of an experimental thing. They didn't use a mix of concrete and sand." He shrugged. "The general theory is that fiberglass, since it's largely artificial, and can be compressed more, will stand up longer to abuse."

Artemis grunted. "An artificial surface...Interesting."

Thorn thought again of the warning from Father Trevor. He didn't actually need any more convincing that something supernatural had been unleashed from beneath his house; he just didn't want to give these holy men the satisfaction of astonishment. Also, he didn't want to rattle Artemis's confidence in him or lessen the ice-cold anger that gave his concentration its edge.

The safe house loomed to the right, and Thorn slowed, careful to make a casual arrival. The last thing he wanted to do was give Rebecca the impression that he was alarmed.

He exited the Town Car first, leaving the shotgun in the back seat. Artemis followed, but his weapons were graciously concealed by his long coat. Cahill, parked on the street, simply staying inside his patrol car. And Thorn was grateful for that—no need to make this a drama.

Rebecca, with Anthony and Malorie beside her, awaited Thorn on the porch. Rebecca [Malone] leaped and ran at Thorn, and he caught her off the ground to swing her in a circle. Then in the next second he was embracing Anthony, kissing his forehead.

He heard a strange sound, realized it was Artemis laughing, and glanced at the oddity. "Ah," the Assassini smiled—a unique sight, "what love was ever love that did not leap at first sight?"

Thorn was struck, despite the happiness of the reunion, to see that side of the Assassini. Then he looked at Rebecca, standing so patiently with arms crossed, smiling.

"Happy to see me?" Thorn laughed.

"Always."

She came down the steps, and they were together again and Thorn was patiently trying to usher them back into the house without *seeming* to usher them.

The kids had other ideas.

"Noooo, Dad," was repeated ad infinitum, and finally Thorn asked, "What's wrong with you guys? It's cold out here."

"We've been inside since we got here!" Anthony exclaimed with no lack of melodrama. "We've been playing games and stuff, but we're bored to *death!* I could die or something!"

Thorn gazed down. "Son, I don't think you're going to—"

"The nuns got us some brand-new gloves and a softball! Can we play catch? Can we? Come on, Dad!"

Rebecca laughed. "I think you'd better play catch." She kissed him gently, straightened the collar of his blue jean jacket. "Then you and I can talk a little, okay?"

A pause, and Thorn knew what that meant—honesty and some real answers that he wasn't even sure that he had. He nodded, "Okay. Just a little while." He looked back to make sure everyone was following the conversation. "Artemis!"

"I know," the Assassini muttered and turned to the east side of the house. He spoke Italian into a compact radio. "It's covered," he added, without taking his eyes off surrounding houses.

From nowhere, Cahill appeared at Thorn's side. His face was gray in the bracing cold, or maybe it was their mutual fear. Thorn couldn't be sure.

"Things are Code One here," he said to Thorn. "I'm gonna run past the office while the professor is getting briefed by the priest. If everything's okay, I'll be back in a couple hours. That work for you?"

Thorn searching Cahill's eyes.

"What's wrong?"

Cahill paused. Thorn rubbed the kids' heads. "Go get the gloves and ball. We have a bat?"

"Yeah!"

"Okay, get that too."

"Cool!"

When they were out of earshot, Thorn gazed curiously at Cahill. "What's wrong, man?"

Cahill studied the house, squinting against the wind. "I figure things are safe here. You got an army, and they don't play. But if that crowd you met this morning is as bad as that old man says it is, they ain't gonna stop just cause you got lucky. They might be picking easier prey to absorb their 'life force,' as that old man said they do. And I got a whole town full of innocent people."

Thorn hadn't considered that, and felt shame. He was, in essence, still a cop. He should have wondered what Jannes and his crew would be doing until nightfall when they would return in the full strength of darkness. It didn't take more than a second to reply.

"Go on and check on things. Use the cell if you need me. We'll back you up."

Cahill turned away as the kids came running outside with four brand-new softball gloves and a bat. Thorn glanced at the black, predatory silhouette of Artemis crouching on a mound beside the rectory, watching over the small field and surrounding houses. His dark, hawklike eyes barely seemed to move, but Thorn knew they saw everything. Then Thorn's face and demeanor expressed nothing but happiness and laughter as he caught the softball.

It was time to change hats.

Time now to be Daddy and forget the rest. And Thorn realized the old priest had been right.

Time enough later for killing.

𓀭 � 𓏏 𓅃 𓅂

Professor Adler was leaning an arm on the back of the couch as the priests moved about the small mansion sprinkling holy water and praying. Placidly sipping tea, Father Trevor sat in the corner.

"We are alone now," Professor Adler said flatly. "What are you not telling the rest about Jannes?"

A long moment.

Finally the priest sighed, "I do not know anything as a fact, my esteemed colleague. And I do not want to confuse these brave men, who face this terrible challenge, with legends of the early Church."

"I understand," Adler said patiently, "but there might be something important that you have simply failed to see. So I think that anything you can share without violating a vow of silence should be shared—at least with me.

"I am not so easily shaken. And as you note, many brave people have taken a stand against this evil—an evil that will not stop, that can't be reasoned with, and will show no mercy. So it goes without saying that we need all the information we can get, Father, legend or otherwise." He waited with conviction. "Do not forget; much legend is rooted in fact."

Seeming to harden, Father Trevor leaned forward in his chair. His gaze strayed to the window. The sun shone brightly, so incongruous to their circumstances. "The most certain knowledge we have of Jannes is what he did against Moses. If you believe that the Holy Scriptures are inspired by God, then the seventh and eighth chapters of the book of Exodus tell us much about our adversary.

"For instance, we recognize that Jannes has access to great power, for he can apparently transform one substance into another, like wood into a serpent. He can also manipulate common things by a process some would call telekinesis. And it would be logical to assume he can communicate with us telepathically."

"Yes," Adler conjectured, "that follows."

Father Trevor continued, "We would be particularly vulnerable in our dreams, when our conscious minds are not on guard and we are not in prayer. Also, where telekinetic powers are concerned, Jannes may be able to start fires, levitate, project images in mirrors and windows. He may even be able to disappear, walk through walls, teleport himself or others. All the wondrous things the world recognizes as masterful achievements of meditation or some other form of ascendancy—the skills of an avatar—he would possess.

"He undoubtedly possesses the wisdom and skill to drive an unprepared person insane by terrifying them beyond the capacity for rational thought. He would use such things as doors slamming, windows breaking, voices, strange signs appearing without noticeable cause, images hurled into every mirror and window, shadows that stalk someone in their sleeping and waking moments...anything to unnerve and eventually shatter one's mind."

"But not this man," Adler interjected. "Thorn, I do not think, is so easily shaken. His mind is strong."

"No...not Mr. Thorn, nor any member of the Assassini. Nor even you and I, I say with grateful humility, because we know the source of this evil and are mentally and, more importantly, *spiritually* prepared." The priest grunted. "I imagine that if a door slammed in front of Mr. Thorn, he'd simply knock it down. His approach to life is quite direct."

Adler's brow revealed his discomfort. "Why is this man, Thorn, so unaffected by this demon?"

Father Trevor waved dismissively. "Mr. Thorn does not care about his own death and is not terrified because his love for his family is far greater than his fear. He fights for love, not his own life. And the threat of physical injury means nothing to him.

"Like our brother, Artemis, he is not shocked by injury or fear. He expects fear, but it does not disturb him. He simply recognizes it, and continues. By benefit of Thorn's experience, even in anger he does not forget wisdom. He does not let rage or fear handicap him from using his physical skill and combat knowledge in its most effective combination."

Adler muttered, "A concise analysis."

"Also, Thorn is a man of inflexible principle."

"And how do you know that?"

"Because Mr. Thorn has lived by a highly developed sense of honor, and I suspect he suffered greatly for it. But now he fights by the strongest principle of all—a principle that even mean members of the animal world adhere to by instinct alone; the principle of defending one's young.

"Yes...Thorn fights to defend his family, so his motivation is the strongest motivation of all—love. He does not believe in ghosts and witchcraft but is intelligent enough to be wary of what he does not know for certain.

"He is the perfect selection for the role the Almighty has chosen him to play. He is neither dismissive of supernatural forces which, in his mind, might possibly be at work, but neither is he hypersensitive to them if they are, which might be worse. The last thing we need to do is start jumping at shadows."

"True," Adler commented soberly, "It is a classic mistake among believers to fear Satan, or even become preoccupied by him." He shook his head. "One thing we do know; this sorcerer has access to genuine power. And we don't know his limitations."

Father Trevor concentrated as Adler continued: "Much of what this demon thing can accomplish through Jannes—those things you mentioned such as doors slamming, noises, images, strange signs drawn on surfaces, visions of devils dancing amid flames—Thorn will not only ignore, he will despise. He will force Jannes to play his most powerful hand."

"And that will be to our advantage," Father Trevor said as if reaching a conclusion. "Jannes has been resting for centuries. He may not totally remember his powers yet. And we know the demon that assists him is limited because it reached that limit with Moses. The demon could not transform dust into gnats or match any plague that Moses called forth afterward.

"We do not know if it was a matter of exhaustion—as if he were drawing water from a well and had simply used up his allotment or power. Or whether, perhaps, God simply stopped his power from working to any affect. It is no matter. With either explanation, we see that God has set boundaries to this demon's power."

"Perhaps it was the power of prayer that stopped him," Adler commented.

Trevor shook his head slowly. "I don't believe that was the sole reason," he muttered. "Surely Moses and Aaron were well in prayer with the Almighty when Jannes transformed his staff into a serpent.

"No, here we have the mystery of God. The Almighty *allowed* this powerful demonic spirit that works through Jannes to perform those miracles, perhaps because the time has not yet come for this specific power to be imprisoned. But let us not forget something significant: God did not allow this demonic force to touch Moses or Aaron with main force."

"What do you mean?"

"I mean that, physically, Moses and Aaron were beyond the reach of this demon. God had established a hedge about them, so that it could not touch their physical bodies. And that is a key."

"What kind of key?"

"Jannes is powerful," he added. "But one who possesses great faith is beyond his ability to affect. Thorn or the sheriff, perhaps even Artemis can be affected by this sorcerer. But Jannes cannot overcome one of great faith."

Adler was staring closely. "Explain what this will mean in a pragmatic sense."

Trevor took a deep breath. "This demonic power cannot kill me with the manipulation of mean objects any more than he could turn dust into gnats. The demon does not have the power. But he can influence the mind of someone to pick up a gun and fire a bullet at me, which could, indeed, kill me. Or Jannes, since he is also physical, could pick up a weapon, such as a knife or gun, and make the attempt himself. But he would be attempting it in the flesh. He would not be empowered by this evil spirit."

"That's what the Assassini are for," Adler responded. "They deal with physical dangers."

"Yes," Trevor nodded, "they are the shield of God against the physical arm of evil. But the Assassini cannot be everywhere at once, or protect everyone at the same time."

"They are brave men."

"Yes...and their place, while tragic, is necessary, for we cannot allow our enemies to heedlessly lay waste to all we hold dear. It is neither Christian nor prudent to stand impotently aside while cruel and evil men tread down the weak of the earth—the orphans and widows." He shook his head with conviction. "No; that is not our mandate, whether we use the Assassini or not."

Adler was aware that he was nodding. "Let's proceed to more of Jannes' weaknesses. You say this demonic power influences the minds of men. How does it accomplish this manipulation?"

"I can only speak from personal experience," the priest continued, and could not mask the remembrance of horror. "First, he will search your past and find what remains most painful to you. With me, it was a woman I once loved, and considered leaving the Church to be with forever. I was only a young man, then, and had not come into a full acceptance of...my place.

"I did love her...truly. But, in the end, I could not forsake what I eventually came to understand as my purpose. And so I told her, with regret, and with tears, that there could be no life for us. At least, not the kind of life she wished for it to be...nor as I had wished for it to be." He paused. "Subsequently...out of a despair that would have faded with time...she took her own life."

Adler beheld a great and poignant sadness in the priest.

"Even now I bear a great sense of guilt and sadness," Trevor added softly. "But, to continue, the demon would manifest her voice; I could hear her crying out to me as she took her own life. I could feel the softness of her tears. Then I would be violently struck in my mind with horrible images of her actions...of her lying in blood.

"Then I would glimpse her surrounded by demons, terrified and tortured, and hear her pleading to me for help. And I would hear voices in my mind telling me I could help her even yet—that she would be released if I would only follow their bidding—if I would only do one thing.

"I knew it was a powerful demon, and I knew what it wanted. It was trying to make me question my judgment. It was trying to make me second-guess myself. It was attempting to make me think of my own pain, my mistakes, everything I have done wrong—to think of anything but what the Scriptures say, and he was succeeding.

"If it could confuse me enough, if it could make me afraid and redirect my thoughts, it would have me. And so I rose up and focused my mind only on what God has written. His words are our greatest defense. Then I prayed and fasted and...in the end, it departed."

Adler spoke quietly, "I thought you said we cannot make this kind depart."

"We cannot command a demon that is a world ruler, it's true," Trevor answered. "But neither can it tolerate the presence of one who is filled with the Spirit of the Lord."

The two old men were covered in silence a long while. Finally, Adler spoke: "I offer my condolences, and I am certain this young woman rests in the arms of our Lord."

Father Trevor nodded slowly. "I only say this because I want you to know what is coming. The attack will combine real regrets from our past—this part will be true. And it will involve fears of our future—this part will also be true. And it will mix these two powerful truths with a believable lie to make the lie seem like the truth. It is a powerful attack, and it can shake you as much as your regrets or fears shake you. If you attempt to think your way out of it, you are lost."

He clenched a fist. "The only hope is to ignore it! *Completely!* You *cannot* argue with your regrets or fears! They are true enough! And lies built on them will also seem true!" With a sigh, he relaxed. "The only defense is Scripture and prayer. Answer him with the words of God—the Living Word. With this he cannot argue, nor does he care to tolerate the presence of it. It is all that will save us."

Adler strolled across the room. "You can quote them by memory under such a psychological attack? Or does the Spirit bring them to mind?"

The priest waved. "I do not trust my mind in moments such as that. I always carry the Bible. I simply read from it. I do not argue with the demon. I do not speak with him. I read from God's Holy Scriptures. In other words, I torment him until he departs."

Adler acknowledged the wisdom with a simple nod. "It must require great discipline."

"I tell you this only because you need to know that the power of this attack is significant. Do not be astonished that you are shaken. *Expect* to be shaken. *Everyone* is shaken. These demonic princes of the air, and who once ruled this planet, are not fools. They have conquered kingdoms and nations for millennium. But do as I do, my friend, and you will be saved."

With respect, Professor Adler smiled: "A heavy millstone to hang around one's neck, Father. And your answer seems...disturbingly simple. It does not seem probable that such a powerful force can be defeated by such a simple thing."

"There are many levels to this battle," Father Trevor said, raising his gaze to Adler. "Satan has fought this war since the beginning. And he engages us in every arena—physical and spiritual, financial and civil. Social. Psychological. Nothing is left untouched.

"For those such as you and I, it is mostly a spiritual battle. And our part is necessary because someone must engage this demonic force on a spiritual level to insure our complete victory. Yet it is not entirely limited to the spiritual. Simply observe the history of the world; it has never been limited to the spiritual.

"For men such as Artemis or Thorn, or even this sheriff, it is largely physical, and they fulfill a righteous role. Some are chosen to fight on the battlefield of the mind, some are chosen to wield the sword. Nor do I presume to believe one place is greater than another. There is a time, and place, for all things."

Adler pursed his lips in silence. "I will ask only one more question," he said finally. "You seem to know a great deal about this type of battle. How difficult will it be to permanently rid the world of this sorcerer, Jannes?"

A frown creased Father Trevor's mouth.

"If any of us survive, you will have your answer."

🪲 ☥ 𓂀 ⸶ 𓅓

When Cahill entered what serviced as the Essex County Jail and Sheriff's Department, his primary thought was not to reveal any of the morning's activities. He walked toward Shirley, who was dispatching. He didn't ask any questions because Shirley wouldn't need to be asked whether something strange had happened; she'd share freely with anyone who would listen.

"Hey, Shirley," he mumbled.

"Guess what?" she shot back.

Cahill stopped. Heavily, he leaned on the counter and sighed. "I give up; what?"

"Taylor called in sick."

"Sick? What wrong with him?"

"Didn't say. Just said he was sick and couldn't come in."

"Huh," Cahill grunted. He couldn't help but think about the morning, and then Taylor, and if they were related. It gave him an uneasy feeling. He knew where Taylor lived, and Taylor was his man. All of his men were his because, despite his tough exterior, Cahill would have died for any of them.

He considered going to his desk and seeing what kind of shift reports came in through the night, but since Shirley hadn't mentioned anything spectacular, he assumed he was probably all right—nothing to call the mayor about, at least. He reached up and lifted his heavy blue coat from a rack.

"I'll be on the radio," he said as he moved toward the door.

"He's probably fishing."

"Then I wish I was him," Cahill muttered, and in a minute he was driving toward a low bank of gray-black clouds.

He had called the weather service and asked why they didn't predict this cold front so he could have prepared his men for it. The public information officer told him they'd failed to predict it because there was no natural cause. The officer added that they were as shocked as Cahill was by the last twenty-four hours.

Cahill got an unpleasant laugh out of that.

Not likely.

A spectral silhouette darkened the window, and Thorn glanced up to see yet another Assassini who, incredibly, didn't seem affected by the bracing cold.

He had finished a rousing game of catch and hit some grounders that entertained Anthony and Malorie until the excitement of seeing him again and the novelty of new softball gloves surrendered reluctantly to shivering and promises of hot chocolate.

At present, Anthony was viciously winning an electronic game and Malorie was wrapped warmly in a blanket with a huge mug of hot chocolate. Touching Thorn's heart, a young, dark-haired nun who had taken a particular liking to the eight-year-old had her arms wrapped around Malorie.

Thorn glanced out the window at Artemis, still perched on the low mound that provided him a complete view of the rectory, and the surrounding fields and homes. He also had a good view of both alleys and all approaching streets. The only entrance he couldn't see was the back door, but three additional Assassini had that covered.

Thorn didn't know, for certain, how many Assassini had arrived for this showdown, but he counted seventeen that were visible, and he assumed there were more. He also counted a dozen nuns and seven priests. He assumed most of them were exorcists, but he didn't forward any questions.

Thorn had been won by the simple faith and courage around him. These people had no stake in this fight—not that he could see. They fought for a purpose and would die for that purpose, and they did not ask for accolades or rewards. At least, Thorn did not see what reward they could gain by laying their lives on the line to defend a family they didn't even know. Or defeat a monster that could destroy them and their brethren with ease. Unless it was a reward that was not of this world.

True, he himself had risked his life many times as a soldier and police officer, but that was different. He had fought only to defend the weak and the oppressed. Noble sentiments enough, but it was not the same to him as what he witnessed now. These people fought for love—just love. What was the verse? "Greater love has no one than this, than to lay down one's life for his friends."

Enough...get your mind back on business...

With a shake of his head, Thorn reviewed the day's events so far. There was a lot to consider, but one thing that impressed him vividly was the manner in which Artemis had stood beside him earlier this morning—the Assassini had proven himself utterly without fear.

And with the thought, Thorn measured the number of Assassini against the support—the priests, exorcists, and nuns. There were almost more of Artemis's group than the other two combined.

The disparity suggested to Thorn that the chief priests in this suspected the end might be more physical than spiritual. In the first place, you don't fly Assassini from the four corners of the earth unless there's going to be a war. They *do* have other responsibilities; they weren't just laying around on couches waiting for a phone call. Carefully setting down a cup of coffee, Thorn looked at Rebecca.

Sitting across the table, she was smiling wanly, but he knew that look. She wanted some answers, and she deserved them.

So far, she'd been patient and supportive, but the time to talk had come. She didn't say a word as she leaned back, staring. "All right," Thorn began, clearing his throat. "It's like this..."

"Let me save you the torment," she said, and Thorn focused with deadpan eyes.

"Go ahead," he said.

She took a deep breath. "Okay, you accidentally found something in that basement. That's a simple start."

Thorn stared. "Well, it was a little more than 'something.'"

"I know," she smiled weakly. "It wasn't your fault, Michael. You didn't know what was down there. No one did. If you'd known...If I'd known..." She shrugged and glanced at Malorie, asleep now in the arms of the nun. "Well, it's water under the bridge. And I think we're pretty well protected for the time being. The only thing I want to know is where do we go from here?"

It took Thorn a long time to formulate a response. He wondered, unexpectedly, what Father Trevor or DeMarco might have already told her.

He was irritated by the intrusive thought, then grateful because it reminded him that, at this moment, it might be a bad idea to soften up the hard truth. The only problem was that he wasn't certain what the truth was, anymore.

He freely recognized the faith and dedication of these people. He recognized the savagery of this maniac who had attacked him and Artemis this morning, and he recognized that something potentially evil had come out of his house. He just had trouble wrapping his mind around it. It was too far out of any experience he'd ever had. Even too far out of any...*beliefs* he'd ever had.

Thorn tried to fill her in on everything that had happened so far. Rebecca had grasped the situation far more than he gave her credit for, and he felt bad for keeping so much from her.

"We had an incident this morning at the house," he finished, surprised that he sounded so weak. He mentally braced before he spoke again: "Babe...this is beyond anything I know. All I can tell you, for sure, is that I'm going to take care of it."

He lifted an arm to the window, and dropped it. "These men are professionals. They're here to—"

"I know why they're here," Rebecca said, following with a slight smile. "You're right; the kids and I are safe with them." She paused. "I'm not worried about us, Michael. I'm worried about you. And what you're going to do."

Thorn debated a dozen things to say; none of them seemed like a good idea. Then Rebecca broke the silence: "I know you're going after it. Just like I know I can't talk you out of it. So I'm not going to try. All I can do is ask you to be careful."

With a heavy sigh, Thorn added, "This is what I'm coming to understand: There are apparently...supernatural things...that I never believed in...but it doesn't matter." He paused. "I mean, it doesn't matter whether I believe in them or not, they're...still there. But I do believe in these people around us, and I believe they sincerely want to help."

He waited for Rebecca to respond, but she seemed content to just listen patiently. And then, gently, she reached out and grasped Thorn's hand. He continued, thinking a slight understatement was a bad idea.

"I don't think this is going to have a peaceful resolution." He opened his eyes and leaned forward to emphasize his point. "These things that are running loose...are a bit *unstable*."

Rebecca leaned forward, too. "Michael, these 'things' aren't *human*."

Silence joined them, and Thorn was significantly impressed by his wife's confidence and her faith and the strength it granted her. He wished it were so easy for him to believe. He wanted to believe. He bowed his head and finally sighed, so tired.

"You're taking this well," he said.

"I believe God is with us, Michael." She paused. "I believe He's with you and what you're going to do."

"Baby, I don't know what I'm going to do."

"What you always do," she said, and for a moment it seemed like she was about to cry—something that came out of nowhere and inflicted both regret and pain into Michael. But she didn't cry. She sniffed, straightened, and clenched his hand more firmly.

"I love you," she whispered. "And despite what you believe and don't believe, I believe God is with you. So you do whatever you have to do... but finish this."

Thorn solemnly nodded. "Yeah...all right."

Thorn saw Artemis gazing at the house as if he could hear every word, and it occurred to Thorn that maybe he could. It would have insured complete security, inside and out, but he didn't think Artemis would have listened in on a private conversation. He didn't forget the Assassini's offhand comment when Anthony and Malorie had ran forward and leaped into his widespread arms: "What love was ever love that did not leap at first sight?"

A deep man...probably a hero to his people.

Thorn felt a rush of admiration for him, all of a sudden.

It was past one o'clock, and Thorn had done what he had to do, for the moment. He had comforted his family and satisfied himself that they were well guarded. If anyone tried to penetrate this security perimeter, the battle would bring down the National Guard. These Assassini didn't play. They couldn't even *spell* play.

Thorn and Rebecca stood. He embraced her a long time before he kissed her forehead, then her mouth. He smiled encouragingly as she wiped away a single tear with the palm of her hand—one that she hadn't been able to prevent.

He gently lifted her chin and smiled.

"I'll bring an ending to this," he whispered.

She looked up at him. "Michael?"

"Yeah?"

"We'll be waiting."

Cahill stopped the patrol car on the gravel road beneath Taylor's one-story plank house.

Built into the single flat piece of a worthless hill crowded with brush and trees, the house had a white plume of smoke billowing from the river-stone chimney. Cahill knew that the cabin wasn't much, but Taylor had inherited it from his father—the *only* thing he'd inherited from the worthless old man—and he didn't have any intention of moving. Not that Cahill blamed him; he didn't much care for city life, either.

He knew why he was so concerned with Taylor. He just didn't want to consciously admit it. So as he climbed the slope of a driveway, he called out loud and casual.

"Taylor! It's Cahill!"

No response, and Cahill tried to ignore the sensation of dread.

"You'd better be sick in there!"

Out of breath and angry, but with a gathering fear, Cahill reached the porch and hit the door with the hammer of his fist. "Taylor! Open the door! Your boat's here! I know you're in there!"

Nothing.

Cahill leaned against the door, gathering breath. He would normally think of how he was getting old and out of shape and there wasn't anything he cared to do about it, either. But his mind was on what might be behind this door.

He backed up a step and drew his gun. He knew that if he was wrong, the county would be paying Taylor for a new door. But after what Cahill had seen and heard this morning, he wasn't in the mood to second-guess.

His kick shattered the doorframe—he glimpsed that it had been dead-bolted—and then Cahill was inside the cabin with his gun out, moving fast. He didn't worry what he'd say to Taylor if his deputy was genuinely sick—probably something like "condolences, yeah, you look terrible, better you than me, see ya Monday, kid." He just wanted to make sure Taylor was *just* sick and not...

Cahill froze in place as he saw Taylor.

His deputy, dressed in a blue bathrobe, was sitting on a crate against the wall, holding an antique, double-barreled, ten-gauge shotgun. A box of stainless steel shells were scattered on a table beside him, within easy reach. With surreal acuteness, Cahill noticed the shotgun first, and then he noticed the rest of the house.

Popcorn lay scattered on the floor in front of the TV, which was hissing on a dead channel. The floor was littered with magazines and the chairs and table were overturned like there had been a fight. The back door was closed and dead-bolted.

This far outside town, it was rare that anyone locked their doors, much less with a dead bolt. There was no reason. For instance, nobody even knew Taylor's place was here unless they lived close by, and the home crowd was pretty neighborly. If they wanted something, they just borrowed it whether you were there or not. But they generally returned it soon enough—within the year, anyway—and if they didn't, you just went and "borrowed" it back.

Still, the locked doors didn't disturb Cahill as much as the fact that Taylor hadn't said a word. And hadn't put down the shotgun.

Cahill took a long moment as he glanced at the open door of the bedroom. The house seemed empty. He heard nothing. The bed was unmade and he saw a uniform lying on the bedroom floor. Slowly, clenching his teeth, Cahill, lowered his gun. He nodded a few times, casual as he could, and said gently, "Just wanted to come out and see if you were okay, Jack."

Taylor's gaze was locked on the far side of the room—on the stone fireplace. Careful not to make any sudden moves, Cahill looked over and saw nothing immediately. But after a second he noticed white pockmarks—.00 buckshot from the 10-gauge—scattered in no accurate pattern across the mantleless chimney.

It was enough.

Cahill didn't know exactly what had happened, but after what he'd heard this morning, he suspected that the same thing that had compelled one priest to attempt suicide had paid Taylor a visit. He turned back very slowly toward his deputy, who still hadn't moved or removed his eyes from the fireplace.

Releasing a deep breath, Cahill slowly holstered his gun. "Jack," he said gently, and took a step forward. "I want you to—"

Taylor came off the crate and leveled the shotgun at him.

"Sheriff, get down!" he screamed.

Strangely—and Cahill even noticed that it was strange—he had the all-too-lucid thought that this is what happens when you're trapped in a room with a mentally unstable person holding a loaded shotgun. He dropped to the floor as Taylor screamed again and fired both barrels, smashing eighteen nine-millimeter rounds into the stones of the chimney.

Cahill had half planned to stay down to avoid a ricochet, but when Taylor fired both barrels, forcing a reload, Cahill gambled that he didn't have his service revolver, too, and leaped to his feet, rushing forward. He kicked the coffee table out of the way as Taylor fumbled, cursing wildly, for another shell. Then Cahill was on top of him.

No time for discussion.

Cahill hit him with a straight right hand an inch below the solar plexus—the flat bone in the middle of the chest that joins ribs together. The impact was solid, and Taylor dropped the shotgun as he pitched forward.

He wasn't hurt; Cahill didn't mean to hurt him. He just wanted to knock the breath out of him, and had. But when Taylor pitched forward, he wasn't stopping, so Cahill grabbed him by the shoulders and half-carried him to the couch, where he collapsed, moaning.

Cahill did a quick search around the couch to insure there were no weapons and then sat heavily on the coffee table. He ignored that he was gasping.

"Jack," he said, "what's wrong with you, man?"

Taylor's lips moved in silent response. His eyes remained glazed.

"Jack!" Cahill shook him by the shoulder. "What's wrong with you? What happened here?"

The words that came from Taylor were so faint that Cahill wasn't sure it was a real response. He had to replay the sound in his mind a few times before he understood the content.

Taylor had said: "I saw them."

Open-mouthed, Cahill realized he was staring. "Saw what?" he asked quietly, suspecting that Taylor didn't know the answer himself.

Another long response: "Them..."

Cahill gazed at the fireplace again. That's where the shotgun had been expended. He didn't see any buckshot holes in the back door or walls, but he didn't really find that too encouraging. Anybody rattled enough to attack a chimney was too rattled to be carrying, or have access to, a gun.

At present, Cahill had to worry about what to do with his deputy. He'd question him later but already had a good idea what he'd get; a lot of talk about visions and images, voices, things that go bump in the night, shadows chasing him with a knife, demons coming out of the fireplace—a full repertoire of haunts.

Taylor must have been easy prey; he'd never been wrapped that tight to begin with, which may explain why he was still alive. Taylor, in the end, hadn't possessed the wherewithal to consider something as quick and merciful as suicide; he'd just cracked up and huddled in a corner. Whatever "life force," as the old priest had explained, that they'd wanted to take from him hadn't been worth taking.

Cahill grimaced and bent to lift Taylor. Forget it, time enough to work through it later. He had to get his boy some help.

"C'mon, Jack," Cahill muttered, and had to bully him to a sitting position. He looked into Taylor's uncomprehending eyes. "I'm gonna take you to the hospital, Jack! Now, I'm gonna have to put the cuffs on you for your own safety. You are not under arrest, son. You hear me? You can hear me, right, Jack? You're not under arrest! I'm just gonna take you to see the doc."

Taylor offered no resistance. In a minute Cahill had him in the backseat, and they were cruising on the hardtop toward the hospital. When they got there, Cahill would brutally pull rank and walk him in fast past security and into a special room reserved for detox patients.

Then he'd officially check him in under another name and advise the doc that it was possibly posttraumatic stress disorder. He'd say Taylor was a danger to himself and others and that he was contacting the Probate Judge this afternoon for a sanity hearing, insuring an initial dose of tranquilizers.

By the time this thing with Thorn and these other goons was finished, Taylor would be recovering and Cahill would straighten out the lies. Right now he needed to get back to Shirley at Dispatch and find out who else had been hit.

Cahill was certain that if they had found Taylor worthless, they hadn't stopped.

They'd found someone else to feast on.

Chapter Fourteen

After long good-byes under watchful eyes and a dozen skillfully concealed guns, Thorn and Artemis arrived back at the house to find Professor Adler and Father Trevor walking over the fifty-five acres of ground.

Thorn donned a short leather coat, took his shotgun from the trunk of the Lincoln, and walked toward them with Artemis in tow. He was close enough to hear them discussing the probability that this was once a Native American burial ground when his cell phone rang. Thinking that it was probably the kids, he answered.

"Thorn?" came an irritated voice.

Thorn scowled: "Cahill?"

"I got big time problems."

"What kind of problems?"

"Are those priests still there?"

"Yeah, I'm watching 'em."

"Put the professor on the phone."

~~Cahill~~ Thorn lowered the phone. He didn't bother with decorum. "Professor!"

Expressing a bit of surprise at the interruption—Adler had obviously had his archeological blood aroused by the discussion—he looked quizzically at Thorn. "Yes?"

"Cahill says he's got problems all over town." Thorn expected a response, but not the one he received.

Professor Adler bowed his head and then raised it tiredly: "Advise the sheriff that we will do what we can. But all we can do at the moment is pray and wait."

Thorn was aware he was staring. He raised the cell phone. "Where are you at, Cahill?"

"The station."

"Artemis and I will be there in a few minutes with some more men. We'll ride with you guys, do back up."

It was Cahill's turn to be surprised; Thorn could hear it in the hesitation, and the reply.

"Consider yourself deputized."

𓆣 𓋹 𓂀 𓊽 𓅃

Thorn only had a minute, but he was going to use it. He walked up to Adler. "What do you mean we're doing all we can do? This town is a powder keg! Cahill's got a bunch of young guys, and he could use some backup!"

"This battle is fought in many arenas, Mr. Thorn."

The words brought an angry stare from Thorn.

"What are you talking about?"

"It would be time-consuming to explain, Mr. Thorn." Adler maintained his calm, but there was no lack of courage or commitment in his face. Thorn blew out a hard breath; he didn't understand these old guys, didn't have time to try. He turned into Artemis.

"You stayin' here or coming with me?"

"The house is my secondary responsibility. This thing and its army want to re-establish a kingdom, but they don't want to reveal their identity. You are one of the few who can blow their cover, so eliminating you will be one of their highest priorities. I will stay with you."

Thorn was already moving.

"Let's give 'em what they want."

The Lincoln was smooth and fast, and as Thorn topped the hill on his way into town he saw the explanation for the tendrils of black smoke that had penciled the horizon.

Fire.

Thorn pulled over to the side of the road and exited. From his vantage point, he saw half a dozen barns on fire and two sprawling farmhouses that must have been built a century ago. Deep inside the woods, he heard gunfire followed by more gunfire.

"Doesn't sound like hunting," he frowned.

"It's not the sound of hunting," Artemis agreed quietly. "It's the sound of killing."

They were inside the Lincoln and in minutes they pulled into the station to see Cahill wrestling with a handcuffed man at the back of the building, attempting to get the prisoner into the steel door. Cahill was on the losing end as Thorn and Artemis walked up and simply grabbed the man by either arm.

Reflexes were automatic as Thorn took Cahill's keys and ushered the man into a cell. He undid the cuffs and—no surprise—the prisoner turned to throw a sweeping right hand that Thorn blocked, pushing him back. He was out of the cell as Artemis slammed the door.

The clang brought back memories galore for Thorn. His next words were reflex as he looked at Cahill: "You okay, man?"

"Yeah," Cahill gasped, hand on his chest, "it's my fourth one this morning, plus Taylor."

"You arrested *Taylor?*"

"No, I took him to the hospital." Cahill waved wearily. "Don't ask. The whole town's gone crazy."

"It is Jannes," said Artemis. "He feeds on this energy. His demon feeds on it. They live for the chaos and terror."

Cahill extended an arm, leaning heavily against the cinder brick wall. He shook his head. "These are good people," he murmured. "They ain't like this...I know them. Don't wanna hurt any of them. But we gotta do something."

No one spoke; the sound of gunfire carried down Timber Avenue outside the station. Cahill raised his head at the sound. Looked at the both of them. Tossed them each a badge. "Yada yada for God and country, you're deputized. I ain't got time for anything fancy."

"Works for me," muttered Thorn.

"For God," said the Assassini and pinned the badge on his black coat. "What now?"

"Shirley had to go home," Cahill responded, loading up his pockets with 12-guage shells. "Contact me; I'm Unit One if you need me. Stay downtown. Just disarm whoever needs disarming and cuff 'em where they are. Cuff 'em to a bathtub, water pipe, whatever. Get some extra flex-cuffs from the board."

Thorn and Artemis loaded up with the plastic cuffs.

"Just make sure they can't hurt anyone and be done with it. Keep moving. Like I say, stay downtown; I'll take care of the outskirts." He pointed at Thorn. "You're Unit 12, and you," he focused on Artemis, "are Unit 13."

"Want us solo or together?" Thorn said, as he lifted an entire box of shells.

"Together," Cahill also took a box. "But handle things fast and keep moving. Remember; no more arrests. Just disarm and immobilize." For a moment he stared out the door. "But what's gonna happen tonight? That's what I'm worried about. This thing is only building right now. By tonight it's going to be county-wide."

"No, it won't," Thorn said sternly. "By tonight I'm gonna make sure that what's causing this is dead."

Without realizing he had even moved, Thorn found himself on the floor beside Cahill as glass rained down over them. It took Thorn a second under the thunder of gunfire to realize that someone had shot out the front windows. He heard Cahill shouting.

"Go out the side and use the cars for cover!"

With the words, Thorn rolled and ran to the side exit. He checked first to insure it wasn't in someone's sights and then he was out and behind the car nearest the street. He was sure to use solid cover, not just concealment, which wouldn't stop a bullet. And there was no better cover than the engine block of a car.

When Thorn glanced over the hood, he was shocked to see an old man—at least eighty—standing in the center of the street with a single shot .410. It was the perfect round for pheasant or quail but a bit outdated for duck and hardly any good at all against a ballistic vest.

Suddenly Thorn wished that he'd grabbed a vest. Too late. He looked at Artemis. "Ideas?"

The Assassini squinted as the old man discharged another aimless shot into the building. He was shouting about being arrested for public drunkenness after he came back from World War II and the one hundred dollars he had to pay the judge. Thorn noticed he was wearing an army cap.

Artemis whispered, "That Smith single shot breeches automatically. He reloads very quickly, and it's at least forty yards to close the distance on him."

"Yeah," Thorn whispered as the old man expertly slipped in another shell and raised aim. He fired again, and the shotgun snapped open at the breech, automatically ejecting the spent shell. He had shells extended between his fingers so that all he had to do was twist his wrist and another shell dropped in the chamber, like that. Two seconds. Thorn couldn't close on him that fast.

Thorn took a minute, thinking it through. "Okay, this is what we do. You show yourself...fire a few rounds high. Get his attention. I'm gonna see if I can get behind him."

No argument.

"Be careful," the Assassini said, drawing a Glock in either hand.

Thorn was gone, moving fast alongside the cars, right to the edge of the sidewalk. When he had as good a lead as solid cover allowed, Artemis stood in the old man's clear line of fire.

"Here!" he shouted and old man spun, raising aim and firing as Artemis dropped smoothly to the parking lot. The blast went over his head and wiped out the windshield on three patrol cars and someone's personal vehicle.

As the old man hastily reloaded, Thorn ran across the street, dropping behind an abandoned UPS van. He didn't even wonder where the driver was—no time. He moved down the far side and followed the old man's position by the sound of the next blast. Then he risked a peek to see the old man walking blindly toward Artemis. To Thorn's alarm, the oldster seemed dead serious on killing the Assassini.

His back was to Thorn now, and Thorn didn't waste time. He knew the guy couldn't hear because he'd fired the shotgun at least ten times. He closed the distance fast and came in low, beneath the eye line even though he was at the old man's back.

"Hey," he said loudly.

With a shout the old man spun, but Thorn was close enough. As the barrel swept around, he just grabbed it and jerked it out of the old guy's hands. It discharged into another building, but Thorn had expected that. Then Artemis was behind the guy and handcuffed him like he'd done it a thousand times.

Thorn blew out his breath, faintly disturbed that he'd held it. A thousand hours of training had conditioned him to control his breathing in combat, but he hadn't.

Not good, he told himself, and was suddenly distracted at how expertly Artemis locked the cuffs to insure they didn't close on the old guy's wrists, cutting off circulation.

"You know a lot," Thorn muttered as they led the man to the side door. Granted, Cahill had told them not to bother with the jail, but they were right beside it so...no sweat.

"We're trained in all the weapons and tactics of civilian authorities," Artemis replied. "That is our purpose; to deal with armies, assassins, all manner of civil threat. It's necessary to know what you know."

The inside information was intriguing.

Thorn asked, "So you research an area before you go into it?"

"Yes."

"And what do you know about these guys?"

"A sheriff and thirty-eight deputies, most of them with less than three years experience because of a pension buyout of veteran officers. Microwave communications are linked to a tower located on a hill two miles from here. Disable the tower, and you will disable their entire communications capabilities. Underground phone lines with access gained through the sewer. White wire is phone, blue is the alarm. They gas their cars at what they call the 'north station.' And we can disable that by pouring a certain chemical in the storage tank. Within minutes after refueling, they will be immobilized."

"They can always commandeer civilian vehicles."

"But civilian vehicles are not equipped for civilian law enforcement, and with communications down—"

"How would you do that?"

"Simply blow up the tower—a negligible-size charge. If the tower is down, the microwaves will have nothing to relay them to the dispatcher."

Thorn thought about all he was hearing; yeah, these guys did their research. He assumed they also knew everything about him, too. They probably even had a copy of his 201, which included his military training and police background.

"You said not to talk too much because these dimensional creatures can hear us, and then they'll know what we're thinking." He watched Assassini, who remained non-affected. "Aren't you worried they'll hear all this and use it?"

Artemis shook his head. "They already know. That is what they're doing right now." He closed the door on the old man. "This man did not attack the building because he was arrested fifty years ago. That was only the manipulation of his mind by Jannes and his followers. The attack is psychological, and uses things from our past to affect our future actions. It is subtle and powerful. Do not underestimate it, for they will try it with you, too."

"They've already tried it with me," Thorn muttered. "It ain't the first time I've ignored how I feel in order to do my job."

Cahill walked in and insured the old man was safe. He turned gruffly away. "Like I said: Stay on Channel One. Remember your unit designations?"

"Unit Twelve."

"Unit Thirteen."

Cahill pointed with the shotgun. "Don't be a hero. If one of these fools breaks into the armory and he's got a Gatlin gun, let him run out of ammo. At six thousand rounds a minute, he'll run out quick. Then try for a leg or something. Don't kill him unless you have to."

They nodded together, and as they were exiting the back to grab their own car, Thorn spoke quietly. "These demons don't affect you?"

"Of course they do," the Assassini replied. "They constantly attack my thoughts."

"How do you handle it?"

Artemis was screwing a silencer onto a Glock, but froze at the question. It caused a tenth of a second distraction for Thorn, since the Glock didn't have a barrel that extended beyond the slide, meaning the silencer had to be threaded inside the barrel itself—a very expensive alteration.

The Assassini sighed, looked directly into Thorn's eyes. "You may think I only deal in violent matters, or that I'm nothing more than a soldier, and I wouldn't blame you. But God knows my heart. I deal with demonic attacks the same way the priests deal with it, Mr. Thorn: I read the Scriptures, just as the Holy Father would do...And I pray. Without ceasing."

Thorn said, "I didn't mean to question your faith."

"There is no offense." Artemis gathered. "It is not easy for you. But if you will remember, our greatest weapons are not guns. Listen to God, hear His voice, and believe. We may defeat this creature."

"How do you know that's it's not this demon whispering to you?"

"By what it tells me," Artemis replied. "If it tells me anything that does not agree with what is written in the Bible, I know it is not God. The Bible is my road map to the truth, Mr. Thorn. It is not more complicated than that. God did not make it hard to hear His voice."

Thorn took a deep breath. Normally he'd be thinking of ballistics and tactics, fuel consumption and manpower and zones. It should have seemed strange that he was mostly thinking about God. But something was even stranger than that...

He didn't find it strange at all.

🪲 ☥ 𓅃 𓏺 𓅐

It was a gray mid-afternoon when Cahill found himself clearing Dead Man's Curve, not two miles from Thorn's house. He'd managed to collect, legally and illegally, an entire trunkload of guns from agitated farmers turned vigilante, and he had helped extinguish a chicken farm fire that threatened to burn down a field of dry corn. He was tired and disheveled, and he'd almost run out of flex-cuffs.

He'd lost contact with most of his men, including Thorn and the Catholic guy, hours ago. He figured someone had disabled the microwave transmitter at the tower. Now, radio contact depended on a distance of two miles and the terrain. If there were a lot of hills, the handheld units just didn't have the juice. But if they were within two miles, as the crow flies, and there were no significant hills, he could reach them.

The last contact from Thorn had been alarming in content but Thorn's monotone, droning voice had made it seem matter-of-fact. It seemed that the pool hall gang had broken into the hardware store for easy shopping. Thorn said he'd let them take what they wanted; no harm in a little theft when there were people running loose with shotguns.

Cahill admired the sense of priorities, and Thorn was right. If somebody's life wasn't in danger, let it go. Cahill himself had just driven off a group of Baptists burning down First Methodist Church. They had a right tidy bonfire going until Cahill had fired his pistol in the air. Those who ran were wise. Those who stayed were flex-cuffed to the water tower, enjoying an unhindered view of the church.

They could stay there until night, when Cahill would send somebody out to take them to jail, or home. He didn't want anybody freezing to death in this cold front.

He was comforted that Thorn and Artemis were veterans; he could trust their judgment. But he was worried about the rest of his boys. They could be trying to do things by the book.

The book went out the window this morning.

What he didn't understand was why some people were tremendously affected by this mental rabies and some weren't affected at all. It was like it targeted one person, then another, and entirely skipped the next. But Cahill had noticed that the ones who seemed most strangely affected also seemed the most devout.

Those he called "heathens"—for lack of a better word—just gazed at the destruction, fighting, and gunfire in astonishment.

Indeed, during the whole of the day Cahill hadn't yet seen any habitual drunks, criminals, or roughnecks causing trouble. It had, almost to a man, been those he considered docile, responsible, religious people—the kind of person who would preside over a PTA meeting before Wednesday night prayer meeting. Perhaps, he considered, the devil really does target those hardest to reach more than the rest.

He grunted when he realized he'd unconsciously reached Thorn's driveway. He gazed up the long black pavement to see the old priest standing on the front porch, hands clasped behind his back. Cahill turned into the drive and in a few minutes exited the patrol car. He gazed about the grounds, saw no one in Artemis's group.

"How are things out here, Father?" he called out. "Had any trouble?"

The priest's eyes narrowed.

"You don't look well, Sheriff."

Cahill grunted. "I ain't." He gazed around the property. "Seen anything unusual?"

"He will not strike us until darkness."

Cahill walked forward. "Yeah, well, being part of a church won't save you, Father. Seems like this...thing...affects religious people even more than nonbelievers."

"It resents those who believe."

"I figured that much." Cahill took a stone-like posture directly in front of the old man. "Let me be frank, Father, because I don't have enough men for another day."

"Thorn and Artemis are...?"

"They'll be here in fifteen minutes."

The old man appraised the sheriff. Cahill was a sad and weary sight. "Jannes has attempted to influence your mind, Sheriff?"

Cahill's gunsight eyes narrowed. "I've had some things go through my head. I just ignored them cause I believe you; I think we're all being influenced by whatever devil came out of that cellar."

"What you're witnessing is only a release of sentiments that are never far beneath the surface," Father Trevor replied. "Most men restrain them; it is one of the things that make us more than animal. But this demon that works with Jannes inspires us to surrender to these animal impulses—our hates, prejudices, fears, old hurts, resentments."

The priest approached. "We suppress these things for a reason; we *must* suppress them or we would be like a tornado going through the lives of those who love us. And when we lose control, the dark half of all that we are decides our actions for us." He sighed. "Jannes does not so much 'create.' He is simply encouraging us to freely release what we keep suppressed...for good reason."

The radio blared at Cahill's hip, and he keyed the mic attached at his collar. It was Thorn.

"This is Cahill. Go ahead."

"Status?"

"I'm at your place. It's Code One."

"Checked the rectory?"

"About an hour ago. They were secure."

"Ten-four."

"What about you guys?" Cahill said quickly.

"Things are calm for the moment. We ended up using the jail. We couldn't have people flex-cuffed all over town."

"All right; get back to your place. It'll be dark soon. You have to end this tonight."

"On our way."

Cahill dropped heavy arms to his sides and stared at the white-robed figure that stood on the porch. He couldn't prevent the question that rose within him: "Why is Jannes doing this?"

Father Trevor released a deep breath. "Jannes does this because he secretly fears what is beyond this world. He, too, fears death. All men do. And he believes by this incredible control over the world, and what others believe and do, he achieves a type of metaphysical security that he is right, and that when he is dead, he is not truly dead forever. He is deceived and secretly terrified that he is wrong—he always has been—but by destroying what does not agree with him, he concludes that his belief system is correct and that he will, indeed, live forever and serve forever at the foot of this spirit that enables him."

Gunfire sounded in the distance, but Cahill didn't remove his eyes as the priest continued so calmly, "What Jannes does not understand is that he is simply a tool; he always has been. The demonic spirit that empowers him knows full well that its time is limited and that Jannes will die a second time when he dies to this world. You see, sheriff, the greatest trick of Satan and his minions is that they never truly unmask their motivations. Or even their presence.

"Satan, if he is truly working in a situation, will never reveal that he is involved. He will appear as an angel of light, not a monster. Indeed, as far as the innocent participant knows, they are only doing what they should have done years ago. It will seem totally justified."

Silence passed, and Cahill turned away like a monument come to life. "All that's beyond me," he growled, and stared at distant spirals of dark smoke. He looked at his watch. "It'll be dark in about four hours. What then?"

"Everyone who has been subjected to this madness today will rest tonight when Jannes and his servants converge on this house to kill Thorn and the rest of us."

"Because we know who he really is?"

"Yes."

"It's that important to him, huh?

"If there is even a suspicion that a demonic force is at work, Satan immediately loses half his ability to influence. Look at yourself; you suspected these thoughts were not your own, so you disavowed them. Your will is not subject to Satan's power—only your mind, and only then if you are determined to resist his influence." He grimaced. "Satan is not the all powerful being he would have us believe. He is limited in what he can do. He cannot *make* us do anything at all. He can merely inspire."

Cahill gazed angrily at distant smoke.

"He's good at it," he said.

𓆣 ♀ 𓂀 𓏏 𓅃

Thorn glanced down Main Street.

Andover looked like a ghost town, with cars burning and smoke spiraling from houses on surrounding hills. He could hear random shouts and an occasional gunshot, but they'd locked up sixty-two people since morning. He didn't think there were enough rioters left to cause much of a problem. Let them shoot out some windows, burn up their own cars. Thorn had bigger things to worry about.

Artemis didn't look much the worse for wear. If anything, he seemed more stoic than he had this morning. His black coat was gray with smoke and ashes and dirt from wrestling about thirty people into handcuffs, but for the most part he was composed. He brushed leaves off his sleeve as Thorn holstered the radio unit.

"Cahill wants us back at the house," he said.

Artemis glanced at the sun, then his watch. "Four hours until sunset."

"Isn't that when you say they'll come?"

"They will come. For you. For me."

There was a question that had been in Thorn's mind all day, and he answered it in the moment. "We'll go by the rectory first. I don't trust that this thing won't go after Rebecca and the kids."

As Thorn moved for the car, Artemis took a single step to block his path. "I don't think that is wise," he said quietly.

A normal man might have become angry at the boldness, and Thorn did have the impulse. But he wasn't a normal man; he was a veteran soldier, accustomed to not reacting to emotions and impulses.

It was also the first time Artemis had disagreed with him in a day filled with split-second life and death decisions, and Thorn gave that a lot of consideration. His second thought was that he had to closely monitor every impulse because he wasn't certain which ones were his, and which ones were suggested to him by Jannes or his followers.

Standing in place, Thorn said calmly. "You don't agree?"

Artemis seemed relieved that Thorn had not reacted angrily. "I think they are safer where they are," he said in a low voice. "They are surrounded by my men and the nuns have them covered in prayer."

From a perfectly logical standpoint, Artemis could be right. Thorn admitted that. But Thorn wasn't perfectly logical in the moment any more than he was overly prone to acting on impulse. He ran over a dozen scenarios in his mind, playing each alternative ending, and considered what tactics Jannes might use at nightfall.

Worse case, Jannes would attack the rectory in full force. At best, Artemis's men would drive them back, but remembering the morning, Thorn didn't count on that. These guys were hard to kill and enjoyed it. Another downside was that if Thorn knew the rectory was under attack he wouldn't be able to prevent himself from leaping into the first car and tearing off down the driveway, which might just be what Jannes wanted. Needless to say, even with backup, Thorn would stand a lot less chance against Jannes in the open field.

"I don't want to argue with you," he said to the Assassini, "but this thing knows us. And it knows that I'll throw my life to the wind if I think Rebecca or the kids are in danger. I underestimated it this morning. But now I think it's either smarter than I thought or getting smarter as it goes."

"It's remembering," Artemis said. "He's lived for more than five thousand years. This morning he was barely alive." He glanced over the ghost of a village. "Now, with all this energy that he's fed upon, he's approaching full strength."

It was enough for Thorn. He stepped around Artemis. "You can go back to the house if you want. I'm going to the rectory to get Rebecca and the kids. I'll be at the house in an hour.

As Thorn slammed the door, Artemis settled in the passenger seat. "You know that this could be what he wants you to do?"

"I know."

"So why are you doing it?"

"Because it's what I wanna do, too."

Cahill set down the radio after Thorn's terse, no-questions transmission. He looked at Father Trevor, who didn't seem surprised. "You don't have anything to say?" Cahill muttered.

"I anticipated as much."

Shaking his head, Cahill mounted the porch. "The last thing I need is two kids and a woman in this house. I've got my hands full as it is, trying to make sure none of you or yours get killed."

"It appears Mr. Thorn would rather have his family under his own watchful eye than under the protection of the Church."

"Can you blame him?"

"No," the priest answered. "Neither can I acquiesce to the wisdom of it, either. Regardless of Mr. Thorn's passion to defend his children and wife, I presume that Jannes would like to have them all in the same place. It would be far easier than dividing his forces, or staging one attack after the next. We must, at all times, remember that just because we sincerely believe our reasoning and motivations are right, they may be influenced. And when we're in highly charged emotional states, it's sometimes best to do nothing at all."

"We don't have the option of doing nothing at all," Cahill growled. "That's his game. He doesn't plan to let us wait or think. He's rushing us. That's what I'm just beginning to understand."

"What do you mean, Sheriff?"

"From the very beginning, he's rushed us." Cahill became angrier with each word. "He's gone the minute we dug him up and then comes back the same day and again the next morning? He tried to kill two of the people that were called out in same day. He hasn't tried to give himself time to recover, organize, anything. From the very first, he's been at this, not giving you folks time to catch up."

Quietly, Adler considered, then, "This tells you what, Sheriff?"

"Tells me two things," Cahill grunted. "First, it tells me he's smart. He knows that when people are rushed, they make mistakes. Second, it tells me he might be afraid of something."

"Afraid?" Adler stared. "Afraid of what?"

Cahill was concentrated. "I don't know—not yet. But he's not moving so fast just cause he wants to kill all of us and protect his identity. There's something he wants—something that he has to have in order to do what he wants to do. Something he *needs*."

Empty stares from Father Trevor and Adler.

"Look," he continued, "this guy, Jannes, he can't do what he wants to do without something that's in this house. That's why he launched an all-out attack while he was still weak. And my guess he's not going to be able to make a more serious move unless he lays his hands on something hidden in this place."

"An artifact," Father Trevor murmured.

"No," Adler muttered. "It would be a talisman—something that connects him to his source! He is...wait...a staff! Of course! Why did it not occur to me! Is not history littered with this? Staffs! Talismans! Potions! Charms! Yes! Of course! He needs the talisman that allows him even greater access to this demon's power! Indeed! History is not filled with such lore for nothing!"

"All this for a staff?" muttered Cahill.

Adler waved it off. "The older the sorcery, the more dependent it seems to be upon talismans and magical emblems. Even demons are limited by cosmic forces, which is why rituals are required. And did not Moses himself use a staff? Moses had the power of God, but God also reached him through the culture of his time, and it was common to use a staff for purposes of supernatural acts! How could I have been so slow to understand?"

Cahill was already at the door.

"I'll be in the basement," he said.

𓆣 𓋹 𓂀 𓏏 𓅢

Artemis had used his cell phone to call his men, so Rebecca and the kids were packed and wrapped up when he arrived. Anthony and Malorie leaped off the porch and Artemis had the door open for them. Thorn didn't bother to turn off the engine as Rebecca was ushered forward by three Assassini guards.

Thorn shook his head at her concerned gaze: "I'll tell you in a few minutes. Let's load up."

Artemis gave terse instructions in Italian to the other Assassini. He glanced at Thorn as he moved around the rear of the Town Car. "One car with four men will lead us. One car will follow. The rest will be at your house within the hour. The nuns will vacate the premises."

"To where?" Thorn asked.

"To a place far too holy for Jannes to invade."

It was enough.

Thorn waited until the lead car tore from the driveway, and then he was on the street. He was tempted to look at the backseat to see how the kids were holding up but decided it might encourage them to express their fear. He kept his eyes on the road, but he heard a soft cry and then Rebecca's soothing voice—the same tone she used with them when they thought they were injured.

He was surprised only when Artemis turned, staring upon Anthony. With a glance into the rearview mirror, Thorn saw the fear he had seen in his beloved son's eyes a hundred times at baseball games, school, races, things that were inconsequential. But this fear was worthy of fear, and Anthony was too young to carry the load. Thorn expected him to burst into tears, and he would have understood. He would rush to the house, and when they were secure Thorn would spend the rest of the time with his kids, and wait for dark. And a man to kill.

Artemis spoke quietly, almost jovially, to Anthony. "I told the others to bring over your electronic games. Were you winning?"

Anthony took a moment to respond. "Uh huh...Dad? Will you play with me?"

Nodding, Thorn turned a corner: "You bet, buddy. Soon as we can set it up. And we'll cook some of those sandwiches you like. And then I want you guys up in your rooms."

Silence.

Malorie was the only one not certain that the night was bringing doom from a dozen directions. Her small voice was endearing with the ultimate trust of a child. "Dad?"

"Yeah, honey?"

Her words were so plain—even matter of fact.

"Are you gonna kill it?"

Thorn kept his eyes on the road, though he knew Artemis had looked over, just as he knew everyone in the car—his wife and children—was watching him, and listening. Something told him to choose his words carefully.

Thorn didn't listen.

"Yeah, baby," he said. "I'm gonna kill it."

🪲 ☥ 𓂀 𓊽 𓅐

"Where are those lights?" Cahill grumbled, throwing a shovelful of dirt past Adler.

"The Assassini will have them working in a moment," the professor responded. "You know, Sheriff, you might want to be more careful on how viciously you slam the shovel into the floor."

Cahill stomped on the shovel. "I know it's here somewhere. I couldn't care less if I break it." He turned to the priests, who were rigging makeshift platforms for extra mag-lights. "Angle that a little ways over here!"

They continued to dig as Father Trevor came into the tomb. He stared at the chiseled walls. "The walls are eaten from the hill and chiseled. So you assume it must be buried in the floor?"

"Yes," said Adler.

The priest did not seem convinced. "Perhaps..." He studied the cellar, itself. "But surely they would not have buried the very instrument of his power with him. What if he had broken the chains?"

271

Cahill continued to sift dirt. But the words seemed to strike a spark in Adler. He gazed about the tomb carefully. "Possibly," he muttered at last. "But where would they have placed it?"

Father Trevor had stepped into the center of the cellar. He looked at the walls, the rafters. "It would be someplace sacred. Someplace that the devil himself would not dare to pass." A pause. "Sheriff!"

Cahill continued shoveling.

"Sheriff!"

Cahill straightened. "What is it?"

"Sheriff, is there any location in this area considered particularly sacred?"

"*What?*"

"Someplace considered holy!" Trevor continued. "Like a revered church! A tomb! A sacred relic! I know there is no place in St. Mark's that would be considered worthy!"

Cahill appeared dumbfounded. "How would I know? I haven't been to church in thirty years!"

"Then is there some place considered cursed?"

Cahill remembered the fence at Andover City Cemetery. He thought it would ridiculous, but everything else seemed ridiculous, too. He tried to think of another place more cursed, but Andover was not replete with cursed tombs.

"Maybe," he said quietly. "There's an old grave. Got a name for being cursed. What do you have in mind?"

Father Trevor nodded at the shovel. "I believe you understand."

Not bothering to drop his shovel, Cahill stood. "I don't buy it, Father."

"What do you mean?"

"If that staff were buried in a grave, then why did that heathen attack Thorn and your man here? If he wanted this stick, he just had to go to the grave and dig it up. He didn't have to come here and risk getting killed." Cahill shook his head, hefted the shovel. "No, what you're looking for is here. That's the only explanation that makes sense."

The logic must have reached Trevor, because he hesitated a long moment. "Nevertheless, I think we should send someone to the cemetery to examine the grave. I could be incorrect—I've been wrong many times—but we can lose nothing by a quick investigation."

Cahill had no problem with that. He lifted his hand to Artemis's men. "You guys know where it's at—off Main Street. Grab some shovels and dig the old geezer up. If it's there, bring it back. If not, get back here. Don't worry about throwing him back. We can do that tomorrow."

No words: Three of them were gone in seconds

Cahill went back to digging and spoke over his shoulder at the priest. "It won't take 'em long. A hundred years ago they didn't bury 'em that deep. They should be back in a couple of—"

An Assassini dropped onto the stairway. "Mr. Thorn has arrived. With his family."

Cahill threw down his shovel. As he moved up the stairs, he wondered how many men he still had in the field and what kind of damage he'd face tomorrow. Then he wondered how low the sun had dropped and hoped he'd see it again tomorrow. When he emerged onto the first floor, he wasn't surprised to see the men he'd come to know as Assassini mobilizing with a host of weapons, priests positioned at entrances, keeping alert eyes on the nearby woods.

Thorn was setting down suitcases and moving with a surprising lack of urgency. By comparison with Thorn's calm demeanor, Cahill felt like he was in a panic. He waited until the boy and girl were ushered into the kitchen with their mother and Thorn stood relatively alone in the foyer. He was checking his Colt and reloading clips. He noticed Thorn carried even more clips inside the top of his cowboy style boots. Cahill's speech was laconic.

"We think there's something here that he wants," he said.

It drew no surprise from Thorn. "And so he's got more than one reason to come back. We'll be waiting."

"What'd you run into in the field?"

"Some of your guys." Thorn seemed unsure whether he wanted to share any more, but Cahill's look settled the issue, and he continued. "Some of them weren't doing too good. We had to disarm them, too. But don't worry. Nobody got hurt." He reconsidered: "Well, nobody got *killed*. But I did have to break a few arms. Other than that, we managed to settle everything peacefully. To tell you the truth, I think most of them were happy to get locked up."

"How bad was it?"

"Same as here." Thorn slammed in a fresh clip, dropped the slide. "People are arguing and fighting about who did what to who forty years ago. Old resentments are being unleashed." He sniffed. "This thing isn't using anything that's not already there. And most of what people are fighting over is the same old stuff that everyone endures at one time or another. He's not causing any of this as much as he's just...encouraging it, I guess."

Artemis had shed his cloak. "He doesn't have to create evil. Man carries enough in his heart. He is merely throwing gasoline on a flame. He can encourage. He cannot compel."

With that, the Assassini walked toward his men. Cahill noticed they'd managed to build a makeshift door to replace the rear entrance Thorn had demolished with the shotgun. Not that he expected a door to slow these guys. This thought inspired him to ask Father Trevor: "Can these goons walk through walls?"

The priest shrugged. "Who knows? They are all different. Like a normal person, one is skilled in this, one in that. Some are adept at throwing images, or perhaps sounds. Some are simply murderers. I suspect Jannes is skilled in all manner of sorcery. If it can be done at all, he is capable."

"He hasn't impressed me so far," Thorn muttered. "Do you guys have this place...covered in prayer, or however you say it, so he can't use sorcery?"

"As much as we know to do," Trevor responded. "There is no means of being certain, but we believe Jannes' ability is greatly limited by the presence of the Holy Spirit. The devil, in general, flees from the presence of God."

"Let's hope you have it, then." Thorn looked at Artemis. "Have your men move Rebecca and the kids upstairs as soon as they get something to eat. They'll be safer in Anthony's room. There's no window."

A nod.

"I'll stay down here," Thorn continued, and lifted the shotgun. He glanced out the window. "Two hours till sunset. We've got a lot to do. Did you find what Jannes is looking for?"

"Not yet," grunted Cahill. "But I think it's in the basement, somewhere. I sent a couple of guys to the cemetery—an old grave—just in case. But I don't think they'll find it there. I think it's here, somewhere."

"Keep looking. We still have a little time." He turned to Trevor. "What else can you do to shut down his sorcery?"

Father Trevor's voice was stone.

"We are doing all that we can do."

"And that is?"

"As I said, Mr. Thorn—prayer."

For some reason he couldn't quite place, Thorn actually had no problem with that as he would have had this morning.

It happened fast.

Like that.

He was faintly aware he'd raised his hand to his head, and then he was gazing through gauzy webs of black crisscrossing before his eyes. He was only dimly aware of Artemis shouting and then he felt he was floating, or falling and...

Then he knew no more.

Thorn was...upstairs?

Yes, he was upstairs. He was gazing at the corner of the crest of the stairway, and beneath him were Artemis, Cahill, Father Trevor, and a host of priests and Assassini. And he could hear them, but when he tried to speak, he was unable to say a word. Yes, he could see them and hear them, but he could not communicate.

A squeaking...

Slowly, Thorn turned and stared down the long, dark hallway. And at the far end of the corridor where the dying sun framed the curtained window in a grave-like white, he saw an old, withered figured sitting placidly in a rocking chair.

The scarlet robed figure was not facing him. Instead, it was facing Malorie's bedroom, the last on the right. Nor was it rocking, or moving, in any way. And somehow Thorn sensed that this was not really happening—not in reality. It was only happening in his mind because the sorcerer, Jannes, had chosen to reach out to him.

Obviously, prayer could not prevent this.

Thorn tilted his head curiously and, in his mind, he took a step toward the silhouette. He could not see the face. And, still, it did not move. But Thorn knew it was waiting for him—just him.

He had taken a half dozen steps down the corridor when, with haunting slowness, the chair turned.

The figure did not move the chair, for the rocking chair seemed to rotate a full ninety degrees, silent and slow and steady with the figure motionless as death, until the shadowed head of the intruder faced Thorn. And still, it had not moved in any way. His hands rested lightly on the arms of the chair.

Thorn heard a soft laugh in the shadows.

"What do you want?" Thorn asked, but his voice echoed in his mind; he didn't need words to communicate with this thing. It knew his thoughts, though Thorn could not discern what it was thinking. He only knew it was inside his mind.

"Will you die for this?" it asked Thorn so quietly.

By reflex, Thorn reached for a weapon. His hand, before he realized he had even moved, had faded behind his right hip where he carried the Colt. But it wasn't there. Then he felt the impulse to look around for the shotgun, and stopped himself—he knew already that it wouldn't be close. He continued to stare at the shadowed shape at the end of the corridor, a black silhouette framed in a gauzy white curtain and a fading sun.

Something about the words had caused Thorn to drop his hand from his hip. He was well aware that he wanted a weapon. He was also aware...of something else. He was surprised when he heard his question echo from the corridors of his mind.

"Die for what?"

The shape laughed.

Thorn understood enough to know it was mocking what he held close to his heart. Whether it was faith or love or friends, it made little difference to Thorn, in that moment.

Its hands tightened on the rocking chair as it leaned slightly forward. Thorn could almost make out a ghastly mask visible in the pale mockery of light.

"You have no faith," it whispered. "He does not care about you. And prayer is worth nothing. Am I not here? Yes...their faith is nothing. Pale hopes...dulcet-colored dreams dressed in shades of fear...

"Don't you understand yet?" the droning voice continued. "I come to you because I want you to join me. I wish you no harm." It lifted a hand. "The others are chattel...The world will be a better place without them. But I will save you and your family. And, then, you will have all that you desire—power, family, health, prosperity. I can provide all these things. All you need do is surrender...to me."

Thorn could think of nothing to say. He felt a vivid rush of fear as the thing's rocking chair seemed to levitate, though it did not actually rise from the floor. Rather, it slid slowly forward, approaching. Then it came forward quickly, in a blink, but the figure had not, himself, moved. He was simply far away and then he was halfway down the corridor no more than ten feet from Thorn.

Breathless, Thorn didn't move, didn't know what to say. He only knew it expected him to be afraid. Then, from nowhere, he heard the words of Father Trevor: *"It will use your fear...your fear and confusion... those are its weapons."*

It lifted a skeletal hand. "Will you die for them?"

Thorn's eyes narrowed.

It rose, solidly and hauntingly, and Thorn heard a low growling like a dead thing emerging so slowly from a dirt-thick grave, wet with decay. It took a step toward him, so slow.

"Will you die for *Him?*"

It was enough. With a frown, Thorn stepped forward, surprised at his own words as he reached out to grab it.

"Come here!"

It vanished as Thorn staggered.

No!

He rolled, swinging his right arm out wildly to grab the thing before he felt hands on him and Thorn opened his eyes, staring at Cahill's pale face. Then Artemis was at his left, kneeling beside him. The Assassini looked concerned. He was the first to speak.

"Michael! Can you hear me?"

Cahill looked like he was on the verge of panic and then Thorn vividly beheld the image of Father Trevor in white, standing behind Artemis. The priest's lips moved in silent prayer. But at the touch of Thorn's suspicious gaze, the old man opened his eyes and nodded slowly.

"God answers prayer," he said lightly. "And now he will not try you, again. You did not fear him, and so he has fled from you. His power has little effect when you do not fear him. He tested you, and you prevailed."

Thorn pushed himself up, surprised that he was so fatigued by an encounter that happened only in his mind. "It seemed...so real."

"Yes," Father Trevor answered. "It always does."

Thorn didn't shake it off as quickly as he'd anticipated. He heard himself from a distance. "Fear can be...a powerful thing..."

Father Trevor laughed lightly, turned away.

"So can prayer," he said.

🪲 ☥ 𓂀 𓉠 𓅃

Standing upon a small rise less than a half mile from the burial mound, he clenched his fists, watching the activity. He turned his head in a circle, loosening. Altogether, he felt rested and ready for what the night would bring, nor was he disturbed by their preparations, which were extensive.

Chapter Fifteen

It warmed Thorn's heart when he entered Anthony's bedroom and saw the kids picnicking on the floor with Rebecca. Three Assassini were positioned at the walls, weapons visible. Only a glance at the kids told Thorn they weren't disturbed by the armament. If anything, they seemed encouraged.

Thorn leaned his shotgun against the wall beside the door and walked forward. He didn't think the kids would be disturbed by it; there seemed to be quite enough weapons on display as it was.

As Thorn knelt, Malorie offered him a potato chip from a big plate of hamburgers, chips and dip, and carrots and dressing. It was a small thing, but encouraging to Thorn; Rebecca was an expert in last minute lunches and emergency snacks. He was confident she'd keep the children happy and warm. And if these three Assassini were half the man Artemis was, they were well protected, indeed.

Thorn was not surprised that Artemis's team seemed to hold their lives so cheaply. He had watched Artemis all day, amazed at the life and death decisions he made without a hint of fear or any other emotion. Thorn had no doubt that the others were much the same; they fought for something more vital—to them, at least—than life in this world.

Although Thorn himself seemed nonchalant about being killed, his decisions were tactical, not spiritual. His indifferent approach arose more from the knowledge that fear is most often what caused a man to hesitate, and hesitation is what usually got you killed. So, his attitude was simply this; when in danger, be decisive and move hard and fast. If you're wrong, there will be plenty of time to lament it later, if you're alive. But do *not* hesitate in the middle of a move, right or wrong.

"Thanks, hon," Thorn said to Malorie, who smiled back.

Thorn was a little amazed at how relaxed the children seemed, and he surmised it was a combination of them knowing they were both high priorities for everyone involved, and extremely well protected.

And ultimately, there was Rebecca's presence, which could not be underestimated. Thorn sensed that, without Rebecca, all the guards in the world would not have calmed them. As it was, however, they seemed fairly content. Rebecca's effortless aura of peace and love just had a way of calming people, including Thorn, himself.

"Are we still going to live here?" Anthony asked.

Thorn shrugged. "I don't know, buddy—maybe. I guess it all depends on whether we want to or not. We've got plenty of money and time; we can live anywhere we want."

"And have horses," said Malorie.

"Yeah, and horses. What kind of horse do you want?"

"An Arabian stallion!"

Thorn laughed. "I don't know about that. They're kinda wild. It might be too much horse for someone your size."

"I can do it!"

It was Rebecca's turn to laugh. She'd been raised with horses and had already made decisions on what kind of horse the children could have. Since Thorn was a city slicker, he had long ago deferred to her authority.

"Well," he began, "your mother is the horse expert. But I'm sure she'll let you pick a horse that's right for you." He looked at Anthony, anticipating the question, "No, you can't have an Arabian stallion. They're too big, too fast, and—"

Artemis's voice was at the entrance.

"Michael," he said quietly, and then waved to the kids. "Hi again."

Anthony and ~~Rebecca~~ malorie waved back. For some reason, perhaps it was Artemis's gentle nature, the children seemed taken with him. Thorn didn't doubt they'd even accept him as a babysitter, and the thought almost made him laugh.

He gave Anthony and Malorie a kiss and leaned forward, staring eye to eye. "I love you," he said to each of them in turn, because he knew somehow that he wouldn't be seeing them again until this was over. Then, hugging all of them together, he kissed Rebecca, and she had the presence of mind to simply say, "See you soon."

"You bet," Thorn smiled awkwardly and rose.

He lifted the shotgun and followed Artemis to the stairs. With a just a narrow glance, Thorn saw the sun was only a hand's breath above hilltops. His voice was quiet; "How long?"

"An hour." Artemis withdrew the MP-5 from his coat. "I think we should double-check our defenses before night."

Thorn nodded.

"Let's do it."

🪲 ☥ 𓄿 𓏏 𓅃

Poised high upon a canopied hill over a mile from the home of Thorn and his family, Jannes folded his arms across his chest. He heard incantations behind him and unconsciously listened to insure they were correctly repeating phrases he had taught them so long ago.

He had fed well during the day, though it would be months before he regained his full strength. Still, he was strong enough to fight this battle tonight. He gained strength with each life force he absorbed from the humans he killed. He did not need to wait an unseemly amount of time before he secured his presence here, and he was increasingly uncomfortable with the presence of these priests.

The last thing he wanted was more of these servants of the Hebrew God scurrying across the countryside hunting him and his followers. He felt he himself was safe, but he was not so confident that his servants could protect themselves.

Three had already been wounded, though he had called upon healing powers that the spirit granted to restore them. Still, each blow cast by Thorn was like an ax at the foot of a tree; a single blow might be meaningless, but a dozen blows would undoubtedly have their effect.

The wisdom made him remember a proverb of the Old One: "Do not despise the day of small things..."

Yes, the Old One had his own wisdom, but he had studied their wisdom, for wisdom was wisdom despite the source. Not that he had ever considered surrendering his life to the God of the slaves. No, he had chosen his god, nor would he forsake him now.

In any case, there was nothing the God of the Hebrews could give him that he wanted and did not already have. He commanded power, immortality, riches. He believed he could conjure anything he needed, unless...

Unless...

Always the memory of that hated defeat cursed him—the memory of Moses. For, even in victory, the old prophet had been the humblest of men. He did not even express satisfaction in the fact that he had so completely defeated the greatest sorcerer in Egypt.

Yes, the power of their God was great, and the certainty of that knowledge constantly haunted him. For he knew that the great "I Am That I Am" could do to him again what He had done in the past.

In Egypt he had not conceived of the God of Israel so utterly cutting off his powers, and he had not been prepared to take the confrontation to another level until it was too late. But that was a mistake he would not repeat. If their God intervened again, he was prepared to attack them on grounds where he was not so easily stopped.

The chest that had contained their blades had long ago rotted into dust, but the bronze swords lined with furnace-hardened gold had endured, so that they were prepared for a more direct resolution. Nor would he hesitate to eliminate his enemy with main force, should it be required. It was something he should have done with Moses, but he had been so astonished by defeat, and the sudden hysteria of the people, that he had hesitated to implement violence.

He had also been unnerved that his god might have deserted him forever, but that had proven an empty concern, for as soon as Moses departed with the people, his powers returned. A few effortless displays before Amenhotep had once more brought the pharaoh back in line with his wishes.

He bowed his head at a cautious approach, and waited for Jaonespur to speak. He did not turn; it was Jaonespur's onus as his inferior to kneel before him before he spoke.

Shaved head lowered as he knelt, Jaonespur held upraised arms before lowering them to rest upon the ground. His voice was restless: "Shall we begin the attack, my lord?"

Jannes laughed. "Have you grown so impatient after three thousand years in the grave?"

"I have grown vengeful, Great Jannes."

With another laugh, Jannes regarded Thorn's white-walled home. Set on a low hill, it was alone except for a half dozen cars parked before it. Also, he could discern shadowy figures moving along the external walkway, some of them heavily armed with these modern weapons. The others, the priests, walked with hands folded before them, counting with the strange necklaces they wore.

There was still much he did not understand about this age, but he did not have time to discover it. He must attack them before Thorn and these men had time to attack him, as he knew they would.

He folded his arms as he considered how this battle would probably fare before the night was over. He'd never fought such a battle as this because he'd never faced so many modern weapons. Even the old Puritan had not possessed such weapons as these men did. And although his men were strong and experienced, these modern weapons gave Thorn and the priests an advantage.

His men were armed with the traditional curved swords of Egypt. The bronze blades had been forged in a secret process that made the metal harder than steel, and they were overlaid with gold. And while the bronze held the edge, it was the gold that had preserved the blades though the centuries. They also had six javelins—spear-like weapons best used for stabbing and short throws, and a few rectangular shields. But after this morning, he'd decided it would be vital that they all donned the lapis lazuli armor plating.

This would not be a slaughter; they would be attacking strong warriors well prepared to make a strong defense. This morning had been a lesson for him; the Puritan and the old Amish grandfather had taken more time to understand and react to his presence. Indeed, he had almost subjugated the entire town before the Puritan had finally cornered him in the cave as he was preparing the girl for ritual.

The fight, while short, had been fierce, as the religious zealot had given no quarter, nor asked any. In fact, he had seemed as indifferent to death as any prophet of Israel, which was a particularly disturbing faculty of the Hebrews. They simply did not care about dying. Even in their final moments they would deny the ultimate meaning of this world, an endlessly frustrating defeat for him. It was no victory to kill a man who loved God more than himself.

"Summon the others," he said finally. "It is time."

"We will attack before darkness?" Jaonespur lifted his face with the question.

"Yes," Jannes said plainly.

Cahill glanced at his watch; he couldn't concentrate on a search for the staff with night getting so close. He felt cold sweat on his back and knew it was from fear, not the digging. He straightened; they still hadn't found anything, but he couldn't continue. He leaned his shovel against the wall and turned to the exit.

"I'm done, professor." He moved toward the cellar. "Keep digging, if you can. But it's getting dark, so I'm going upstairs to wait." He had an afterthought. "Don't put too much into it. I don't want you dropping dead from a heart attack in the middle of all this. I got enough problems."

The professor leaned forward on the shovel. "Perhaps Father Trevor was right," he said, a bit out of breath.

"Or there's nothing here at all," Cahill muttered. "Either way, we don't lose anything by looking."

Cahill was out the exit and up the stairs. In a second he'd found Thorn and Artemis on the back porch. He checked the job the other Assassini had managed with the door. It was solid wood, and they'd installed medieval-style crossbar. It looked like they'd done this kind of work before.

Thorn was pointing to the woods and discussing tactics as Cahill reached into his pocket and pulled out a cigar. He lit it without saying a word and tried to follow Thorn's analysis.

"I don't think we'll see their approach," Thorn said slowly. "If they didn't know, before, that bullets can put them down, they do now. So, this next time, they'll take precautions."

"They'll wait for complete darkness," Artemis nodded. He looked to the tree line on the east side of the house. "They can project their reflections; it would not be unreasonable to assume they can also project their images."

"Which is why I've broken all the mirrors," Thorn frowned. "But you're right. They might be able to get us shooting at shadows. And the thing is, we've got ammo; but we don't have *that* much ammo."

Thorn's eyes were flicking over the tree lines as if he could already see phantoms. His words came in coalescing thoughts that never made it to a coherent sentence: "...lot of ground to cross...be exposed...have to coordinate..."

"Down!" Cahill shouted and raised his shotgun toward Thorn and Artemis, who hit the porch together.

Cahill's blast tore rails from the porch.

Thorn had rolled to the north end; Artemis went to the south, but they rose at the same time, spinning and raising aim in the direction of Cahill's fire. Asking no questions, Thorn clicked off the safety as he raised the shotgun and saw...

Nothing.

Although Artemis must have seen nothing as well, the Assassini ran forward without hesitation and vaulted the railing. He came down on the other side in a crouch, searching. Thorn spun toward Cahill: "What'd you see?"

"He was at the wood line," Cahill shouted, shoving another shell in the smoking chamber of the shotgun. Only then was Thorn aware of screaming; it was the children. He moved fast into the house as an Assassini emerged at the crest of the stairway.

"They are all right!" he shouted to Thorn. "The gunfire just frightened them. Now they are prepared. They are safe. Their mother is calming them down."

Turning away, Thorn only barely heard Father Trevor's words as he turned back to Cahill. The priest rose from his chair and in a moment was climbing the steps, scepter in hand.

"He will target the children," he said. "I will be with them."

Thorn started forward. The priest sharply raised his hand. "No! That is exactly what he wants you to do!"

Thorn pointed at the priest. "Protect them with your life!"

"Done," said the old man curtly, and moved with surprising swiftness up the stairs. Thorn turned to the balcony to see Artemis rush forward.

"They're not going to wait for nightfall," he said. With a single deft move, he extended the shoulder stock of the MP-5, giving it a steadier front sight alignment for long range shooting. It didn't need to be said; if they were coming now, then Thorn and Artemis's people needed to take advantage of it. With this much light, they had a good chance at picking one of them off in their approach.

Thorn was on the porch as six more Assassini emerged, each of them raising weapons to their shoulders, each of them knowing that this would involve long range hits. Within two steps, Thorn's heart sank, and he realized why Cahill was simply standing there, speechless.

In the entire surrounding wood line, Thorn saw white silhouettes—hundreds of them.

Thorn blinked, disbelieving, and focused again. Yes...he wasn't seeing things. There were hundreds of sorcerers—literally hundreds and hundreds. All standing in clear view. All holding weapons. All waiting for some signal they had not received. Thorn saw Artemis shake his head, swearing softly.

A quick review of their tactical situation gave Thorn two things to think about: one, they didn't have enough bullets to take a shot at every image; and, two, closing the doors wouldn't do any good because if they could project these images in a field, they could probably project them inside a house.

As one man, they began walking toward the house.

Cahill's explosive curse was outright.

"What now?" Artemis shouted.

Thorn reached a single conclusion: If Jannes had wanted to teleport, or whatever you call it, his men into the house, he would have done so, already. But they didn't because Jannes wanted Thorn and his men to open fire on the images, expending their ammo. It was an attempt to make them empty their guns. And although Thorn didn't know the full scope of the attack, he was certain that they didn't need to fire a weapon yet.

"Fall back!" he said to everyone. "Everybody inside the house and barricade the doors!"

It was done in seconds, and the bar dropped over the back door as they backed into the center of the living room. As Thorn and Artemis focused on doors and windows, Cahill spun toward the front foyer, shotgun leveled at his hip. Thorn was thinking furiously, wondering what could be next. Something told him that they had probably just frustrated Jannes for a moment's respite; the sorcerer would think of something else.

"Don't shoot unless one is on top of you," Thorn muttered. He looked at Artemis. "Tell your men!"

Artemis repeated the command in his microphone; there was no question it would be followed. In the upstairs bedroom, Thorn heard footsteps and glimpsed a wisp of black coat. The Assassini were positioning themselves in the hall. Or, at least, two of them; the last would remain beside the kids.

Then something so logical occurred to Thorn that he cursed himself that he hadn't thought of it earlier. "These things are an *image!*" he shouted.

"We know that!" Cahill shouted back.

"No! I mean; they're an image! They don't have substance!"

"So?"

To answer, Thorn spun and smashed a canister on the counter and whirled back, hurling the shattered pottery into the living room. And at the violent cloud of white that cascaded over the floor and furniture, Cahill leaped back. In the next moment the cloud had settled over the floor and doorway and everything else that stood between them and the walls.

"A phantom won't leave a footprint!" Thorn snarled. "They can throw an image, but they can't throw substance! If you see something move the flour, shoot!"

Cahill and Artemis decided to increase the advantage. Both grabbed flower pots and smashed them on the floor, kicking showers of dirt until the three of them held a tight circle in the middle of the room, surrounded by a field of flour and dirt. Nothing could approach without leaving a track.

"Yeah," Cahill muttered hatefully, "like to see you get through that!" He nodded. "Good thinking, Thorn."

Thorn was too busy watching the floor to reply. And he glimpsed a shadow outside the back door but didn't fire because images and faces and sounds and phantoms couldn't hurt them. He couldn't have cared less if there were a thousand phantoms. All he wanted was one clear shot at one real sorcerer. And he'd wait for it.

Whatever hit the back door held the force of a runaway truck, and the crossbeam was ripped away from the frame. Thorn didn't so much hear the sound of the impact as see the crossbeam swing low and then away to clatter on the floor. He saw Artemis swing around, raising aim, and knew the Assassini was going to fire.

The blaze of the MP-5 was brighter than Thorn remembered from training, but he didn't allow himself a distraction as Artemis finished with the clip and slammed in another, chambering just as quick. Thorn was aware Cahill hadn't also fired at the back door, and realized the sheriff had kept his aim centered on another entrance.

Deafened by the machinegun, Thorn heard himself shouting to the basement stairway. "Professor! Get up here!"

They waited in trembling silence. No voice answered them from downstairs. No shape shifted in the darkness near the crest of the steps. The professor had not heard or he had chosen not to comply. Or he was unable to comply.

It was the last possibility that electrified Thorn. He knew what one of them had to do just as he knew there was no good way to do it. Whoever went alone into this was easy prey, and he didn't intend to surrender to circumstance. For a moment he considered leaving the professor to fate, but decided against it just as quick. He wouldn't leave a man behind.

Still, there was no time to debate a move that he knew he'd eventually have to make. Thorn lifted the aim of his shotgun to sweep past Artemis and hit the first step to the basement. He called back over his shoulder as he descended.

"Hold it for two minutes!"

Artemis didn't take his eyes from the back door.

"Hurry!"

Thorn hit the landing at the basement and instantly knew something was wrong. There was light burning in the tomb, but it wasn't moving. He stopped in place, reflexes working on automatic.

Never run into a situation. Walk...

Thorn said loudly enough, "Professor?"

No reply.

He reminded himself he'd already racked a round in the shotgun and eased forward, searching for sight or sound. Artemis and Cahill were just going to have to hold the fort until he got back. He wasn't going to rush through this darkness, not even when the professor was in immediate danger. If the old man was hurt, it wouldn't do much good to get hurt trying to rescue him.

Thorn heard shuffling inside the tomb.

"Professor?"

A muffled reply.

Thorn knew; knew in his heart, where it really mattered. Knew that there was more than one way in and out of this house, and he didn't know where it was. That was how Jannes had managed to slip out beneath him. The sorcerer had slipped into the woods through some kind of hidden door that Thorn had yet to find.

Another six steps and he'd be in the entrance of the tomb, but he knew they'd be the most dangerous six steps. If someone is going to attack you, they're going to wait until you're focused. They won't hit you while you're looking. They'll leave a clue, a weapon, a note, something to make you bend and examine it—something to draw your attention for a single moment.

It was a slight alteration on the old military tactic of placing a weapon on the trail when one was being pursued, then placing a grenade beneath the weapon, and pulling the pin. When the enemy caught up to the weapon, they'd pick it up, allowing the pin to eject on the grenade—a simple and effective booby trap.

Thorn barely looked at the entrance of the tomb until he was a single step away from it. Instead, he'd been focused on the rest of the cellar, allowing his eyes to acclimate to the darkness. He closed one eye when he moved into the brightly framed tomb, keeping night vision in one eye if he had to turn and meet an attacking coming out of the blackened corners of the cellar.

He was not amazed at what he saw.

Jannes stood there with the tip of a long sword like a fingernail moon poised at Professor Adler's neck. The old man was blackened with dirt and sweating. His white shirt was torn.

Thorn noticed that Jannes held a long black staff in his left hand, behind the professor. He was dressed in a flowing scarlet robe that descended almost to the floor, and wore a wide gold gauntlet on each forearm. His shaved head and face glistened in the dim half-light of the tomb.

"Thank you for finding my staff," he smiled.

Thorn frowned. He was thinking furiously of a dozen tactics, but there were two wildcards he couldn't factor. One, what the professor's reaction would be. Two, what new extremes of power the possession of this staff granted Jannes.

He'd already seen that the sorcerer's power was significant, even without the staff. But now he had what he had lost so long ago. Undoubtedly it was a substitute for the staff Jannes had lost in his conflict against Moses, but Thorn didn't think that would be much of an advantage.

Whatever Jannes had imbued into one staff, he'd undoubtedly imbued in the replacement. It was probably like a sword; a master sword maker could make one masterpiece after another. Thorn sized up the armored Egyptian servants that stood on the left and right of the professor, swords low. They were as large as Jannes and heavily armored, but Thorn doubted that they also possessed the sorcerer's incredible powers. Still, that armor looked solid enough, and it was plated, almost like chain mail, allowing quick movement.

Enough; there was only one move to make.

"What do you want?" Thorn asked.

"You," Jannes smiled. "You and your family. But you rejected me, so...I came for what is mine."

"So take it and leave."

"Have you reconsidered joining me?"

"No."

Jannes took that with surprising disappointment, which Thorn found curious. The sorcerer continued: "Strange...I have influenced servants of your God all this day...I have done it across centuries. How is it you resisted me?"

"I guess I don't much like what you're selling," Thorn muttered, listening close for another approach.

"No?" Jannes said more seriously. "Why not tell me the truth? It hardly matters, anymore. There are no more secrets."

"The truth?" Thorn took a cautious step, closing the distance. "The truth is, you don't have the power to overcome anyone's will. You can plant thoughts, steal thoughts, intimidate people. I don't doubt that you can make someone want to kill. But you can't make them do it. What we do is up to each of us. It always has been."

Jannes laughed. "Really..."

A grating, rustling sound in the darkness behind him made Thorn's skin crawl and the hair rise on his arms. He almost turned before seeing that the guards had come up on their feet, prepared to rush forward. He listened closer and heard a slight crash—the sound of something falling to the ground and rolling.

Thorn saw the professor's eyes widen.

He spun.

It was one of those moments where you simply react with the sense that you're dead, anyway. Thorn didn't have time for distinct impressions, but in the half darkness it looked like a King Cobra—some kind of extinct snake. It was almost forty feet long and ivory in color and, reared to strike, its fanned head was at the same height as his.

Thorn knew the two guards would be rushing as soon as he turned his back to them, so he fired point blank, blowing its head—and it was a real snake—from its body. Then he ran out of time for thought because he dove forward, figuring one of the guards had already swung a curved sword for an angled blow.

He sensed sharp movement passing behind him as he gained his feet quick, coming up on top of the twisting body of the serpent and spun to fire from the hip. The blast caught one of the guards full in the chest, and he staggered backward. Thorn was dimly aware the cellar was shredded by ricochets.

So, their armor could stop a shotgun.

Thorn didn't have time to consider how their armor could resist a 12-gauge round because the first guard was already on top of him, arm drawn for a downward cut.

Stepping into the attack, Thorn hit the sword as it descended with the barrel of the shotgun and twisted back, shoving the barrel of the Mossberg under the front of the faceplate. The butt of the shotgun was pointed at the floor; the barrel was pointed up underneath the man's chinstrap.

The guard attempted to jerk his head out of the way.

Thorn pulled the trigger.

The impact was tremendously bright and bloody, and the guard fell backward like a tree, sword clattering to the floor. Thorn didn't waste one second to verify the damage but heard Jannes bellow in rage from the tomb.

"Heal that!" Thorn shouted.

The second guard had leaped to the side to avoid the same damage and Thorn took advantage of the distance. He cast the shotgun to his left hand and fast drew the Colt from behind his back with his right.

In a split second he fired two rounds point blank and center mass—a double tap. The rounds cut into the armor, and Thorn had expected them to penetrate where the shotgun had failed but, although the man staggered back as any man would have to, he didn't fall.

No more time for this dance.

At the last second Thorn dropped and raised a solid aim to where... Jannes was gone.

So was the professor.

Alive and sweating and breathless, Thorn spun to see the second guard running hard across the darkness of the basement. Thorn pulled the trigger of the Colt, tracking. Thorn fired the six remaining shots, not sure if he hit or missed, and then he was standing in shadow holding a smoking Colt in an outstretched arm. He didn't search the tomb. He knew he was alone.

Too late to help the professor.

The second guard had used the secret entrance. He was gone, too. Frantically holstering the heated Colt, Thorn shoved another two shells into the magazine of the Mossberg and mounted the stairs fast.

As gunfire broke loose in the house.

🪲 ♀ 𓂀 𓏏 𓅃

Monsignor DeMarco was staggering up the stairs, attempting to reach Anthony's room where three Assassini had taken position, firing down the far direction of the corridor, as Thorn finally crashed into the living room.

Thorn only dimly noticed that Cahill wasn't present when he gained his footing and saw Artemis wrestling with one of the sorcerers. Bigger and stronger, the sorcerer simply picked the Assassini up from the floor and hurled him across the room, where Artemis smashed against the wall and collapsed to the floor.

Raising the shotgun, Thorn almost leveled for a shot but then he heard DeMarco yell and saw yet another sorcerer—or an image?— standing over the fallen monsignor. Only the faintest presence of mind enabled Thorn in the rush of events to look at the floor to see if the flour was disturbed by the attacker.

Sword upraised, it moved.

So did a cloud of white at its feet.

In five rushing steps, Thorn was behind it to the side and grabbed the back collar of its breastplate, spinning it away from DeMarco. Thorn knew better than to try the shotgun on its armor; it was useless. So as he spun it back, he swung the shotgun in low and jammed the barrel against the back of its unprotected knee and pulled the trigger. A wide ragged hole was blown into the stairway because the blast almost took its leg off at the shin.

Thorn ignored its hideous scream and jerked it again to send it tumbling down the steps. He couldn't help firing another round into it, even though he knew it'd be useless against the lapis lazuli and whatever metal was beneath it.

When the wounded sorcerer hit the floor, it simply bounded up and ran to the stairwell and the basement. It was lost from sight almost immediately; it would use the secret door.

Thorn spun into to a shaken DeMarco.

"Fall back to the kids!"

Without a word the priest was on his feet and moving fast. Thorn was able to catch movement again in the room just as Artemis reached his feet and squared off with the sorcerer.

The sorcerer moved forward, lifting its sword. Thorn saw that Artemis had lost the MP-5 in the exchange and expected him to fast draw the Glocks. But when the Assassini's hand came out of his coat it held the two-and-a-half-foot tanto. The abbreviated version of a katana was a fearsome weapon; the twelve-inch hilt was followed by a blade two feet in length and at least an inch wide.

Like Roman gladiators or biblical warriors of an age long lost to the world, Artemis and the sorcerer met in the middle of the living room. The circular blows were almost too fast for Thorn to follow, but Artemis seemed equal to the sorcerer in skill and speed.

Then the katana struck hard and true, slicing off a section of the lapis lazuli and Thorn saw why the shotgun had failed him, for underneath a blue-green of the lapis lazuli was a sheet of what appeared to be bronze, but it was apparently harder than steel. He didn't have time to think, but tactical training mechanically registered that it was a bronze-like material heat-treated in some unknown way and only a solid, supersonic round would penetrate it.

In the split-second it took to discern the strength of their armor, the sorcerer and Artemis exchanged a half-dozen blows and clashed shoulder to shoulder, attempting to tie up the other's sword arm. The sorcerer tried head butting, but Artemis expected the attack and twisted, turning his shoulder into the blow.

The sorcerer was dazed as Artemis's shoulder slammed the faceplate into his face, and Artemis didn't miss the opportunity to follow up. He used the impact to spin away from the blow, and the katana came around in a backhand blow aimed at the sorcerer's neck. But at the last second the sorcerer sensed it and threw himself forward, blocking the back of Artemis's arm.

Thorn would have taken a shot, but they were moving too fast, and then Cahill staggered back into the room, bleeding from the chest. He held his smoking .45, and the slide was locked back. Even as Thorn rose to check the sheriff's wound, the back door was blasted open and two more sorcerers rushed in, expertly swinging blades.

"Artemis!" he shouted as the Assassini dove and rolled beneath a blow.

Hurling the shotgun aside, Thorn fast drew the Colt and fell into a solid stance, firing instantly. He was only dimly aware that Cahill had fallen back against a wall, raising the .45 and was firing as fast as he could pull the trigger.

Artemis was smart enough to roll back to his feet, ducking to avoid another sweeping blow from the sorcerer what could have cut off the head of a wild bull. Thorn didn't visually follow the Assassini's next movement but glimpsed him rolling far to the side and then Artemis was firing, too, and Thorn knew he'd gotten his hands back on the MP-5.

Thorn was aware that he changed two clips, that the house was shredded by the combined gunfire—the flashes of armor spinning in the air at the impacts of the .45s and the nine millimeter rounds by Artemis, and he sensed rather than saw gunfire cascading from the staircase. Then in a rush and with the sound of wounded cries, the sorcerers crashed back through the doorway. In a last futile act of hatred one of the sorcerers threw his curved sword at Thorn. He ducked, and it hit the banister perfectly to stick, and then they were gone.

It was solid dark outside now, and as Cahill staggered forward with a curse to chase them into the night, Thorn shouted.

"Cahill! No!"

The sheriff needed no more. He came down hard on his left foot to brake his movement and then collapsed, it seemed, into the couch. His right hand, still holding the .45, came up to clamp down on his bleeding left shoulder. Thorn wasn't sure whether it was just a cut or Cahill had been stabbed, but he wanted to organize before they attacked again. First priority; check on the status of the children and Rebecca, but he had to cover things down here.

Artemis must have understood his thoughts because he swept forward, black cloak lifted. He dropped the slide on a fresh clip he'd slammed in the MP-5.

"Check the kids," Thorn said, breathless.

No words.

Artemis mounted the stairs.

Grimacing, Thorn took a painful step forward and wondered why he was hurting so badly. He glanced down to see a wide, wet patch of black on his blue jeans. He'd caught a slashing blow in the thigh and hadn't even noticed. Still, he didn't feel it, but it was stupid to ignore it. Adrenaline killed pain, but blood loss just plain killed.

By habit, as always, Thorn kept a wide blue handkerchief in his back pocket. He stuck the smoking Colt in the front of his pants, and in twenty seconds had a crude but tight bandage wrapped around the wound. No time for cleaning; he just wanted to slow the blood flow. He heard an Assassini moving down the stairs. When he glanced up, he saw the man carried the black medical kit.

Wearily, Thorn pointed to Cahill.

"Take care of him," he gasped. "I'm fine."

No questions. The Assassini moved to Cahill, who collapsed back into a chair as Artemis appeared at the crest of the stairs and descended to stand beside Thorn.

"They're fine," he said, and glanced at Thorn's leg. "You?"

Thorn shook his head.

"They'll be back. Soon. We need to...we can't keep this up. And there's another way into this house. There's a tunnel in the cellar. We need to close it up."

Artemis nodded. "I'll take care of that."

"Yeah; blow it."

"Yes."

Thorn wiped sweat from his brow with a forearm. "Jannes got his hands on a staff. I don't know what that means."

A voice came from the stairway.

"We may be doomed."

Chapter Sixteen

Pale and sweating, Father Trevor stood at the crest of the stairway, leaning on his scepter. He didn't follow his dark words with another apocalyptic statement, and Thorn was glad of it.

From the single comment, he knew that the staff Jannes had claimed in the basement would somehow enhance his power, or enhance access to his power. Biblical images of the supreme sorcerer summoning snakes to fill the halls of his house flowed through Thorn's mind.

Enough…nightmares could go forever and never helped anything. Experience and temperament had conditioned Thorn to have low expectations.

He looked over to see Cahill seated on a chest. The Assassini was working meticulously and quickly on his left shoulder, sewing the wound. The rest of Cahill's shoulder was orange with Bedadine, an antibiotic and antiseptic. The Assassini was quick and skilled; Cahill would be back on his feet in a couple of minutes.

Priorities…

Thorn could question Trevor in a few minutes; no rush for that. Right now they had to close the tunnel in the cellar; first things first. Thorn didn't even have to say anything to Artemis as he moved to the kitchen.

The Assassini pulled a hand grenade from his vest and handed it to Thorn. With a glance Thorn confirmed it was a standard U.S. Army

GR-2M issue. It had a three to five second fuse, depending on luck and whether the sun was shining, which meant, basically, three seconds.

With Artemis slightly behind him, and holding another grenade, they descended the stairs fast. Thorn fully expected an entire contingent of sorcerers in the cellar, but when they hit the floor there was nothing but a feeling of emptiness. There was no air movement, no sound, no warmth, and no shadows shifting in the mag-lights.

Thorn calculated two things: First, the sorcerer had run to the right and disappeared. Second, Thorn had been down here a dozen times and he had seen nothing that resembled a door. But there were shelves in that particular corner and simple logic told him they were just a crude mask for a tunnel. He put the hand grenade in his coat pocket as he felt along the wall.

He didn't look for a hidden lever like a book you tilted, a candlestick, or any other implement that might release a catch. He stuck out his hand and felt for a draft.

A tunnel always drew air out of the ground to the surface, and since this cellar was deep beneath the surface, any exit would be pulling an air current. In a moment Thorn had found it, a draft flowing softly over the back of his hand.

It was in the corner, at the farthest section of shelves and almost flush against the wall. Thorn shook his head and stepped back, raising the shotgun.

"Get back," he said to Artemis.

Thorn's first blast tore a huge section from the center of the panel, and he took one second to shine his mag-light through. Yeah; it was a tunnel. "Back," he repeated to Artemis, who had turned away to watch the rest of the cellar.

Thorn's next five blasts reduced the shelves to splinters, and then he flipped the Mossberg, holding the empty shotgun like a baseball bat to swing straight down, ripping a huge hole in the shredded wall. A tunnel loomed beyond it, and he turned to the Assassini.

"Here!" Thorn tossed the shotgun.

Artemis caught it and tossed him the second grenade. Thorn pulled both pins. He looked steadily at Artemis.

"You ready?" he whispered.

Artemis nodded.

"Watch the rafters," Thorn said, and he tossed both grenades into the tunnel. He was moving before the levers, spinning into the shadows, hit the ground. With Artemis beside him, Thorn threw himself across the stairs.

The explosion, compounded by the solid walls of the cellar, was like a fluid thing, engulfing them in an unbelievable surge of air pressure and heat and a riot of noise that was accompanied by a long rumbling that continued. After fifteen seconds, the cellar was filled with something like fog; a thick combination of smoke and dust.

Thorn was on his feet first and moved forward to make sure the other shelves weren't on fire and that the tunnel had collapsed. Just a faint glance told him the tunnel was still intact enough for a man to slide over the mound of dirt. He shook his head.

"Need another one," he said, and Artemis handed him another grenade.

Thorn was more meticulous in his pitch this time, and they managed to make the staircase before the explosion amplified air pressure and the smoke strangled them. Staggered and a little deaf, Thorn managed to rise and shine his flashlight into the opening.

The tunnel was sealed, and not by dirt. The second explosion had brought down ripped slates of flint that laid tons of hard rock on top of the softer dirt that the sorcerers could have conceivably tunneled through. Thorn didn't know if Jannes could somehow make the cave-in disappear, but something told him that the sorcerer was limited by what he could do with the earth itself. Which is why silver could bind him; the earth was both his strength and his weakness.

Then, very strangely, Thorn thought of something he had not noticed earlier: Jannes, when Thorn had observed him beside the professor, had not been wearing anything on his feet—not even Egyptian-style sandals.

It had not seemed significant to Thorn at the time, but it seemed important now. Then he thought of the other five sorcerers he'd seen so far. They hadn't been wearing anything on their feet, either. Again, not even sandals.

This was important; Thorn knew it, somehow. Then he remembered the tunnel and Artemis waiting. He took his shotgun and moved toward the stairs.

"That did it," he said.

They were up the staircase quick, and as they exited the kitchen into the living room, Thorn saw Cahill jamming more forty-five rounds from a box into empty clips. The bloodied sheriff had positioned himself beside the stairs so he could see every entrance. His shirt was sliced, but the Assassini who had tended to Cahill gave Thorn a quick nod as if to say, "He's okay."

For the moment, Thorn ignored Father Trevor. He moved straight to Cahill. "You all right?"

"Ah," Cahill grunted, "guess I zigged when I should have zagged. I put a few rounds in him, hurt him. But he crashed through a window before I could finish him. They're quick...for dead men."

"Not dead yet," Thorn said, and turned sharply to Father Trevor. "What is it about dirt, or metals?" he asked. "Why don't they wear shoes or sandals? Why can't Jannes do anything about silver?"

Father Trevor thought for a moment. "I cannot answer you regarding silver except to say that silver seems to be representative of Christ, just as gold is associated with the kingdom of heaven." He lifted a hand. "Did you not know about the significance of earth?"

"No, priest. And I *still* don't know."

Trevor gestured widely with his words. "The power of the natural cosmos, and thus the power linked to Jannes through his sorcery, is indicated in the construction of the tent and tabernacle of Moses. When Moses built the tent and the tabernacle, it was to hold the ark, the altar, the laver, the table of showbread, and candelabrum, and there were four square posts surrounding the Holy of Holies, which was itself representative of—"

Thorn interrupted. "Get to the *point*."

"The pillars of the tent never touched the earth because the earth was symbolic of man!" The priest gestured high on the walls. "In other words, the earth was separated from God by the veil, and could not join directly with God because God was holy. But with silver foundations, like flower pots, the posts of the Holy of Holies could be erected on the earth!"

"What does that have to do with Jannes?" Thorn scowled.

"Jannes' power is linked to the earth," Father Trevor said. "Nor can the earth, or that which is not holy, touch God. But through the use of silver, God was able to erect his sanctuary. The silver, which was the foundation for the posts, represents Jesus becoming the bridge between God and man. In the same way the power of Christ joined God and man, it separates Jannes from God."

"You're saying that Jesus," Thorn repeated, "Jesus joins us to God, and separates Jannes?"

"Yes! And that is why Jannes cannot wear sandals. It is the earth that gives him his power and not God. Not Christ. Cosmic powers, which were set in motion in this world long ago, are the power of Jannes' sorcery. And they flow from the earth, not from Christ."

Thorn was a little confused. "I thought you said Jannes' power was from a demonic spirit. And demons are supernatural."

"Demons are also a part of nature," Father Trevor continued. "What is not God is *created* by God. So demons are *also created* by God. They, too, are a type of nature. And the term 'supernatural' has no real meaning. Demons are just as 'natural' as we are and must obey rules just as we do. They only inhabit another dimension.

"They are like the currents of the ocean." The priest swept his hand back and forth, stirring the air in front of him. "With great effort man can redirect the currents for a little while, but he cannot alter the course of the ocean. The ocean will fight back, and the ocean will *win!* But for a short time, a current can be redirected. That is all that Jannes does; he simply redirects a certain power of nature for a short time."

Thorn was listening close. "What happens if Jannes isn't in contact with dirt? What if he's not in contact with the earth?"

"I cannot say."

By combat reflex, Thorn got cold: "Take a guess."

"Even demons must obey laws," Father Trevor said. "And laws specify that, in order to channel the power of his demon, Jannes must be in contact with the earth. If he were not barefoot, Jannes would have to place dirt inside his shoes. That is how important it is to him. I would surmise that if he is not in contact with the earth, the demon cannot channel through him because this demon must channel his power *through* nature."

It all made sense to Thorn.

"That's why Jannes has never attacked inside the house," he said, almost to himself. "That's why the others have only used their swords when they attacked us in here. It's because...in here...they aren't in contact with the earth, and can't use magic."

Thorn looked hatefully at the shattered back door. "That's *it*...They can't use their sorcery if they're not in contact with the earth. And that's why Jannes was able to conjure that snake in the cellar. He was standing on the ground. But in here..."

Artemis spat: "On this artificial floor he is like any other man!"

"We got him!" Cahill shouted, and clambered to his feet. He looked like he could barely stand, but the news had riled him up; in the moment, he looked like he could go another nine rounds. "We got him, Thorn! He *does* have a weakness!"

Thorn was silent; he stared at the door. "It won't be that easy, Cahill. If we know it, I can guarantee Jannes knows it. He wants to get us outside. On his ground."

"Then how come they keep coming to us?" Cahill was more fired up by the minute.

"I don't know," Thorn said. "Maybe they're trying to make us retreat—make a run for the cars. Maybe they want to make us pursue them into the woods...I don't know."

"He *did* project images inside the house," said Monsignor DeMarco, who had appeared at the upstairs railing. "We saw them ourselves up here. So he can obviously manifest magic at a distance."

Thorn was building a concrete theory. "Yeah, but that's the rub," he said. "At a distance he can project images, reflections, even sounds. He can even move a few small things if he can see them. But he can't change the substance of something—not at a distance. And he can't do anything at all if he's not in contact with the earth."

"You sure about that?" asked Cahill.

"Yeah," Thorn said quietly. "Jannes' real power is that he can transform one thing into another. But if he's standing on an artificial surface, he can't turn a car into a crocodile or a staff into a snake. Also, he wouldn't be able to use his power to heal up so fast, which would make him..."

"Mortal," said Artemis grimly and terribly. He nodded, "You were right, Michael."

Thorn turned, staring determinedly.

"If it lives, it can die."

🪲 ♀ 𓅿 𓏏 𓅃

Jannes paced a slow, calm path inside the tree line, casting unreadable glances at his apprentices. Occasionally he would glance at the house where every light burned brightly.

The last of his servants had stumbled in several long moments ago, wounded and breathless. He had felt the faint impulse to kill them for their failure, as he had done in Egypt. But he reminded himself that this was not Egypt, and he had only a limited number of servants thus far. There was a time and place for all things.

After they settled, exhausted, on the ground, he stretched out his staff, as they were accustomed to him doing in battle, and he felt his god's power flow through him and into them, healing their cuts and broken bones. It was not a simple incantation, for it dealt with human flesh, which was ultimately under the dominion of the God of Israel. But he was able to manipulate flesh and blood to a degree among his followers.

He hadn't even tried to resurrect the servant Thorn killed in the cellar. In the first place, his apprentice's body was still in the bowels of the house, and Thorn had destroyed the tunnel. Second, it was one thing to fix a cut or broken bone; it was another thing entirely to attempt to repair a brain. Regardless of how he made it appear, his healing powers were limited. And, as always, the Hebrew God could intervene and, quite simply, stop him.

He could not argue it; the Old One was easily capable of stopping his sorcery, nor did he know whether He required a prophet to stretch out his hand to accomplish it. Perhaps their God could simply stop him, prophet or no prophet. He did not know. He only knew he did not want another confrontation with the God of Israel, and he was very glad that Moses was dead.

That he had not encountered anyone with the faith of Moses had never surprised him. In the dim six hundred years that he wandered the land after the Hebrew prophet had departed Egypt, he had come to understand what a titanic figure the shepherd had been to his people.

He had seen the rise of David, Elijah, Daniel, Ezekiel—all men of astounding power, just as Enoch and Melchizedek, king of Salem, had been, and none of them were held in such reverence as Moses—a greatness that only grew with the passage of generations.

No wonder the Hebrew God had sent his greatest warrior, Michael, to claim the body of Moses from Satan after the prophet fell before the border of their Promised Land. For certain, the Hebrews would have taken his body and built a shrine about it and worshipped it. His greatness had known no bounds.

In fascination he had watched the succeeding prophets, marveling like the others at their miracles, unable to deny true power when he witnessed true power. And when Elijah had cut up his bull upon an altar of twelve stones to be burnt by fire sent from the God of Israel, he had tactfully retreated from Mount Carmel before the four hundred fifty priests of Baal met their deserved doom.

It was not for nothing that he slipped unnoticed into the forest before the killing began. He had seen the awesome wrath of the God of Israel before. It had been nothing less than stunning.

He saw that depthless wrath after the flood, when the land was made void of the great kings and the Nephilim. He had seen it at Babylon, when the Hebrew God confused the common language, dooming the tower. He had seen it after Isaiah wandered the land naked for three years to pronounce the judgment God would bring on the land because of their adulteries and depravities—depravities that he himself had so carefully planted, nurtured, and flamed.

He sidestepped the bloodthirsty Babylonian invasion of Nebuchadnezzar by dazzling military leaders with childish parlor tricks, which they found nothing less than amazing. Also, he was not Hebrew, so not a worthy target of their wrath. And then, afterward, he had returned to Egypt to find the country in ruin, a fool for a pharaoh, and a skeleton for an army.

It had taken him little time to reinstate himself as Court Magician since Amenhotep, Thothmes, Hatshepsut, Merneptah, and Ramses were dead and forgotten. He had even laughed to learn that the fool Egyptians could not tell him that it was Ramses' young face carved on what they now called the "Sphinx."

He remembered the ancient nation that was his home—and his first kingdom—and he once more saw them carving the Lion of the Desert more than a thousand years before Egypt condensed itself from a ragtag group of homeless transients.

It was by his early leadership that Egypt first gained government, magic, wealth, religion, weapons, cities, and roads. In time they had progressed enough so that he could quietly monitor them from the shadows as he established idiot pharaoh after idiot pharaoh, and ruled them secretly.

All these things passed through his head in the space of a heartbeat as he considered the dark terrain and the white-walled house before him. Then he became aware again of Jambres' expectant face.

Yes, his apprentice desired an answer.

Beyond the house, the night was silent. He was confident that the chaos he had sown this day would keep the occupants disoriented until sunrise. To his good fortune, those who originally buried him in that mound had picked a township that had never become large enough to command its own palace guard—or whatever they called it in this day and age.

In truth, he was still not fully oriented to this society. It would take him time, though his spirit was communicating with him in sensations that piqued his curiosity to enter a certain building, or a certain person's life, and explore until he understood the reason for his curiosity.

Then, with the needed knowledge, he would continue building block upon block until he understood all he needed in order to tear them down from within by threatening, withholding, and delivering three of their most fearful needs—food, clothing, and shelter.

It was a simple and incredibly effective way to control their lives. But controlling their minds was a far greater challenge; to control their minds he had been forced to attack their very greatest fear: the fear that they were utterly alone in the universe.

He had been the remedy for that, providing them with mass companionship through religion or politics or social coalitions. Amusingly, the coalitions subsisted remarkably well on the illusion of brotherhood and hope for eternal life, despite the voice that told them this was fear and not faith.

But so great was their fear that they ignored the reality of it. And if they could not convince themselves of faith in whatever he had provided, crocodile, dog, hawk, or the Nile itself, he would invent something new like he'd invented "Ra," the sun-god who gave life to the entire earth.

Did not the forests and reeds and the desert itself live because of the sun? And was not gold the metal that most perfectly worshipped Ra, mirroring his majesty? And was not the pharaoh Ra's regent in the land, dispensing Ra's life-giving judgments so that there would be no death, but only a journey to the Underworld?

A journey...and there would be no death...

Yes, but he knew differently.

He knew very well what the wrathful Hebrew God had done at Babylon—unleashing a destruction he had never imagined was possible, and that when the God of Israel delivered death, it was a final death unless you were delivered by another power...as he was.

So great had been the terror of that night that they had beheld each other with faces of flame, amazed at the horror of what was surely a final deliverance to death. He had watched Nephilim who had been born after the flood staggering with their hands over their ears, trying to escape the roaring night—giants framed by flame that rained down from white holes torn in swirling black clouds, utterly destroying city and king.

Yes, the God of Israel could deliver death beyond imagining when He so desired, and virtually nothing could withstand Him.

Still, even the faintest flicker of hope that they might be right, that they might retain eternal life by whatever belief he tossed to them like a bone to dogs, had been enough to placate their fears, to control them. Until, of course, Moses, and then the succeeding prophets, and eventually the world had changed.

He was protected as well as he could be protected by the great spirit that guided him and gave him the power for his sorcery. He could create life from lifeless things; he could change water into blood and command lesser beasts; he could influence the minds of men, terrorizing or satisfying; he could even overcome physical death.

True, he was limited...but so were the prophets of Israel. And he would eventually see whether his god could deliver him from death, as he had promised him.

He focused on what was before him. Jambres awaited instruction.

Thorn and the priests were in the house, where he would not go. But they were wounded now. And their primitive weapons would not suffice. He understood enough about this time period to know they must reload their strange metal weapons, and they did not have enough "ammunition" to last forever. And that was their weakness; they put faith in their weapons, but what would do they do when they exhausted their weapons?

Then again, another problem presented itself with this particular group; the one known as Thorn was particularly resistant to his influence. But none of them were easily subjected, which was why he had tried to silence them quickly.

If the common people knew their thoughts were influenced by his god, then they would simply pray or execute their wills, and he would have to resort to force, which could expose him.

Invisibility was his truest weapon; he always tried to avoid force because each use of force had to be followed by a greater use of force to maintain the same effect, and eventually he ran out of people to kill. Force was, quite simply, counterproductive. Persuasion was much wiser, and easier, to accomplish, which was why he enticed them to indulge their rage, lusts, greed, and any other desire that might come between them and their God.

But Jambres' impatience reinforced one thought; yes, he *did* have to silence Thorn and these people, force or no force.

He had briefly considered turning Thorn, but that had been a failure. No matter; he had failed before. Some simply would not turn; they would die first. And that, too, was no matter. He would simply kill them. But he had hoped to spare himself the trouble, and the work—a hope he no longer held.

He gazed upon the five sorcerers who surrounded him, each fearsome and powerful in their own right. They, too, knew some of his secrets, though he was careful about how much to reveal. He did not want his own sorcery used against him, which was possible.

Just as a man can forge a sword, and that sword can be used by another man to kill him, so could his sorcery be used to destroy him. It was a danger he had long ago frustrated by never revealing the secrets of his power.

The prophets of Israel had presented an entirely different kind of danger—the same danger he faced, tonight. If he could overcome their will, he could easily destroy them. But that had always been the problem; it had been the problem with Moses, Ezekiel, Isaiah, Daniel, David—all of them together.

They had, quite simply, held to what was written by the Old One. They were instantly on guard against indulging instinctive desires and tested every thought against the written Word of their God.

He had thought to avoid that morass, again. When he had recovered from awakening, he had almost indulged the hope that he had risen within another dark and primitive land where the minds of the superstitious would be easily swayed. But the hope had died when he'd overheard ~~heard~~ the two men speaking in front of the house, and a careful search of the surroundings revealed that this was no primitive culture.

Even worse, he had not expected to encounter such religious conviction so quickly. It had taken him off guard, and he was too weak for an open conflict, which was one reason he had tried to offer Thorn a truce. Still, it hadn't worked. And there was no time to lament the force that he had encountered.

If it had been one of the name-only groups, he would have been triumphant already. But these people were sincerely dedicated to what they believed and, even worse, they did not build or enhance upon the words of the Old One. They held simply and truly and totally to what was written. And, so, he would kill them. He had no choice.

Enough musing...

It was time to organize his men.

Turning, he bowed his head and frowned over them. His meaning was clear in his posture; he would not accept failure, and they had failed. But he was here, and so they would overcome, in the end.

It was by his foresight that these servants had not been with him when he'd been confounded by the power of Moses. There were no surviving witnesses of his defeat. It was bad enough that the Hebrews had recorded it in their books.

All his men stood as he raised his face and gazed upon them. When they were alert and ready, he spoke.

"The priests have fortified themselves within this home, so we must draw them outside. Only, we must do it quickly. For by sunrise this country will be swarming with members of their army.

"As it was when Alexander and his thousands stormed Egypt and overcame us by sheer numbers, so it will be with them. I will not be able to control them all. But I can control their leaders as long as they are unaware of my influence."

Jambres bowed and spoke, "And how shall we lure them outside, Jannes?"

The sorcerer shook his head. "While we may use sorcery when sorcery is required, we can also use the weapons of man to achieve our ends. We will do what they do not expect. We will set fire to their home, forcing them outside."

"And then you will kill them?"

"Yes," Jannes said, with a step toward the home. He stared over it a long moment. "Then I will transform their weapons and cars and even their clothing into creatures that will turn and rend them—creatures that will kill them all. Man, woman, and child."

They gathered silently behind him.

"Go! Burn them out."

Thorn didn't like the look of things when he entered the bedroom where the kids and Rebecca had huddled together on the bed. He was unexpectedly glad that he'd taken the extra time during the previous night to assemble the four-poster.

That night felt like it was so long ago. Nothing he'd ever faced as either a soldier or police officer seemed half as dangerous as what he faced now. He tried to hide that thought as he walked up and hugged his kids.

Anthony attempted bravery and let go of Thorn soon enough, but Malorie hung on. She wasn't going anywhere, or letting him go. Rebecca smiled encouragingly, but Thorn could tell she'd been fighting back tears. With a glance, he confirmed that the Assassini were disposed at a respectful distance, leaving them relatively alone.

Thorn patted his boy's back. "Holding up, champ?"

"Yeah," Anthony rubbed his eyes. "I'm okay."

He didn't bother asking Malorie; it was obvious how she was holding up. He focused on Rebecca and decided he could speak frankly. There was no more hiding it from the kids; best that he put it on the table and hoped they understood it.

"They tried," he said, simply enough. "They fell back, probably to reorganize. But they'll try again."

"When?" Rebecca asked quietly.

"Soon...before morning," Thorn answered.

"It's not over, then," she said to herself.

Thorn tried to reassure her. "These are good people, babe. We can do this."

Rebecca wiped an eye with the heel of her hand. "I know...And so are you...You're a good man."

Thorn wanted to lie down on the bed, holding them all in his arms. And although he knew his adrenaline level would never allow him to sleep, he could have used the closeness, and the rest. It was going on two and a half days now without sleep. And he knew he'd need to catch a catnap at the first opportunity.

To stay on his feet, he'd been drawing on the same mind-set he'd developed during qualifications for Special Forces when they'd had to run fifty miles with a fifty-pound pack in less than eight hours. Somewhere in the pain he'd stopped caring about pain. He'd stopped caring about the heat, the blisters, and the numbness—stopped caring about life or death. He'd just picked up one foot, set it down, and moved up a step. It hadn't even mattered how far or fast he moved... Just a little, if that's all he could do. Just keep moving, don't quit. That was all there was to it, and that was what he was using now—just keep moving.

Malorie lessened her hold just a little, and Thorn was aware she was looking at the Assassini. Her voice was timid and frightened. "What are they going to do now?" she asked.

Thorn smiled over her. "They're going to watch over you and Anthony and Mommy—same thing they've been doing." He held her face in his hands. "No one's going to hurt you, honey. I promise. You have a dozen men in this house determined to protect you and Anthony and Mommy. We are not going to let any bad guys get in here."

"Here, Malorie," said Anthony. "I want you to have this." He removed the silver cross that he had worn for years, sleeping and waking. "It's always reminds me that Jesus is with me."

Astonished and encouraged, Malorie tentatively took the necklace and held it before her face. "This is mine? You're giving it to me?"

"Sure."

"But...why?"

"Cause it'll make you feel better. And you're my sister."

Thorn barely heard Malorie's words.

"Wow, Anthony...Thank you."

"You're welcome," he smiled.

Overcome, Thorn hugged them all, knowing he'd better get back downstairs before Cahill decided to launch a storm trooper attack on the woods. "I'll be back up here in a little bit, okay?" He looked from one face to the next. "I'm not gonna leave you guys. I promise you we're gonna be okay."

Malorie held the cross. "You'll kill it?"

Thorn held back his emotions.

This animal had already done the most terrible of all things to his children by forcing this upon them. They would recover, to a degree, with a lot of time, patience, and love. But they would never forget the horror of this night.

Thorn thought of the sorcerer.

His jaw tightened.

"You bet," he said.

🪲 ♀ 𓂀 𓏤 𓅃

Thorn wasn't the only one in a killing mode.

When he reached the living room, Cahill had positioned two extra shotguns beside windows. Now, the sheriff only needed to run from one window to the next and keep firing; he didn't have to worry about taking his weapon with him.

Thorn had seen the technique before, mostly among old-timers or mountain men cornered in a cabin, but he didn't care for it. He preferred to keep his weapon in his hand. He just preferred to carry at least three weapons and plenty of ammo for each.

Poised before windows, Artemis and his men stood guard. Father Trevor was seated in a chair along a windowless wall, and Monsignor DeMarco was moving up the stairs as Thorn reached the floor. The monsignor appeared weary and pale as he mounted the first step. Thorn placed a hand on his shoulder.

"You okay?" he asked the priest.

DeMarco nodded tiredly and grasped the rail, as if he needed support. "It is one thing to believe something is possible...It is quite another to witness it."

That brought a mild laugh to Thorn; his first. He didn't say anything more as the priest moved slowly up the stairway and in a moment was lost from view. Then Thorn moved up to Cahill.

Cahill looked to be holding up and nodded curtly as Thorn stood shoulder to shoulder with him.

"We got good visibility for about a hundred feet," the sheriff muttered. "It doesn't give us much, but it's enough if they don't look like there's a thousand of 'em, again."

"I wouldn't count on that," Thorn said without tension. "They know it's the only way they can get close without catching a round, and they've learned that a round can slow 'em down."

"Or kill 'em," Cahill added.

Thorn stared. "You checked the basement?"

"Sure did."

"He still there?"

"Dead as a mackerel."

Thorn nodded. "Good."

Artemis had his back turned, and there was something alert but somehow downcast about the Assassini's posture. Thorn didn't like it, and patted Cahill once on the shoulder as he moved away.

"Holler if you see anything."

"You bet."

As he closed the final steps to Artemis, Thorn tried to relax. Maybe it would be contagious. But when he reached the Assassini he felt the tension in the air and became tense, himself. Whatever was on Artemis's mind was not good.

"What is it?" asked Thorn.

Artemis shook his head, silent a long time. When he spoke, he didn't remove his eyes from the darkness. "They know everything we know," he began, "so they should realize that we know the sorcerer's weakness."

"I know," said Thorn. "Jannes can read our minds, right?"

"I don't think so," the Assassini grimaced. "But the spirit that empowers him can listen in on our conversations. He's like...part of the air. He can pass through, listen in, tell Jannes all that we're planning—all that we hope to accomplish."

It took a moment for Thorn to come up with a reply, and he was fairly surprised at his own words: "Didn't help him much with Moses," he said at last.

Artemis turned his head to stare at him. Thorn didn't blink. "Well, it didn't," he added. "You keep talking about how powerful this thing is, but maybe he's not as powerful as you think." He paused a long time. "I mean, do you think he knew that he wasn't going to be able to turn dust into gnats? That God was going to wipe out pharaoh's entire army at the Red Sea?"

"I never said he could read the future."

"Maybe he's not so hot at reading the present, either." Thorn gestured toward Father Trevor, bowed in prayer. "Aren't you the one who believes this sorcerer can be shut down by the power of prayer? Well, we've got a ton of prayer, right there in that old man. And if I had to make a guess, I'd say God listens to him."

Something about the words seemed to have struck the Assassini. He continued to stare at Thorn, and then spoke slowly: "I thought you said that you did not have faith."

"I never said that, man. I said that I didn't have *your* kind of faith—that I didn't have my *wife's* kind of faith." Thorn laid a forearm on the windowsill, gazing out. "I've *always* believed in God. But it's hard to believe in a God that actually intercedes in the lives of men, heals folks, raises people from the dead and feeds them...and in some six-thousand-year old sorcerer who turns water into blood."

Thorn slowly shook his head. "Now...*that's* faith. And I don't have that." He paused. "I've always believed God just pretty much set all this in orbit and stood back and...we're on our own. But what you believe... what Rebecca—and even what the kids believe—is difficult to accept."

"You only need faith," Father Trevor said quietly. "If you will be still, you will feel the presence of God. He is always available to you, Mr. Thorn. Faith has its own life, and it will respond to God if you take the time to listen...for one moment."

Cahill's bearish voice rumbled from the foyer. "I feel it just fine, tonight."

Too quietly, because it indicated fear, Thorn walked closer to the old man, and Thorn wondered why he was afraid. Perhaps, something whispered to him, he was afraid of the answer he might find in his question.

Father Trevor stared at space before him—an empty space to Thorn. But he wondered what the priest saw there, and he spoke slowly: "And this Jannes? Does this demon tell him what we've talked about in the last few hours? Or is your...your faith great enough to stop him?"

Father Trevor gazed up. "I have prayed that the blood of Christ would protect us from this creature knowing what we plan and discuss. Indeed, I have prayed that the Almighty would shut its ears and eyes to what we would do and restrict its power to affect us."

Thorn was aware of a lightness in the air. "Do you think he answered you?"

"I do," the priest nodded. "Just as I believe that you will be Jannes' doom."

No movement outside; Thorn could sense it. He tilted his head slightly at the priest. "What makes you say that?" He lifted a hand toward Artemis, dropped it. "You people have your own soldiers."

Father Trevor laughed.

"Only God knows why He chooses His warriors." The priest nodded, with a knowing acceptance. "But I would say you were chosen before you were born. As with all of us."

In the silence, Thorn lifted his head. He was listening, and he wasn't surprised at Artemis's quiet words.

"They are coming."

Thorn hefted the shotgun and walked to the window. His voice was bitter; "I know." He didn't look at Cahill as he added, "You ready?"

"Bring 'em on," Cahill answered.

The sorcerers emerged from the edge of darkness, over a thousand of them, daggers in the left hand, torches in the right. Thorn knew immediately what they were planning and gave the sorcerer credit for the idea. He spoke more to verify that Artemis understood.

"They plan to burn us out."

"Yes. Any ideas?"

Thorn was calculating. He turned back to Father Trevor. It was time for power now. No more words. "You said you could restrict his sorcery. Can you or not?"

Trevor was silent. He bowed his head and prayed. "Since the beginning," he began, "men have died resisting his evil. I can only pray."

Thorn saw them coming in the last hundred feet, torches blazing. He knew that only five of them would be physical, but he didn't want to wade out among them and begin shooting. One bad decision, and he'd be dead under a real blade that he had bet was a mirage.

But he was out of options.

He reached out and grabbed Artemis's MP-5, the submachine gun, as he handed the Assassini the shotgun. "Hold this," he said. "I'm going out. Cahill!"

"I've got you covered!"

Thorn hit the back door. And as he cleared the rail and hit the ground, he had already arrived at a different plan: This guy could manifest images, but he couldn't move flour on the floor. He could bring these phantoms, but Thorn was betting he couldn't manufacture heat.

He crouched on the ground, watching for anything that might give away what was real. But it was impossible. They all moved as one, every step in cadence, like an army, and now they were fifty feet from the house, almost close enough to throw a torch to the porch or roof. And despite how they might fight the blaze, it'd be over fast enough.

Concentrate...

Thorn raised his face, staring.

Watch them. Something will give them away...

Scent...

The thought came to him, and he turned to the right, sensing rather than knowing...

It was there, somewhere. One of them was real. The sorcerer had covered everything—almost—but not this. His spells were powerful, but he wasn't omniscient. He only covered what he could think of, and he hadn't thought of manufacturing the scent of smoke. Maybe he just couldn't do it. Thorn didn't know and didn't care; it was enough.

He leveled the MP-5 and fired at a cluster.

One of them fell back with a cry, and Thorn saw lapis lazuli plates pinwheeling through the air. As he ran forward to finish it, he heard a cry from inside the house and turned to see the east side of the porch on fire. Several Assassini rushed outside; one kicked the torch back into the grass, and the second began beating at the flames with a blanket. Then Thorn didn't have any more time as he reached the fallen sorcerer.

The man was already rising.

"Not this time," Thorn said, and emptied the MP-5 to put him down again. Then he fast-drew the .45 to fire a full clip. Even that wasn't enough.

Against his better judgment, Thorn whirled to see Cahill on the porch with a fire extinguisher. Somehow the sheriff had managed to find it among moving boxes and crates.

As he moved down the porch Thorn was firing indiscriminately into images and reflections. He obviously had chosen to shoot at anything, image or not, that even appeared hostile. And, although Thorn didn't know where Artemis was, he figured the Assassini was doing the same.

When he whirled back to the downed sorcerer, the man was already on his feet and came at Thorn with sword upraised. Almost with contempt, Thorn dropped the slide on a new clip and waited for the blow.

The man was staggering, and as his arm came around in a windmill move, Thorn stepped up to catch the wrist with his left hand. In the next split second he placed the barrel of the .45 against the sorcerer's chest and pulled the trigger five times.

The blasts were tremendous and deafening at close range, and the sorcerer stood in place until the last one punched cleanly through his back and then it was over.

In slow motion, the sorcerer fell back. And if he had had the time, Thorn would have taken a moment to curse him. But he didn't. He turned before the sound of the .45 faded from the trees and moved toward the porch. He had taken less than a dozen steps when a hissing sound made him freeze.

Standing in place, Thorn debated running. He didn't know what was behind him, and didn't want to. He was standing in the open—the sorcerer's territory—and he was vulnerable. And, somehow, he knew he couldn't outrun what was behind him.

Moving his head only, Thorn looked back over his shoulder and saw a tree at the edge of the wood line bending forward. And in the next moment the limbs began to move in a downward spiral, becoming snake-like, coiling and uncoiling.

Even in the dim half-light Thorn could determine that some of the limbs had thick, muscular substance the size of an anaconda, and some were the size of twigs and moved like mambas or moccasins—small and deadly.

Thorn didn't want any part of this. He ran.

When he reached the porch, Cahill was rounding the corner, spraying the last of the fire extinguisher. He'd managed to control the blaze on the east side and held something in his left hand that Thorn immediately noticed. It was a piece of broken mirror.

Thorn didn't have to ask as Cahill lifted it and shouted. "The phantoms don't cast a reflection! The real ones do!"

Thorn was grateful for Cahill's discovery. He was willing to do whatever he could to gain the faintest advantage in this maelstrom. He glanced through the back door to see Artemis positioned on the stairway. The Assassini had backed up enough to keep an eye on Anthony's door and the living room, and it seemed to be the best position he could take at the moment.

As Cahill reached his position, the sheriff dropped the broken mirror on the deck and it shattered again. He tossed one half to Thorn and kept the other. He was breathless and angry: "You gotta angle it and don't be too close when you do, but the real ones cast a reflection. It gives you a good idea where to shoot."

The hissing sound that Thorn had heard arose again, and Thorn turned on the porch as Cahill's mouth opened in shock. And as Thorn turned, he knew what he was going to see, but nothing, in the end, could have prepared him for it.

The tree had moved to within twenty feet of the porch, but it was no tree. It swayed and undulated with a life of its own. The limbs that reached into the night were like living things, each hissing and coiling. Thorn glanced toward the forest at a rending sound and saw other trees uprooting themselves. It was an uncanny, slow motion phenomenon as horrific in sound as it was to behold. Cahill's voice sounded dim and shaken.

"We're dead," the sheriff whispered.

It seemed as if the forest itself were alive in a long, twisting movement, absent from the wind, independent of the night, and angry at their presence. At least a hundred trees were moving on their own, and a ragged, tearing sound—like trees uprooting themselves—rasped from the depths of the woods.

Thorn didn't want to agree with Cahill that they were doomed, so he didn't say anything at all. He turned at a sound at the back door and saw Father Trevor step into the night.

Cloaked in white, the priest stared at the trees as they moved with the darkness. He stood a long moment, and Thorn couldn't determine if he was frightened or amazed or horrified. Then the priest lifted his scepter and began intoning a low prayer.

It had happened before Thorn was aware that the sound had ceased, but he reflexively searched the tree line the silence registered in his mind; the forest was still. It had happened in a breath, no drama, no lights, no sense of divine intervention. It had just happened.

At that, Father Trevor lowered his scepter and turned to gaze at the mass of sorcerers who encircled the house.

"*Minimus homo, crux dominus,*" he said.

And suddenly Thorn and Cahill and the priest were staring over empty fields.

It took Thorn a moment to understand what had happened, but then he realized the priest was countering the power of the sorcerer with the power of prayer. And as the surreal sight of it was taking hold inside him, Thorn saw a single flicker of movement behind Cahill.

"Cahill!" he shouted, and the sheriff needed no more. He whirled, knowing without seeing that another of the sorcerers was close. In the next second he was grappling with an armored image that held a curving blade in a bloodied hand.

Cahill fell back at the attack, and Thorn caught the sorcerer under his ribs with a kick. In a twisting bundle of arms and legs and chaotic blows thrown and missed, they crashed through the railing of the porch and onto the grass.

Thorn wasn't sure if he or Cahill fired first, but ten rounds exploded in the night and then the fight was over. Thorn staggered to his feet, staring down. He saw the sorcerer lying motionless and Cahill's .45 smoking, close to its head. He reached down and gave Cahill a hand to his feet. "Did you kill him?"

Cahill muttered as he rose, "If I didn't, it wasn't from a lack of trying." Upon reaching his feet, he coldly nudged the dead sorcerer with a foot. "They can take a bullet...I'll give 'em that."

As he wiped a forearm across his forehead, Thorn noticed that Father Trevor had reentered the house. "With these guys, you just empty the clip."

"Let's get inside."

"I'm ahead of you."

When they entered the house, Thorn wasn't surprised to see the priests in close conference. He didn't know what they'd be discussing now, and he didn't care. He had his own conference to attend.

He set the .45 on safety as the Assassini gathered around him. Artemis had shed his coat so that his arsenal was in full view; it also occurred to Thorn that his arsenal was more easily reached without the encumbering cloak.

"We used a variety of techniques," Artemis said. "First, we just fired among them. If they're massed together, you will hit one if you don't leave man-size holes in your firing pattern."

"But you expend a lot of ammo," Thorn said.

"Yes. But we have a lot of ammo in the cars. At least ten thousand subsonic nine millimeter rounds."

One of the Assassini who used a Street-Sweeper—a 12-gauge shotgun with a circular drum that fired twelve rounds on semi-auto— handed Thorn a full box of shells for the Mossberg.

"We expected that we'd need extra rounds," he said simply.

Thorn looked at the box; double-aught buckshot. "Good enough," he said, then focused on Artemis. "If we hold out until daylight, what kind of reinforcements can we expect?"

With a sigh, Artemis said, "They will send reinforcements by tomorrow if they don't hear from us. But if we haven't killed this creature by tomorrow, Jannes will massacre our reinforcements quickly. He grows stronger every hour, and more of our people won't even have the advantages we have, which are few enough."

"What advantages do *we* have?" Cahill grunted. "This guy can turn a tree into a snake! I know! I saw it!"

"We've deduced, correctly, that Jannes is powerless unless he is in touch with the earth," Artemis replied coolly. "We have men who are holy and can counter some of his sorcery. Plus, we know how his sorcerers move, their tactics and weapons, their style. And we know how they can be defeated in combat because we've done it."

"He's right," Thorn said, with bitterness. "If we let other people in this—including your deputies, Cahill—we'll just be setting them up to die. We have to take care of this tonight."

Cahill glanced out the window.

"Then we better get ready...cause here they come."

Chapter Seventeen

Slides of shotguns and automatic weapons snapped angrily at the words, and Thorn was at the back door, staring out. He glanced at the wood line to see if the forest remained in place; it did.

"Thank God," Thorn said by reflex.

Jannes' most terrible ability—the power to transform inanimate objects into living weapons—was apparently shut down; Father Trevor's prayer had been answered. But Thorn knew it'd take more than prayer to finish this. Although the priest could hold back this sorcery on a certain plane, Jannes wasn't limited to sorcery. And as the night grew older, the sorcerer would eventually resort to any means necessary to finish this fight.

He'd try again to set the house on fire, but Thorn was confident they could hold them back.

These guys were smart and adaptive, it was true, but they were still from another time period and they weren't omniscient. They didn't know what this century contained.

In fact, it would take Jannes and his people months—maybe years—to understand the twenty-first century. Not only did he have to catch up with the ever-changing world of politics, there was science, machinery, technology, law, transport, and the varied customs of a hundred societies. And religion would present a new, unique problem.

Instead of a single rebellious nation of slaves led by Moses, there was a new, convoluted world of countless churches, denominations, Bibles, pastors, scholars, teachers, nuns, priests, and even holy warriors. And, for all that had changed, Thorn had come to understand that some things hadn't changed at all: the Church still had its prophets, and Jannes could still be shut down by the power of God.

So, in addition to new problems, Jannes still had to compete with the old. But there was something about this line of thought that tugged at Thorn's mind.

Something new...

The thought orbited Thorn's mind with the sorcerers that circled the edge of darkness.

Something new...

What was it about the thought that continued to snag his imagination? There was something solid, there a weakness he could exploit. But he didn't have time to develop it as he glimpsed a gray shape running toward the west side of the house.

Thorn was already moving in that direction as Cahill shouted from the foyer.

They were rushing the house, no more phantoms to mask their approach. They were taking their chances that they could get inside before they took a round.

Not a good bet; Thorn heard automatic gunfire open from an Assassini at the west window, and then Cahill was firing from the front. It was chaos, and Thorn raced into the foyer to back up Cahill.

He hit the doorway in a rush to see the bloodied sheriff with his back against the near wall, two sorcerers attacking from opposite sides. Cahill drew the .45 in one hand and leveled the shotgun in the other and began pulling the triggers as fast as he could, eyes flashing like wildfire.

Without missing a step the sorcerer who took four blasts from the semiautomatic shotgun turned and leaped high. Thorn followed the move but drew up to avoid shooting Cahill. Then there was a pillar to support the balcony above them blocking his shot, and then the sorcerer crashed cleanly through a window.

As Thorn spun back to aim at the second sorcerer, Cahill was frantically pulling the trigger of an empty pistol. Thorn saw Cahill react in shock, as if he hadn't expected to run out of ammo so soon, and Thorn fired a fast shot at the second attacker but knew he'd missed before he fired. Then the sorcerer was on top of Cahill.

With an enraged curse, the big sheriff reached out at the last moment and grabbed a huge vase of flowers. Then his hand swept forward and smashed the urn over the sorcerer's forehead.

The impact was tremendous—Thorn almost felt the shock from where he stood—and Cahill followed it with a hard kick to the guts. As he grabbed the sorcerer by the throat, he shouted to Thorn.

"Thorn! Get to the kids!"

Arms intertwined, Cahill and the sorcerer crashed through a huge oak table, scattering chairs across the foyer. And again Thorn tried to get a shot, but they were too close and entangled.

It took both of them a moment to recover, then Cahill came up holding a disjointed chair leg; Cahill was obviously accomplished at dirty fighting. He turned anything he touched into a weapon.

As the sorcerer rose, the burly sheriff swung the chair leg like a club to tear a chunk of forehead from his attacker. Then he shot another glare at Thorn.

"*Go! I've got this one!*"

At almost the same moment, continuous gunfire erupted on the balcony, but only lasted a few seconds before Thorn heard a series of crashing sounds and panicked shouts. And, staring up, Thorn was frozen by an ominous silence.

A single glance confirmed Cahill was doggedly holding his own—good enough.

With a quick spin, Thorn hit the stairway fast to behold something he hadn't expected. The three Assassini assigned to protect his family lay unconscious on the landing. Confused, Thorn raised his face, searching for an explanation, and his heart skipped a beat.

No image in gray this time.

Jannes stood unmoving at the far end of the corridor. Dressed in a scarlet robe, his bald head reflecting the dim light, he had one hand inside the heavy folds of his cloak and held the long black staff with his other hand. Beneath the sharp shadow of his hawkish brow, his eyes were hidden.

The boldness of the attack stunned Thorn; surely Jannes knew he had no power unless he was in contact with the earth. Then the alarming thought occurred to Thorn that maybe they were wrong. Maybe Jannes *didn't* have to be in contact with it.

Thorn didn't have time to check on the condition of the fallen Assassini. Instead, he took a slow step over one of the bodies, toward the door of Anthony's room. Then he froze as the sorcerer spoke. The sound of gunfire continued downstairs, but Thorn had no trouble discerning the words.

"We meet again," Jannes laughed, as Thorn slowly raised aim with the shotgun. "Perhaps you should have chosen to live..."

Thorn heard nothing from Anthony's bedroom. And despite the surreal threat before him, he had to know about his family before he engaged Jannes. He took another tentative step.

"They are still here," Jannes continued, and sighed. "What a pleasure it would have been to have someone so strong-minded at my side. You would have become pharaoh, Mr. Thorn."

Thorn's frowned: "What'd you do with the professor?"

"Ah," Jannes laughed, "He died without pain. And his sacrifice was not in vain. The life force I absorbed from him has almost restored my healing powers. Which were, of course, in need of strengthening."

Gunfire raged downstairs, and Thorn reached Anthony's door in a single step. He glanced in quick, searching. They weren't on the bed, and then he glimpsed Rebecca's leg peeking from behind the closet door. They were hiding—the three of them.

He could live with that; they were alive.

Thorn's glance had only taken a split second, and he had never fully removed his peripheral vision from Jannes. But when he looked back, the sorcerer was gone. He seemed to simply vanish—that simple, that quick.

"Nice parlor trick," Thorn whispered.

A tremendous collision beneath the balcony made Thorn twist and glance over.

Immediately Artemis and a sorcerer crashed through the kitchen door and into the living room. The Assassini had lost his machinegun and was trying to toss the larger, stronger sorcerer back, but the sorcerer clearly had the advantage in hand-to-hand combat.

Thorn only had seconds; he had to hit the sorcerer at this range with the shotgun, but the shotgun fired a pattern of what was equivalent to eight 9-mm rounds at once. He had to be careful with the pattern to avoid hitting the Assassini.

With his back to Rebecca and the children, Thorn raised aim and waited until Artemis threw the sorcerer back the narrowest space. He aimed for the sorcerer's leg and as he fired the man twisted in place, bellowing at the buckshot that ripped through his thigh. Then Artemis moved—moved so swiftly and smoothly that Thorn only saw a flashing ribbon of silver trailing red.

Thorn wasn't sure what had happened since the sorcerer was still standing in place, motionless, and Artemis was only five feet away, staring. Then in an eerie, slow motion cascade, the sorcerer's head tilted back and fell, thudding as it struck the floor behind his feet.

His body crumbled forward.

Thorn turned back to his family to…

Jannes smiled into his eyes.

Thorn didn't move. Then Jannes withdrew his arm from his cloak, and Thorn saw that he held a handful of dirt.

Dirt…

He *was* in touch with the earth!

With a shout Thorn brought up the shotgun. His next sensation was that he had been shot from a cannon. He was aware that he had crashed through the railing, which disintegrated as if it'd been hit by a force of nature.

He saw the twenty-foot ceiling less than arm's length from his face and in the amazingly long moment tried to remember what was on the floor. He twisted in the air, trying for a glimpse as he descended with remarkable presence of mind and saw the coffee table directly beneath him. It was almost as if Jannes had planned for him to crash through the glass—had hit him with such a trajectory in mind—and there was nothing Thorn could do about it. Once a man is in the air, he's committed to the direction.

The vague thought flashed through Thorn's mind to toss the shotgun wide, but he couldn't imagine why as he braced himself for a deadly impact.

If the fall didn't kill him, the shattered glass would. Then he sensed a shadow sweeping in fast and something hit him hard from the right, carrying him wide of the table. In the next minute Thorn and Artemis were rolling, entangled, on the floor. The Assassini had seen the danger and caught Thorn's body enough to deflect him from the glass.

Thorn was on his feet first, raising the shotgun.

"He's upstairs!"

They moved together.

"No mere man could have struck such a blow!" Artemis managed, drawing a Glock with either hand.

"He can use his sorcery inside the house!"

Artemis hesitated: "But he's not in contact with—"

"He's got dirt *on him!* He's in touch with the earth!"

No time for anything else as Thorn hit the crest and was instantly in Anthony's room. He didn't even need to see it to confirm it; he just knew. And as he ripped open the door of the closet, he braced himself to not faint with fear...

It was empty.

Artemis reacted with a shout. Thorn was already out the door, sighting the hallway's only window at the far end.

From a distance, it appeared to be locked from the inside but that wasn't good enough. Thorn raced to it to make sure. He checked the windowsill; yeah, it was locked. But it was no assurance that Jannes hadn't used it to exit. As far as Thorn knew, Jannes could have telekinetically locked it after he left.

"Come on!" he yelled to Artemis as he rushed down the hallway. "He's gotta be close!" As they descended, Thorn dimly realized the gunfire had stopped and called out: "Cahill!"

A moment later the sheriff staggered into the living room with a smoking .45 in one hand and one of the sorcerer's swords in the other. He was bleeding from a half dozen shallow cuts, but Thorn didn't have time for first aid.

"You get him?" Thorn shouted.

Exhausted, Cahill waved at the foyer. "They die like snakes," he gasped.

Thorn scanned the room: Father Trevor was gone.

That was the first thing Thorn realized after Cahill entered the room, and he wondered that he hadn't noticed it before. He searched the kitchen and west side of the house. Nothing. As he raced toward the back door, he snatched up a handful of shotgun shells and thrust them into his pocket. He shoved three into the Mossberg as he spoke.

"Jannes killed the professor!" He almost racked the shotgun, then remembered it was already chambered.

"Are you certain?" Artemis asked.

"Yeah...He killed him once he got what he needed."

Artemis stared. "What did he *need?*"

"We hit 'em hard enough to exhaust Jannes' healing powers." Thorn gave the house a last look. "He needed the professor's life force or whatever you call it to rejuvenate. So he's strong now—real strong. We have to separate him from the ground."

Cahill grunted: "That ain't gonna be easy if he's carrying dirt on him, Thorn."

"It won't be easy *anyway*, Cahill. But we have to do it or he's gonna wear us down one by one and kill us all. He can make all the mistakes in the world and he'll heal up. But we're vulnerable. We can't make *one* mistake."

"No kidding."

Artemis was scanning the hallways and doorways and, as Thorn lifted the shotgun, he moved straight for the porch. He was certain Jannes had taken the kids and Rebecca outside; he wanted this confrontation on the ground, where he was strongest. Thorn didn't bother to see if anyone was following him.

As Thorn hit the wraparound porch, he was over the railing and took in the entire sight before he hit the ground. In the middle of the field, Jannes stood with Anthony and Malorie and Rebecca. Two of his sorcerers stood behind him, which added up. Artemis had killed one, Thorn nailed one, and Cahill killed the other one in the foyer.

Another thirty feet and Jannes would have been into the woods, where he was all but unstoppable. But he'd been confronted by an implacable wedge of black-robed priests. And at the tip of the wedge, Father Trevor's spear-like scepter shone silver in the light of the moon. It was clear that he would not let the sorcerer pass.

Thorn caught the conversation as he rushed forward, aware that Artemis and Cahill were close behind. In the final few feet, Father Trevor said to the sorcerer, "Your power has no affect against me, beast. Strong faith and the blood of Christ is power to those who believe." A pause. "The days of your empire have gone the way of all things...to dust."

Jannes laughed. "I am not yet dust, priest."

"Yes, beast...Dust you were, dust you are, and to dust you shall return. Now, release the woman and her children. You will not hold them while the spirit of Christ is with me."

Jannes frowned. "I am not limited to sorcery, old man. Did you not know the pyramids are mortared with the blood of slaves I killed with my own hands?" He shook his head and glanced at Thorn. "While my sorcery has no affect on you, priest, faith only works for those who possess it."

He extended a hand toward Thorn, and Thorn shouted in pain, falling to his knees. Dropping the shotgun, he clutched his head at a searing, blinding pain that lanced his forehead. He blinked, trying to focus, but the pain flowed like lava through his head.

Rebecca cried out, "What are you doing to him?"

"Killing him," said Jannes calmly. "It is a simple thing when I am in full contact with the source of my power. Perhaps the priest's faith makes him invulnerable. But not everyone possesses such faith."

Artemis had bent over Thorn, but he obviously didn't know what to do as Thorn arched his back, mouth open in shock. Then Cahill stepped up, motioning quickly for Rebecca and the kids to stand clear. Yet with the movement the remaining sorcerers grabbed the children, holding them as shields.

"I underestimated your powers, creature," said Father Trevor quietly. He did not seem disturbed by Thorn's agony as he stretched out his scepter and said, "In the name of Jesus of Nazareth, I command you to release him."

With a shout, Thorn shook his head. He blinked repeatedly for a minute, focusing, and saw the sorcerer once again. By reflex he reached for the shotgun as he stood up.

It wasn't necessary to say anything about Father Trevor's intervention. Wasn't necessary to despise Jannes' attempt at power. Wasn't necessary to declare that the power of the God that defeated the sorcerer at the hand of Moses had defeated him again. Now, Jannes could show how he mortared the pyramids with the blood of slaves.

"Kill me," Thorn said as he closed, "if you can."

One of the sorcerers leaped toward Artemis and swung the scythe of a blade, but the Assassini was prepared. He dove in low, under the blade, and literally picked up the sorcerer to slam him into the ground. Thorn didn't see what happened next because he reached Jannes, who violently jerked Malorie in front of himself.

Thorn had expected it, just as he'd hoped he would reach the sorcerer before he reacted. Now, Thorn didn't have much choice. With the sorcerer's blade poised at Malorie's throat, he stopped in place. Artemis stood, looking defeated, and Thorn glanced over to see the sorcerer rising, too. The fight had carried them twenty feet to the side, and at this distance there was no reason to fear a stray round hitting either Rebecca or the kids. As the sorcerer grabbed his sword, Artemis fell to a knee and extended a hand holding a Glock.

The Glock was a high capacity nine-millimeter that fired a seventeen-round clip, and Artemis had an extended clip, giving him thirty rounds.

As the sorcerer stood, sword in hand, the Assassini fired the full clip into his chest. It seemed to go on a long time, and then the sorcerer collapsed forward, bloodied almost beyond recognition. Thorn grunted; yeah...they might die hard, but they did die. And as he fell, Thorn looked back to Malorie.

Thorn couldn't rush in and try for a wild shot any more than he could try and wrestle away his child. He gazed into Jannes' face. "You're not gonna make it," Thorn said dully.

Jannes smiled, "We'll see." He looked at the trees. "When I am safely inside the trees, I will release your daughter. But only if you give no pursuit."

"Aren't you afraid we'll talk?"

The sorcerer laughed. "The more I learn about your time, the more I become convinced that no one will listen to you." His smile was ghastly. "In the beginning, I'll admit, I was concerned. But it seems that so many of you are shamans or witches or wizards or prophets...I truly don't believe you will be noticed among the multitudes who declare their idiocies."

Thorn shifted his weight. "I guess you know a little about prophets."

"That is close enough," the sorcerer warned

Barely moving, Thorn settled back.

"Good," Jannes smiled, tightening his hold on Malorie. "To answer you, since we have no more time; yes, I've known your greatest prophet, for Moses was genuine, and the God of Moses was the one true God. But the world will not see his kind again. In this age it is rare to find someone who even believes, much less a prophet to be feared."

"I'll make sure the world believes in you, Jannes. I'll make it my mission from God to make them believe."

Jannes chuckled. "Satan's greatest trick is convincing the world that he does not exist, Mr. Thorn. And I have been told by my lord that the master, the father of lies, will assist me in my deceptions."

"It won't be enough."

"We will see."

Jannes had taken three steps back.

Thorn knew only one thing; there was no way Jannes was taking his daughter into that forest. He glanced at Rebecca, who was holding Anthony back. The boy would have rushed forward to rescue his sister, but he was waiting for Thorn to make the move.

"Malorie?" Thorn said loudly.

His daughter nodded as Thorn followed the sorcerer's retreat a single step, carefully maintaining the distance. His hand shifted on the Colt .45, tightening, insuring the safety was off. Mentally he counted the rounds he'd fired to affirm—without glancing down—that a round was chambered. In seconds he was certain that three rounds remained; he was ready.

He spoke with meaning to Malorie: "Do you remember what Anthony gave you tonight?...The gift?"

Tears in her eyes, Malorie nodded.

Thorn spoke clearly: "I want you to look at it."

Jannes' eyes narrowed at the cryptic command. He tightened his arm around the little girl as he backed another step and then Malorie's hand came away from her neck and over Jannes' arm, holding the silver crucifix. And as the crucifix touched Jannes' hand, the sorcerer reacted as if he'd been scorched to the bone.

He howled, and his arm flew from Malorie's throat as he staggered back. Then he seemed to realize and recovered, leaping toward Malorie again. But as he moved, Thorn smoothly dropped to a knee with his arm extended and fired the Colt.

At the range—at least fifteen feet—the 248-grain bullet passed less than four inches from Malorie's head to hit Jannes solidly in the chest. Shocked by the sheer impact, Jannes dropped his staff and staggered back. Thorn fired two more rounds, each hitting center mass.

The slide locked, and Thorn reached for another ten-round clip as Cahill lifted his shotgun. But Jannes was far from dead. With a shout, he swept out an arm and Cahill's shotgun pinwheeled through the air as if snatched by an electromagnetic current. Then Jannes thrust out his open hand and Cahill shouted as he flew backward, struck hard by an invisible force.

With just this short distance from Father Trevor, Jannes seemed to already regain a significant portion of his power. He focused hatefully on Thorn, seething with pain and anger.

"Fool!" His hands clenched like talons as he started forward. "You think this can defeat me? Strike me down and I will only heal myself! I will always heal myself!"

Thorn leaped forward and tore the silver scepter from the hands of Father Trevor and spun, hurling the silver shaft like a javelin into the chest of the sorcerer.

His aim was true.

The scepter hit Jannes hard beneath the sternum to split the lazuli plates and the skin and heart beneath to protrude a foot out his back. And as the sorcerer spun screaming, trying to pull the silver from his chest, he dropped the sword.

Thorn reached him in a linebacker rush and hit him full in the chest, propelling them both across the field in a swirling, murderous exchange of blows taken and received and, with real fear, Thorn felt Jannes growing stronger with each blow.

It was obvious that, no matter what kind of limits the priest had summoned to prevent Jannes from manipulating the forest itself, the sorcerer could still use his incredible healing power. With a volcanic effort, Thorn threw Jannes back, but Jannes only seemed to increase in size and confidence.

He smiled.

"I will recover from your wounds," he gasped. "Can you not see?" He inhaled deeply, and Thorn could see the wounds closing as they spoke. "No wound can kill me as long as I touch the earth."

With a curse in a language unknown, Jannes turned and ran for the forest. Thorn turned and pointed at Artemis and Cahill: "Stay with Rebecca and the kids!"

Cahill started forward. "But—"

"*Do it!*"

Snatching up the MP-5, Thorn rose up to pursue the sorcerer, determining in the same moment that only one of them would survive this. He turned at a shout from Artemis and caught a clip for the machine-gun from the air, slamming it in the receiver. Now he had another fifty rounds, and knew he'd need every one of them.

Still, he didn't know what he could do to reduce Jannes further. He'd already hit him with everything he had, including silver, and it only had minimal affect because as long as the sorcerer remained in touch with the earth, he retained the power to heal himself. Thorn didn't know what could possibly hurt him, but he had to find something. He'd have to improvise, so he took one second to snatch up the sorcerer's staff lying on the ground. It might come in handy.

In seconds Thorn hit the forest, virtually blind in the heavy canopy of night. But he glimpsed Jannes running for a clearing ahead, and heedlessly swept low-hanging limbs from his face, running all out over uneven ground. He kept his bearing by sighting the four-hundred-foot water tower so close beside them, and a desperate idea occurred to Thorn with the sight of it.

Something new...

Thorn bowed his head in thought.

Something he doesn't know is artificial...

Thorn studied the grounds of the water tower.

Something to separate him from the earth...

Jannes was about to reach the wood line on the far side of the clearing. Thorn knew it was now or never.

He dropped and leveled the MP-5 to take aim. The shot was long—forty yards—and he couldn't afford to miss because he wouldn't get another opportunity.

He fired with a slow, controlled squeeze of the trigger and knew immediately that he'd hit where he was aiming because Jannes somersaulted in the air with a wounded howl and landed hard on his back. But almost immediately the sorcerer began to rise, so Thorn lifted the long black staff horizontally above his head.

"I've got your staff!" Thorn shouted across the small clearing and then, in a quieter tone, added; "Why don't you come get it..."

For a moment Thorn thought the sorcerer would choose discretion instead of defiance, but then Jannes was walking toward him without hesitation or fear, healed already from the gunshot wound to his leg.

Thorn backed up, matching the approach step-by-step. He only glanced over his shoulder one time to measure the final few feet to the water tower, and then he felt pavement under his feet.

It was the access drive.

Although Jannes had healed himself from the damage Thorn had inflicted, he was a gory, surreal sight in black as he mounted the low rise, stepping on the grass bordering the driveway.

"Surrender my staff," he rasped.

Thorn laid the staff on the drive.

"Come and get it."

Grimacing in disgust, as if sickened by the thought of descending to battle this meaningless soldier, Jannes stepped onto the pavement and approached with angry strides. Flakes from his ravaged armor were separating with the movement, exposing his chest. He glanced down as they clattered on the drive. He blinked, focusing, and shook his head.

"Stone and dust," he grunted, with contempt. "I rule them both."

The staff lay on the ground between them.

Thorn's hand tightened on the machine gun.

"You would have lived if you had remained with your family," Jannes said as he bent to his staff. "Now they will die for the trouble you have given me."

Thorn leaped forward and fell to his knee, shoving the barrel against the sorcerer's chest. Jannes' face opened in surprise. Then he laughed loudly and grabbed the barrel with his strong right hand.

Their eyes held.

"*Fool!*" he raged into Thorn's face. "You *cannot* kill me! I will heal as long as I stand on this earth!"

"You're not standing on *earth!*" Thorn rasped. "Ever heard of *fiberglass?*"

Jannes' eyes flared as he stared down to see that he stood upon a substance not natural to the earth and upon which his sorcery was useless. Horrified, he raised his face as Thorn's shouted.

"*Heal this!*"

Thorn pulled the trigger hard, and the sorcerer's body rose with the automatic fire of the MP-5. Thorn stood, following the barrel to continue firing and firing. Even in the blinding blaze of gunfire, Thorn could see bullets blasting armored plates from the sorcerer's back. It was enough to massacre a dozen men, Thorn knew, and something told him it was more than murderous.

Thorn didn't listen.

In a haunting, surreal moment Jannes' face twisted to the side, staring at the grass *the earth*, so close but so far because he couldn't escape the devastating assault. And Thorn *still* held the trigger down, firing and firing as he walked forward, following Jannes step for step until the sorcerer finally fell back.

Arm extended, Thorn gazed through smoking, superheated air at the sorcerer. There was simply nothing left of Jannes' chest. The armor was blasted into jagged plates, and the blue-green of the lapis lazuli was black in the white light of the tower. With his opened chest and bloody armor and clenched hands, Jannes resembled some kind of gigantic, grotesque moth, its talons curled in death.

It took a moment, but Thorn began to breath again as he stared at the still body of the sorcerer. He didn't know if he was dead beyond reviving or how to confirm the death of such a creature. Then, as if from nowhere, Artemis was silently at his side. His short sword gleaned silver in his fist. His ruby red ring seemed to glow with a preternatural light.

Thorn managed, "The kids and Rebecca?"

"Safe," Artemis stated. "Cahill is guarding them. And they are surrounded by those who are holy...Those who await your return."

Thorn only had to glance into the Assassini's cold eyes to know his intent, and Thorn realized he didn't really care to see this last, necessary act. It was enough. He turned away.

"You do it," he said.

Artemis nodded coldly.

Heedlessly tossing the MP-5 aside, Thorn moved toward the wood line. It took a moment, but Thorn suddenly realized that there was a quiet prayer being spoken in the night. Almost from the center of him, he felt a single, severing blow struck and the last word of the prayer blended softly with the wind and the forest that embraced him and he whispered.

"Amen..."

Epilogue

It had been almost a year, and so much had changed that Thorn could hardly remember the life he once lived. But he didn't forget the horror of what they survived, and he used every available moment with the kids.

Rebecca had survived the ordeal with remarkable strength, and recovered faster than even Thorn himself. He calculated it was because her faith had given her a strength that he was only now slowly coming to understand. It wasn't easy to understand the power of her faith, and Thorn had come to look at it more as a journey than a place you ever truly reached.

Anthony and Malorie still had nightmares, and had come to sleep with them in their bedroom when they were scared. Thorn had no complaints; if that was the only after-affect of something as horrible as what they endured, he knew they'd eventually shake it off. But it'd take time, and they had all the time in the world. There was no rush to fix anything. In time, and with love and patience, they'd be okay.

Thorn still had nightmares, himself, but he didn't share them. Not with Rebecca, and not with the kids. Not that he had a need to be Superman, but he did have a desire to inspire strength and courage instead of fear. And now, also, he had a need to help his children grow in faith, because he'd come to believe, as well.

He would never forget what he had encountered. Not only the evil, but the good. Although Artemis had gone back to his world, they remained good friends and kept in touch. And it made Thorn laugh sometimes that even Cahill had become a regular churchgoer.

Thorn could say safely that he didn't quite understand faith, and maybe he never would. But he could say that he *did* have faith. And after what he'd seen, faith was enough, at least for the time being. And one day, yeah, he might be wise and prophetic and have some answers; right now he was willing to settle for the fact that he believed, and was trying to live his life in the light God gave him to see that life.

Yeah...it was enough.

The rest would come, in time.

About the Author

A veteran novelist and best-selling author, James Byron Huggins' life story reads more like fiction than fact. His career as a writer began normally enough. He received a bachelor's degree in journalism and English from Troy State University, and then worked as a reporter for the *Hartselle Enquirer* in Hartselle, Alabama. Huggins won seven awards while with the newspaper before leaving journalism in 1985.

With a desire to help persecuted Christians in Eastern Europe, Huggins moved to Texas to work in conjunction with members of the Christian underground in that region. From the Texas base, Huggins helped set up a system used to smuggle information in and out of Iron Curtain countries.

In 1987, Huggins was finally able to leave the United States to offer hands-on assistance in Romania. As a jack-of-all-trades, Huggins photographed a secret police installation, took photos of people active in the Christian underground, and also continued his work as an orchestrator of smuggling routes. Huggins was instrumental in smuggling out film and documentation that showed the plight of Christians in Romania. He even found time to create a code that allowed communication with the United States. As in Texas, Huggins' life had few creature comforts. To survive, he would often remain hidden in the woods or in secure basements for days at a time.

After his time in Romania, Huggins returned to the United States and took up journalism once more. He again worked for a small newspaper and won several awards as a reporter. Later on, he worked at a nonprofit Christian magazine before becoming a patrolman with the Huntsville Police Department in Huntsville, Alabama. After distinguished service as a decorated field officer, Huggins left the force to pursue writing novels.

His first three novels—*A Wolf Story*, *The Reckoning*, and *Leviathan*—achieved best-seller status in the Christian marketplace. From there, Huggins broke into mainstream science fiction with *Cain* and *Hunter*. Huggins then released *Rora*, a historical novel depicting the harrowing life of a European martyr. His novel, *Nightbringer*, is currently being made into a film. His recent novel, *The Scam*, delves into the suspense-filled world of government, conspiracy, crime, and intrigue on an international scope. *Sorcerer* is Huggins' eighth book.

Huggins currently lives in Kentucky.

*One of the top five
Christian fiction
books of the year!*
—Library Journal

Nightbringer
a novel by
James Byron Huggins

An ancient evil has darkened the halls of Saint Gregory's Abbey in
the Italian Alps. The once-peaceful monastery becomes a murderous
battleground as the monks and a group of visiting tourists find
themselves locked in a hopeless battle with an unstoppable force.
Cut off from the outside world by a sinister snowstorm, the group
of defenders must fight for their survival and for their very souls.
But from among the defenders arises an ageless holy warrior who
alone has the skill and power to stem the bloody tide of evil. In the
epic battle that will decide the fate of all involved, the warrior must
not only struggle against a familiar foe of mythic might, but also
rediscover the faith and love that have carried him
through a thousand battles.

ISBN: 0-88368-876-X • Hardcover • 304 pages

WHITAKER
HOUSE
www.whitakerhouse.com